Praise for *New York Times* bestselling author RaeAnne Thayne

"[Thayne] engages the reader's heart and emotions, inspiring hope and the belief that miracles *are* possible."
—#1 *New York Times* bestselling author Debbie Macomber

"A solid plot, realistic, compelling characters and strong tension make this story hard to put down."
—*RT Book Reviews* on *A Cold Creek Baby*

"Plenty of tenderness and Colorado sunshine flavor this pleasant escape."
—*Publishers Weekly* on *Woodrose Mountain*

Praise for *New York Times* bestselling author Maisey Yates

"Yates's thrilling...contemporary proves that friendship can evolve into scintillating romance... This is a surefire winner not to be missed."
—*Publishers Weekly* on *Slow Burn Cowboy* (starred review)

"Fast-paced and intensely emotional... [One] of the most heartfelt installments in this series, and Yates's fans will love it."
—*Publishers Weekly* on *Cowboy to the Core* (starred review)

RaeAnne Thayne finds inspiration in the beautiful northern Utah mountains, where the *New York Times* and *USA TODAY* bestselling author lives with her husband and three children. Her books have won numerous honors, including RITA® Award nominations from Romance Writers of America and a Career Achievement Award from *RT Book Reviews*. RaeAnne loves to hear from readers and can be contacted through her website, www.raeannethayne.com.

Maisey Yates is a *New York Times* bestselling author of more than seventy-five romance novels. She has a coffee habit she has no interest in kicking, and a slight Pinterest addiction. She lives with her husband and children in the Pacific Northwest. When Maisey isn't writing, she can be found singing in the grocery store, shopping for shoes online and probably not doing dishes. Check out her website, www.maiseyyates.com.

New York Times **Bestselling Author**

RaeAnne THAYNE

RETURN TO STAR VALLEY

Previously Published as *Cassidy Harte and the Comeback Kid*

**HARLEQUIN
BESTSELLING
AUTHOR
COLLECTION**

HARLEQUIN®
BESTSELLING
AUTHOR
COLLECTION

Recycling programs
for this product may
not exist in your area.

ISBN-13: 978-1-335-99985-6

Return to Star Valley

First published as Cassidy Harte and the Comeback Kid in 2002.
This edition published in 2020.

Copyright © 2002 by RaeAnne Thayne

Want Me, Cowboy
First published in 2018. This edition published in 2020.
Copyright © 2018 by Maisey Yates

This edition published by arrangement with Harlequin Books S.A.

For questions and comments about the quality of this book,
please contact us at CustomerService@Harlequin.com.

Harlequin Enterprises ULC
22 Adelaide St. West, 40th Floor
Toronto, Ontario M5H 4E3, Canada
www.Harlequin.com

Printed in U.S.A.

CONTENTS

Also available from RaeAnne Thayne

Harlequin Special Edition

HQN Books

For a complete list of books by RaeAnne Thayne,
please visit www.raeannethayne.com.

RETURN TO STAR VALLEY

RaeAnne Thayne

To Angela Stone and her band of angels,
especially Merrilyn Lynch, Dorothy Griffiths,
Terri Crossley and Leslie Buchanan,
for nurturing my family when I couldn't.

Chapter One

Forget bad hair days. Cassidy Harte was having a bad *everything* day.

The ancient commercial-grade oven had been giving her fits since lunch; the owner of the small grocery in town had messed up her order, as usual; and her best assistant had decided to run off to Jackson Hole with a hunky, sweet-talking cowboy.

And now this.

With a resigned sigh, she set the spoon down from her world-famous, scorching-hot chili bubbling on the stove and prepared to head off yet another crisis.

"Calm down, Greta, and tell me what's happened."

One of the high school students Jean Martineau had hired for the summer to clean rooms and wait tables at the Lost Creek Guest Ranch looked as if she was going to hyperventilate any second now. Her hair was even spikier than normal, her eyes were huge with panic behind their horn-rimmed glasses, and she was breathing harder than a bull rider at the buzzer.

"He's here. The new owner. A whole week early!" she wailed. "What are we gonna do? Jean and Kip took the guests on a trail ride before dinner, and there's no one else here but me and I don't know what to do with him," she finished on a whimper.

Is that all? From the way the girl was carrying on, Cassie would have guessed a grizzly had ambled into the office and ordered a cabin for the night. "It's okay. Calm down. We can handle this."

"But a whole week early! We're not ready."

It *was* pretty thoughtless of the Maverick Enterprises CEO to just drop in unexpectedly like this. But the man hadn't done anything in the usual way, from the moment his representative had made Jean Martineau an offer she couldn't refuse for her small guest ranch in Star Valley, Wyoming.

All of the negotiations had been handled by a third party—the few negotiations there had been, since the company hadn't so much as raised an eyebrow at Jean's seven-figure asking price.

She turned her attention back to Greta. "We'll just have to do our best. Don't worry about it. Maverick has made it clear it wants the ranch pretty badly. The company has already invested buckets of time and money into the sale. As far as I know, it's basically a done deal. Even if we tried, I don't think we can possibly blow it at this late date."

The girl still had the wide-eyed, panicky look of a calf facing a branding iron. "You know how much I need this job. If he doesn't like the service here, he could still fire every single one of us after Maverick takes over. I don't want to go back to making ice-cream cones at the drive-up."

True. And Cassie would really hate to lose her job cooking meals for the guest and staff at the ranch. Finding a well-paying job she was qualified for in rural Wyoming wasn't exactly easy. Especially one that included room and board.

She knew she could always move to a bigger town but she didn't want to leave Star Valley. This was her home.

If she had to, she knew she could *really* go home, to her family, but the idea of crawling back to the Diamond Harte appealed to her about as much as sticking one of those branding irons in her eye.

Besides that, she loved working at the Lost Creek. These last few months on her own had been so rich with experiences that she couldn't bear the idea of losing it all, just because some spoiled, inconsiderate executive decided to drop in on a whim.

She sighed. What a pain in the neck. He'd ruined her plans. With a twinge of regret she remembered the great menu she had planned for the new boss's first night at the ranch—rack of lamb, caramelized pearl onions and creamed potatoes, with raspberry tartlets for dessert.

Tonight's dinner was good, hearty fare—chili, corn bread, salad and Dutch-oven peach cobbler—but it was nothing spectacular. It would have to do, though. She didn't have time to whip up anything else.

"You have to help me," Greta pleaded. "I don't know what to do with him and I'm afraid I'll ruin everything. You know how I get."

Cassie winced at the reminder. Two weeks before, the president of a fast-food chain from back east had rented the entire ranch for a family reunion. In the midst of a severe case of nerves, Greta had ended up accidentally short-sheeting his bed, leaving out towels altogether and overcharging his credit card by a couple of extra zeros. Then at breakfast she'd topped it off by spilling hot cocoa all over his wife.

"Where is the new guy now?"

"I left him in the gathering room. I didn't even know which cabin to put him in, since that doctor and his family have the Grand Teton for another two nights."

Their best cabin. Rats. "What's left?"

"Just the Huckleberry."

One of the very smallest cabins. And the one next to hers. She blew out a breath. "That will have to do. He can't expect to drop in like this and have the whole world stop just for him. Check to make sure the cabin sparkles and then send one of the other wranglers up the trail after Jean. I'll go out and try to keep him busy until she gets back."

With a last quick stir of the chili—and a heartfelt wish that she were wearing something a little more presentable than jeans and a T-shirt with her favorite female country band on the front—she headed for the gathering room.

It didn't matter what she was wearing, she assured herself. He was probably a rich old man who only wants to play cowboy, who wouldn't notice anything but the ranch unless a stampede knocked him over. He had to be. Why else would his company go to so much effort to buy the Lost Creek Guest Ranch?

The ranch consisted of a dozen small guest cabins and the main ranch house that served as lodge and dining hall. The centerpiece of the split-log house was the huge two-story gathering room, with several Western leather couches set up in conversational groups, a huge river-rock fireplace and a wide wall of windows overlooking the beautiful Salt River Mountain Range.

At the doorway Cassie found the new owner standing with his back to her, gazing out at the mountains.

Okay, she was wrong.

This was no pudgy old cowboy-wannabe, at least judging by the rear view.

And what a view it was.

She gulped. Instead of the brand-spankin'-new Western duds she might have expected, the new owner wore faded jeans and a short-sleeved cotton shirt the same silvery green as the sagebrush covering the mountains. Dark blond hair touched with gold brushed the collar of his shirt and broad shoulders tapered down to lean hips that filled out a pair of worn jeans like nobody's business. The long length of faded denim ended in a pair of sturdy, battered boots built more for hard work than fashion.

Whoa, Nellie.

By sheer force of will she managed to rein in her wandering thoughts and douse the little fire of awareness sparking to life in her stomach. What in the world was the matter with her? She wasn't the kind of woman to go weak-kneed at a pretty, er, face. She just *wasn't*.

Standing in a hot kitchen all day must have addled her brain. Yeah, that must be it. What other excuse could there be? She couldn't remember the last time she had experienced this mouthwatering, breathless, heart-pumping reaction.

On some weird level, she supposed it was kind of comforting to know she still could. For a long time she'd been afraid that part of her had died forever.

Still, it was highly inappropriate to entertain lascivious thoughts about her new employer, tight rear end notwithstanding.

She pasted on what she hoped was a friendly, polite smile and walked toward the man. "Hello. You must be from Maverick Enterprises," she said. "I'm Cassidy Harte, the ranch cook. I'm afraid you caught us by surprise. I apologize for the delay and any inconvenience. Welcome to the Lost Creek Ranch."

Oddly enough, as soon as she started to speak, the man completely froze, and she saw the taut bunching of muscles under the expensive cotton of his shirt.

For one horrified moment, she wondered if he was going to ignore her. When she was within a half-dozen feet of him, though, he finally began to slowly turn toward her.

"Hello, Cassie."

The world tilted abruptly, and she would have slid right off the edge if she hadn't reached blindly for the nearest piece of furniture, a Stickley end table that, lucky for her, was sturdy enough to sustain her weight.

She couldn't breathe suddenly. This must be what a heart attack felt like, this grinding pain in her chest, this roaring in her ears, this light-headedness that made the whole room spin.

Even with the sudden vertigo making her feel dazed and disoriented, she couldn't take her eyes off him. In a million years she never would have expected him to show up at the Lost Creek Guest Ranch after all this time.

"Aren't you going to say anything?" her former fiancé and the man who had destroyed her youth and her innocence asked her with that same damn lopsided smile she'd fallen in love with ten years before.

She gulped air into her lungs, ordered oxygen to saturate her brain cells once more. Still gripping the edge of the oak table, she finally forced herself to meet his gaze.

"What are you doing here, Zack?"

Zack Slater—ten years older and worlds harder than he'd been a decade ago—angled his tawny head. "Is that any way to greet me after all these years?"

What did he want from her? Did he honestly think she would embrace him with open arms, would fall on him as if he were a long-lost friend? *The prodigal fiancé?*

"You're not welcome here," she said, her voice as cold as a glacial cirque. She had ten years of rage broiling up inside her, ten years of rejection and betrayal and shame. "I don't know why you've come back but you can leave now."

Get out before I throw you out.

For just an instant she thought she saw the barest hint of a shadow creep across his hazel eyes, then it slid away and he gave her a familiar, mocking smile. "Funny thing about that, Cass. Welcome or not, I'm afraid I won't be leaving anytime soon. I own the place."

Her heart stumbled in her chest as instant denial sprang out. "No. No, you don't."

"Not yet, technically. But it's only a matter of time."

Owned the place? He couldn't. It was impossible. Fate couldn't be that cruel. She wouldn't believe it.

"I don't know what kind of game you're playing this time," she snapped, "but you're lying, something we both know you're so very good at. How stupid do you think I am? Maverick Enterprises is buying the Lost Creek."

Again he offered nothing but that hard smile. "And I'm Maverick Enterprises."

She wouldn't have been more shocked if he'd suddenly picked up the end table still supporting her weight and tossed it through the eighteen-foot window.

Zack Slater and Maverick Enterprises? It wasn't possible. Jean had done her research before she agreed to sell the ranch. She might be in her seventies but she wasn't some kind of doddering old fool. According to the papers provided by the lawyer who had brokered the deal, Maverick had more investments than Cassie's oldest brother had cattle—everything from coffee-houses to bookstores to Internet start-ups.

The one common thread among them was that each business had a reputation for fairness and integrity, things the man standing in front of her would know nothing about.

"Nice try, but that's impossible," she snapped. "Maverick is a huge operation, with its fingers in pies all over the West."

"What's the matter, Cass? You don't think a money-grubbing drifter who could barely pay for his own wedding might be the one licking the apple filling off his fingers?"

She scowled. "Not you. You never had any interest in business whatsoever."

"Sorry to shatter your illusions, sweetheart, but it's true. Do you want the number to my office so you can check it out?"

In the face of his cocky attitude, her assurance wavered. This couldn't be happening. He had to be lying, didn't he?

"Why should I believe anything you say?" she finally snapped. "You don't exactly have the best track record around here. I made the mistake of trusting you once, and look where it got me."

He shifted his gaze away, looking out at the mountains once more. After a moment he turned back, his expression shuttered and those long, dark lashes shielding his vivid eyes.

"Would it help if I said I was sorry for that?" he asked quietly.

For what? For leaving her practically at the altar...or for asking her to marry him in the first place?

She gazed at him, words choking her throat like Western virgin's bower around a cottonwood trunk. Did he honestly have the gall to stand in front of her and apologize so casually, as if he'd simply bumped shopping carts or pulled in front of her in traffic?

She thought of her oldest brother and those first days *after,* when Matt had walked around in a state of dazed disbelief. Of a tiny, frail Lucy, just a few months old, wailing shrilly for the mother who would never come back.

Of her own shock and the agonizing pain of complete betrayal, those days and months and years when she knew the whole town looked at her with pity, when the whispers behind her back threatened to deafen her.

Sorry? Zack Slater could never be sorry enough to make right everything he and Melanie had destroyed.

"You're about ten years too late."

Zack winced inwardly at the bitterness in her voice, though it was nothing more than he expected. Or than he deserved.

He wanted to kick himself for blurting that out so bluntly. He should have slowly worked up to his apology, waited until she had time to get to know him again before he tried to explain away the decisions he'd made that summer.

But since the moment she had walked into the vast room with its cozy furniture and spectacular view, his brain seemed about as useful as a one-legged chicken and he had to fight with everything inside him not to reach for her.

And wouldn't *that* have gone over well? He could just picture her reaction if he tried to pull her into his arms. Knowing Cassie, if he tried it, she would probably scratch and claw and aim a knee at a portion of his anatomy he was fairly fond of.

She said he was too late for apologies, for explanations. He hoped not. He *really* hoped not, or all his work these last few months would have been for nothing.

Before he could answer, she drew herself up with the unconsciously sensual grace that had been so much a part of her, even as an eighteen-year-old young woman just growing into her body.

Eyes glittering with fury, she faced him. "I don't know what kind of scam you're trying to pull here, Slater. But I'll warn you, Jean is not some feeble-minded old lady to sit by and just let you waltz in and swindle her out of the ranch she has loved all her life. And even if she were, you can bet, I'm not. Jean has people who love her, who look out for her. Whatever twisted scheme you've come up with, you won't get away with this."

At that, she stalked out of the room, her wildflower scent lingering behind her.

He blew out a sharp breath. So much for a warm welcome. Not that he'd expected one. But then, he'd never imagined Cassie would be the first one to greet him when he arrived, either. He'd thought he would at least have had a little more time to prepare for the shock of seeing her.

She had changed.

What had he expected in ten years? Time didn't stand still except in his entirely too-vivid imagination. There,

Cassidy Harte had remained as fresh and innocent as she'd been at eighteen, when she had stolen his heart with her mischievous smile and her boundless love and her unwavering loyalty.

That Cassie—the one who had haunted his dreams for so long, through the dark months when he had nothing else—had worn her hair long, in a sleek ponytail he used to love to pull from its binding and twist his fingers through.

Sometime during the long years since, she had cut it off. He wondered when, and felt a little pang of loss he knew he had no right to.

Her hair was still as dark and luxurious as it had been ten years ago—as glossy and rich as fine sable—but now she wore it in a sexy little cap that, on any other woman he might have called boyish.

There was nothing remotely boyish about Cassidy Harte, though. From her high cheekbones to her full lips to her body's soft, welcoming curves, she was one hundred percent woman.

Her eyes were the same. Blue as the spring's first columbine, fringed by long thick lashes that didn't need any kind of makeup to enhance their natural beauty.

Ten years ago those eyes would have softened when he walked into a room, would have lit up with joy just at the sight of him. Now they were hard and angry, filled with a deep betrayal he had put there.

This had to work.

He shoved away from the couch and turned back to the mountains, looking out at the magnificent view with the same yearning he imagined was in his gaze when he looked at Cassie.

It had to work. He couldn't imagine the alternative.

He had made mistakes—he would be the first one to admit them. But he had paid for them, and paid dearly. Could he make it right with her? What were the chances that she would ever be able to find it in her heart to forgive him, after the hurt he had caused her?

Slim to none, he figured.

He rubbed a hand over the ache in his chest. He would just have to do his best. No matter how tough, how seemingly insurmountable the task might seem, he had to do everything he could to make it work.

No matter the risk, he must take this chance.

To see if somewhere inside this hard, angry woman still remained any shred of the one person in the world who had seen something in him worth loving.

Chapter Two

It was true. All of it.

To her shock and dismay, it turned out he was telling the truth this time. By some sadistic twist of fate, Zack Slater was indeed the CEO of one of the most powerful companies in the West—and the man who would be signing her paycheck from here on out.

What kind of warped sense of humor must Somebody have to mess up her life so completely? Just what, exactly, had she done to deserve this?

She tried to be a good person. She didn't lie, didn't cheat on her income taxes, didn't swear—much, anyway. She obeyed the Golden Rule, she was kind to the elderly and small children and she really made an effort to go to church as often as she could manage. And for all her effort, this is what she got?

She should have raised a little hell when she had the chance.

Jean Martineau, steel-gray hair yanked back into her usual ruthlessly tight braid, frowned at her with concern in her snapping brown eyes. "I had no idea, Cassie. I swear I didn't. The man who signed the papers went by William Z. Slater. Other than the last name bein' the same, why would I have any reason to think for one minute that he might have anything in common with Zack Slater, the no-good drifter who caused Star Valley's biggest scandal in years?"

Thank you so much for bringing that up again. Cassie pounded out more of her emotional uproar on the hapless ball of dough for the next morning's sweet rolls. At this rate, the poor things would be as tough and stringy as cowhide.

"It's not your fault," she assured her friend and employer slowly. "I'm sure he concealed his identity on purpose."

But why? That was the question that had been racing through her head all afternoon. If this whole thing wasn't a scam—and apparently it wasn't—why would Zack put himself to so much trouble to buy a small guest ranch that would probably never be more than moderately successful? It didn't seem like the kind of savvy investment a fast-track company like Maverick Enterprises would make.

The ranch was geared toward families, with plenty of activities for all ages. Jean had the philosophy that children needed to be exposed to the history of the West, to what life was like on a real working cattle ranch, in order to preserve appreciation for the old ways.

To that end she tried to keep her rates affordable, well within range of the average family's vacation budget.

Cassie would hate to see Zack come in and turn the

ranch into some kind of exclusive resort for the rich and famous, like some of the other guest ranches in the area had become. It would be a shame, not to mention take a huge investment in capital.

But why else would he want it, especially when he had to know he wouldn't be welcomed back by many of the good people of Star Valley?

And why all the secrecy?

Maybe for that very reason—if Jean knew he was the one buying the ranch, she never would have agreed to the sale.

Cassie pounded the bread one last time, wishing it were a certain man's lean, masculine, *treacherous* features.

"I can try to back out of the sale, if it's not too late." Jean didn't sound very confident. Her frown cut through her wrinkled, weather-beaten face like sagging barbed wire.

Cassie shook her head. "You won't get another offer to match the one Maverick made for the ranch."

"Well, I can get by without the money."

Maybe, but both of them knew Jean wouldn't be able to run the ranch much longer, at least not with the same hands-on approach she had always maintained. Some days her arthritis was so bad she couldn't even raise her arms to saddle a horse.

"I can't let you back out of the sale," Cassie said gently. "Not on my account. I'll find a job somewhere else. Wade Lowry is always after me to come cook for the Rendezvous Ranch."

Jean touched her shoulder. "I'd hate to lose you. I wouldn't be able to find anybody else with your gift in the kitchen."

"I'm sorry," she said helplessly. "I can't work for him. Surely you understand that."

Jean squeezed her shoulder, then stepped back to lean a bony hip against the table. "The past is past, honey. Nothing you can do to change what happened ten years ago. You got to move on."

It was so much like the lecture Matt always used to give her, she wanted to scream. "Maybe I can't change the past. But I also don't need to have it thrown in my face every day when I go to work."

"True enough. Can't say as I blame you."

Still, the disappointment in the feisty rancher's eyes gnawed at Cassie's insides. Guilt poked at her. Leaving right now in the middle of the ranch's busiest season would create a bundle of problems. Jean would have to find someone else fast to fill her position, which meant she would have to take time from the ranch's guests for hiring and training someone new.

She wavered. Maybe she could stick it out a little longer, just for Jean's sake.

Then she thought about working for Zack, having to see him regularly. Ten years ago she had been nothing short of devastated when he jilted her. She had worked hard during the intervening years to get to this place where she had confidence again, where she could see all the good things about herself instead of constantly dwelling on what it was she had lacked that had driven the man she loved into the arms of her brother's wife.

Seeing him all the time, working for him, was bound to undermine that confidence. She couldn't do it. Not even for Jean.

"I'm sorry," she said again.

Jean shrugged and managed a weathered smile. "We'll

just have to make the best of a bad situation. That's all we can do. Now, it's been a heck of a day. Why don't you go back to your cabin and I'll finish up here?"

"No. I'm almost done. You get some rest."

Jean touched her shoulder again. "Good night, then," she said, then hobbled from the kitchen.

After her boss left, Cassie quickly finished her prep work for breakfast, then turned the lights off and walked out of the kitchen toward her own cabin next to the creek.

She considered her little place the very best perk of working for the ranch. It was small, only three rooms—tiny bedroom, bathroom and a combined kitchen and living room—but all three rooms belonged to her.

For another few days, anyway.

The cabin was more than just a place to sleep. It represented independence, a chance to stand on her own without her two older brothers hovering in the wings to watch over her, as they had been doing for most of her life.

She was twenty-eight years old and this was the first time she had ever lived away from home. How pathetic was that? She had never known the giddy excitement of moving into a college dorm and meeting her roommates for the first time or the rush of being carried across the threshold of a new house by a loving husband or repainting a guest bedroom for a nursery.

She didn't like the bitter direction her thoughts had taken. Still, she couldn't help thinking that if it hadn't been for Zack Slater, her life might have turned out vastly different.

She had just graduated high school when he blew into her life. She had been young and naive and passionately in love with the gorgeous ranch hand with the stunning gold-flecked eyes and the shadows in his smile.

To her amazement he had seemed as smitten as she. The fierce joy in his face whenever he saw her had been heady stuff for a girl who had never even had a serious boyfriend before.

Right from the beginning they had talked of marriage. He had wanted her to finish college before they married, but she couldn't stand the idea of being away from him for four long years. She had worked for weeks to persuade him that she could still attend college after they were married, that he could work while she went to school since she had a scholarship. After she graduated, she would work to put him through.

Finally she had worn down his resistance. She flushed now, remembering. Maybe if she hadn't been in such a rush, had given him time to adjust to the idea of settling down, he wouldn't have felt the need to bolt.

But he did, taking her dreams—and her brother's wife—with him, and leaving Matt a single father of a tiny baby.

What else could she have done but stay and try to repair the damage she had brought down on her family? If she had the choice to do all over again, she honestly didn't think she would change anything she had done after he left.

She sighed and let herself into the cabin, comforted by the familiar furnishings—the plump couch, the rocker of her mother's, the braided rug in front of the little fireplace. She had made the cabin warm and cozy and she loved it here.

Functioning more on autopilot than through any conscious decision, she walked into the small bathroom and turned on the water in the old-fashioned clawfoot tub, as hot as she could stand. When the tub was filled almost to overflowing, she took off her clothes and slipped into the water, desperate to escape the unbelievable shock of seeing the only man she had ever loved, after all these years.

Taking a bath was a huge mistake.

She realized that almost as soon as she slid down into the peach-scented bubbles. Now that she didn't have her work in the kitchen to keep her busy, she couldn't seem to fix her mind on anything but Zack and the memories of that summer ten years ago, memories that rolled across her mind like tumbleweed in a hard wind.

The first time she had talked to him—really talked to him—was branded into her memory. He had worked at the Diamond Harte for several months before that late spring evening, but she had been so busy finishing her senior year of high school that she had barely noticed him, except as the cute, slightly dangerous-looking ranch hand with the sunstreaked hair and that rare but devastating smile.

Matt liked him, she knew that. Her oldest brother had raved about what a way Zack had with horses and how he worked the rest of the ranch hands into the ground. And she remembered being grateful that her brother had someone else he could trust to run things, while he had so many other worries on his mind.

Melanie had been in the advanced stage of a pregnancy she obviously hadn't wanted. Never the most even-tempered of women, her sister-in-law had suddenly become prone to vicious mood swings. Deliriously happy one moment, livid the next, icy cold a few moments later. Her brother definitely had his hands full, and she was grateful to Zack for shouldering some of that burden.

Then, in late May, the week after her high school graduation when the mountain snows finally began to melt, Matt had asked Zack to take a few of the other ranch hands and drive part of the herd to higher ground to graze. Because it was an overnight trip, they would need someone to cook for them, and Cassie had volunteered, eager for the adventure of a cattle drive, even though it would be a short one.

When she closed her eyes, she could see every moment of that fateful trip in vivid detail...

She loved it up here.

With a pleasant ache in her muscles from a hard day of riding, Cassie closed her eyes and savored the cool evening air that smelled sweet and pure, heavy with the rich, intoxicating perfume of sagebrush and pine.

The twilight brushed everything with pale-rose paint, and the setting sun glittered on the gently rippling surface of the creek. Hands wrapped around her knees, she sat on the bank and listened to the water's song and the chirp and trill of the mountain's inhabitants settling down for the evening.

She would miss this so much in the fall when she moved to Utah for college. The campus in Logan was beautiful, perched on a hill overlooking the Cache Valley, but it didn't even come close to the raw splendor of the high country.

This was home.

So many of her most pleasant memories of her parents were built on the firm foundation of these mountains. Every summer and fall on the way to and from their grazing allotment they used to camp right here where the creek bowed. Her mom would cook something delicious in a Dutch oven and after supper her dad would gather her and Matt and Jesse around the campfire and read to them out of his favorite Westerns.

She smiled softly. Her memories had begun to fade in the six years since her parents had died in a wintry roll-over accident, but she could still hear Frank Harte's booming voice ring through the night and see his broad, callused hands turn the pages in the flickering firelight.

She missed them both so much sometimes. Matt did his best. Both her brothers did. She knew that and loved them fiercely for working so hard to give her a good, safe home for the past six years.

Matt had only been twenty-two, Jesse seventeen, when their parents died, and she knew a lot of men would have figured a grieving twelve-year-old girl would have been better off with relatives or in the foster care system. Their aunt Suzie over in Pinedale had offered to take her in, but Matt had been determined they would all stick together.

It must have been so hard for him. She thought of how rotten she'd been sometimes, how often she'd snapped at him when he told her to do her homework or make her bed.

You're not my mother and you can't make me.

She owed him big-time for putting up with her. Someday she would have to find a way to repay him.

She sighed, resting her chin on her knees. She was reluctant to leave this peaceful spot, even though she knew she should probably go check on the stew and see if the ranch hands had eaten their boots yet.

When she walked away from camp a half hour earlier, Jake and Sam Lawson had been snoring in their tent in a little before-dinner nap after beating the brush all day. But they were probably awake now and wondering where she'd wandered off to.

She smiled at the thought of the two bachelor brothers, who were in their early sixties and had worked for the ranch her entire life. They treated her like a favorite spoiled niece, and she loved them both fiercely.

And then there was Slater.

A whole flock of magpies seemed to flutter around in her stomach whenever she thought of the lean, hard cowboy leading the cattle drive. This was the longest she had ever spent in his company, and she had to admit she had spent most of the day watching him out of the corner of her eyes.

The few times he'd caught her watching him, he had given her that half smile of his, and she felt like a bottle rocket had exploded inside her.

He made her so nervous she couldn't think straight. What was it about him? She'd been around cowboys all her life and most of them were simple and straight-forward—interested in horses, whisky and women, not necessarily in that order.

Zack seemed different. Despite the way he joked with the older cowhands, there was a sadness in his eyes, a deep, remote loneliness that probably made every woman he met want to cuddle him close and kiss all his pain away.

She rolled her eyes at the fanciful thought. If a woman wanted to kiss Zack Slater, it wasn't to make him feel better. He was totally, completely, gorgeously male, and a woman would have to have rocks for brains not to notice.

Well, she couldn't sit here all night mooning over Zack Slater. Not when she had work to do.

Just as she started to rise, the thick brush ten yards upstream on the other side of the creek begin to rustle with more than just the breeze. A few seconds later, a small mule deer—no more than a yearling doe, probably—walked out of the growth and picked her way delicately to the water's edge. After a careful look around, she bent her neck to drink and Cassie watched, smiling a little at the ladylike way the doe sipped the water.

The deer so entranced her that she almost missed another flicker of movement, again on the opposite side of the creek, at the halfway point between her and the deer. She narrowed her eyes, trying to figure out what other kind of animal had come to the water, then inhaled sharply. She caught just a glimpse of a tawny hide and a long swaying tail as something slunk through the brush.

A mountain lion!

And he had his sights on the pretty little doe.

Even though she knew it was all part of the rhythm of life—hunter and hunted, another link on the food chain and all that—she couldn't bear to watch the inevitable.

She squeezed her eyes shut for a moment, then changed her mind and jumped to her feet, waving her arms and hollering for all she was worth. As she'd hoped, the doe lifted her head from the water with one panicked look, then bounded back into the trees with a crash of branches.

"Ha, you big bully," she said to the cougar. "Find your dinner somewhere else."

The big cat turned toward her and she could swear there was malice in those yellow eyes. With a loud, deep growl that made the hairs on the back of her neck stand at attention, the animal turned, his long tail swaying hypnotically.

Uh, maybe drawing attention to herself with a cougar on the prowl wasn't exactly the best idea she'd ever had.

"Nice kitty," she murmured in a placating tone. "Sit. Stay."

The big cat paced the bank on the other side, staying roughly parallel to her. For the first time Cassie began to feel a real flicker of fear, suddenly not at all sure the eight-foot-wide creek would be enough of a barrier between them if the cat decided she made a better snack.

Moving slowly, she scooped up a softball-sized rock, just in case, and began backing toward camp and the men.

She had only made it a few yards when the cat tensed his muscles as if to spring back into the brush. Before she could breathe a sigh of relief, he turned at the last minute and spanned the creek in one powerful leap. With a strangled shriek, she threw the rock but it only glanced off the cougar's back before landing in the water with a huge splash.

Cassie didn't wait around to see if her missile found a target. She whirled and took off for camp, heart racing and adrenaline pumping through her in thick, hot waves. The cat was gaining on her. She knew it and braced, expecting jagged teeth to rip into her flesh at any second. This was it, then. She was going to die here in these mountains she loved, all because of her stupid soft heart.

And then, when she thought she could almost smell the predator's breath, fetid and wild, and feel it stir the hair at the back of her neck, a gunshot boomed through the twilight.

For an instant time seemed to freeze and she became aware of the total silence on the mountainside as the echo died away. A few moments earlier the evening had buzzed with activity but now nothing moved except the soft wind rustling the new leaves of the aspens.

She stopped, gratitude and relief rushing through her, then shifted her gaze to see which of the ranch hands had come to her rescue. She wasn't at all surprised to see Slater just lowering a rifle.

What did surprise her was the yowl behind her. To her shock, the cat wasn't dead, just royally teed-off. Apparently he decided he'd had enough of interfering humans. With a last angry screech exactly like one of the barn cats tangling with the wrong cow dog, the mountain lion skulked back into the trees.

She whirled back to Zack. "You missed him!"

"I shot into the air."

"Why?" she asked, incredulous.

He shrugged those broad shoulders. Despite the fierce need to pump every ounce of air to her oxygen-starved cells now that the danger had passed, her heart skipped a beat at how big and strong and wonderful he looked leaning there against a rock. "I saw you scare away his prey. You can't blame the guy for going after the consolation prize."

She stared at him. "You were going to let him take a chunk out of me just because I didn't want to watch him kill a poor, helpless deer in front of me?"

"Naw." He grinned and she began to feel a little shaky. "I probably would have gotten around to shooting him once he caught up to you."

"Well, that's comforting."

He only laughed at her snappish tone. "You okay?"

"Swell. Thanks so much for your help." The panic of the moment, coupled with the fact that she hadn't had time to eat anything since breakfast, combined to make her feel a little light-headed.

Zack walked closer to her, then frowned. "You're shaking."

"I think I need to sit down."

To her complete chagrin, she swayed and would have fallen over if he hadn't suddenly moved as fast as the cougar had—and with exactly the same lithe grace—and reached for her.

He guided her to the soft meadow grass. "Here we go. Just sit here for a minute until you feel more like yourself."

She hissed in fast breaths between her teeth, thinking again of that terrible moment when she thought her number was up. Remembering it wasn't helping calm her down, any more than having Zack Slater crouching so close.

She knew she was trying to distract herself from her scare but she couldn't help noticing his hard mouth, just inches from hers. A little wildly, she wondered what it would be like to have those lips on hers, how he would go about kissing a woman.

"Deep and slow." His voice broke through her thoughts, and she stared at him, suddenly terrified he'd read her mind.

"Wha-what?"

"You're going to hyperventilate if you keep breathing so fast. Slow down a little."

Wrenching her mind away from any thoughts of the man's kisses, she focused once more on the cougar. "Do you think he'll be back? We should watch the calves."

"I think between the two of us, we've probably scared him clear to Cody by now."

They sat there for a moment longer until she felt she had enough control of herself to return to camp.

To her amazement Zack had stuck close to her all evening, as if afraid she might have some delayed reaction to almost becoming cat bait. He was sweetly protective, even insisting on going with her to bury the remains of their food from any wandering bears.

Later they sat around the campfire long after the Lawson brothers had gone to bed, talking softly while each glittering star came out and the wind mourned through the tops of the pines and the fire hissed and sputtered.

She told him of her parents and her grief and how tough it had been after their deaths. He shared snippets of his own childhood, of moving from town to town with a saddle bum for a father and of being on his own since he was fifteen.

And then, when the campfire burned down to embers, he walked her to her tent, pushed her hair away from her face with a work-hardened hand and softly kissed her.

It had been worlds better than anything she could have imagined. Sweet and tender and passionate all at once. Just one kiss and he had completely stolen her heart.

That had been the beginning. They were inseparable after that and had tumbled hard and fast into love. It had been the most incredible three months of her life, filled with laughter and heady excitement and slow, sexy kisses when her brothers weren't looking.

Until it ended so horribly…

Cassie came back to the present to several depressing realizations. The water in the tub was now lukewarm, bordering on cool, and any bubbles had long since fizzled away.

And, much worse, silent tears were coursing down her cheeks as she relived the past.

Oh, cripes. Hadn't she cried enough tears over Zack Slater? It was a waste of good salt. The man wasn't worth it ten years ago, and he certainly wasn't worth it now.

She climbed from the tub, wrapping herself in a thick towel, then splashed her face with cold water to cool her aching, puffy eyes. She hadn't indulged in a good, old-fashioned pity party for a long time, and she figured she must have been long overdue. But enough was enough. Now that it was all out of her system, she could move on.

She put on her robe and decided on a glass of milk before bed. Just as she was opening the refrigerator and reaching for the carton, she heard a knock at the front door.

Rats. It was probably Jean coming to check on her one more time. The last thing she wanted was to have company, with the mood she was in tonight. She thought about ignoring it, but the knocks only grew louder and more insistent. Gritting her teeth, she looked out the small window at the cabin next to her, thinking of the man who now stayed there.

The man who now owned the whole blasted place.

What if he decided to venture outside to investigate the commotion? She didn't need another encounter with him today. Swearing under her breath, she went to the door and swung it open, then her breath seemed to tangle in her lungs.

Well, she didn't have to worry about Zack coming out to see who was banging on her door, since he was the one standing there, fist raised to knock one more time.

Chapter Three

As he'd expected, she didn't look exactly thrilled to see him. Her eyes turned wintry, her mouth went as tight as a shriveled-up prune, and her spine stiffened, vertebrae by vertebrae.

Even so, she looked so beautiful he had to shove his hands into his pockets to keep from reaching for her.

She must have only just climbed out of the bath. Her still-damp hair, a few shades darker than normal, clung to her head, and she had wrapped herself in a silky robe of the palest yellow. The delectable smell of peaches wafted to him on the cool, early-summer breeze, and his mouth watered.

Framed in the light from inside her cabin, she looked warm and soft and welcoming, just as he had imagined her a thousand times over the years.

Her voice, though, was as cold as her eyes. "What do you want?"

Just to see you. To hear your voice again. He shifted his weight, alarmed at the need instantly pulsing through him just at the sight of her. He would have to do a much better job of controlling himself if he wanted this plan to work.

"I just spoke with Jean." Despite his best intentions, his voice came out a little ragged. "She said you tendered your resignation."

He didn't think it was possible, but that prune-mouth tightened even more. "What else did you expect?"

"I expected you to show a little more backbone."

She stared at him for several seconds. In the porch light her eyes looked huge, those dark lashes wide with disbelief, and then she laughed harshly. "Oh that's a good one, coming from you. Really good. Thanks. I needed a good joke tonight."

Okay. He deserved that. He had no right to lecture her about staying power when he had been the one who walked away just days before their wedding. Still, that was a different situation altogether.

He plodded gamely forward. "So you're just going to walk out and turn your back on Mrs. Martineau when she needs you?"

Her gaze shifted to some spot over his shoulder. "Jean has nothing to do with this. You're the new owner. That means I'm turning my back on *you*."

"We need to talk about this."

"No, *we* don't." She started to close the door, but his instincts kicked in and he managed to think fast enough to shove a boot in the space. Still, she pushed the door hard enough to make him wince.

"We don't have anything to say to each other," she snapped.

"I think we do. Come on, Cass. Let me in."

After a long pause where she continued to shove the door painfully against his foot, she finally shrugged and stepped back. He followed before she had a chance to change her mind.

Inside, he saw the cabin's floor plan matched his. Here, though, it was obvious Cassie had decorated it to suit her personality. It was warm and comforting, with richly textured rugs and pillows and Native American artwork covering the walls.

Cassie was a nurturer. She always had been, even as a girl just barely out of high school. She used to talk about her brothers raising her, but he had spent enough time with the family to know she took as much care of them as they did her. The Hartes looked out for each other.

The cabin reflected that nesting instinct of hers.

He smiled a little at an assortment of whimsical, ugly, carved trolls filling an entire shelf above her mother's rocking chair. She'd been collecting them since she was a girl and he recognized several new ones since he had last seen her collection.

He narrowed his gaze, looking closer. Where were the little kissing trolls he'd given her as a gift during their first month together? He couldn't see the piece here with the rest of the figurines.

He almost asked her what she'd done with it—why she hadn't set it out, too—but then clamped his teeth against the question. He had no right to ask her. Even if she burned it and flushed the ashes down the toilet, nobody would have blamed her.

"This is nice," he murmured instead.

"You must live in some grand mansion somewhere, now that you've hit the big time."

He thought of his cold, impersonal apartment in Denver, with its elegant furniture he was never quite comfortable using. Her little cabin held far more appeal.

"Not really," he answered. "It's a place to sleep and that's about it."

There was an awkward pause between them, and he thought about the little trailer home they'd planned to buy in Logan while she finished school. She had decorated it in her head a hundred times, talking endlessly about curtains and furniture and wallpaper. He had even gotten into the spirit of things, something that still amazed him. Neither of them had cared how cramped the little trailer would be. They were too excited about starting their lives together.

She finally broke the silence, her expression stony and cold. "Can we skip the small talk? I've had a long day and need to be up at five to start breakfast over at the lodge."

He pushed away his memories. If he wanted this to work, he had to focus on the present. "Okay. Let's get down to business. I don't want you to quit."

"What you want hasn't mattered to me for a long time, Zack."

He ignored her clipped tone. "From all the research my people did before we made the offer, we know that the food at the Lost Creek is one of the main draws of the ranch. In just a few months you've developed quite a reputation for delicious, healthy meals."

He paused, waiting for her to respond, but she remained stubbornly silent. After a moment he went on. "I want to build on that reputation. Use it as a selling point. That's been one of my goals for the ranch from the beginning."

She rolled her eyes. "Come on, Zack. You didn't really think I would stay here and work for you, did you?"

At his continued silence she gazed at him for a moment, then her jaw sagged. "You did! I can't believe this!"

He had hoped. Now he realized how completely foolish that had been. "You used to be the kind of woman who would never back down from a good fight."

Her mouth hardened again. "I used to be a lot of things. Ten years is a long time. I'm not the same person I was then. I've become much more choosy about the things I'm willing to fight for."

"And your job isn't one of them?"

"I won't lie to you. I like working for the Lost Creek. Jean is a sweetheart and gives me all the freedom I could ever want to create my own menus. But I would rather take a job cleaning truck-stop toilets than stay here and work for you."

He deserved everything she dished out and more. He knew it, but her words still stung.

"Is there anything I can say to change your mind?"

She shook her head firmly and he chewed the inside of his cheek. He hadn't wanted to play this card but she was the one folding way too early in the game. "Fine," he said, his voice cool and detached. "I'll let Jean know in the morning that Maverick will have to pass on the ranch."

Her eyes widened, and that stubborn little jaw threatened to sag again. "You can't! You've already signed papers. Jean already has a check."

"Earnest money, that's all." He refused to let the shocked outrage in her voice deter him. "We had thirty days to reach a final decision on the sale. I'll just tell Jean I've changed my mind."

"You're willing to walk away from the whole deal just because I refuse to work for you?"

"I'm a businessman, Cassie, as unbelievable as you seem to find that. The food you provide is an important component of the ranch's appeal to its guests. Who knows what kind of an impact your resignation will have? I don't want to take that risk."

"You can't be serious."

"Do I look serious?" He brushed an imaginary piece of lint off the sleeve of his shirt while she continued to gape at him.

"This is blackmail," she hissed.

"Call it what you want." He smiled as if his whole world wasn't riding on this moment.

"You bastard." Her voice quivered with fury.

Her reaction cut deep, but he only smirked. "You think I've never been called that before?"

"I'll just bet you have."

"I never would have made it this far without a thick skin."

"Just like every other snake in the world, right?"

Her eyes were bright with anger, and hot color flared high on her cheekbones. He wanted to reach across the distance between them and kiss away her anger, wanted it so badly his bones ached with it. He clamped down hard on the need for some kind of contact—any kind—between them.

"Think what you want about me—"

"Oh, I do. You can bet I do."

He went on as if she hadn't interrupted him. "But as far as I'm concerned, you're part of the package deal." He paused. "However, I can understand your reluctance, given our unfortunate history."

She snorted. "Unfortunate, my eye. The day you ran out on me was the luckiest day of my life."

A muscle in his jaw twitched. "I'm trying to be reasonable here, Cassie, but you're not making it very easy."

She remained stubbornly silent.

"As I was saying," he said, "I understand why you might want to find a new position. So I'm willing to make a deal with you."

"What kind of deal?" Suspicion coated her voice like a thin sheet of ice on a puddle.

"You stay the thirty days until the sale is finalized, and Maverick won't back out. In the meantime you can hire someone as your replacement, someone who can learn your menus and build on your success."

"And what do I get in return, besides the oh-so-appealing pleasure of your company?"

The Boy Scouts probably would have laughed themselves silly if he'd ever tried to join up, but he certainly believed heartily in their motto about being prepared.

Through a little casual conversation with Jean during the negotiations for the guest ranch, his lawyer had learned Cassie's job at the ranch was always considered temporary between the two women, that she was saving for a down payment on the diner in town.

Why she didn't use some of the vast Diamond Harte resources was beyond him, but in this case her typical dogged determination worked to his advantage.

"Stick it out for thirty days, and I'll give you a bonus of five thousand dollars."

Only the slightest flicker in her gaze betrayed that she had even heard him. "I don't want your money."

He shrugged. "Then stay for Jean's sake. I'm sure I don't have to tell you it will probably be a long time before she'll see another offer as good as the one we've made."

Not just a long time. Never. Cassie drew in a breath, trying to gather the thoughts he seemed to scatter so easily. Maverick had offered far more than the appraised value for the ranch. And who knew when Jean would even get another offer? The ranch had been on the market for a year already with little to show for it but a few nibbles.

He had her backed against the wall, and he damn well knew it. Would he be ruthless enough to make good on his threat to renege on the deal, even knowing he would hurt a sweet, feisty woman like Jean Martineau in the process?

Yes. She didn't doubt it for a second.

She wasn't stupid enough to buy his argument that the ranch's reputation would suffer without her. She was a good cook but there were plenty of others who could pick up right where she left off. No, he wanted her here for his own sinister reasons. She couldn't begin to guess what they might be. Just thinking about his motives made her stomach flip around like a trout on the end of a line.

On the other hand, Jean was her friend. She had been kind to her and given Cassie a chance to prove herself, when all she had for experience was ten years spent cooking for her family's cattle ranch.

How would she be able to live with herself if the deal fell through because of her?

Anyway, what did it matter who signed her paycheck? She probably wouldn't even see him during that thirty days. The president and CEO of Maverick Enterprises most likely didn't have a spare second to spend hanging around supervising a dude ranch in western Wyoming.

He would probably be here for a few days and then crawl back under whatever rock he'd been hiding under.

The realization cheered her immensely. She could handle a few days. She was a strong and capable woman. Besides, he didn't mean anything to her anymore. Any feelings she might have had for him so long ago had shriveled up and blown away in the endless Wyoming wind.

"Ten thousand dollars," she said promptly. With that much, she'd have all she needed to make the down payment Murphy wanted.

"You really think you're worth that much?"

She refused to let him see her flinch at his words. "At least."

"Okay. Fine. Ten it is."

She had never expected him to agree. The very fact that he did left her as wary as a kitten in the middle of a dogfight. "One month, then. For Jean's sake."

At least he didn't spin her platitudes about how she wouldn't regret it. Instead his dazzling smile sent a chill of premonition scuttling down her spine. She ignored it and held the door open for him to leave in a blatant message even Zack Slater couldn't disregard.

After a pause he sent her another one of those blasted smiles and obediently trotted for the door. As he walked out into the cool June night toward his own cabin next door, she couldn't help wondering if she had just made the second biggest mistake of her life.

He was already up and dressed when he heard her leave her cabin an hour before sunrise.

From his comfortable spot in the old wooden rocker, Zack listened to the squeak of her screen door, her footsteps on the wooden planks of her porch, then her sleepy, muffled curse as she stumbled over something in the predawn darkness.

He grinned into the hidden shadows of his own front porch. His Cassidy Jane had never been much of a morning person. Apparently, she hadn't changed much in the past decade.

His smile slid away. Wrong, he reminded himself again. Maybe she still wasn't crazy about getting up early, but she was no longer the same girl he had loved ten years ago. Everyone changed. He couldn't come back after so long and expect her to have waited for him in suspended animation like some kind of moth trapped in glossy amber.

She was a different woman, just as he had changed drastically from that wild, edgy ranch hand. The only thing they shared was a bittersweet past ten years old.

But last night in her house he had seen glimpses of the girl she had been, like some kind of ghostly reflection shimmering under deep, clear water. The way she tucked her hair behind her ear. The stubborn jut of her chin as she had argued with him. Those luminous blue eyes that showed every emotion.

She was the same but different, and he wanted to find out all the ways she had changed over the years.

He would see this through. He had come too damn far to back down now. If nothing else, he could at least explain to her why he had left. He owed her that much.

On impulse, he rose from the comfortable old rocker and followed her on the gravel pathway toward the lodge, maintaining a discreet distance between them.

The early-morning air was cool, sharp and sweet with pine pitch and sagebrush. He inhaled it deeply into his lungs, listening to the quiet. He had missed this place. More than he realized, until the day before when he returned.

He bought his own ranch in the San Juans a few years ago and he escaped to it as often as he could manage, but it wasn't the same. Western Colorado had never felt as comfortable to him as Star Valley.

As right.

The months he spent working the Diamond Harte were the best of his life. Not just because of Cassie, although he had watched her and wanted her for a long time before that fateful trip into the high country when he had kissed her for the first time.

Cassie was a big part of his bond to this place, but there was more. Her brother Matt had treated him well, far better than any other man he'd worked for over the years.

Wandering ranch hands without their own spreads generally had a social status roughly equivalent to a good cow dog. He'd become accustomed to it as a boy following his father from ranch to ranch across the West. He didn't like it but he accepted it.

At the Diamond Harte, everything had been different. Zack had been given more responsibility than he'd ever had before. He'd been treated as an equal, as a trusted friend.

And he had repaid that trust by abandoning the boss's sister a week before their wedding.

He frowned and pushed the thought away, concentrating instead on moving quietly several yards behind her. By now they had reached the lodge. Instead of going in the main door, Cassie slipped around the back of the big log structure and unlocked a door on the side, going straight into the kitchen, he assumed.

After a moment's debate as to the wisdom of another confrontation with her so early in the game, he gave a mental shrug, twisted the knob and walked inside.

He found her standing across the large, comfortable kitchen with her back to him, her arms reaching behind her as she tied on a crisp white apron.

She didn't bother looking up at his entrance. "I'm glad you're on time this morning, Greta. We've got a lot of work ahead of us for breakfast if we're going to do this right today. As much as I would love to serve a steaming bucket of slop to Zack Slater, I can't do that to Jean."

He paused several seconds, then couldn't resist. "I appreciate that," he drawled. "How about we save the bucket of slop for tomorrow? I think I'd prefer bacon and eggs this morning."

She whirled around at his voice, her blue eyes going wide. Color soaked her high cheekbones but she didn't apologize, just tilted her chin a little higher as her cool beauty punched him hard in the gut. "You're up early."

He leaned a hip against one of the wide counters. "I spent too many years as a ranch hand. Old habits, you know. It's tough for me to sleep past six these days."

"It's only half past five," she pointed out. "You have another half hour to laze around in bed."

"Must be all this fresh, invigorating mountain air." Or something.

"Well, I'm afraid you're too early for breakfast." Her voice was sharp as she reached for a metal pan on a shelf. "We don't start serving until seven."

"I can wait."

She studied him for a moment, then pursed her lips together. "If you're starving, there might be a few muffins left over from yesterday. And the coffee will be ready in a few moments."

Despite the grudging tone of voice, her words still reached in and tugged at his heart and he saw another ghostly reflection of the woman he had loved, the soft-hearted nurturer who hated to see anybody go hungry on her watch. Even him.

"I'm fine," he assured her. Better than fine. He thoroughly enjoyed watching her bustle around the kitchen, even though her movements were jerky and abrupt, without her customary elegant grace.

His presence unnerved her. He could see it in the way she fumbled through drawers and rummaged blindly in the huge refrigerator.

Under ordinary circumstances she probably knew this kitchen like she knew her own name, but you'd never be able to tell by her movements this morning.

He found it very enlightening to see her composure slip. Enlightening and entertaining.

Somewhat ashamed of himself for finding secret pleasure in the knowledge that he could fluster her so much just by invading her space, he straightened from the counter. "Can I help you do something?"

She peered around the chrome door of the refrigerator to stare at him. "You mean like cook?"

He shrugged. "I have been known to rattle a few pots from time to time."

Her gaze narrowed. "Why would the CEO of Maverick Enterprises volunteer to cook breakfast for ten hungry families?"

Because the CEO of Maverick Enterprises has spent ten years mooning over the chef. "Maybe I'm bored."

"Don't you have some kind of leveraged buyout or hostile takeover to mastermind somewhere?"

"I'm all leveraged out this morning. And I've found takeovers to be generally much less hostile once I've had my morning coffee."

She didn't return his smile, just watched him with that suspicion brimming out of her blue eyes. Finally he decided not to argue with her. Instead, he picked up a knife and went to work cutting up the green peppers she'd pulled from the refrigerator.

"Am I doing this right?"

She watched him for a moment, a baffled look on her features, then she shrugged. "You're the boss. If you want to play *souschef,* don't let me stop you. Dice the pieces a little smaller, though."

She returned to rifling through the refrigerator, and they worked in silence for a few moments, the only sounds in the kitchen the thud of the knife on the wooden cutting board and the delicate shattering of eggshells from across the room.

He had a quick memory of other meals they had cooked together, when he had been free to sneak up behind her if the mood struck him. When he could wrap his arms around her and lift her long, thick hair to plant kisses on the spot right at the base of her neck that drove her crazy, until she would turn breathlessly into his arms, the meal forgotten.

They had ruined more than one meal at the Diamond Harte together. He smiled at the mental picture, and of the slit-eyed look her older brother would give him when he would come in and find something burning on the stove and the two of them flushed and out of breath.

Not caring for the direction of his thoughts or the awkward silence between them, he looked for a distraction, finally settling on what he thought would be a benign topic of conversation.

"So how's your family these days?" he asked.

The egg she had just picked up slid out of her fingers and landed on the floor. She made no move to clean it up, just stood across the kitchen staring at him with her eyes murky and dark.

He only meant to make a casual inquiry. What had he said? "Was that the wrong question?"

"Coming from you, yeah, I'd say it's the wrong question." With color again high on her cheekbones, she snapped a handful of paper towels off a roll and bent to clean up the egg mess.

He set the knife down carefully on the cutting board and frowned at her. "What's that supposed to mean? I'm not allowed to ask how your brothers are doing these days?"

She rose, her eyes hard, angry. "I will not let you do this to me, Slater. I can't believe you have the gall to show up here after all these years and act like nothing happened."

While he was still trying to figure out how to answer that fierce statement, she shoved the paper towel in the garbage, then returned to cracking eggs with far more force than necessary.

"My brothers are fine." Her voice was as clipped as her movements. "Great. Jess is the police chief in Salt River. He and his fiancé are planning a late July wedding. Matt remarried a few months ago, and he and his new wife are deliriously happy together. She's a vet in town and she's absolutely perfect for him."

He wondered about the defiant lift to her chin as she

said this, as if daring him to say something about it. "So he and—what was her name? Melanie, wasn't it?—aren't together anymore?"

She didn't say anything for several moments. At her continued silence, he looked up from the cutting board and saw with some shock that she was livid. Not just angry, but quaking with fury.

The woman he'd known a decade ago rarely lost her temper, but when she did, it was a fierce and terrible thing. He only had a second to wonder what had sparked this sudden firestorm when she turned on him.

"No, they're not together anymore." Her voice sounded as if it was coated with ground glass. "They haven't been *together* since you ran off with her."

He blinked at the cold fury in her eyes. "Since I *what?*"

She turned away from him. "I'm really not in the mood for this, Slater. I have too much to do this morning if I'm going to feed your guests."

His own temper began to spiral. "The hell with the guests. I want to know what you're talking about. Why would you say I ran off with Melanie?"

"Hmm. Let me think. Maybe because you did?"

"The hell I did!"

"Drop the innocent act, Zack. People saw you. *Jesse* saw you. The two of you were making out in the parking lot of the Renegade. There are variations on the story but from what numerous people told me, she was climbing all over you like the bitch in heat that she was, and you weren't doing much to fight her off. Before Jess could beat the living daylights out of you, you and my darling ex-sister-in-law climbed into your truck and drove off into the sunset, never to be seen in Star Valley again."

His mind reeling, he scrambled to come up with something to say to that stunning accusation.

Before he could think past the shock, the side door swung open and the teenager who had greeted him the day before with such dumbstruck inadequacy whirled in, tucking a T-shirt into her jeans as she came.

"Sorry I'm late, Cassie. I slept through my alarm again."

The kitchen simmered with tension, with the fading echoes of her ridiculous claims. The idea that he would take up with that she-devil Melanie Harte was so ludicrous he didn't know where to start defending himself.

"No problem, Greta. You can take over for Mr. Slater. He was just leaving. Isn't that right?" she challenged him, her lush mouth set into hard lines.

He wanted to stay and have this out, to assure her he would rather have been hog-tied and dragged behind a pickup truck for a couple hundred miles than go anywhere with Melanie. He didn't want to do it in front of an audience, though. And since he couldn't figure out a polite way to order the poor girl out of the kitchen, he decided their shoot-out could wait.

"This isn't over," he growled.

Her eyes were still hot and angry. "Yes, it is, Zack. It was over ten years ago. You made sure of that."

He studied her for a few moments, then set the knife down carefully on the cutting board and walked out of the room before he said something he knew he would regret.

As Cassie watched him leave, a vague unease settled on her shoulders like a sudden summer downpour.

Why did he seem so astonished when she told him

she knew he left with Melanie? Was he honestly dense enough to think they could both disappear on the same night and nobody would be smart enough to put two and two together and come up with four?

He had definitely been shocked, though. That much was obvious. He couldn't have been faking that dazed, dismayed expression.

She shrugged off the unease. She had too much work waiting for her, to sit here trying to figure out what was going through the mind of a man who was a virtual stranger to her now.

"Do you want more green peppers?" Greta asked.

She saw that Slater had diced a half dozen, far more than she really needed for the *huevos rancheros*.

"No. That's plenty. Why don't you start putting together the fruit bowl?"

While Greta moved around the kitchen gathering bananas and strawberries and grapes, she kept sending curious little looks her way. Cassie ignored them as long as she could, then finally gave a loud sigh. "What?"

Greta yanked a grape off a cluster and popped it into the bowl. "Just wondering what that was all about. What's the story with you and the new boss?"

For a moment she was surprised at the question, then she realized the teenager would have been only a child a decade ago, too young to hear about the biggest scandal in town. "Nothing. No story."

Greta raised her eyebrows doubtfully. "What were you saying has been over for ten years, then?"

She didn't want to talk about this. Especially not with someone who had a reputation for garbling stories until they had no resemblance whatsoever to the original.

On the other hand, Slater's return was a rock-solid

guarantee that the whole ugly business was going to be dredged up all over town, anyway. She might as well get used to answering questions about him. "It was a long time ago," she said tersely. "We were engaged, but it didn't work out."

There. That was a nice, succinct—if wildly understated—version. It seemed enough for Greta. "You were engaged to the CEO of Maverick Enterprises?"

"Like I said. A long time ago."

"Wow! That's so romantic. Maybe he came back to try to win your heart again."

When pigs fly.

"I strongly doubt it," she murmured, then tried desperately to change the subject. "When you're done there, you can start squeezing the orange juice."

Greta wasn't so easily distracted. "For what it's worth, I think he's gorgeous. Like some kind of movie star or something."

Gorgeous he might be. But Cassie didn't have the heart to tell the starry-eyed teenager that beyond that pretty face, Zack Slater was nothing but trouble.

She was telling the truth.

Two hours later Zack poked at a runny omelette and half-cooked hash browns with his fork, trying hard to pretend he didn't notice the sullen whispers and the not-so-subtle glares being thrown his way by the Salt River locals.

When he had lived here before, Murphy had a well-earned reputation for good, hearty meals. Either the service and the menu had drastically gone downhill or Murphy was saving all the edible food for his other customers.

He supposed he was lucky to get anything, given the overwhelmingly hostile atmosphere in the diner.

When he walked into the café—with its red vinyl booths and mismatched paneling—the breakfast conversation of the summer crowd had ground to an awkward halt like a kid cartwheeling down a hill and hitting the bottom way too fast.

At first he figured everybody focused on him only because he was a new face in town. It was a sensation he was well acquainted with after spending most of his life being the worthless drifter who would never quite belong.

By the time the waitress slammed a menu down in front of him, the tension in the diner still hadn't eased a bit, and he began to suspect the attention he was receiving had its roots in something else.

So a few people remembered him from a decade ago. Big deal.

Soon the whispers began to reach him, and it didn't take long to hear his name linked with Melanie Harte's.

Cassie hadn't been making it up. Judging by the reaction at Murphy's, everybody in town thought he had not only had been chicken enough to run out on his sweet, loving bride-to-be less than a week before the wedding but that he'd stolen her brother's wife in the bargain.

The one taste of greasy eggs he'd managed to choke down churned in his gut.

Son of a gun.

He had known that leaving so abruptly a decade ago would cause a scandal, that Cassie would be hurt by it. He'd had his reasons for going, and at the time they had sure seemed like good ones.

Hell, when it came right down to it, he hadn't really been given much of a choice, had he?

At the time—and in the years since—he had tried to convince himself that leaving was the least hurtful option. He was going to break her heart eventually. He knew it, had always known it, even as they had planned their future together.

This way was best, he'd decided. Better to do it quick and sharp, like ripping off a bandage.

But he would have stayed and faced all the grim consequences if he had for one moment dreamed everybody would link his disappearance with a twisted, manipulative bitch like Melanie Harte.

What the hell were the odds that they both had decided to run off on the same night?

Cassie would never believe it was only a coincidence. He couldn't blame her. He had a hard time believing it himself.

Giving up on the eggs, he sipped at his coffee, which was at least hot and halfway decent. Of course, Murphy and his glowering minions probably hadn't had time to whip up a new pot of dregs just for him.

What was he supposed to do now? Going into this whole thing, he'd been prepared for a tough, uphill climb convincing Cassie to give him another chance.

To forgive him for walking out on her.

Tough was one thing. He could handle tough, had been doing it his whole life.

But he'd never expected he would have to take on Mount Everest.

Maybe he ought to just cut his losses and leave. He had plenty of other projects to occupy his mind and attention. Too many to waste his time on this hare-brained idea.

This little hiatus from company headquarters was playing havoc with his schedule. Maybe it would be best for everyone involved if he just handed the Lost Creek over to one of the many competent people who worked for him and return to what he did best.

Making money.

He sipped at his coffee again. Why did the idea of returning to Denver now seem so repugnant? He had a good life there. He'd worked damn hard to make sure of it. He had a penthouse apartment in town and a condo in Aspen and his ranch outside of Durango.

He had a company jet at his disposal and a garage full of expensive toys. Everything a man should need to be happy. Yet he wasn't. He hadn't been truly happy since the night he drove out of Star Valley.

"You want anything else?" The waitress stood by the table with a coffeepot in her hand and surliness on her face.

Yeah. He wanted something else. He wanted a woman he couldn't have. Was there anything more pathetic?

"No. I'm finished here."

"Fine. Here's your tab. You can pay the cashier." She yanked the ticket from the pocket of her apron and slapped it down on the table, then turned away without an ounce of warmth in her demeanor.

Okay. So this little junket into town had established he wasn't going to be welcomed back to Star Valley with open arms by anyone. He fingered the tab for a moment, tempted to climb into his Range Rover parked outside and just keep on driving.

No. That's what he had done a decade ago, and look where it had gotten him. He wouldn't give up. Not yet.

He could show Cassidy Harte—and everybody else in town, for that matter—that his stubborn streak would beat hers any day.

With new determination he slid out of the booth, reached into his wallet and pulled out a hundred, just because he could. He left it neatly on top of the ticket then walked out the door, leaving the whispers and glares behind him.

The morning air was clean and fresh after the oppressive atmosphere inside the diner. It was shaping up to be a beautiful summer day in the Rockies, clear and warm.

He nodded to a man in uniform walking through the parking lot toward him, then did a double take.

Hell.

Cassie's middle brother, Jess, was walking toward him, fury on his features. Great. Just what he needed to make the morning a complete success.

Chapter Four

Uncomfortably aware of the patrons inside the café craning their necks out the window to watch the impending scene, Zack straightened his shoulders and nodded to the other man.

Hard blue eyes exactly like his sister's narrowed menacingly at him, and Jesse folded his arms across his chest, a motion which only emphasized the badge pinned there. "Slater."

"Chief," he answered, remembering that Cassie had told him her brother now headed the Salt River PD.

The other man stood between him and his vehicle and showed no inclination to move out of the way as he stood glowering at Zack. Yet one more person who wasn't exactly overjoyed to see him turning up in Star Valley again.

Zack couldn't say he was surprised. For while he

hadn't known Jesse as well as Matt, Jesse had at least tolerated him.

Even so, neither brother had been exactly thrilled at the developing relationship between their baby sister and the hired help—a penniless drifter without much to his name but a battered pickup and a leather saddle handed down from his father.

Although they hadn't come right out and forbidden the marriage, they hadn't been bubbling over with enthusiasm about it, either. He hated to admit their attitude had rubbed off on him, making him feel inadequate and inferior.

He'd gotten their unspoken message loud and clear. Their baby sister deserved better.

Jesse had been a wild hell-raiser back then. Hard drinking, hard fighting. In a hundred years Zack never would have expected the troublemaker he knew ten years ago to straighten up enough for the good people of Salt River to make him their police chief.

Of course, the fact that Jesse was a cop didn't mean a damn thing. Not around here. Zack knew more than most that a Salt River PD uniform could never completely cover up the kind of scum who sometimes wore it.

He shifted, wary at Jesse Harte's continued silence. Either he was gearing up to beat his face in or he was going to order him out of town like a sheriff in an old Western.

The irony of history repeating itself might have made him smile under other circumstances.

And while he was definitely in the mood for a good, rough fight, he had a feeling Cassie wouldn't appreciate him brawling with her cop of a brother on Main Street.

If he had learned anything after ten years of building

a successful business from nothing, he'd learned that sometimes diversion was the best course of action. "I understand congratulations are in order," he finally murmured, stretching his lips into what he hoped resembled a polite smile. "When's the big day?"

Jesse continued watching him with that stony expression. "Next month."

"Lovely time of year for a wedding."

The other man had apparently contributed all he planned to in the conversation because he didn't respond. Zack finally gave up. "Nice talking to you," he murmured coolly, prepared to walk through him if he had to.

Jesse stepped forward, shoulders taut and his face dark. "You're not welcome here, Slater."

Big surprise there. He felt about as wanted in Salt River as lice at a hair party.

Jesse took another step forward, until they were almost nose to nose. "Now, why don't you make this easy on yourself and everybody else? Just go on back wherever you came from and forget about whatever game you're playing."

He tensed. "Who says I'm playing a game?" he asked, even though he was. It was all just a risky, terribly important game.

"I don't care what you're doing here. I just want you to leave. No way in hell will I stand by and let you hurt my family again."

The hands he hadn't even realized he had clenched into fists went slack as he remembered what people thought of him. What Cassie thought of him. That he had run away with Melanie, destroying her own dreams as well as her brother's marriage.

What a mess. Damn it, Melanie had left a new baby,

no more than a few months old. He remembered a sweet little thing with dark curly hair and big gray eyes who had immediately stolen her aunt Cassie's heart.

Melanie had abandoned her husband, her baby daughter, her whole life here in Wyoming. And everybody thought she did it because of him.

No wonder the whole town despised him.

"I'll be keeping an eye on you," Jesse muttered. "You screw up one time—drive one damn mile over the speed limit—and I'll be on you like flies on stink. I'll tie you up in so much trouble you'll be begging me to let you leave town."

He didn't doubt it for a minute. "Good to know where we stand." He offered a bland smile but wisely refrained from holding out his hand. "Nice seeing you again."

Since the police chief still showed no inclination to step aside and let him pass, he finally moved around him and headed for his Range Rover.

Leaving would be the easy thing, he thought as he pulled out of the parking lot and headed on the road back to the Lost Creek. The smart thing, even. But he'd taken that route once and lived with the guilt and self-doubt for a decade. He wasn't ready to do it again.

Not yet, anyway.

Cassie hung up the phone in her small office off the main kitchen of the ranch and fought the urge to slam her forehead against her messy desk three or four dozen times. If she received one more call about the scene in front of Murphy's between Slater and Jesse that morning, she was afraid she couldn't be held responsible for the consequences of her actions.

She had a whole afternoon of work ahead of her, planning menus and ordering supplies, and she didn't have the time—or, heaven knew, the inclination—to sit there listening to salacious gossip.

What had Jesse been thinking to confront Zack in front of the most popular hangout in Salt River, where he could have optimum visibility? As if all the busybodies in town needed a little more fuel to add to the fire. She was sure the grapevine was just about buzzing out of control over Zack Slater's triumphant return.

It all made her so furious she wanted to punch something. She had spent ten years trying to live down the past, hoping people were starting to forget the scandal.

Hoping *she* was starting to forget.

And now here he was again, stirring them all up like a boy poking at a beehive with a stick.

Still, Jess had no business pulling his protective, big-bad-cop act in front of Murphy's. She could just picture him scowling and threatening, trying to intimidate Slater into leaving town.

As if he could. She leaned her head back in her chair with a grimace. Two of the most stubborn men she had ever known going at it like a couple of bull moose tangling racks.

And Slater. She blamed him even more. None of this would have happened if he had stayed clear of town.

Why did he have to go into Murphy's for breakfast, anyway? Didn't he think the food at the Lost Creek was good enough for him? He was sure willing to pay a heck of a lot of money for it.

With a stern reminder, she caught herself just before she could build up a good huff. She didn't really give a flying fig what Zack Slater thought of her food. He could eat at Murphy's three meals a day if the mood struck him.

It was none of her business. She ought to be grateful to him for staying out of her way.

She forced her mind back to her work and dialed the number to the small grocery store in town. Alvin Jeppson, the owner and produce manager, was a good man. She'd gone to school with one of his five daughters and Al had coached her ponytail softball team several years running. Maybe it was all that cheering he did back then—or maybe just the din created by five daughters—but over the years he had become a little hard-of-hearing.

In typical stubborn Western male fashion, he refused to turn his hearing aid up loud enough, which resulted in some interesting twists whenever she tried to purchase supplies from him.

When he picked up the phone, she automatically raised her voice several decibels. "Mr. Jeppson, this is Cassie Harte at the Lost Creek. I need to check on my order."

She smiled while Alvin greeted her with warmth and affection. The smile faded to a grimace when he immediately launched into a diatribe against that "no-good cowboy who done her wrong" daring to show his face in town again.

"If he turns up in my store, he'll wish he hadn't. I can tell you that much for darn sure."

She had a quick, undeniably gratifying mental picture of old, deaf Mr. Jeppson whacking Slater with a can of cream of mushroom soup. "Like it or not, it looks like he's going to be the new owner of the Lost Creek," she said loudly. "You're going to have to do business with him."

"What's that? You say I'm going to have to learn to swim? What does that have to do with anything."

"No! I said you'll have to do business with him when he takes over the ranch," she repeated in a near-shout.

"I won't do it. Not after the way he treated you and your kin. He can buy what he needs over in Idaho Falls and that's that."

Even though she was touched by his loyalty, she knew Jeppson's couldn't afford to give up the guest-ranch account. She was about to tell him so when her shoulders began to itch and she sensed someone standing behind her in the doorway. She swiveled slightly and spied a pair of worn jeans covering long, muscled legs.

They ended in a pair of scuffed boots that had definitely seen better days. She knew before her gaze traveled up the rest of that frame who was standing in her doorway leaning against the jamb.

How long had he been there? She felt hot color climb up her cheeks, grateful he couldn't hear Alvin Jeppson's diatribe against him. "Mr. Jeppson, I'm going to have to go. I just wanted to let you know there was a mistake on our order. I need two hundred pounds of potatoes, not tomatoes. Potatoes," she enunciated carefully. "Idaho russets. Yeah. That's right. I'll send someone to pick them up this afternoon. Okay. Byebye."

She hung up while he was still ranting about the injustice done to her by the man standing in front of her. It would probably take Alvin at least five minutes to realize she was no longer on the line.

She swallowed hard and turned toward Slater, cursing her pulse for jumping at the sight of those hard, masculine features. "If you're looking for something to eat, there are box lunches in the refrigerator," she said curtly. "We never fix a formal meal for lunch since most of our guests are busy with sight-seeing or riding around the ranch."

He continued watching her out of those gold-flecked eyes like a cat ready to pounce on a helpless mouse. "Thanks, but I'm not hungry right now."

"No. I imagine you had your fill at Murphy's, didn't you?" She couldn't resist the gibe any more than she could keep the bitterness out of her voice.

He didn't respond other than to raise an eyebrow. "News travels fast."

"This is Salt River, Zack. What else did you expect? I imagine phones started ringing the moment you passed the city limits sign yesterday, and they haven't stopped since."

"So you've probably heard I had a little chat with big brother number two."

"Yes, I heard. Repeatedly." She glared at him. "Congratulations. The two of you and your little contest have now replaced Peggy Carmichael and her hernia operation as the biggest news in town."

"Well, *that's* something," he murmured, his voice dryly amused.

She wanted to ask what they had talked about, since none of her informants had been close enough to hear the conversation, but she figured she could guess. "It's a good thing Jesse wears a badge now, or you'd be smiling with a few less teeth from now on."

He demonstrated his still-intact dentistry by flashing her a devastating grin. "I think it's fair to say he was still sorely tempted to take a swing or two at me, badge or not."

The smile faded as suddenly as it appeared. He was

silent for a moment, his face solemn, then his gaze met hers. "And I would have deserved it."

Before she could answer that startling admission, the phone rang again. She gazed at it with loathing, wishing fiercely that she could ignore it. The last thing she wanted to do was try to appease someone else's prurient curiosity about Zack Slater in the presence of the man himself.

It might be important, though. Maybe Alvin needed to double-check something. Something that couldn't wait.

She glared at the phone for a few more seconds but finally picked up the handset after the fourth ring. "Yes?" she asked, her voice sharp enough to slice through concrete.

"Cassie? Is that you?" a deep voice asked, and she barely managed to choke down her groan.

She definitely wasn't in the mood for this. She almost thought she would prefer talking to the worst gossip in town rather than Wade Lowry right now.

"Yes, Wade," she murmured, her voice as stiffly polite as an army cadet. "How are you?"

Out of the corner of her gaze, she saw Slater stiffen suddenly, but she didn't have a chance to figure out why.

"You'll never believe what I heard at the bank this morning," he exclaimed, shock and dismay in his voice.

"Oh, I'm sure I will," she murmured.

He went on as if he hadn't caught her sarcasm, which was probably exactly the case. "I heard Zack Slater is back in town. Is it true? Have you seen him?"

"Yes. And yes." She'd seen way too much of him in the last twenty-four hours for her sanity's sake.

"How does he have the nerve to show up around here again after everything he's done?"

"That's something I'm sure you'll have to ask him,"

she murmured, surprised by the depth of his outrage. She and Wade were friends and had dated on and off for the past few years, but she would never have expected the bitter fury in his voice when he talked about Slater.

"You can be sure I'm going to do exactly that if I see him," her would-be champion answered.

He continued in the same vein for a few more moments, apparently expecting little more than monosyllabic responses from her. Good thing, since she couldn't come up with anything more intelligent to offer. Not when Zack stood in the doorway, arms crossed over his muscled chest as he blatantly eavesdropped.

She was more than a little annoyed with herself for finding the conversation so awkward and for the low, subtle tension that always seemed to draw her shoulders back whenever she talked to Wade.

He was a very nice man. Considerate, decent, hardworking. The very antithesis of Zack Slater.

He had made it clear several months earlier that he wanted more from their casual relationship, and she was furious with herself that she couldn't manage to drum up more feelings than friendship for him, no matter how hard she tried.

Wade would be perfect for her. They shared common interests, common background, common goals in life. He was good-looking and even owned his own very successful guest ranch just a mile or so from the Lost Creek.

If she married him, she could have his entire modern kitchen at her disposal. Could probably have free rein doing what she loved for the rest of her life.

But the no-good-cowboy-who-done-her-wrong currently standing behind her, listening to every word, had left a gaping hole in her heart that no one else had ever been able to fill.

Wade began to wind down, and she forced herself to pay attention as he reached what she discovered was the real reason for his call. "One of the repertory companies in Jackson Hole is doing a production of *Shenandoah*. It's getting fairly good reviews for a small theater, and I've got tickets for Sunday night. Would you be interested?"

His voice was tinged with a faint hesitation that only intensified her self-disgust. These days Wade offered each invitation with the wariness of a child whose fingers had been slapped one too many times, but who still couldn't help hoping this time he might be able to reach the cookie jar.

What was worse? she wondered. Continuing to turn down his tenaciousness in the hope that he would eventually give up? Or dating him when she knew she would never be able to feel anything more than friendship for him?

She opened her mouth to decline once more, then she caught sight of Zack leaning against the door frame, looking lean and tawny and gorgeous. The heartless, cheating son of a gun.

She jerked her gaze back to her desk and winced as she heard her next words tumble out. "Sure," she told Wade. "Sounds like fun."

An awkward pause simmered across the line and she knew he was taken aback that she had agreed but he quickly recovered. "Great. Show starts at eight. I'll pick you up at six and we can have dinner first. Will that work?"

"Yes. Oh, no. Wait a minute." Her Sunday commitments jostled through her memory. "I'll be having dinner at the Diamond Harte on Sunday with my brothers. We always do."

"Oh." The disappointment in his voice was painful to hear.

She caught sight of Zack again and swallowed her resigned sigh, trying to inject enthusiasm in her voice. "We can eat early and finish up by six-thirty. Why don't we skip dinner together and just go to the show? You can pick me up at the ranch."

The polite thing would be to invite him to dinner with her family but she didn't want anybody—especially not Wade—getting the wrong idea.

"That would be great. I'll spend the rest of the week looking forward to it."

"Me, too," she lied. "I'll see you then."

As soon as she hung up the phone, Zack uncoiled from the wall to loom over her. "Big plans?"

"A show in Jackson." She busied herself pretending to tidy up her desk, just to give her hands something to do.

Zack was quiet for a moment, then his mouth tightened. "I don't want you going anywhere with Lowry. Call him back and tell him to forget your plans."

It took several moments for the sheer audacity of his words to pierce her brain. When it did, she could do nothing but stare at him. "Excuse me?" she finally managed to exclaim.

"He's trouble. Stay away from him."

"Trouble? You're warning me that *Wade Lowry* is trouble?" She didn't know whether to laugh or scream. She thought she had been as angry as she'd ever been that morning in the kitchen, but when it came to Slater she was discovering all her emotions were on a short fuse, just looking for any excuse to come brimming to the surface.

"I'm serious, Cass. I don't want you going out with him."

"And I don't want to be the topic of dinner conversation at every house in Star Valley tonight because you showed up again," she snapped. "Here's a little life truth for you, Slater. One I learned the hard way. We don't always get what we want."

A muscle in his jaw flexed. "What would you think if I told you Lowry is one of the reasons I left town?"

She eyed him skeptically. "If I believed you—which I absolutely don't—I would probably think I should just run over to the Rendezvous right this minute and give Wade a big, sloppy, wet kiss for doing me the biggest favor of my life."

His face went completely still, and she thought she saw a glimmer of hurt in his gold-green eyes. For one terrible moment she had to fight the urge to apologize to him. As if she had anything to be sorry about in this whole awful mess!

"Stay away from him," Zack finally growled. "I don't trust the man. You shouldn't, either."

He turned on his heels and walked out of her office, taking with him any soft feelings toward him she might have been crazy enough to entertain for even a second.

Furious with the blasted man and with herself for being such an idiot about him, she picked up the paperweight shaped like a chef's hat that Lucy had given her for Christmas. With all the strength and technique Alvin Jeppson had tried to drum into her head through those years of coaching, she threw it as hard as she could at the door frame where Slater had just been leaning.

It bounced off with a loud thud, leaving a big, ugly nick in the wood, then clattered to the floor.

She'd chipped it, she saw when she went to pick it up. Just a little on one side, barely noticeable, but still, tears pricked behind her eyelids. She blinked them back. She refused to cry over a silly little paperweight, even though it had been a gift from her beloved niece.

And, damn it, she wouldn't cry for Zack Slater, either.

He had no business here.

In Star Valley, at the Lost Creek, and especially not camped out on the front porch of Cassie's cabin. The porch swing chains rattled as he shifted position, watching moonlight gleam like mother-of-pearl across the gravel pathway leading to the main lodge.

Why wasn't she home? The dining room had closed more than an hour ago and all the guests at the ranch were either taking an evening ride around the lake or playing board games at the main lodge or relaxing in their cabins.

So where was Cassie? If these were the kind of hours she kept, he was going to have to do something about it. It wasn't healthy, physically or mentally, no matter how much she loved her work.

He heard his own thoughts and grimaced at the irony. He was a fine one to talk. He'd spent just about every moment of the past ten years pouring his blood and sweat and soul into Maverick, trying to make it a success.

The magnitude of what he had accomplished still sometimes made him sit back in wonder. The kid of a dirt-poor drunk had no business wheeling and dealing with the big boys.

While he listened to the night seethe and stir around

him, he thought of the strange, twisting journey that had begun when he left Salt River a decade earlier. He had wandered aimlessly for a while, then had joined up on the rodeo circuit, looking for a bit of quick cash.

Amazingly enough, right out of the gate he'd won a couple of fairly decent bronc busting purses, fueled more by reckless despair than any real skill on his part. He wasn't aware of any kind of conscious plan at the time, but some instinct had led him to him plow the money into investments that had paid off.

He had turned around and invested those dividends again, then again and again, hitting big on just about everything he turned his hand to. Much to his surprise, he discovered he had an uncanny knack for predicting market trends. Through that knack, a lot of hard work and a few mistakes along the way, he had built Maverick into a huge, highly successful company.

By all rights, he should be deliriously happy. He had just about everything a man could want. Everything he'd ever dreamed about.

Hell, more than that. A decade ago, he hadn't had any dreams. Whenever he pictured the future—something he didn't like to do much back then—he figured he would turn out just like his father, a penniless drifter always looking to see what was over the next hill.

Cassie had given him the rare and precious gift of faith. She had believed in him, had seen potential he'd never even suspected lurked inside him. Even after he left her, he had cherished that gift. Without it, he probably would have lived out that prophesy and become just like his old man.

Yeah, he had just about everything he'd ever wanted.

Except Cassidy Harte.

He gazed out at the moonlight, remembering the silk of her skin and the slick, incredible heat of her mouth under his. Even after a decade, the memory of her enthusiastic, wholehearted response to his touch was still as strong and as vivid as it had been the day he drove out of town with his heart shredding into little pieces.

The way things were going, he had a fairly strong feeling he would never again taste her mouth or feel those small, competent hands caress him. He blew out a breath, cursing again the tangled whims of fate.

Why the hell did Melanie have to leave the same night he did? It would have been hard enough trying to explain everything to Cassie, trying to make things right again, without the onus of trying to explain away the unbelievable coincidence.

Maybe he should give this whole thing up. Just go on back to his life in Denver and get on with things, forget about trying to repair the damage of his decisions.

He fiddled with a loose link on the swing's chains. He didn't want to give up. Not yet. He needed to talk to her, at least. He owed her an explanation that was ten years overdue.

He had tried to tell her earlier in the afternoon. That's why he had gone in search of her after his dismal trip into Murphy's, to set the record straight. He'd gotten a little sidetracked, though, when he had overheard her on the phone with Lowry.

Fierce jealousy hadn't been the only emotion curling through him when he pictured the two of them together. He didn't like the idea that Cassie could ever be mixed up with scum like Lowry.

He sighed and shifted in the swing again. Jealousy hadn't been the only emotion but it had been by far the strongest. Even though logic told him he had no right to be jealous—absolutely no claim over her—he had about as much control over it as he did that moon up there.

He leaned his head back, watching the path for some sign of her and listening to the chirp of crickets, the tumble of the creek behind the cabins, the far-off whinny of a horse...

He must have dozed off. He wasn't sure how long he slept but he awoke to find her propped against the porch rail watching him, her arms folded across her chest and her face in shadows.

"Hi." He heard the sheepishness in his voice at being caught in a vulnerable moment and tried to clear it away. "You're late."

The moon slid from behind a cloud, and he saw her raise an eyebrow. "I didn't realize I had a curfew."

"You put in long hours. Too long. Is it like this every day?"

"No. Not usually. Claire Dustin, one of the wranglers' wives, usually helps out with breakfast but she's in Bozeman catering her sister's wedding this week." She paused. "I'm thinking she'll make a good replacement for me. I'll talk to her about it when she gets back Monday. If she's agreeable, I can start training her right away."

"That eager to be gone, are you?"

She said nothing for several moments, then straightened from the porch railing. "I'm tired, Slater. As you said, it's been a long day. To be perfectly honest, I'm not sure I have enough energy left to tangle with you again tonight."

"I don't want to fight. I just want to talk to you. Explain a few things."

"I don't think I have the energy for that, either."

He should just let her go inside and sleep. But he didn't want this ugliness between them any longer. Not if he had any chance of clearing it away. "Please. Sit down."

She was quiet for a long time watching him across the width of the porch with only the night sounds between them—the cool sigh of the wind, the crickets' chatter, the creek tumbling along behind the trees.

Just when he began to fear she would ignore him and march into her cabin, she blew out a breath and slid onto the swing next to him.

Now that she was there, he didn't know where to begin.

"Gorgeous view from here," he finally said, which wasn't at all what he wanted to talk to her about. Still, it was the truth. He could see the Salt River Range behind them. Even in mid-June, the mountains still wore snowcaps that gleamed bluish white in the moonlight.

The Lost Creek had a prime location on a foothill bordering national forest land. From here he could see small glowing settlements strung along the Star Valley like Christmas lights.

"I like it," she finally murmured.

"I would have to say it's almost as nice as the view from the Diamond Harte."

"Almost. Not quite."

The pride in her voice for her family ranch made him smile. Although he knew she wouldn't be able to see much in the darkness, he could feel the heat of her gaze on him. What she could see apparently displeased her because her voice was curt when she spoke. "I'm tired, Zack. What did you want to talk about?"

This wasn't the way he wanted to do this, with her

already testy and abrupt. But it didn't look as if she was going to give him much of a choice.

"I'm sorry about this afternoon. About Lowry."

"You should be."

He winced at the residual anger in her voice. He wasn't sorry for warning her about the bastard, just that he had gone about it the wrong way.

She didn't give him a chance to explain. "I find it unbelievably arrogant that you think you can blow back into town like nothing happened and start ordering me around," she snapped.

"I don't think that."

"Don't you?"

"No!"

"Let's see." She ticked off his shortcomings on her fingers. "In the thirty-six hours since you showed up again, you have blackmailed me to keep me from quitting my job, you have once more dredged up old, painful gossip about me all over town and you have commanded me not to go out with a man I've known most of my life. Seems to me you're working pretty hard to control me."

Put so bluntly, he could understand why she would be more than a little annoyed with him. Maybe he *had* been a little heavy-handed since he'd seen her. What other choice did he have, though?

"I didn't come to fight with you, Cass. We need to talk. I'd like to clear the air between us."

"I really don't think that's possible." Her voice was small and maybe a little sad, which gave him some hope.

"Will you let me at least try?"

She remained silent, which he took as assent. Where to start? he wondered, gazing out at the mountains. At the crux of the matter, he figured.

"I didn't leave town with Melanie."

She froze, stopping the swing's motion mid-rhythm. "We went over this earlier. I don't want to hear it again."

She started to rise but he held a hand out to keep her in place, brushing the denim of her jeans as his hand covered her leg. She jerked away from his touch but stayed in the swing beside him, which he took as a good sign.

"Please. Listen to me. I know you're going to find this an amazing coincidence—hell, I have a hard time believing it myself—but I left alone. I swear it."

"So how did Melanie leave town? Teleportation?" A thin shear of skepticism coated her voice. "Her car was left in the parking lot of the Renegade. She was last seen climbing into your pickup truck, then the two of you were observed going at it inside the cab like a couple of minks. Are you saying everybody else who saw you two drive off together was lying?"

"No. They weren't lying. We did drive off together."

She made a *hmmph* kind of sound and folded her arms across her chest. He sighed. This was going to be much harder than he expected.

"You know what Melanie was like. She was wild. Out of control. That night she was drinking like a sailor with a three-day pass and throwing herself at anybody in sight. I offered to give her a ride home because I knew she was too drunk to be safe behind the wheel of a car. When she climbed into my truck, she attacked me."

"Oh, you poor helpless man. I'm sure that was just terrible for you."

"It was, dammit! I couldn't stand her. I was engaged to marry the woman I loved and didn't want to have anything to do with someone like Melanie Harte."

Cassie remained stubbornly silent, her arms folded

tightly, and he knew with grim certainty that she didn't believe a word he was saying.

"She kissed me," he tried again. "Started grabbing me as soon as she climbed into the truck. I told her to stop. I thought she was going to behave herself but as soon as we pulled out of the parking lot, she started all over again. Eventually I told her I would just leave her on the side of the road if she didn't cut it out. She laughed and said I wouldn't dare, that if I did, she would tell you I put the moves on her."

His memory of this was hazy because of what had happened later that night but he tried his best to reconstruct it. "I laughed at her. I told her you'd never believe it. She was crazy that night, though, and wouldn't stop. About the third or fourth time she tried to grab my crotch, I pulled over just outside the city limits, yanked her out of the truck and drove away, to hell with being a gentleman. That's the last time I ever saw her. I swear."

She didn't answer for several moments. When she spoke, her voice was subdued. "And somehow in the middle of all that, you just decided to keep on driving, right? Tell me, Zack. When did you decide you weren't really in love with me? When did you realize you couldn't stomach the idea of being married to me and decided running was a better option?"

Was that what she thought all these years? *Of course,* he answered his own question, his heart aching. What else could she have thought?

"It wasn't like that, Cass," he murmured, wondering how much to tell her about the other events that had unfolded that night. Ten years later it all sounded so inconceivable, even to him.

Who would she be more willing to believe the worst

about? People she has known and cared about all her life or the man she had spent years believing had betrayed her in the worst way possible?

He didn't want to make her have to choose. Truth was, he was afraid where he would stack up. But he had to give her some kind of explanation. If he didn't, the past would remain an insurmountable wall between them and she would never let him through.

"After I dropped Melanie off, I drove back to the Diamond Harte, then started to feel a little guilty about dumping her out like that in the middle of nowhere. Once I cooled off, I realized I couldn't leave her alone in the dark to find her own way home. I imagined her falling into the river or something else terrible happening to her, so I turned around to go look for her."

"And did you find her?"

"No. I just figured somebody else must have given her a ride. But while I was looking for her, I stumbled onto something else. Something illegal."

"What?" She sounded every bit as skeptical as he expected.

"When I didn't find her on the main road, I thought she might have wandered off in the wrong direction so I decided to look along this gravel road near where I dropped her off. I was feeling pretty guilty by then, when I saw a little puddle-jumper Cessna landing in a field a mile or so down the road. I figured they must have had to make some kind of emergency landing so I went to investigate."

"And?"

"It wasn't an emergency. It was a planned drop site. The plane was delivering a large shipment of cocaine. I was in the wrong place at the wrong time and stumbled on a crew transferring it from the Cessna to a truck."

She was silent for a moment then she began to laugh, low and rich and full of disbelief. "Okay. You might have had me going there for a moment but this is too much. What kind of idiot do you take me for? This is Star Valley, Slater. I'll admit, I'm not naive enough to think we don't have any illegal narcotic use in the valley but certainly not enough to make it some drug smuggling hub."

"Maybe not here. But I imagine there are plenty of tourists and movie stars just over the mountains in Jackson Hole who wouldn't care how their drugs arrived as long as they had a ready supply."

"Assuming I believe you—which I don't—it still doesn't explain why you just decided to take off. Why not go to the police? Someone would have helped you."

Oh, yeah. Salt River's finest would have helped him, all right. Helped him right into a five-to-life prison sentence for drug smuggling. He doubted Cassie would believe the depth of corruption in the small-town police department. Hell, he still had a hard time believing it and he had witnessed it firsthand.

Trying to figure out the best way to answer, he gazed out at that sliver of moonlight on gravel and the shadows beyond.

She wasn't ready for the whole truth, he thought, so he slipped her something a little more palatable. "Back then I didn't trust a man in uniform the way you did. Call it cynicism or whatever you want. I suppose I could have gone to someone, but I really didn't think anyone would believe me."

"Why not?"

"I knew what people said about me. What everybody

in town was saying. That I was some kind of gold digger after your share of the ranch."

"Nobody really thought that."

He studied his fist resting on the armrest of the swing, not willing to shatter that last illusion of hers. She had been a sweet, loyal eighteen-year-old girl in love who hadn't wanted to see what everyone was saying behind her back.

He suddenly missed that girl fiercely.

"Maybe not. Maybe that's only how I interpreted things. Like I said, I guess I was too cynical. I thought I would end up in jail if I came forward. That I would take the fall."

Not that such a conclusion had just sprung into his head out of the blue. After he'd been beaten so badly he could hardly move by four masked police officers wielding billy clubs and pistol butts, he'd been given the message loud and clear. Leave town or go to prison for drug smuggling.

What else could he have done?

"So you decided it would be easier to just leave, to hell with me and all our plans." Her voice was low, bitter, and ripped through his heart like a ricocheting bullet.

"Either way you would have despised me, whether I walked out or whether I stayed and ended up in jail. I figured leaving would be the best thing I could ever do for you."

"How thoughtful of you."

This time her bitterness made him wince. "Cassie—"

"Let me ask you one question. Why on earth would you want to marry a woman you thought so little of?"

"I thought the world of you! I loved you!"

She was the one shining light in a life that had been gray and colorless before their paths collided.

"You couldn't have loved me. You didn't even know the first thing about me."

"Sure I did."

"If what you say is true—if you really did stumble onto some drug ring and were afraid of taking the fall for it—you should have known that you didn't have to run. I would have stood by you, no matter what happened. No matter what anybody said about you."

He tried to see her expression in the dim porch but her face was just a pale blur in the moonlight. "I thought I did the right thing. I didn't want you to have to endure the shame of having your fiancé arrested the week before the wedding."

"What do you think would have been worse for me?" Her voice was just barely audible above the sighing wind. "The shame of you being arrested on some trumped-up charge that any good lawyer could have beaten? Or the shame I've lived with for ten years, of believing you preferred my brother's wife to me?"

Aw, hell. He closed his eyes against the pain lodging thick and heavy in his chest.

"If I'd had any idea everyone thought I jilted you to run off with Melanie, I would have come back and faced any consequence. I'm so sorry you had to deal with that."

"And that's supposed to mean something to me now, after all this time?"

"I don't know. I hope so."

She rose from the rocking chair and stood over him, a slender shadow in the night. "You still left, Zack. Whether you left with Melanie or not. You still left without a note or a phone call or anything. You owed me that much, at least."

She was right. He had wanted to call her a thousand times that first year but had always stopped before dialing the number. A clean break would be best for her, he had rationalized. She would move on with her life and forget about him.

Find someone better.

It sounded good in the abstract. Noble and selfless, even. But he had faced some fairly ugly truths about himself a long time ago. He hadn't refrained from making contact with her out of some high-minded desire for her to heal. He'd been a coward. Pure and simple. Afraid that the moment he heard her soft voice, he would turn around and head back to the Diamond Harte like a compass finding north.

"I'm tired, Zack," she finally said into the silence. "As I told you, it's been a long, hard day."

She moved past him for the door, and he felt his last chance with her slipping through his fingers. He stood and reached out to grab on to something—anything—and found the soft, bare skin of her forearm.

"I'm sorry I hurt you, Cass," he murmured. "I never wanted to do that. I thought I was protecting you."

Now that they were face-to-face, he could see the fatigue on her face, the purplish circles under her eyes. He wanted to smooth a hand over that tousled cap of hair. To hold her on his lap and tuck her head close to his chest and listen to her breathe against him while she slept.

His gaze locked with hers, and he realized some of what he was feeling must have shown in his expression. Her mouth opened just a little, and a breathy little sound escaped.

He could no more keep from bending toward that mouth than he could yank the moon from the sky.

If he'd been thinking at all, he would have expected her to jerk away when his mouth met hers. Knowing Cassie, he might have expected at least a slap or a knee to the groin. Heaven knows, he deserved all that and more.

She didn't lash out at him, though. Instead she whispered another of those little sighs and her lips softened under his.

He kept the kiss gentle. Slow and tender. Nonthreatening. A shadowy remembrance of other kisses.

She leaned into him just for a moment—just enough for his blood to begin singing and his body stir to life—and then she wrenched away from him so abruptly her elbow caught the door frame with a hard whack.

Chapter Five

She wasn't sure exactly when awareness slipped over her like a chilling mist.

One moment she wanted to weep from the tenderness of his kiss, from the unbelievable wonder of being in his arms once more. Of tasting his lips and feeling his skin and absorbing the taste and smell of him that had haunted her dreams for so long after he left.

The next, her spine stiffened, her muscles tensed, and she wrenched away. The impact of her elbow hitting wood jarred her completely back into reality.

Damn him for kissing her like that.

And damn her right along with him for allowing it.

"Don't touch me again." She meant to sound strong and determined, but she heard the quaver in her voice and cursed herself for her weakness.

"Cassie—"

"I'm serious, Slater. You want me to stay and work here, fine. I'll stay. We made a deal, and I, for one, always try to keep my word. But I don't want you near me."

She didn't wait for him to answer, just opened the door to the cabin and hurried inside before she did anything else stupid. Inside she slammed the door and stood for a moment, then slumped to the floor, one trembling hand covering her mouth that still burned from his kiss.

She felt stunned, immobilized by shock. As if every illusion she had ever had about herself had just disintegrated into a fine, chalky dust.

What just happened here?

Had she really just let Zack Slater kiss her? Not just let him, she corrected herself with dawning horror. She had been a willing participant, had wanted to dissolve in his arms like sugar in warm water.

She closed her eyes, remembering the heat of his mouth, the strength of his arms around her. The overwhelming sense of rightness, of belonging, that had seeped through her skin—through her bones—like spring sunshine.

As if she were home again after a long and treacherous journey.

What the bloody blazes had come over her? She blew out a shuddering breath. There was nothing *right* about kissing Zack Slater. It was wrong in every single definition of the word.

Her hands trembled as she pressed them over her face. Where was her pride? Her self-respect? Her sense of self-preservation, at least?

She meant what she said. She couldn't allow him to touch her again. Especially now that she realized her body still responded to him with all the enthusiasm of dry tinder to a match.

She wouldn't let him do this to her again. She had worked too hard the last ten years to become someone she could like and respect again. Now, when she finally felt as if she could hold her head high again, that she was a strong and capable woman—not that needy, trusting girl who had given her heart so completely—Slater had to turn up again.

She thought of the unbelievable story he had told her, sick to realize how desperately she wanted to believe him. It would still sting to know he chose to leave her rather than give her the opportunity to prove to him she loved him enough to stand behind him, no matter what happened.

It would still hurt, yes. But at least she wouldn't have to live with the constant, deep, burning shame of knowing he had preferred a woman like Melanie to her.

She let her hands drop and shuddered out a breath. She wanted to believe him, but she couldn't. The story was too outlandish. Too contrived. He and Melanie must have been carrying on a sordid affair, just as everyone had said. Melanie made no secret of her desire to leave Star Valley, and she had finally found someone willing to take her.

Cassie leaned her head back against the door. She couldn't believe him. She had to stand strong and solid as the mountains she loved. Ten years ago Zack Slater had left her bruised and broken, had nearly destroyed her and her family and had turned her into the laughingstock of Star Valley. She couldn't forget all that just because of a few self-serving words of explanation and a soft, tender kiss that left her yearning for something she could never regain.

She wouldn't let her heart be vulnerable to him.

This time she might not survive.

"So are you going to tell us how you're really dealing with all of this?"

In the big, comfortable kitchen of the Diamond Harte, Cassie looked up from the potato salad she was throwing together. Though her sister-in-law, Ellie, had been the one who asked the question, she and Jesse's fiancé Sarah were both watching her with identical expressions of concern on their faces.

She knew exactly what they were talking about but she wasn't at all in the mood to get into it right now, so she pretended ignorance, even though she knew it wouldn't fly with them for long. "Dealing with what?"

"Come on, Cass," Ellie muttered. "You know what I mean. With that man showing up again after all these years!"

Here it comes. She sighed. She should have known she couldn't get through the regular Sunday afternoon Harte family gathering without Zack Slater starring as the main topic of conversation.

Trying to avoid the question as long as possible, she looked out the window where her brothers, beer bottles in hand, went through the strictly male ritual of manning the steaks on the grill. She almost wished she were out there with them.

But whose inquisition was she more willing to face? Her stubborn brothers' or that of their equally persistent women?

Finally she turned back to the table, pasting a smile

on her face that probably fooled nobody. "I'm fine. Really. I can't say I'm thrilled Slater has the gall to come back and I'm not crazy about everything being dredged up again, but I'm coping."

Sarah's green eyes darkened with sympathy. "This must be so difficult for you. I can't even imagine it."

A quick image of their soft, late-night kiss of earlier in the week flickered through her mind. *Difficult* didn't even come close to describing the tumult shaking around her psyche since Zack Slater had shown up at the Lost Creek Ranch, rich and self-assured and as gorgeous as ever.

"I'm coping," she repeated, as blatant a falsehood as she had ever uttered.

She was fairly certain her friends saw through it, but they loved her too much to call her a liar to her face.

Instead Ellie stuck her chin out with a pugnacious tilt. "I know I, for one, would love to spend an hour or two locked in a room with the man, giving him a piece of my mind. Turning up again after all these years as if nothing had happened! How does he dare show his face around here?"

She remembered the regret she thought she'd seen in those eyes that night on her porch as he had told her his version of events. If he were telling the truth—that he hadn't left with Melanie—he had been judged unfairly.

It was one thing for a man to get cold feet about his wedding and decide to bolt. Better before the wedding than after, most people would say.

It was quite another if he took off with someone else's wife in the process.

But he couldn't have been telling the truth. Where else would Melanie have gone?

She looked out the window again at her brothers. Matt stood at the grill ready to turn the steaks, smiling at something Jesse must have said.

She adored both of her brothers, but she and Matt shared a special bond. After their parents' death when she was twelve, he had been the only authority figure in her life and she loved him deeply for taking on the responsibility of a young girl when he could easily have handed it off to someone else.

Deep in her heart she had always suspected he'd married Melanie in the first place to provide Cassie with a more normal home life than just that of an impressionable girl living with her two young bachelor brothers, one of them a wild hell-raiser.

He had never said as much—and he never would, she knew—but deep down she had always feared she was the one responsible for his disaster of a marriage.

Guilt washed through her as she realized she had given very little thought to Matt and how *he* must feel to have Slater back in town.

His marriage to Melanie had been over a long time before Zack Slater entered the picture—that much had been glaringly obvious—but it still couldn't be easy for Matt to live in the same town with the man everyone believed had run off with her.

No, she corrected herself again, angry at the part of her still clinging to that wild, foolish hope. The man who *had* run off with her brother's wife. She couldn't forget that. She wasn't ready to give up ten years of betrayal just because Zack claimed their mutual disappearance on the same night had been strictly coincidental.

"What has Matt said about Slater coming back?" she asked Ellie, her voice subdued.

Her sister-in-law shrugged. "Not much. He's upset about it of course, but mainly I think he's worried about you."

"Still, it must sting his pride a little bit to have all those old, ugly bones dug up."

Ellie's mouth tightened. "I don't think he had much pride left when it came to Melanie."

She couldn't dispute that. Cassie knew there were plenty of folks around Salt River who thought Slater did them all a big favor by taking away Matt's wild, troubled wife.

The silence in the kitchen was broken by Sarah ripping open a bag of chips and pouring them into a serving bowl. "What puzzles me," she said with a thoughtful frown, "is why the man would come back to Salt River at all. I would think anyone with a kernel of sense would stay as far away from here as possible. He had to know he wouldn't exactly be Mr. Popular. Not with all the lives he hurt when he left. He must have a very good reason to come back. Either that or he's crazy."

"Maybe that's it," Ellie said, crunching on a chip. "Maybe he's bonkers. Or maybe he's just a heartless bastard who doesn't care about who he's hurting by coming back."

Cassie remembered that flash of vulnerability she thought she'd seen as he had kissed her, and had the sudden, insane urge to defend him. He wasn't crazy or heartless. She opened her mouth to say so, then clapped her lips shut again.

She wouldn't defend him. Anything she said was bound to be misinterpreted by her family.

Why *had* he come back, though? It was a darn good

question. One she was ashamed to realize she didn't have the courage to explore.

"Can we change the subject?" she finally asked. "Those steaks out there smell delicious, but I'm afraid I won't have much of an appetite if we keep talking about Zack Slater."

Sarah was quick to apologize. "Don't mind us," she said softly. "We're just a couple of nosy old busybodies."

"Speak for yourself," Ellie said with a teasing grin. "I'm not old."

The conversation quickly drifted to other subjects, especially Sarah and Jesse's upcoming nuptials. But even while Sarah described the dress she had finally picked out and the shower Cassie and Ellie were throwing her in a few weeks, Cassie couldn't shake the memory of that breathless moment on the porch right before Slater had kissed her.

They were discussing the menu Cassie planned to serve at the wedding dinner when her nieces burst into the kitchen, dusty and sunburned from their favorite activity, horseback riding.

The girls were a contrast in appearance—Dylan red-haired like her mother, with freckles and a snub nose, and Lucy with curly dark hair and big gray eyes. But they were partners in crime in just about everything. They'd been best friends since Ellie and Dylan moved to town the summer before and had connived and schemed to bring their parents together.

Cassie had a feeling they also secretly took credit for bringing their fourth-grade teacher, Sarah, together with Jesse.

She shuddered to think what would happen if they

ever decided to turn their fledgling matchmaking skills in her direction.

"We're starving," Dylan moaned dramatically. "When are we gonna eat?"

"Yeah," Lucy chimed in. "I'm so hungry I could eat my boots."

"From the looks of it, those boots have been in places I don't even want to think about," Ellie said. "Why don't you take them off in the mudroom and then scrub all that barn grime off your hands and faces?"

They groaned but quickly obeyed, then both reached for the potato chip bowl at the same time. Before they could reach it, Cassie whipped the bowl behind her back with a grin. "Nope. Neither one of you is getting anything to eat until you give me my hug."

This time they obeyed without the groaning. She put the bowl back on the table and gathered them close. Dylan was quick to return to the chips, but Lucy lingered in her arms and Cassie planted a kiss on the top of her dark curls, smelling shampoo and sunshine.

All too soon Lucy pulled away and Ellie stepped into the breach. "Why don't you girls help carry some of this food out to the picnic table and tell your dad and uncle to hustle with those steaks?"

Cassie watched the girls obey, trying hard to ignore the sharp little niggle in her heart.

It shouldn't still bother her. Not after all these months. Everything had changed now that Matt had married Ellie. Lucy had a different family now—a stepmother and a sister. The four of them had forged a loving family and she couldn't be happier for them.

But she still couldn't help an aching sense of loss

that pinched her heart every time she was around her niece now.

After Melanie left, she had taken over caring for Lucy. What else could she have done? There was no way Matt could handle a three-month-old infant by himself and run the ranch, too.

And giving up her college plans and devoting herself to her niece hadn't been completely unselfish on her part. She had needed the distraction, a firm purpose, something to help restore her shattered self-esteem. She found it in mothering the poor lost little baby.

For nearly ten years she had been Lucy's mother in everything but name. She had held her chubby little hands when Lucy took her first fledgling steps, she had cuddled her at night and read her bedtime stories, she had nurtured her when she was sick. She had given the little girl all the love in her heart and had it returned a thousandfold, with sticky kisses and tight hugs and whispered secrets.

Everything was different now. She had moved away to give Matt and Ellie space to build their new life together. It was the right thing to do, she knew. But a part of her still grieved to know Ellie was the one who now heard those secrets of Lucy's, who now received those sticky kisses and tight hugs, while she was relegated to the role of maiden aunt.

Now Jesse and Sarah were getting married, and she knew it probably wouldn't be long before they added their own little branches to the Harte family tree.

She would love their children, just as she did Lucy and Dylan. She would spoil them with presents and take them to the movies and baby-sit so their parents could have a night on the town.

And she would always be on the outside looking in.

She ground her teeth, angry at the direction of her thoughts. She was childish to think such things, even for a moment. Her family loved her. She had absolutely no doubt about that. Lucy loved her. Their hearts would always be knit together by those ten years she had nurtured her niece. Nothing could change that.

"Are you sure you're all right?" Sarah asked in her quiet voice while Ellie was occupied loading the girls up with plates and silverware.

Cassie pushed away her thoughts and summoned a smile. "Sure. I'm fine. Just hungry."

Sarah didn't look convinced, but to her relief, her future sister-in-law was too tactful to push her on it as they finished preparations for dinner.

As usual, the meal was noisy and rambunctious, full of heated debates, good food and plenty of laughter. Cassie joined in, but a part of her sat back, watching her brothers with the women they loved.

Matt and Ellie never seemed to stop touching each other. Ellie's hand on Matt's arm as she made a point. Matt's quick caress of his wife's shoulder as she leaned back in her chair. A soft kiss when they thought no one was looking.

It still amazed her to see her big, gruff oldest brother teasing and smiling at his spunky little wife.

Jesse and Sarah were the same, and she whispered a quick prayer of gratitude that her middle brother had finally realized he deserved better than the wild, bubble-headed party girls he usually dated, that he had been wise enough to latch on to someone as soft and good as Sarah.

She was jealous of them for their happiness. All of them. For a few brief months she had known that same deep connection with Slater, but she was terribly afraid she would never find it with someone else. The knowledge had her picking at her steak and barely touching the homemade ice cream Dylan and Lucy had churned.

She had a good life, she reminded herself. Thanks to Slater, in just a few weeks she would have enough money to put the down payment on Murphy's and finally realize her dream of running her own restaurant. She would have purpose in her life again. Direction.

"You gonna eat the rest of that?" Jesse asked, gesturing with his spoon toward her melting ice cream.

She grinned at her bottomless pit of a brother. And wasn't it just like a man that for all he ate, he never gained an ounce of fat, just hard muscle? "What will you give me if I let you finish it off?"

"How about a ride in my police Bronco with all the lights and sirens blaring?"

"Ohh. As tempting as that sounds, I just don't think my poor heart could stand so much excitement."

Jesse pondered for a moment. "How about I let you keep Daisy while we're in Vancouver for our honeymoon?"

She laughed, looking toward the shade of the sycamore where his big golden retriever lounged with Dylan and Lucy. "Again, a very enticing offer. But I think your baby would be happier here on the ranch where she can chase the cats and play with the cow dogs. Is that the best you can do?"

"Come on, Cass. Your ice cream is just sitting there going to waste, melting all over the place. Why don't you just tell me what you want?"

She hadn't want to bring this up in front of the rest of the family but she couldn't pass up the chance. "Promise you won't make any more scenes in town like the one in front of Murphy's this week with Slater, and it's all yours."

Jesse glowered, all teasing forgotten. "I can't make a promise like that. I should have pounded the bastard's pretty-boy face in."

She glowered right back. "It's not your battle to fight, Jess."

"The hell it isn't."

"All you did with your little chest-pounding demonstration was stir up more gossip. You're not helping anything."

"I'm not about to sit by and let him hurt you again."

"I can take care of myself," she snapped, even though she wasn't at all sure of that, as evidenced by her response to that slow, sexy late-night kiss.

Before Jesse could argue, Matt broke in. "Neutral corners, you two. Looks like we have company."

From here she could see the long, curving driveway into the ranch and she recognized Wade's truck kicking up dirt as he roared toward the house.

"Who could that be?" Ellie wondered.

Color climbed up her cheekbones. "Um, that would be my date."

"Who?" Jesse asked suspiciously, and she fought the urge to dump the rest of her melting ice cream in his lap.

"Wade Lowry. We're going to a show in Jackson. You have a problem with that?"

Jesse made a face but didn't say anything. She knew he and Wade didn't get along, something to do with the days when Wade worked for the police department.

"That's great!" Ellie interjected, with just enough enthusiasm to make Cassie wonder if her family thought she had zero social life. Which was basically the truth. "You should have invited him to dinner."

She made a noncommittal sound, heartily glad she hadn't. "I'm sorry I can't stay to help clean up."

"Don't worry about it," Ellie said. "Just go have a great time."

She rose from the picnic table and plopped her bowl of what was now plain vanilla cream without the ice in front of Jesse. "Here you go. Enjoy."

And that's just what she would do, she thought as she walked out front to meet Wade. She would do her best to enjoy their date and try to summon more than just friendly feelings for him.

She wanted to grab for happiness where she could find it, not spend the rest of her life pining for something she could never have again.

Chapter Six

This was getting to be a bad habit.

Zack sat on the little front porch of his cabin, uncomfortably aware he was lurking in the corner like some kind of peeping Tom. He had pushed the comfy rocking chair as close to the wall as he could without the rockers hitting it. Nobody could see him, he assured himself as he watched the small driveway for any sign of Lowry's pickup truck.

He wasn't spying on her.

He *wasn't*.

He was simply savoring the quiet of the night, enjoying a beautiful cool summer evening in the mountains, with the fresh, intoxicating smell of sage mixed with pine, and the stars twinkling overhead in a vast glittering blanket. He was only enjoying the soothing sounds of the crickets and the creek and the soft wind tinkling the wind chimes Cassie had hung on her porch.

Right. Who was he kidding? He had been sitting out here all evening trying to convince himself his motives were pure, even while one part of him kept watch like a nervous father for Cassie to return from her night out.

He had maintained his solitary vigil while the ranch guests returned in pairs or small family groups to their own cabins after a hard day of recreating. Now, just past midnight, the ranch was mostly quiet. Peaceful.

Even with this edginess that forced his gaze toward the driveway a dozen times a minute, he still found himself enjoying it.

A barn owl hooted somewhere in the night, a low, mournful call, and a few seconds later it was answered from one of the big cottonwood trees near the creek.

At least somebody wouldn't be alone tonight.

He found himself smiling at the whimsical thought but sobered quickly. He, on the other hand, was still alone. Always alone, just as he'd been from the age of fifteen, except for that brief, magical time when his life had merged with Cassie's.

Before he could dwell on that grim reminder he saw headlights flash into the driveway and shifted a little deeper into the shadows.

Lowry drove a late-model pickup truck with a fresh wax job that gleamed in the pale moonlight.

Zack watched him climb out and hurry toward the passenger side to open the door for Cassie, ever the gentleman, and Zack had to clench his hands into fists to keep from marching down the steps and slugging the bastard.

Cassie hopped out of the truck with what he thought might be just a little too much eagerness, as if all she wanted was to be home.

Or maybe that was just wishful thinking on his part.

No. Everything about her body language spoke of a woman who wasn't eager for any post-date clutch. She shoved her hands in the pockets of her sweater and walked briskly up the walk toward her cabin.

"I had a great time, Wade," she murmured when they reached the steps to her porch. "Thank you for inviting me."

Lowry edged a little closer, and Zack went completely still so he could hear his next words.

"We need to do this more often," Lowry murmured, and Zack didn't realize he was holding his breath until he heard her make a little noncommittal sound in response.

"Well, good night," she said, somewhat breathlessly. "And thanks again."

Zack couldn't help his smirk as she hurried up the steps of her cabin as if she wanted to put as much distance as possible between them. His smirk faded quickly when Lowry bounded after her to the door.

In the gleam of the porch light she had left burning, Zack could see her unease. Her shoulders were tight, and she was already reaching to unlock her front door.

She might have made it through the door unscathed. He would never know. At that moment he leaned forward slightly for a better view, and the rocker squeaked on a loose floorboard under his feet.

It was just a tiny sound in the night, no louder than the wind rubbing two limbs together, but she whirled her head toward his cabin. Though the lighting was dim, he was fairly certain her eyes narrowed suspiciously at the corner of darkness where he lurked.

When she turned back to Lowry, her smile was unnaturally bright, with none of the hesitation that had been there before. "I really did have a wonderful time, Wade. I know the Applewood Players in Jackson are performing a melodrama this summer. I've heard good things about it. Maybe we could go sometime."

Wade looked slightly dazzled. "I'd like that."

After an awkward pause he angled his head and Zack held his breath, knowing with grim certainty what was going to happen next. Sure enough, the bastard leaned down and brushed his lips against Cassie's.

It wasn't a long kiss, only a few heartbeats, but it went on long enough that Zack was forced to curl his hands into fists on the armrests to keep from throttling both of them.

He wasn't sure through the haze of green over his eyes which of them broke it off. The next thing he knew, Cassie had unlocked her door slicker than spit on a griddle.

"Have dinner with me this week."

"I don't know," she answered, and he wondered if that breathy note in her voice stemmed from reaction or nervousness. "My schedule's pretty full for a while. Jean wants everything to be perfect for…for the new owner, plus I'm going to be busy training my replacement."

"When is your next day off? I'm flexible. We can work around your schedule."

"I'll have to let you know. Good night, Wade," she finally said with firmness, then slipped inside her house, leaving her clean wildflower scent floating in the air, torturing him even across the distance between their cabins.

Lowry stood on the porch for just a moment, then bounded down the porch steps, whistling cheerfully as he climbed into his pickup. He revved the engine a little too much, then drove away.

Zack stayed in his dark corner a few moments longer, wondering when he could safely get up and go inside without her hearing him. He was still mulling it over when her door opened again and she peeked her head out.

"You can come out now. He's gone," Zack called softly. He only meant to tease her a little, but he immediately realized he had made a severe miscalculation in judgment.

His old man always warned him not to yank a barn cat's tail unless he was in the mood for some damn good scratches.

With both hands, she shoved open her screen door the rest of the way then marched down her steps and up his until she loomed over him, angry tension in every tight line of her body.

"How was the show?" she snapped. "See anything interesting while you were lurking out here in the dark?"

He leaned back in the rocking chair with a grin. "To be honest, it didn't look real thrilling from here. But then, I wasn't the one with Lowry's tongue down my throat, either."

The sound she made was somewhere between a growl and a cussword. "What are you doing out here, Slater?"

He shrugged. "Can't a man sit out on a warm summer evening and just enjoy the night?"

"You have no right to spy on me."

He assumed an injured tone. "Spy? Why would I want to do that?"

"Beats me. Why do you do anything? Why come back to Star Valley in the first place? Why go to so much trouble to buy the Lost Creek? Why force me to stay and work for you?"

Because I'm still crazy about you, after ten years. He heard the words in his head and shifted in the rocking chair, swallowing them back.

"I like it here," he muttered. "I've always liked it here."

"No. It's more than that. You're up to something. Why not just admit it and tell me what it is you want?"

What would she say if he told her what he wanted was to pull her into his lap right now and show her a real kiss, not that thing Lowry gave her?

Since he was pretty sure she wouldn't appreciate it, he opted to change the subject. "How was your date?" he asked instead.

She was quiet for a moment, her eyes narrowed as she studied him. "Fine. The musical was good."

"And the company?" he couldn't resist asking.

"None of your business, Slater."

Every instinct in him warned him to hold his tongue, but his next words slipped out, anyway. "I thought I told you it wasn't a good idea to go out with him."

"And I thought I told you I don't give a damn what you want. Good night, Slater."

She whirled to go, but he reached out and grabbed her arm before she could march back down the steps. "Just be careful around him, okay? I don't think he's the nice guy everybody seems to think."

She slid her hand from his loose grasp. "You've been gone for ten years, Zack. You don't know Wade at all. And you don't know me, either."

He watched her walk back into her cabin then purposefully move about the place yanking every curtain closed.

That barn owl hooted again but this time there was no answering call.

The silence made him feel more alone than ever.

She was cutting radishes into flowery garnishes the next afternoon when Jean walked into the kitchen, her gray hair yanked into its regular braid and a smile on her weathered face.

"Hear you went into Jackson with Wade Lowry last night to see a show. Have a good time?"

She sighed. She had answered that very question half a dozen times already that day. Why was it she couldn't even buy a new toothbrush without everybody hearing about it?

"They have a talented group this year, even though those college kids seem to get younger and younger every year."

"Time marches on, whether we want it to or not."

True enough. Just that morning she had ruthlessly yanked a solitary gray hair from among her short dark cap like a gardener after weeds. Maybe that's why she couldn't seem to shake this black mood. It surely didn't have anything to do with her snoopy next-door neighbor or the insane urge that had come over her the night before to kiss that smirk right off his face.

"Anyway, it was very professionally done," she said, hastily dragging her mind from those dangerous waters. "I was thinking maybe some of the guests might enjoy an outing into town one of these nights. You could probably get a good rate on tickets for a large group."

"Good idea. Maybe I'll try to set something up next week." With a long sigh, Jean settled into a chair and plucked one of the radishes from the tray, then popped it into her mouth.

It was so rare to see the Lost Creek owner—well, the lame duck owner, anyway—sit down for any length of time that Cassie set down her knife and studied her boss carefully.

"Everything okay?" she asked.

Jean shrugged. "Sure. Just fine."

"How are you feeling, really?"

The older woman was quiet for a moment and Cassie ached for the weary frustration flickering through those steely gray eyes. "I won't lie to you. Some days are better than others. Without this damned arthritis I'd feel half my age."

No matter what she might think about Zack Slater, she couldn't forget that Jean really didn't have a choice about selling the ranch to his company. She wasn't sure if he would be ruthless enough to make good on his threat to back out of the sale if she didn't stick it out for a few short weeks, but she couldn't take that chance.

"Just think." She summoned a smile for her friend. "In a few months you'll be in San Diego with your daughter and can take it easy just soaking in the ocean breezes."

A spasm of worry tightened the older woman's features. "I suppose. If everything goes through with Maverick and young Slater."

"Has there been a problem?" Cassie asked carefully.

"Don't know. He's a man who plays his cards pretty close to his chest. Hard to know what he's thinking."

Wasn't that the truth? There was a time she thought she knew him as well as she knew herself. She could see now exactly how foolish and young she'd been. Age had taught her that people could be married for years and still keep a large chunk of their souls to themselves.

"You know," Jean went on pensively, "I couldn't figure out at first why he wanted the ranch, but the more I see him around the place, I think I'm beginning to see it."

Cassie hated the curiosity prowling through her. At the same time she couldn't quite manage to control it. "What have you figured out?"

"I don't think it's about money at all. I think he loves it here. I think maybe he feels he belongs."

Cassie chopped so hard she mangled the pretty little radish flower under her hands. Zack Slater would never belong. Not at the Lost Creek, not in Salt River, not in the entire Star Valley. He couldn't.

Jean was wrong. It had to be the money. He was a greedy opportunist who knew a good deal when he saw it. And if he could find a way to hurt her in the bargain, so much the better.

She opened her mouth to say so but shut it again. She had no call to hurt Jean's feelings. If the woman wanted to believe Zack's motives for buying the guest ranch were so pure, Cassie didn't have the heart—or the cruelty— to disillusion her.

Besides, after their agreement ended in just three more weeks, he would have no more hold on her than their shared past. What he did wouldn't concern her at all.

"Anyway, the reason I stopped by is to ask how you'd feel about going up with the cattle drive tomorrow. I was planning to go as camp cook but I'm just not sure I can manage it, the way I've been feeling the past two or three days."

The idea held instant appeal. She hadn't gone on an overnight ride into the mountains since the previous fall's roundup at the Diamond Harte. The thought of a night spent breathing clear, high-altitude air seemed exactly what she needed to make some order of her chaotic thoughts.

She could have Matt bring her favorite mare over from the ranch and her pack tent and camping supplies.

"What about the meals here while I'm gone?" she asked, warming quickly to the idea.

"Claire can cover for you. Most all the guests have signed up for the roundup, anyway. I know it's short notice, but it would really help me out."

"No problem." She was already running through possible menus in her head. "I can easily put together all the supplies this afternoon."

Since the roundup would leave before first light in the morning, she spent the rest of the afternoon planning the four meals she would need to fix, then carefully loading the necessary ingredients into large panniers to be carried by two packhorses.

While she worked, eager anticipation curled through her like black-eyed Susans on a fence, lifting their cheerful faces to the sun.

If nothing else, a trip into the mountains would help put some distance between her and Slater. And maybe a little physical distance would be all she needed to keep the blasted man from invading her thoughts every fifteen seconds.

Cassie stepped back and surveyed her handiwork in the pale early-morning light while the sturdy packhorses nickered softly to each other and to the other mounts being saddled for the trip.

"Does the load look even to you?" she asked Marty

Mitchell, one of the oldest of the Lost Creek wranglers. A horse that wasn't loaded right would tire too quickly on the climb into the mountains.

He spat a wad of chew on the ground. "Far as I can tell. You sure you remembered everythin'?"

"I think so." She did a quick mental inventory. She was probably forgetting something—she usually did on the Diamond Harte cattle drives, anyway—but she had double-checked her list as carefully as possible the night before.

"The dudes are rarin' to go." Marty spat another wad of chew to the ground. She followed his gaze and saw that Jean had been right the night before. While she'd been finishing with the packhorses, most of the Lost Creek guests had shown up and were being matched by one of the other wranglers with appropriate mounts for their riding skills.

"Those two are gonna be trouble," Marty said, pointed to a pair of towheaded twins, a boy and a girl a few years younger than Lucy and Dylan. The twins wore matching Western regalia—vests, chaps, and jaunty little red cowboy hats—and looked as if they were ready to come to blows over a pretty black-and-white speckled pinto pony.

As Cassie watched, ready to step in as peacemaker, the girl took matters into her own hands by shoving her foot into the stirrup of the pony they both obviously wanted, gripping the saddle pommel and mounting up before her brother had a chance to blink.

Cassie grinned.

"You would appreciate such a dirty trick," a low voice murmured in her ear. In an instant her blood turned to ice and then just as quickly to molten fire.

She whipped her head around, and dread clutched

her stomach when she saw Slater leading one of the Lost Creek geldings, a big, muscular blood bay. Zack wore jeans, a denim jacket and a battered Stetson, and the horse he led was outfitted just like the others, with a bedroll, tent and all the supplies a person would need for an overnight stay in the mountains.

She found herself made speechless by the implications.

He *couldn't* be going on the cattle drive. Fate wouldn't be that cruel to send the two of them into the same circumstances that had brought them together in the first place a decade ago.

How could she possibly spend two days with him in the mountains? She couldn't. Her mind raced around in circles trying to figure out a way to escape the inevitable.

Even as she wildly examined her options, she knew she had no way to get out of it. She was trapped, just as surely as a wildcat treed by a pack of hounds. She had promised Jean she would do it and she couldn't back out now. Her assistant couldn't handle the trip on such short notice, and she had seen by the trembling exhaustion on her friend's face the day before that Jean simply wasn't up to it.

It was far too late in the game to find anyone else.

Had Jean known Slater planned to ride along? Or had he only decided to join the expedition when he found out she was going, as part of his general plan to torment her?

"What's the matter? You look surprised to see me."

Surprised was far too mild a word. *Horrified* fit much better. "Doesn't the owner and CEO of Maverick Enterprises have far more important things to do with his time than go with a bunch of greenhorns on a mock cattle drive?"

"I can't think of a one," he answered with a small smile and a funny look in those hazel eyes.

He held her gaze for just a moment longer than necessary, until heat soaked her cheeks and she had to look away. Her gaze landed on his mouth, and for one crazy instant she could remember nothing but their brief kiss the week before on her porch.

Not just that kiss, but a hundred others. Slow, drugging kisses that sent her blood churning through her veins. Quick ones that made her heart flutter like a trapped bird in her chest.

Once she had known that mouth as well as her own, had tasted every inch and savored every curve and hollow.

Her insides trembled in remembered heat. She closed her eyes, willing him to disappear. When she opened them, he was—to her everlasting regret—still standing beside her, reins held loosely in his hands and looking as gorgeous as ever.

"If you need some suggestions for what to do with yourself, I can come up with plenty," she snapped.

His grin only added to his looks, she was disgusted to admit. "I'm sure you could, sweetheart," he answered, then swung into the saddle with a power and grace that left her a little light-headed.

It was going to be a very long two days.

She tried her best to pretend Zack Slater didn't exist throughout most of the day.

It wasn't easy, especially since she and her string of packhorses brought up the rear of the haphazard group that stretched along the wide trail like worry beads.

From back here, she had an excellent rear view of him riding ahead of her. Not that she was paying the least bit of attention. She most certainly was not. But if she *had* been, she might have had a hard time not observing how the blasted man still sat in the saddle as if he had been born there, loose and easy and natural.

She didn't notice, though. Any more than she saw the way the bright summer sun gleamed off that tawny hair under his hat like August wheat or the way his smile flashed at something one of the Carlson twins said to him or the way her breath seemed to catch in her chest every time he turned around and speared her with a hot look from those murky gold-flecked eyes.

He didn't exist, she reminded herself. Instead of focusing on him, she tried to turn her attention to the thrill of a cattle drive—even a light version like this one, where there were almost more drivers than cattle.

The Lost Creek guests loved this, living out their own version of the movie *City Slickers*. Jean didn't keep a big herd at the Lost Creek, maybe one hundred and fifty head. Not like the Diamond Harte, with its herd four times that size.

Jean moved her Herefords only about twenty at a time. Half the summer was spent moving them up to higher ground, the other half bringing them back to the ranch in small groups so that guests throughout the season had the opportunity to participate in a cattle drive.

The formula seemed to work, to the exhilaration of all—except maybe the somewhat bewildered-looking cattle.

It was exciting, Cassie had to admit. Even though she had always participated in the Diamond Harte roundup on a much more massive scale, this was still fun—the bawling of the cattle, the creak of saddles and jangle of tack, the barking of the three low-slung cattle dogs who did most of the actual work.

What was there not to enjoy? They were on a wide trail—a Forest Service fire road, really—surrounded by spectacular scenery: fringy Douglas firs, white-trunked aspens with their pale-green leaves fluttering in the breeze, and wild carpets of wildflowers spreading out in every direction.

She breathed in the scent—of horse and sagebrush and mountains. It was a smell so evocative of summer she had to smile. Oh, she had missed this. She wasn't going to let Slater ruin her delight in something she had always loved.

She was so busy trying not to pay attention to him that she didn't notice that he'd pulled away from the rest of the group until he was coming toward her.

She stiffened in the saddle enough that Solidad grew fractious, both at Cassie's sudden tension on the reins and at the presence of the big bay Slater rode.

"Easy, girl," she murmured, but she wasn't sure if it was a message aimed more at herself or at her mare.

Now beside her, Zack gestured toward the ranch guests whooping and hollering and yippy-cay-aying. "Not quite like a Diamond Harte cattle drive, is it?"

She looked for derision in his eyes, in his voice. To her surprise, she found none, just genuine enjoyment. It reminded her of what Jean had said the day before about his motives for acquiring the ranch.

"It's what keeps people paying the big money to stay at the Lost Creek and all the other dude ranches like it. Traditions like this and the romance of the Old West."

"It's not hard to understand why the ranch is such a success. Who wouldn't enjoy this?"

How in the heck was she supposed to ignore him when he flashed that smile in her direction?

She tried not to acknowledge the heat sizzling through her or the way her legs suddenly trembled in the stirrups.

"I figured the kind of slick, high-dollar guests Maverick Enterprises is planning to bring in probably won't have time to bother with something as noisy and smelly as an old-fashioned cattle drive. What with all those facials and massages, right?"

She heard her words, snippy and childish, and wanted to yank them back, but they lay between them like the rocks strewn across the trail.

He tipped his Stetson back and speared her with a glittering look. "Is that what you think? That I'm going to turn the place into some kind of ritzy spa?"

"How should I know? It's not my business, anyway. A few more weeks and I'm gone."

That funny look appeared in his eyes again. He opened his mouth, but she had the feeling he changed his mind about whatever he was going to say and chose another topic instead.

"I like the Lost Creek just the way it is," he said after an awkward moment. "I wouldn't have decided to buy it otherwise. Once my company takes over, I don't expect we'll make many changes."

She pondered that surprising snippet of information while they rode abreast through the dust kicked up by the small herd a hundred yards ahead of them now.

She wanted to study him, to gauge his sincerity, but she wasn't exactly sure she trusted herself to spend too much time looking at him.

Riding so easily in the saddle in his battered Stetson and Western clothes, this man seemed to have appeared right out of her memories. It was too easy to forget old heartaches and pretend she was riding once more beside the lean, hungry cowboy she had loved so fiercely.

No. She wasn't going to think about that. Casting about for another topic of conversation, she remembered what Jean had said the day before. "What made you decide to buy the ranch?" she asked, before she'd really had time to think the question through.

He frowned as if disconcerted by the question. "What do you mean?"

"There are probably a dozen other guest ranches for sale across the West. Why the Lost Creek? Why come back to Star Valley after all this time?"

He was quiet for a moment, then tilted his head and studied her, his eyes as bright as jade under the shade of his hat. "You haven't figured it out yet?"

She blinked at him, suddenly wary. "Figured what out?"

The power of his smile snatched the breath right out of her lungs. "I came back for you, Cassidy Jane."

Before she could absorb the sheer stunning force of his words, a confused dogie broke away from the main herd and headed into the sagebrush. Zack spurred the big bay and took off after it.

She watched him go, not sure whether she should be furious at his shocking admission.

Or scared to death.

Okay, he'd screwed up. Big-time.

At their campsite on the shore of a small mountain lake rimmed by sharp, white-capped peaks, Zack split his time between helping the Lost Creek wranglers as they set up camp and sneaking little looks at Cassie preparing the evening meal.

He knew he was staring at her but couldn't seem

to help himself. She moved like water—graceful and smooth and fluid.

And every time she caught him looking at her, she flushed brighter than the red-hot embers of the campfire.

He had made a tactical error of major proportions. He never should have opened his big mouth about his true reasons for coming back. He should have just bided his time, let her get to know him again. See if, by some miracle, she might be able to trust him again.

Now she was jumpier than a grasshopper on a hot sidewalk.

He hadn't meant to tell her so bluntly, but the truth had just slipped out when she'd asked him why he returned to Star Valley.

Well, part of the truth, anyway.

How could he tell her he had never stopped loving her? How the memory of those few months he'd spent with her had been burned into his mind and had set the course for his entire life?

By the world's standards he was a successful man. He had money, he had power, he had influence. The dirty, white-trash kid in hand-me-downs had yanked himself up by the proverbial bootstraps and made something of himself.

Ten years ago he was nothing. Or that's what he felt like, anyway. Now when he walked into a room, people sat up and took notice.

But it wasn't enough. Nothing he did had ever seemed enough since he'd left Star Valley and Cassidy Harte.

She didn't want to hear that from him. He had seen the shock in her eyes. Hell, it went beyond shock. Her pupils had widened with something close to horror.

Could he blame her? A decade ago he had left her heart shattered, the subject of gossip and speculation.

Zack knew what small towns could be like; his father had carted him through enough towns from Montana to Texas. He knew damn well how the scandalmongers had probably circled around her like a howling pack of wolves, just waiting their turn to gnaw at her.

She had every reason to be bitter.

He was crazy to think he could make right in just a few precious weeks what he'd done to her. How could he make her see past his desertion and the terrible wrong he had unwittingly done her by leaving the same night as Melanie?

He might have had a chance if people thought he'd just taken off, gotten cold feet and wandered off to greener pastures. After all, he was the son of a drifter, a rambling man.

But there was Melanie. It was a far different matter for everyone to believe he'd taken her along for the ride.

Where *was* the blasted woman? he wondered again. He had already contacted the discreet team of private investigators he used to see if they could get a lock on her current whereabouts.

If he could find her, she could corroborate his story—that they hadn't run off together and it was just lousy timing that they'd both decided to leave Salt River on the same night.

So far the investigators had come up dry. They couldn't seem to find any trace of her after she left the Star Valley.

Anyway, even if he managed to locate her and somehow drag her here, what reason would Cassie have for believing Melanie, anyway, when she obviously had no inclination to think *he* was telling the truth?

With a sigh he finished hammering the final tent stake and stood back while two of the Lost Creek wranglers quickly shoved in the poles and erected the structure.

"Thanks for your help, Mr. Slater. I think we can handle it from here." Like everybody else, Kip Dustin, the lead wrangler, couldn't seem to look him in the eye as he offered the words.

Zack ground his teeth at the "Mr." business. All the wranglers—hell, all the employees of the Lost Creek—teetered on an awkward, precarious line, torn between loyalty to Cassie and showing proper respect for their new boss.

"Call me Zack," he ordered.

"Yes, sir," the wrangler mumbled, his big ears going red under his slouchy felt Stetson.

He didn't want to make the man uncomfortable. He only wanted to be clear that he didn't expect to be treated any differently from the rest of the guests on the trip.

One of the other wranglers called out a question to Dustin about a couple of the horses, and the man escaped with alacrity to answer it.

With most of the work setting camp finished, Zack was left with little else to do. While they waited for the evening meal, some ranch guests had headed down to the small mountain lake to fish with tackle supplied by the ranch. Since he hadn't brought along waders or his own custom-built fly rod, the idea of drowning a worm didn't hold much appeal.

Others were holed up in their tents, probably stretched out on their sleeping bags as they tried to relax sore muscles unused to spending a hard day's work in the saddle.

He knew if he retired to his tent, he wouldn't be able to think of anything but the woman twenty feet away who was bustling about cooking. He'd rather sit here and watch her, he decided, and settled back against a tree trunk.

He loved looking at her.

With her face a little rosy from the sun and her short cap of dark hair tousled from the breeze, she looked sexy and mussed, like she'd just come from a lover's arms.

He closed his eyes while memories haunted him of watching her sleep tucked against him, her breathing deep and even and a soft smile on her face as she nestled closer.

She had loved him so generously, without reservation, throwing her whole heart and soul into it. The first time he had kissed her, in the hushed silence of the night on that other long-ago cattle drive, she had looked at him with dazed delight in her eyes.

"Wow!" she had said in a breathless voice. "So that's what all the fuss is about."

He remembered laughing roughly and giving her another light kiss on the tip of her nose. After she had gone inside her tent, he had stood outside for a long time under the moonlight studying the vivid red marks on his palms where his nails had dug into skin to keep from devouring her.

He opened his eyes, chagrined to realize he had clenched his hands into fists again just at the memory.

He jerked his mind from the past and saw that the Carlson twins, Maddie and Max, were now pestering her at the camp cookstove, apparently bored with fishing.

Their parents were among those resting in their tent. He suspected it had more to do with taking a short break from the twins' incessant chatter than with aching muscles.

He sympathized with them. The twins were two ferocious bundles of energy. Their blond curls that had looked so shiny and clean that morning were now coated with dust, and they each had pink cheeks that would probably be a full-fledged sunburn in the morning.

They looked hot and dusty and cranky. He rose with

some vague idea of rescuing Cassie from their clutches, though he didn't have the first clue where to begin.

As he drew closer he could hear them bickering about who would be able to eat more peach cobbler. Cassie stepped in before the argument could get more heated. "I could use a couple of strong hands to bring me more water from the spring to purify. There might be a cookie reward in it. Anybody interested?"

They both jumped at the chance, bickering now about who could carry more water without spilling it. She handed them each a blue-speckled enamelware coffeepot, and they rushed eagerly down the trail toward the cold spring at one end of the lake.

"That ought to keep them occupied for fifteen minutes or so," he murmured.

Her shoulders stiffened and she looked up at his approach. "I can only hope."

"You're good at that."

She raised an eyebrow. "Cooking Dutch-oven potatoes? I've had plenty of practice."

"I meant with the kids. You're a natural."

"I've had plenty of practice with that, too."

He was confused for a moment, then remembered. "That's right. You helped your brother with his little girl. Lucy, right?"

"Yes." For a moment he thought she might have forgotten his presence. Her mouth curved into a wistful little smile while she peeled and sliced potatoes in a steady rhythm. She was so preoccupied that she didn't seem to notice when he picked up another knife and began doing the same.

"Is she as much of a handful as those two?" he asked after a moment of working beside her.

The smile became more pronounced. "She was always

the sweetest little girl. So loving and eager to help. She still is, but now that she has Dylan for a stepsister and partner in crime, I have a feeling Matt and Ellie are in for one heck of a wild ride."

"You miss her, don't you?" he asked quietly.

Her hands went still. "Why would I miss her? I see her all the time. Every Sunday at least, when we all get together for dinner."

Though she spoke with casual acceptance, he thought he saw a deep ache in her eyes. This was boggy, tricky ground, made even more treacherous by her stubborn refusal to listen to him about Melanie. Still, he longed to comfort her. Or at least to acknowledge her pain.

"It's not the same, is it?"

"No. It's not the same." She was quiet for a moment, the only noise the solid thunk of the knife slicing through a potato. Her expression softened, her columbine-blue eyes turned thoughtful. "For nine years she was my child in everything but name. I taught her to read and to do cartwheels and to always tell the truth. I suppose in some ways she'll always be the daughter of my heart."

The softness vanished as suddenly as it appeared and her movements became brisk, even though he thought he saw just the faintest sheen of moisture in her eyes. "Anyway, now she has Ellie and Dylan. The four of them are a family. A wonderful family. And Ellie couldn't be a better mother to both girls."

His heart twisted for her, for those tears she wouldn't shed. Despite her brave talk, it couldn't have been easy to leave the Diamond Harte. To leave the child she had nurtured and loved for ten years into another's care.

He knew all about walking away and how it could eat away at a person's soul.

He almost reached out and pulled her into his arms, but he knew she wouldn't welcome the sympathy or the gesture. "She was lucky to have you," he murmured.

The sloshy ground he'd been worried about suddenly gave way. Her gaze narrowed as she seemed to remember who, exactly, she was talking to. "I didn't have much choice. Thanks to you and Melanie, there was no one else, was there?"

The fragile moment of shared intimacy shattered like a bird's egg toppling from a high tree, and he mourned its loss.

"I didn't leave with her, Cassie. What is it going to take to convince you?" He set down the knife and sighed, more defeated than angry. "I couldn't look at any other woman but you. I still can't."

She hitched in a sharp breath, and for a moment their gazes locked. Awareness bloomed in those blue depths like the carpets of wildflowers they had ridden past earlier in the day.

He wanted to kiss her.

He *had* to kiss her.

The urge to step forward and take her in his arms trampled over him with more force than a hundred bawling Herefords. Before he drew breath enough to move, though, two bickering voices heralded the return of the Energizer Bunny twins.

"We brought your water, Miss Harte," Maddie reported, arms straining to carry the full coffeepot.

Cassie jerked her gaze away from his, her color high. "Thanks," she said to the twins. "I really appreciate your help."

"Max spilled some on the trail but I didn't. I didn't spill a drop."

"Did so," her brother argued.

"Did not! I was way more careful than you."

Because she looked about ready to pour the rest of her water all over her brother—and because he had a feeling Cassie would prefer to dump the other pot on *his* head—Zack intervened. "I was just going to see how the fish are biting at the lake. Anybody want to come with me and help put the worms on my hook?"

"That's so easy!" Max exclaimed, showing off a couple of empty holes in his grin where a tooth used to be. "My dad showed me when I was just a little kid."

He swallowed his smile at that. "All right. The job is yours, then. Fifty cents for every worm you put on the hook for me."

"Wait!" Maddie exclaimed, not to be outdone by her brother. "I know how to put worms on hooks, too!"

He pretended to consider. "I don't know. I think one fishing guide is probably enough."

She looked so disappointed he had to relent. "All right. You can each take turns. And then when we come back, Cassie, here, will fry up all our trout for us, right?"

She sniffed, but he thought he detected just a hint of a smile wrinkling the corners of her eyes. "I'm fixing barbecued chicken and potatoes tonight. If you're in the mood for fish, you can fry them yourself."

He whistled as he walked down to the lake followed by two little chattering shadows. He was making progress with her, he knew it, despite the occasional bumps along the way.

Chapter Seven

Hours later Cassie sat on a fallen log at the lakeshore, listening to the darkness stir around her.

Night creatures peeped and chirped, small waves licked at the pebble-strewn shore in a steady, comforting rhythm, and a cold wind whistled in the tops of the pines. All of it was punctuated by the occasional soft slap of a fish leaping to the surface for a midnight snack.

She huddled in her denim jacket, unwilling to face the warm comfort of her sleeping bag just yet even though she knew she was crazy to linger out here in the cold.

The rest of the Lost Creek guests and wranglers had turned in long ago. She had watched the last flashlight flicker out inside a tent at least fifteen minutes ago.

And still here she sat.

A gust of wind whistled down the mountain toward her, and she shivered. If she wanted to sit up all night, she could at least stir the glowing embers of the camp-fire back to life and enjoy its warmth a little instead of lurking down here at the water's edge alone.

But there was something restful about watching that pale spear of moonlight gleam across the rippled surface of the lake. Something soothing, calming.

Heaven knows, she needed anything peaceful she could find.

She wouldn't be able to sleep. Even as tired as she was after a long day on the trail, she recognized her own restlessness far too well to think she might even have a chance, not with all these thoughts chasing each other through her mind.

And every single one of them centered on the lean, dangerous man sleeping a hundred feet away.

Damn him. Damn him straight to the burning hell he deserved for shaking her up like this. He had no right to say what he had earlier in the day. To mention so coolly that he had come back for her—as casually if he were talking about the low-pressure system building over the intermountain West or how his favorite baseball team would fare in the conference championships this year.

What did he expect from her? That she could just blink her eyes and make the past disappear, all the heart-ache and loss and disillusionment she had suffered because of him?

She drew a ragged breath. Why was she letting the blasted man tangle up her thoughts like fishing line jumbled into a pile? Zack Slater could say anything he wanted. He could say he came back to Salt River to plant palm trees down Main Street for all she cared. She felt nothing for him. Nothing but anger and the echo of a long-ago hurt.

She closed her eyes to the night and huddled lower in her jacket. Who was she kidding? A part of her wanted to do exactly that—snap her fingers and make the past disappear. To recapture that magical summer when the world stretched out in front of them, full of joy and promise.

There were invisible ties between them. She had felt them tug at her even over the ten years since she'd seen him last. Since his return, they wound tighter and tighter, until she was beginning to fear she would never be able to break free.

Maybe it was because he was the only man she had ever slept with. The only one she had ever wanted to be with.

How pathetic was that? She had remained faithful to a man who had deserted her.

Not that she'd ever dreamed he would come back. She had dated in those ten years. Not a lot—she'd been busy with Lucy, after all—but she had been out more than a few times over the years.

But nothing serious. Nothing lasting. She had never made love with any man but Zack Slater.

Her first and her only.

Back then he had been as cautious about intimacy as he was about everything else, wanting to take things slowly. Finally, with the single-minded purpose only an eighteen-year-old girl in love can claim, she had decided to take matters into her own hands.

On her suggestion, they had taken his pickup up the network of dirt roads crisscrossing the foothills overlooking Salt River, looking for the perfect spot to watch the town's annual July Fourth fireworks display. She had packed a picnic of sorts. Fresh strawberries. Crusty

French bread. A bottle of wine she had been forced to ask the clerk at the store to pick out for her.

All carefully designed with seduction in mind.

She felt ridiculous that it had come to that, to seducing her own fiancé. They were getting married in less than a month. She had her dress picked out, the flowers had been ordered and she was in the middle of addressing all the invitations.

But while they had done just about everything else together, from sweet, tender kisses to long makeout sessions in his pickup that left them both trembling with need, Zack had stubbornly refused to take things all the way.

He wanted to wait, he said. She had to be sure.

"You're so young," he had said with those rough, callused hands tracing bare skin just above her hip. "I don't want your brothers or anybody else saying you rushed into this just because of this…heat between us."

In those miserable weeks and months after he left, she finally realized that even then he must have been having doubts that he would be able to go through with the wedding. His feet must have already been chilling in his boots even as she set out to remedy her lack of experience.

At the time, though, she had known only the frustration of thwarted desire and had finally convinced herself to take matters into her own hands.

She had loved Zack Slater. Completely and forever. They were going to spend the rest of their lives together and she wanted to take this natural step with him more than anything. So she had packed a thick blanket and her seductive food and suggested they drive above the town lights, where they could watch the fireworks away from the noisy, boisterous crowd.

She closed her eyes now and could see it as vividly as that morning's trail ride.

The evening sky was streaked with purples and reds as the sun began to set in a blaze of glory. After driving around for a while, Zack had finally parked his battered old pickup on a plateau high above the valley.

She sat next to him, her nerves dancing. She wanted to do this. Wanted it more than she wanted her next breath. But she had to admit she was also scared to death.

"Does this look like a good spot?" he asked.

"Yes," she mumbled through a mouth that suddenly felt full of dusty rocks. "I think so."

He spread the thick blanket in the bed of the truck, then lifted her up easily with those powerful hands that could touch her with such breathtaking tenderness.

He seemed a little distant at first, maybe picking up on her own nervousness, but as the sky began to darken and the stars came out one by one, they both began to relax. They laughed and talked and fed each other strawberries.

When she produced the wine and the plastic cups the clerk at the liquor store had graciously provided, he raised an eyebrow but didn't say anything.

He must see right through her, she thought, a blush scorching her cheeks. All this time she thought she was being so clever, he knew exactly what she was planning.

She knew they would get around to kissing eventually—they couldn't seem to be within a few feet of each other without their mouths connecting. Still, the stubborn man let her set the pace.

She laughed and chatted the way she had every other time they'd been together, even while her insides shivered every time she looked at those hard, chiseled features and felt the heat of his gold-flecked eyes on her.

She was right in the middle of a breathless story about the time she'd been caught skinny-dipping with her friends in the mayor's pond by the mayor and his wife, who had obviously come down to the pond with the same idea, when Zack suddenly yanked her into his lap.

"I can't take any more," he murmured against her mouth, and she tasted wine and the sweetness of the berries. "I've got to kiss you."

"Who's stopping you?" she murmured back, and was rewarded with a fierce, possessive kiss. The shivers in her insides turned to devastating earthquakes of awareness.

That kiss had led to more. And more.

She could remember every second of that night. Every gliding touch, every drugging kiss. Before long, the buttons of her lacy shirt slipped free, and those wonderful hard hands found her unbound breasts.

"No bra tonight?" he murmured against her neck with a surprised laugh.

"It's the Fourth of July," she said on a gasp as his fingers danced across a nipple. "My own little celebration of freedom."

"I'm not sure this is quite what the Founding Fathers had in mind, but hey, I'm as patriotic as the next guy."

Her laugh turned into a gasp when he slid down her body and drew the nipple into his mouth, sending shock waves rippling through her. He had never gone this far and she knew this was it.

While he licked and tasted her skin, desire exploded inside her, building and building until she was afraid she would shatter. Finally she couldn't stand this aching tension. She reached down and cupped his hardness through the thick material of his jeans, her fingers fumbling with the button fly so she could really reach him.

He groaned and shoved against her hand for a moment, then eased away, flopping back on the blanket to stare up at the sky. "Stop. Slow down."

She sat up, her shirt still unbuttoned and her long hair flying loosely around her face. "Why? I'm so tired of slowing down! I love you, Zack. We're going to spend the rest of our lives together. This is right. Why do we have to wait?"

She leaned over him, and this time she kissed him with all the fierce love in her heart. "I love you, Zack Slater," she murmured. "I will never stop loving you."

With a groan, he fisted his hands in her hair and devoured her mouth. Lit by only the moonlight and the last glowing rim of sun streaking the mountains, he quickly removed the rest of her clothing.

Though July, it was chilly at this higher elevation, and she shivered a little as a cool wind kissed her bare skin. But only for a moment. Then he covered her with his hard, muscled body and the shocking, incredible sensation of his naked flesh against hers warmed her completely.

She clutched him to her tightly and kissed him while a thousand sensations burned themselves into her brain. He had been so careful. So gentle. Even though she could feel the need trembling through him, feel the strength of his arousal against her, he still moved slowly.

She was far from naive about what went on between a man and a woman but she wasn't prepared for Zack Slater and that dogged determination of his. He took his dear, sweet time, touching every inch of her skin, until she was ready to weep from frustration.

Finally his hand slid between her thighs, to the slick, aching center of her need. She shattered apart instantly, crying out his name.

While her body still pulsed and trembled, he knelt over her. "Are you absolutely sure, Cass? We can still wait."

She groaned and bit his shoulder hard enough to leave two little crescent-shaped marks. "Yes! I'm positive! Will you just do it?"

With his glittering hazel gaze locked with hers and his hands crushing her fingers, he entered her slowly, carefully, just as the first booming fireworks exploded far below them in town.

They spent the next three weeks finding every opportunity they could to be alone together. Each time they made love was more incredible than the last, and those invisible bonds tightened even more.

And then he'd left.

Something stirred behind her in the brush, and Cassie jolted back to the present, horrified to feel the wet burn of tears in her eyes. She swiped at them with the sleeve of her denim jacket, furious at herself for dredging that all up again and for the low thrum of remembered heat that had burrowed under her skin while she relived those moments in his arms.

With the instincts of one of the small, scurrying creatures of the night, she sensed who was coming long before she saw him. Maybe it was his scent of cedar and sage carried by the breeze. Or maybe it was just the hum and twang of those bonds between them.

Whatever the reason, by the time he broke through the brush to her spot by the lake, all her defenses were firmly in place.

"You should be in bed, Cassie. Aren't you freezing out here?"

"It's not so bad," she answered, relieved that her voice only trembled a little.

The wind whistled through the pines as he stood looking at her. "May I join you?" he finally asked.

No. Go away and leave me in peace. "I was just about ready to turn in."

He reached out as if to touch her arm, then checked the movement. "Stay a moment with me. Please?"

She studied his features, wishing the moon were full so she could see him a little more clearly. Every instinct warned her that lingering here would be dangerous, especially when her thoughts were filled with the remembered passion between them and the feel of his hands upon her skin.

But she couldn't walk away.

Oh, sweet mercy. She couldn't leave. What was wrong with her? She hated Zack all over again for the ache in her throat, the heaviness in her chest. For breaking her heart into tiny jagged pieces, which she still couldn't seem to make fit back together completely.

He sat beside her on the wide log, sending out an ambient heat that seemed to seep through her jacket. She wanted to burrow closer to that warmth, but she knew it wouldn't be enough to thaw the cold that had been inside her for ten years.

They sat in silence for several moments, lost in the night and the past. He was the first to break it.

"I thought I could forget you," he murmured.

She stiffened at his quiet words. She didn't want to hear this. The urge to run back to the safety of her tent was overwhelming, but pride and something else—an unwilling compulsion to know—kept her glued to the log.

"I *wanted* to forget you," he went on. "That was my plan. Move on to the next town, bury myself in hard work and forget all about the Diamond Harte and Star Valley and the pretty blue-eyed girl with the long brown hair and the smile that could make me feel a hundred feet tall."

"Why?"

The word was wrenched out of her, and she hated herself for asking it and hated him more for forcing her to ask. Why did he want to forget her? Why had he left in the first place?

"Survival," he answered, his voice grim. "It was sheer torture remembering those nights I held you in my arms. Remembering all the dreams we made together and the future we planned. Somehow I ended up on the rodeo circuit. Those first few months after I left, I think I probably spent more time in the bottle than sober."

She pictured him ten years younger, desperate and drunk. "If you were so miserable, why didn't you just come back?"

"I almost did a hundred times. But I knew nothing had changed. I was still the wrong man for you."

She bit her tongue to hold back the bitter words that wanted to flow out like vinegar from a spilled bottle.

"I tried my damnedest to forget you. But I couldn't. For ten years I remembered the way you always smelled like wildflowers. The way you tucked your hair behind your ear when you were concentrating on something. The way your mouth would soften like warm caramel when I kissed you."

He finished on a murmur, his voice just a hush, barely audible above the wind. The low timbre of it reached deep inside her, plucking at those strings only he had ever found.

She shivered, not from the cold this time but from a slow, achy heat she didn't want to face.

"Is that supposed to matter to me?" she snapped, to cover her reaction. "That once in a while you spared a thought for the stupid, naive girl you left behind?"

"Not only once in a while. Much more often than that."

She drew in a shaky breath. "Slater, you could have tattooed my name across your forehead for all I care. It still wouldn't change the basic fact that you left."

His mouth tightened. "I had reasons. I told you that. At the time it seemed like the best decision all around."

"Oh, right. I almost forgot. Salt River's evil drug cartel that was going to arrange things so you were thrown in jail."

"Damn it, Cassie. I'm telling the truth. I was threatened with exactly that. Ask yourself this. How would you have faced your friends, your brothers, if the man you planned to marry went to prison?"

"We'll never know, will we?"

He opened his mouth as if to say something, then snapped it shut again. An uneasy silence descended between them again, and he picked up a stone and skipped it into the lake, where it bounced five times, one more than her own personal best. Where the stone hit water, ripples spread out in ever-widening circles that shimmered in the moonlight.

"I figured you'd be long married by now to some prosperous rancher," he finally said. "Even though that was what I wanted for you, I hated picturing you with a house and a husband and a pack of kids."

She had to close her eyes at the raw note in his voice. She wouldn't let him get to her. She couldn't.

"When I found out you never married, that you were working at the Lost Creek, I realized I had to come back to find out why."

Why had she never married? Because no one else had ever asked her. Maybe someone might have if she hadn't always constructed an invisible wall of protection around her wounded heart that no man had ever been able to breach.

"Wait a minute." Her attention finally caught on his words. "How did you find out I never married?"

In the moonlight she thought she saw his color change slightly, and he refused to meet her gaze, looking out at the water instead.

Finally he shrugged. "I sent out private investigators. You weren't very hard to find."

Of course she wasn't hard to find. She had never gone anywhere. All her life, the only time she had been beyond a hundred-mile radius of Star Valley was the time she and Lucy spent a week with Matt at a stock show in Denver.

She hadn't been anywhere, hadn't done anything, hadn't lived beyond the insular world she had known all her life. The world had marched on in the last ten years—just look at how much Slater had changed—while she had stayed behind, forever frozen in ice.

Waiting for him.

No. No she wasn't. She denied it vehemently. She had done what she had to do, stayed and raised her niece and helped her brother. She couldn't regret that.

She loved it here. She had a good life. Good friends, her family. Once she bought Murphy's in town, she would have everything she had ever needed.

Still, her face burned and she wanted to press a hand to the sudden slippery self-disgust flipping around in her stomach like one of those trout.

It was far easier to focus her anger at him. "You sent hired dogs after me?"

He grew still, his eyes suddenly cautious over her tone. "Cassie…"

"Am I supposed to be flattered by that?"

"You're not supposed to be anything."

"So that's why Maverick decided to buy the Lost Creek. You found out the ranch was for sale and figured maybe I was, too."

"No. Of course not."

"I don't care how much money you have, Slater, and I never did. You're the only one who cared about that. If you bought the ranch with some crazy, misguided idea that I would fall back into your arms, you've wasted your money."

Now she wasn't cold anymore. She was burning up, an angry inferno, and she embraced the heat. She only prayed it would blaze hot enough that the little part of her still clinging to the past would burn away into cinders.

She rose and glared at him. "I was stupid enough to fall for you once, Slater. You can be damn sure I won't make the same mistake again."

She whirled and marched away, leaving him sitting by the small mountain lake, watching after her.

Chapter Eight

Zack lay in his sleeping bag, watching his breath puff out in little clouds in the cold predawn air.

He hadn't slept more than an hour or two all night, and those had been restless, tortured with dreams of her. In one, she had been standing above him on a high glassy tower flanked by hundreds of giant steps, each taller than he was. Every time he tried to hoist himself up and managed to make it within a few steps from her, she moved a little higher up the tower.

Forever out of reach.

The dream's symbolism didn't escape him. He huffed out a breath, grimly aware that he'd messed this whole thing up from the day he came back. What had seemed like such a great idea in Denver—doing everything he could to persuade her to give him another chance—now seemed quixotic in the extreme.

How could he undo the past? Even if he had the power to do so, she wouldn't let him close enough to try healing the wounds his desertion had inflicted on her spirit.

His presence here was torture for both of them. He was beginning to see that. She wanted him to leave so she could get back to the life she had made for herself.

And he wanted to stay so badly he ached with it.

He should just give up. Cut his losses and go on back to Denver. Every time he considered it, though, he remembered the way she had responded to his kiss earlier in the week. The way she shivered if they accidentally touched. The color that climbed her cheeks whenever she caught him looking at her, as he knew he did far too often.

She wasn't immune to him. She'd be lying if she said she was. Even if her mind and her heart couldn't see beyond his past sins, her body was more than willing to forgive and forget.

If only he could manage to convince the rest of her that he deserved that forgiveness.

Or convince himself.

He sighed and rolled over just as he heard the zip and rustle of someone climbing out of a tent nearby.

Cassie.

It had to be. As camp cook she was probably trying to get a head start on breakfast before the rest of the guests and wranglers woke up.

Without stopping to debate the wisdom of confronting her again so soon after their encounter the night before, he moved quietly. He slipped his jeans on over the thermals he'd been wise enough to pack, grateful once more that he had remembered how cold it could get in the Wyoming mountains, even in June.

He shoved his boots on quietly, then grabbed his denim jacket and Stetson.

Outside in the frosty mountain air, he saw her crouched at the fire ring, busy trying to coax the embers back to life. She wore a forest-green ranch coat but her head was bare, her short-cropped dark hair tousled and sexy from sleep. He imagined it would probably look exactly like that after making love all night.

A low groan rumbled in his chest as his unruly body stirred at the mental image. After a moment of fierce concentration, he managed to force it away and offered what he hoped was a harmless smile.

If he expected a smile in return—or any sign at all that she was happy to see him—he was doomed to disappointment. She glowered but went back to work trying to kindle a blaze.

Undeterred, he stepped closer. "Need help?"

For a moment he thought she was going to refuse his offer, then she shrugged and rose to her feet. "Knock yourself out. I need to get some water for coffee."

He took her place, then watched as she grabbed a small bag from inside her tent, then picked up one of coffeepots. She flipped on a flashlight against the early-morning darkness, then disappeared through the trees toward the lake.

She hadn't left matches for him, he noted with a wry grin. And the embers were as cold as her heart.

Little brat. Did she expect him to rub a couple of sticks together? Joke's on you, sweetheart, he thought, and dug into the pocket of his jacket for his lighter. A few moments later he had a nice little fire snapping to ward off the chill.

A slightly ridiculous sense of pride glowed in him as

brightly as the flames while he warmed his hands in the heat emanating from the fire.

When she returned a few moments later carrying the coffeepot filled with water, her hair was wet and under control, her face damp and clean.

A memory flashed through his mind of that first cattle drive they went on, the one that had started everything between them. He had been amazed and intrigued that she had somehow managed to stay fresh and clean and pretty even when trail dust covered everyone else in a fine layer.

He had noticed the boss's younger sister long before then—how could he not?—but he had kept those very facts uppermost in his mind. She was the boss's sister. And she was young.

He was far too wise a man to mess up a good job over a girl, no matter how pretty and fresh she might be. Besides that, she was far too young and innocent for a rough man like him.

Still, on the trip he had seen another side of her. She had been funny and gutsy and mature beyond her years. And she had looked at him with a wary attraction in her blue eyes that he had been helpless to resist.

She still looked at him that way, whether she was conscious of it or not. That, more than anything else, kept him in Star Valley when he knew damn well he should have given up and gone back to Denver days ago. As soon as he found out about Melanie.

He shoved his hands in his pockets and approached her at the big four-burner propane camp stove, with its prep counter and griddle. "What else can I do to help?"

"Nothing. Everything's under control here."

Except me, he thought. "Can I get you more wood for the fire?"

She shrugged, which he took as assent. He spent the next few moments gathering a few more armfuls of wood. By the time he returned, the enticing aroma of coffee and sizzling bacon reached him.

None of the other guests or wranglers had ventured out yet, he saw. Cassie still stood at the camp stove, mixing together ingredients for flapjacks, and she barely looked up when he returned to camp. He set the wood atop the dwindling pile and joined her.

He longed to kiss that pink, sunburned nose but he didn't want a spatula covered in batter across his face so he contented himself by just leaning back against a tree trunk and watching her graceful movements.

"Do you remember that first cattle drive we went on together?" he finally asked. "You and your cougar friend?"

She paused for just a fraction of an instant in stirring the pancake mix. "I remember."

"I think that's the moment I fell in love with you," he murmured. "When you faced an angry mountain lion with your chin out and that smart mouth of yours going a mile a minute."

When she returned to the batter, her movements were brisk, almost agitated. "Shut up, Slater."

He moved closer, until he was only a few feet away. She edged away as far as she could without her post at the stove. He was making her nervous, but he didn't care.

He was desperate, fighting for his life here.

"That's when I fell in love with you," he repeated. "On that trip. But I knew even that first time I kissed you by your tent that there wasn't a chance for us. Not then."

"And not now," she snapped.

"I had nothing to offer you. No money, no prospects. Nothing to provide you the future you deserved."

Her eyes were hard blue flames in an angry face. "And just because you're Mr. Big Shot Businessman now, because you have enough money to buy whatever you want, you think that's going to make a difference to me? That I'm shallow enough to care? Are you honestly arrogant enough to think I'll just fall into your arms now that you've so magnanimously decided to return like some kind of damn conquering hero?"

He couldn't keep his hands away from her another second. He reached out and curved a finger along the silky skin under her high cheekbones, aware he was taking the biggest chance of a life filled with risky choices.

"Not because of the money," he said quietly, his heart beating a mile a minute. "Because you never stopped loving me. Any more than I ever stopped loving you."

She froze at his words and stared at him, her eyes huge and stunned. A small, distressed sound escaped her mouth, and he moved faster than that mountain cat she'd confronted to catch it.

He kissed her tenderly, gently, trying to show her the fierce emotions in his heart. At first she remained motionless under the slow assault, then, just when he was beginning to feel a little light-headed from holding his breath, her hands crept around his neck like tiny, wary creatures coaxed out of hiding.

With a hushed sigh, she settled against him, and her mouth softened under his. He wanted to shout in triumph. Wanted to grab her tightly against him and mold her body to his, to devour that soft, sweet mouth.

He didn't want to send her running back for cover,

though, so he forced himself to keep the kiss slow and easy while his blood sang urgently through his veins.

She wanted to weep from the tenderness in his kiss and from his words. She wanted the soft, devastating kiss to go on forever while the sun burst above the mountains, bathing them in its warmth. She wanted to stay right there for the rest of her life with his hands cupping her face and his mouth soft and gentle on hers.

When he eased away, both of their breathing came in shallow gasps. "Don't lie to me, Cassidy Jane." His voice was low, compelling, and his hazel eyes gleamed with an emotion she didn't want to acknowledge. "No matter what happened ten years ago, you still have feelings for me, don't you?"

She blinked at him as reality came crashing back. Dear heavens. He was right. She did. Part of her had never stopped loving him, even when she hated him.

Heat soaked her skin, and she wanted desperately to escape, to hide away until she could come to grips with this horrifying realization. Before she could, she heard two high-pitched voices already bickering, then the zip of a tent flap. An instant later the Carlson twins burst out into the clearing.

She barely had time to step away from Zack before their mother crawled out of the tent after them.

"Is that bacon? We're starving! When will it be ready? Can we have some?" The twins punched questions at her in rapid succession.

The jarring shift from the sensuous, dream-like encounter with Zack to the very real demands of two nine-year-olds left her disoriented. She blinked at them for a moment, then quickly composed herself.

She had long practice with hiding her feelings, after all. Even from herself.

"Yes, it's bacon. And if you each wash your hands with one of those wet wipes, I might let you snitch a few pieces now, before breakfast."

The next hour passed in a rush as she prepared pancakes and hash browns and pound after pound of bacon to feed sixteen people. She welcomed the hard work, grateful for something to keep her mind away from Zack and the stunning truth he had forced her to finally admit to herself.

While she was occupied with cooking and cleaning up breakfast and then reloading the food supplies, the Lost Creek wranglers broke camp. The sun was still low in the east when the group began the trail ride back to the ranch.

Without the excitement of the cattle to prod along, the guests were far more subdued during the ride back. Even the dogs plodded along without much energy.

Cassie didn't mind. She had far too many thoughts chasing themselves through her mind to concentrate on anything but a slow, easy ride down the wide trail.

After that cataclysmic kiss, Zack's low words had unleashed a flood of emotions that still whirled and cascaded through her. She thought she had been able to exorcise him from her heart after he'd left. But with just a few words, he had shown her how foolish and naive she was for clinging to that notion.

She still loved him. Had never stopped. Now what was she supposed to do about it?

Absolutely nothing, the cautious side of her warned. She couldn't afford to do anything about it.

"You know who he is, don't you?"

Cassie hadn't noticed Amy Carlson, the twins' pretty, frazzled-looking mother, had fallen behind the rest of the riders and was riding abreast of her. The twins were up closer to the line, being closely monitored by their father and a couple of the wranglers.

She followed the woman's gaze right back to Zack riding ahead of them in that loose-limbed way of his and felt a blush climb her cheeks as she realized she must have been staring at him.

"Who?" she asked, pretending ignorance.

Amy made a fluttery gesture with her hand. "Mr. Gorgeous. Zack Slater. I just about died when I recognized him at the ranch the first night we arrived, eating in the dining hall just like the rest of us mortals."

"I know who he is."

"Besides being every woman's secret fantasy, the man is close to a legend in Denver," Amy went on. "Every single thing he touches seems to turn to gold. I read a piece on him in the business section of the *Post*. It was fascinating stuff."

She had always thought him fascinating, even when he'd been a rough-edged ranch hand. Though she suddenly discovered she desperately wanted to hear about the life he had made for himself, she didn't want to appear too obvious. "Really?" she asked blandly.

Amy didn't appear to need much encouragement. "He keeps to himself for the most part. Reclusive, almost. I never see his picture on the society pages. But he has this really gorgeous apartment in Denver and a big ranch in western Colorado. According to the reporter at the *Post*, although he keeps it a secret, he's also a big-time philanthropist who gives huge amounts of money to all kinds of pet projects. A couple of alcohol rehab centers. The children's hospital in Denver. A mentoring program for kids living in abusive situations."

Alcohol rehab centers? Abused children? The little crack in her heart widened even further.

Zack had never wanted to talk much about his childhood, even when they were engaged. He had no family left, she knew that. His mother had died of cancer when he was six and his father hadn't taken her death well. From what she had pieced together, Zack's father had packed up his little boy and carted him from ranch to ranch across the West, never staying long in one place.

Zack had finally struck out on his own when he was just fifteen, although he had never told her why he dropped out of high school or left his father somewhere in Montana.

He had mentioned one time, almost in passing, that his father used to drink too much. She wondered now if his father had been a mean drunk. If he had taken his frustrations with life out on his son.

Was that the reason Zack had preferred the hardscrabble life of a rambling cowboy to staying with his father?

She wanted to rub a hand at the sudden ache in her chest for that young boy. He had passed a high school equivalency test before she met him, she knew, but it had still bothered him that he hadn't graduated in the traditional way or gone on to college.

He had considered himself uneducated, rough.

She thought of what he had said the night before, that he hadn't been the kind of man she deserved a decade ago.

She hadn't cared a thing about his education level or his bank balance. She had loved his solid core of decency, his honor and his sense of humor. His inherent kindness. The way she always felt cherished and protected in his arms.

A hundred things about him were far more important than what he had or had not accomplished with his life.

But with stunning clarity she finally realized that the things she had considered inconsequential had been anything but to Zack.

She jerked her attention back to Amy Carlson and her recital of his success.

"But why am I telling you this?" Amy said with a rueful smile. "You probably know all about the mysterious Zack Slater."

Ten years ago she thought she knew him. Now she wasn't so sure. "Why would you say that?"

Amy sent her a knowing look. "The two of you have something going, right?"

More heat soaked her cheeks. "What do you mean?"

The other woman grinned. "I have the two eyes God gave me, sugar. I saw the way you two were looking at each other this morning before breakfast. You were both putting out enough heat, I was afraid for a minute there you were going to start a forest fire. Besides that, the man hasn't stopped watching you for longer than a few minutes this entire trip. I'll tell you, there are plenty of days I'd trade both my twins plus my left arm to have a man like Zack Slater looking at me like that."

Cassie barely resisted the compelling urge to see if he was watching her now. "You're mistaken. We don't have a relationship. We…knew each other a long time ago. That's all."

"Well, if I'd had half a chance with a man like him before I met my Paul, you can bet I would have grabbed hold with both hands and not let go for all the pine needles in Wyoming."

That's exactly what she wanted to do, she realized with

sudden panic. He was asking for another chance. And, heaven help her, she wanted desperately to give it to him.

But how could she? She wasn't that heedless, optimistic eighteen-year-old anymore—that girl who was confident that everything would work out exactly as she wanted.

Ten years ago she had gone after what she wanted with single-minded purpose. She'd decided she wanted Zack Slater, and she hadn't been about to let anything stand in her way.

Not even him.

She had pushed them both into a relationship, then into an engagement. Maybe if she hadn't been in such a headlong rush—maybe if they had taken more of a chance to build a stronger foundation—he wouldn't have run.

She had been a different person then. What had happened to that reckless, spirited girl who took chances, who embraced every day with boundless excitement and joy?

A few weeks ago she might have said Zack Slater destroyed her when he left.

Now, as she rode along the trail lined with towering spruce and ghostly pale aspen, she faced some grim facts about herself. She had let that girl wither away, until she had become a cold shell of a woman afraid to take any chances for fear of something going wrong.

So terrified of being hurt again that she never let herself dream.

That's why she hadn't made an offer on the café in town yet. Heaven knows, she had enough money from her share of the Diamond Harte revenue over the years that she could have paid cash for the café the day she moved away from the ranch.

Taking the job at the Lost Creek had just been a stall tactic.

She sat a little straighter in the saddle, stunned by the realization. She forgot about the raw beauty of the mountains around her as the cold truth settled in her chest. She had been too afraid of failure, of taking chances. Zack hadn't done that to her. She had done it to herself.

No more. She wasn't going to hide behind the past anymore. Excitement began to churn through her like the creek still swollen with runoff. She was obligated to stay at the ranch for another few weeks, but after that she would start negotiations with Murphy. By the end of the summer she would have her own restaurant.

After her brother's wedding in a month, the cute little rental Sarah lived in would be available. Maybe she could take over Sarah's lease—or even make Bob Jimenez an offer to buy it.

Suddenly the day seemed brighter, the air more fresh. She could do this. She wanted to be that fearless girl again.

And Zack. Did she dare take a chance with him, too?

With her heart pounding hard, she thought of the sweetness of his kiss that morning, the thick emotion in those green eyes. He hadn't been lying when he said he still cared about her.

Trying again with him would take a huge leap of faith. Could she trust him to catch her on the other side?

Zack sat on his favorite chair on the porch watching the stars come out one by one and trying like hell not to spend too much time watching the windows of the cabin next door for an occasional shadow to move past the closed curtains.

What was the matter with him? He was turning into some kind of sick and twisted voyeur, hoping to catch even a glimpse of her. Where was his pride? His dignity?

He didn't have much of either left when it came to Cassidy Jane Harte.

Going along on the cattle drive the day before had turned out to be a complete bust. He was no closer to regaining her trust today than he'd been a week ago when he first arrived at the ranch.

He sighed into the darkness and thought of the stacks of messages Jean Martineau had handed him as soon as they rode back to the ranch. Claudia, his very competent assistant, was frantic to have him back in Denver, with a dozen projects needing his urgent attention. He couldn't keep putting off his return to real life.

He hated to admit defeat at anything, but he was beginning to think this was a battle he couldn't win.

The thought left an acid taste in his mouth. The future stretched out ahead of him, stark and lonely and colorless, but he didn't know what else he could do to change it.

If only he could find Melanie. But one of the messages from Claudia contained another worthless report from his P.I. So far it looked as if the woman had either changed her name and moved out of the country or had been abducted by aliens.

He was betting on the aliens at this point.

Either way, he figured he was damned. If he couldn't find her, Cassie would have to take his story on blind faith. He couldn't see that happening anytime soon.

The only bright spot about the cattle drive had been the way she'd responded to his kiss that morning. He had seen awareness and some deeper emotion flicker in her eyes before she had shielded them with her lashes and surrendered to him.

He shifted in the chair, remembering the sweetness of her mouth and the fluttering of her hands against his chest. She hadn't been exactly bubbling over with enthusiasm during the kiss—hadn't participated much at all, really—but she hadn't poured hot coffee on him, either. That had to count for something, right?

And a few times on the ride down the trail, their gazes had met and he thought he saw something else there besides anger and disdain. A different light. Softer, somehow.

No. That was probably only wishful thinking on his part. He hadn't seen her since they arrived back at the ranch several hours earlier, when she had treated him with the same cool reserve.

Her porch light suddenly flickered off, leaving only a soft glow through the window. Damn. Now she was going to bed before he had a chance to come up with any kind of half-rational excuse to knock on her door in the middle of the night.

He should do the same. He hadn't slept much all week, and his muscles ached from two days in the saddle. Still, something kept him planted here, watching the stars and regretting the past.

With a sigh he planted his hands on the armrest of the old rocker and prepared to rise, when he suddenly heard the squeak of hinges. An instant later his breath caught and held somewhere in the vicinity of his throat as she stepped out onto the porch.

Though her porch light and his were both out, he could see her clearly from the soft light still on inside her cabin. Her hair was damp around the edges as if she had just stepped out of the tub, and she was wearing a loose, flowing white cotton robe that glowed iridescent in the moonlight.

He opened his mouth to greet her, then paused for just a moment, struck by the stunning picture she made. Sensual and sweet at once. Wistful and wanton. As he watched her move to the porch railing, he couldn't seem to remember how his voice worked. All he could do was stare, his throat dry, as she leaned out and gazed up at the vast glittering night sky, her attention fixed on the same stars he had watched appear.

What was she wishing for? he wondered. He would give anything to know, to be the man she shared her secrets with.

He couldn't sit here like this, lurking in the corner and watching her in such a solitary moment. Remaining silent was an unconscionable invasion of her privacy.

"Hey," he finally called out, his voice sounding rough and ragged to his ears.

She froze for an instant, then turned toward him with something like resignation in her eyes. "Zack. Isn't it past your bedtime?"

"Probably. The night was too gorgeous to ignore." And so are you, he thought, and unfolded his length from the rocker to go to her. When he joined her at the railing, he was heartened considerably when she moved aside to make room for him.

For a moment they were silent, both contemplating the mysteries of the heavens, then she sent him a sidelong look. "Why do we always keep meeting in darkness?" she murmured.

He was going to say something flip, but stopped and gave her question a little deeper consideration. "Maybe it's easier facing each other and ourselves at night than in the harsh glare of daylight."

She lifted one slim, dark eyebrow. "That's very philosophical, Slater. And surprisingly insightful."

He shrugged. "I'm just chock-full of surprises, Cassidy Jane."

"Yes. I'm beginning to see that," she murmured.

Just what did she mean by that? he wondered. Before he could ask, she spoke again.

"I heard quite an earful about you today from Amy Carlson on the ride down the mountain. She read all about you in the business section of one of the Denver papers, apparently."

"Oh, no." His oath was low and heartfelt.

Her soft laugh drifted over him like imported silk. "It was very educational, I must admit. I never would have pegged you for such a philanthropist."

"Have I just been insulted?" he asked, with an inward curse at the business reporter at the *Post* for being so damned good at his job and ferreting out that closely held secret.

She laughed again. "I don't know. Maybe. Sorry. You know, in all these years, I just never pictured you as a pillar of the community, giving bundles of money away like some modern-day Robin Hood."

He couldn't control the sudden tension rippling through him. He hated talking about this. What the hell was the point of giving anonymous donations if they weren't going to stay that way?

So what if he contributed to a few causes he cared about? That didn't make him any kind of hero. Just a man with astonishing good luck in a lot of ways that seemed hollow and unimportant unless he could share that luck.

He blew out a breath, turning away the conversation before it became any more uncomfortable. "How did you picture me?"

"Oh, plenty of ways. All of them very creative, you can be sure. I believe staked out naked on an anthill somewhere with buzzards circling around your head was always a personal favorite."

He heard the humor in her voice. But he also heard the thin thread of pain woven through it, like a pale, out-of-place color on a rich tapestry. Regret washed over him again, bitter guilt that he had been the cause of that pain.

He shifted to face her, leaning a hip on the railing. A wild yearning to reach out and caress that face, to touch her soft skin, welled up inside him. He almost did it but checked himself at the last moment, afraid she would shy away from him like an unbroken colt.

"I never meant to hurt you, Cassie. I should have high-tailed it out of Star Valley the minute things started to get serious between us. Before everything went so far."

She didn't answer him, just watched him out of those solemn blue eyes that had always seen deep inside his soul.

"I thought about leaving a hundred times but I couldn't do it. For once in my godforsaken life, something right had happened to me. Something real and beautiful. I was too selfish to give that up—to give you up—even though I knew I would end up hurting you in the end."

"But you did give it up. You left and you never looked back."

"I left," he allowed. "But I've spent every day of the last ten years looking back, Cassie. Knowing I made the biggest mistake of my life walking away from the only woman I have ever loved. And wondering how I could ever make it right with her again."

After he finished speaking, her eyes turned murky and dark. A second later one fat tear slipped out. Dismayed, he stared as it caught the moonlight, wanting to call back whatever he'd done to make it appear.

His Cassie hardly ever cried. He couldn't bear this, the heavy, unforgiving weight of knowing he had hurt her. Not just once, but a thousand times over the past ten years. Self-disgust filled his chest, his throat, even as he had to force himself not to reach for her.

She didn't want him here. He was only hurting her more every day by his stubbornness.

"Don't cry, sweetheart. Please. I'm sorry. I should never have come back. I'll leave in the morning, I promise. I won't bother you again."

She swiped at the tear and glared at him. "Don't you dare walk away from me again, Zack Slater. Not when I was just trying to gather the courage to give you another chance."

He froze, afraid to believe what he thought he just heard her say. It took every ounce of energy within him to remember to breathe. "You mean that?"

"I must. Why else would my legs be shaking?"

A shocked joy exploded inside of him, fierce and bright and buoyant. He drank in her tousled beauty, wanting to burn every second of this into his brain.

Her smile trembled just a little, like a small, tender wildflower in a mountain breeze. With a groan, he reached out and clasped her face in both hands and lowered his mouth to hers.

He kissed her slowly, reverently, savoring every inch of her mouth. She kissed him back, this time with no hesitation or wariness. Her lips moved under, opened for him.

Welcomed him home.

He wanted to weep from the torrent of emotions gushing through him. This was where he belonged. Right here, with her arms around him and her mouth soft and giving beneath his.

This was where he had always belonged.

Entwining his hands in her sexy little cap of hair, he deepened the kiss. Her breathy sigh of response acted on his already inflamed body like a rush of hot wind on a grass fire.

Her arms pulled him closer, then closer still, until he could feel her soft curves through the thin cotton of her robe. He folded her against him, marveling again at how perfectly they fit together.

Gradually, through the haze of joy and desire engulfing him like coastal fog, he realized she was shivering against him, ever so subtly but enough to make him draw away. "Is that from the cold or from nerves?"

She blinked at him. "What?"

"Your legs aren't the only thing shaking, sweetheart." He looked closer and realized she had come outside with no shoes. The wooden porch slats must be freezing beneath her bare feet.

"No wonder you're trembling. Here, let's get you inside."

He picked her up and opened her door. The soft glow inside came from a trio of slim candles she had left burning on the mantel.

"You didn't have to do that. I'm not helpless."

"I know. You've always been so strong and determined. It's one of the things I love most about you."

Strong? He must have her mixed up with another woman. She had been anything but strong in those days and months after he had left, when she had kept herself from shattering apart only because Matt and poor Lucy needed her.

In the intervening years she had cowered in her safe little life like a rabbit in a hole. And like that rabbit, while she might have felt free from the danger of heartache in that insular world, she had also been slowly starving to death.

Depriving herself of the very things she needed to survive.

Even knowing that—even with the vow she had made to herself that morning—she didn't feel very strong right now. A low, constant fear hummed through her but she refused to give in to it.

The simple truth was, she believed him. About Melanie. About the crime ring he stumbled onto. About how he thought he was doing the right thing for her by leaving.

She would never agree with the choice he had made. But that morning as they had ridden through the mountains where she had fallen in love with him so long ago, she had finally come to understand it.

Maybe he had to leave so that he could finally learn to see himself the way she always had—as a good, decent, honorable man who deserved whatever happiness life had in store for him.

The candles' glow burnished him in gold, catching in his hair and the gold flecks in his eyes. That beautiful, sculpted face she had loved for so long.

She smiled suddenly. She could be stronger than fear. She would be.

She wrapped her arms around his neck and kissed him fiercely. He remained still for one instant then he groaned and dragged her against him, his mouth ardent and demanding as he pressed her down to the plump cushions of her couch.

Eventually kissing wasn't enough. It had been too long and her emotions were too raw, too close to the surface. She gasped when his hand shifted from the skin at her hip until he was barely touching the curve of her breast. Heat pooled in her stomach, in her thighs, and she arched against him.

He groaned against her throat and trailed kisses along her jawline, then back to her waiting mouth while his fingers touched her.

Oh, dear heavens, she had missed him. Missed this. The fire and the closeness and the sweet churn of her blood.

Only with Zack had she ever felt so stunningly alive, and she wanted it to go on and on forever.

His fingers danced over her nipple, and the shock of it was like leaping into an icy mountain lake without testing the waters first. She couldn't seem to catch her breath, and for a moment she was afraid she was in way over her head.

"Zack, stop," she gasped.

The slow torture of his fingers stilled instantly. Wariness crept into his eyes.

"I'm just not… I don't think I'm ready for…for more. Not yet."

He gazed at her for a moment, his eyes glittering, then he drew in a ragged-sounding breath. "I can understand that. I'm sorry. I've just dreamed of touching you for so long."

He stepped back from the couch and raked a hand through his sun-streaked hair. When she saw his hand trembling slightly, she had to admit to a certain completely feminine sense of power.

"Thank you for understanding," she murmured. "We rushed into things before. I don't want to make that mistake again."

"You're right. You're absolutely right." With a lopsided smile he reached out and grabbed her hand and pulled her to her feet. "Slow and easy. I can handle that."

He kissed her forehead and wrapped his arms around her tightly. At the feel of that hard, muscled body against her, she suddenly wasn't so sure "slow and easy" would be enough.

The next week was as close to heaven as she could imagine.

The pace of life in the Lost Creek kitchen didn't slow at all just because she and Zack were busy rediscovering each other. She still put in long hours cooking for the ranch guests, ordering supplies and training Claire Dustin to take over for her.

Zack was busy, too. Although he didn't put it in so many words, she had a feeling his continued absence from his business interests in Denver was causing problems, because a few days after that momentous kiss at her house, he moved his office to one of the extra rooms in the ranch, installing computers, phone lines and a crisp, efficient, somewhat snooty assistant named Claudia.

While she devised menus and tested out recipes, his days were filled with conference calls as he ran his little empire in absentia.

And it *was* an empire, she was coming to realize. It

was one thing to know in the abstract that Zack had built his own very successful business from the ground up. It was quite another to watch him in action, with his sleeves rolled up and a pair of wire reading glasses perched on the tip of his nose as he talked on the phone about capital outlays and IPOs.

She had to admit she found the contrast between the rough-edged cowboy she had known and this high-powered executive very sexy.

Even with their respective workloads, they still tried to spend every available moment together. In the past week they had managed to squeeze time to go riding together several times, to take moonlit hikes into the mountains around the ranch, and the night before they had taken a drive through the massive splendor of Grand Teton National Park to have dinner at Jenny Lake Lodge inside the park.

Although they spent long, drugging hours kissing and rediscovering each other, he always stopped before things went too far. While she was touched—and amazed—at his restraint, she was also growing increasingly frustrated.

She was falling for him again, and hard. A part of her still quaked at the thought, but the rest of her couldn't deny that she was happier than she had been since she was that fresh-faced eighteen-year-old girl head over heels in love.

Just now they were on their way to the Independence Day parade in Salt River, set to begin in just under fifteen minutes.

She had almost said no when he'd suggested it after breakfast that morning. Not because she didn't want to go—the small-town parade was usually one of the highlights of her year—but she was fairly sure gossip about poor Cassidy Harte and her long-lost fiancé was still running rampant around town. She wasn't sure if she had the fortitude to face the inevitable stares and whispers.

Small-town life definitely had certain advantages over living in a big city. But the endless buzzing grapevine—where everyone thought they had a God-given right to dabble in everybody else's business—wasn't among them.

Most people in Star Valley still believed Zack Slater had run off the week before their wedding with her brother's wife. What would they think when they saw the two of them together?

Trying not to pay attention to the butterflies step kicking in her stomach, she folded her hands tightly together. She didn't care what anyone said. She was strong. She could handle a few stares and whispers.

If she was going to show up in the middle of the Independence Day parade with Zack Slater, she wasn't going to have much of a choice.

Chapter Nine

It wasn't quite as bad as she had feared.

Once they'd walked the short distance from their parking space to the parade route, her nerves had settled somewhat. They still received their share of raised eyebrows, and she could hear more than a few whispers behind their backs. But no one was outright rude to them.

Either Zack didn't notice or he didn't care. He placed a hand at the small of her back as they looked for a spot to watch the parade, both to guide her and to stake his claim, she suspected.

He looked gorgeous, as usual, in weathered boots, faded jeans and a tailored short-sleeved navy cotton shirt that stretched over the hard muscles of his chest. Her mouth watered just looking at him as he set up the folding lawn chairs they had borrowed from the Lost Creek at an empty spot in front of the grocery store.

She settled into the chair and tried to put the murmurs and prying looks out of her mind, content just to bask in the moment.

She enjoyed all of Salt River's little celebrations—from the summer concerts in the park to the homecoming football game to the Valentine's Day carnival at the elementary school—but the Independence Day parade was always a highlight.

Folks here took their patriotism seriously. They hadn't been sitting for five minutes when one of the elderly American Legion members rushed over with a couple of small flags for them to wave along with everyone else.

Cassie smiled as she took it, scanning the crowd for some sign of her brothers. She couldn't see them and wasn't sure if that little fact relieved her or disappointed her.

Jesse would be busy directing traffic away from Main Street, she remembered. But Matt and Ellie and the girls were probably planted somewhere along the crowded parade route, Sarah watching along with them.

She hadn't seen them in a week. Guilt pinched at her as she realized how isolated she had become from them, how she had ducked out of their regular Sunday barbecue and had declined Ellie's invitation to go to the annual rodeo with them later that night.

Although she winced at the realization, she was too terrified about their reaction if they saw her with Zack. She still hadn't told her family the two of them were in the slow process of renewing their relationship. She couldn't. Not yet.

She might have forgiven Zack for walking away ten years ago but she was fairly certain her overprotective brothers wouldn't be so quick to let bygones be bygones.

Not when it came to Zack Slater.

But since they were nowhere in sight, she didn't have to worry about it right this minute. She had a parade to enjoy.

Half an hour later she was smiling at the antics of a couple of clowns who looked remarkably like Reverend Whitaker and his wife when she happened to glance at Zack. He was watching her intently, an odd light in his hazel eyes.

Heat soaked her cheeks. "What's the matter?"

He gave her one of those soft, beautiful smiles that made her catch her breath and feel more than a little light-headed. "Nothing. I just like watching you."

What was she supposed to say to that? She could feel more heat crawl up her cheekbones and figured she was probably as red as the stripes on her little flag.

"You belong here, don't you?" he asked quietly.

"Jeppson's? Well, I do spend plenty of time inside yelling out my produce order."

He smiled, then turned serious again. "No, I mean all of it. Salt River. The whole small-town thing. You're very lucky."

"Lucky? Because I've never been anywhere in my life?"

"Because you're part of this and it's a part of you. You belong," he repeated.

She narrowed her gaze, giving him a closer look. That odd light in his eyes was envy, she realized. He was envious of *her?* A woman whose entire life had been spent within a sixty-mile radius? Who couldn't walk a block through town without having to stop and visit with at least three or four people along the way and who had to schedule at least an extra half hour for any shopping trip just because she knew she was bound to run into someone who wanted to chat?

Zack had never had any of that. She was barely aware of the high school band passing by with its enthusiastic rendition of "Stars and Stripes Forever." Instead she remembered his childhood. His drunk saddle bum of a father with the itchy feet, who had dragged his young son from ranch to ranch across the West, never content to stick long in any place.

Zack had gone to nine different elementary schools, he had told her, in six different states.

He had never experienced this. The sense of continuity, of community. Of being inextricably linked with something bigger than yourself. A wave of pity for him crashed over her, and she wanted to gather him close in her arms right there in front of everyone and cradle him against her.

"You belong in Denver now," she offered. "You have a big apartment there and your business. Oh, and your ranch in the San Juans. You belong there."

He was quiet for a moment, then he gave her another of those slow, serious smiles. "I've never felt as much at home in either of those places as I do right here in Salt River when I'm with you."

Unbearably touched, she felt the hot sting of tears welling up in her eyes. She blinked them back and reached across the width between them to place her hand on his where it rested on the arm of his lawn chair. He turned his hand over and clasped hers, and they stayed that way, fingers locked together, for the rest of the parade.

She always grew a little melancholy when the last float passed by, when people gathered up their little flags and their lawn chairs and headed home. It was the same ache that always settled in her chest as she watched the last leaf fall from the big sycamore outside her window at the Diamond Harte at the knowledge that she wouldn't see another until spring.

Where would she be a year from now when the parade again marched down Main Street? Would the man who sat beside her still be a part in her life? Or would he march on just like the parade?

Her chest felt tight and achy at the thought. She knew she was going to have to face that possibility, but right now she didn't want to think about anything beyond the moment.

"So what's next?" he asked as they packed up their own chairs and began the trek back to his Range Rover. "Do you have to hurry on back to the ranch to fix dinner?"

"No. Jean told all the guests they were on their own today. I think most of them were coming into town for the Lions Club barbecue later."

"So you're free for the rest of the day?"

She nodded. "What did you have in mind?"

His grin somehow managed to be mischievous and seductive at the same time, something only Slater could pull off. "Well, if I had a pickup truck, we could always take a picnic up in the mountains later and make out while we watch the fireworks."

An instant image of their first time together flashed through her mind and an answering heat curled through her stomach. Drat the man for stirring her up like this right on crowded Main Street!

"What's that old saying? If wishes were horses then beggars would ride?"

He laughed. "Not a horse. A pickup. I have this sudden, overwhelming compulsion to buy a truck. Where's the nearest dealership?"

"Matt always buys his ranch vehicles in Idaho Falls. It shouldn't take more than an hour to pick out a truck, right? I should think we can make it there and back before the fireworks show with time to spare."

He stopped dead and stared at her. She met his gaze squarely, wondering if he could correctly read the message in her eyes. She was ready to move forward, to take the next step with him. The sooner the better, as far as she was concerned.

"Are you sure?" he murmured, as if he could read her thoughts.

With a slow smile she nodded. An instant later he dropped the folded lawn chairs and yanked her into his arms, right in the middle of town, and lowered his head for a fiery kiss.

She would have stood there all afternoon just basking in the hot promise of that kiss—with no thought at all for where they were and who might be watching—if a carload of teenagers hadn't chosen that moment to drive past honking and catcalling.

With a flustered laugh she broke the kiss. "Whoa." That was the only coherent thought she could put into words.

Before he could answer, she saw his gaze sharpen on something behind her. Fearing one of her brothers had stumbled onto them, she turned and saw with relief that it was only Wade Lowry.

Her relief was short-lived.

Wade stepped forward, his hands clenched into fists and his handsome face twisted with anger. "I heard the rumors but I couldn't believe they were true. How can you stand to be seen with this…this son of a bitch after what he did to you?"

She blinked, stunned by his words, his animosity. A regular churchgoer, Wade hardly ever used profanity. It was so out of character that she didn't know how to answer him.

Why would he be so furious? Was it jealousy? Maybe he thought they had more of a relationship than they did. She went out with him occasionally but she had always tried to be clear that she wasn't interested in anything more serious with him. He was her friend. She hated the idea that she might have hurt him.

"Wade—" she began, but he cut her off.

"He took Melanie away! She never would have left if it hadn't been for him."

She blinked, disoriented by his words. Melanie? This was about *Melanie?* Had Wade been one of the many men ensnared in her sister-in-law's twisted, sticky web of destruction?

She couldn't believe it. The man she knew was far too decent and principled to sleep with another man's wife, no matter how alluring she might be. But the emotions in his eyes told a different story. Of betrayal and loss and something else she couldn't recognize.

"Wade, he didn't leave with Melanie," she said gently.

He turned his anger toward her, and she drew in a shaky breath at the force of it blazing at her. "Of course he did! Everybody knows that! People saw the two of them go. Your own brother saw them leave together!"

Zack stepped forward. "You know exactly why I left town ten years ago, don't you, Lowry? And it wasn't because of some imaginary tryst with Melanie Harte."

Zack's voice was sharp, his eyes suddenly as hard as granite.

Wade stiffened. "I don't know what you're talking about."

"I'm sure if you put your mind to it and thought real hard, you could probably figure it out."

"You're crazy. Everybody knows you ran off with Melanie. The only mystery is why a woman like her would be willing to settle for a no-account drifter like you."

"That's what I might have been then," Zack murmured, pure ice against Wade's fiery anger. "But not anymore. Now I have money and power. And a very long memory."

Wade flexed his hands into fists, looking as though he was ready to lash out any second and turn the verbal confrontation physical.

She could just imagine Jesse's reaction as Salt River chief of police if he had to come break up a fight between the two men. She huffed out a breath, furious with both of them—Wade for starting it and Zack for tossing fuel onto the fire.

"This is ridiculous. You two are not going to brawl in the middle of Main Street. Not if I have anything to say about it. I'm sorry you're upset, Wade. I don't know what was between you and Melanie. That's your business. Just as what is between Zack and me is mine."

She didn't give him time to respond, just grabbed on tightly to Zack's arm. "Come on, Slater. If we're going to make it to Idaho Falls and back, we had better hurry."

He looked down at her as if just remembering her presence. With one last stony look at Wade, he opened the door to his glossy Range Rover for Cassie, then climbed in and drove away, leaving the other man standing in the street glaring after them.

They were almost to Tin Cup Pass before she finally lost patience with his continued silence. "Okay. Spill it. What was that all about."

He gripped the wheel. "You tell me. He's *your* boyfriend."

She barely refrained from slugging him while he was driving. "He's my friend. You want to tell me what you have against him?"

He said nothing for several moments while yellow lines passed in a blur. "I'm fairly certain he was one of the men I saw that night unloading that airplane full of drugs," he finally said.

She stared at him. "Wade? You're telling me you think *Wade Lowry* was part of some vicious criminal operation? A drug smuggler? That's impossible! You must be mistaken."

"Why?"

She could give him a hundred reasons. A thousand! Wade was a kind and gentle man. A little stuffy, maybe, but generally considered to be one of the nicest men in town.

She was struggling to put it into words when she suddenly remembered something else. "It's impossible! Ten years ago he was on the other side of the law. He was an officer with the Salt River PD."

He kept his eyes on the road but his mouth hardened. "So were the rest of them."

Her jaw sagged. "What? You're telling me the Salt River Police Department was running drugs?"

"I don't know about all of them. There were only four men there that night, all wearing masks. The only one

I recognized for sure was Chief Briggs. He was the one giving the orders."

She didn't find that such a stretch of the imagination. Jesse had told her enough horror stories about his predecessor that she could certainly believe Carl Briggs would have been capable of anything. He had been completely dirty, as crooked as a snake in a cactus patch.

Briggs had been under indictment on multiple counts of corruption five years earlier when he'd dropped dead of a heart attack.

Jesse was still trying to repair the damage Briggs had done to the small police department's reputation during his tenure.

But Wade? The image of him involved in any kind of criminal enterprise just didn't fit the man she knew. "You said they were all wearing masks," she said slowly. "So you can't be sure Wade was there."

"Not one hundred percent," he admitted. Damn, he wished he could remember that night more vividly, could put faces and names to the men who had so gleefully taken turns beating him.

If he could, he would find a way to even the score now that he was no longer that no-account drifter Lowry had called him. What was the saying? Vengeance was sweeter when it was savored. He would love to be able to savor a little delayed justice.

His memories were just too hazy, though. He only had vague impressions of Briggs ordering one of the men to cuff him. Then the chief had circled around him a few times, just for intimidation's sake, before offering him three choices that were really no choices at all.

They could kill him right then and bury him deep in

the mountains surrounding Star Valley where nobody would ever find him.

They could let him take the rap for the drugs.

Or he could leave Salt River and never come back.

Cocky bastard that he'd been a decade earlier, he had spat in the chief's face. Briggs had eased back on his heels, his pale blue eyes narrowed.

"Boy, you just made a big mistake," he murmured softly, then had ordered the other men to finish him off.

They had all taken turns beating on "Cassie Harte's pretty-boy boyfriend" who stuck his nose in the wrong place.

He must have passed out from one too many kicks in the head. His last thought before he had surrendered to the pain had been for Cassie.

When he regained consciousness, he'd been alone. No plane, no handcuffs, no Briggs. Only his beat-up truck and a note staked to the ground in front of him that said only five words. "Jail or bail. Your choice."

He had no doubt in the world Briggs could make a charge of drug smuggling stick against him. He wanted to stay and fight it. But then he thought of the expression he would see on Cassie's face if she saw him behind bars. The hurt and the dismay. The disillusionment.

He couldn't make her endure that kind of shame. She deserved better than to have to go through that.

She deserved better than him.

It had taken him a good fifteen minutes to make his shaky way into the driver's seat of his old truck and start it up, pain shrieking through him with every second from what he would later learn had been a half-dozen broken ribs, a concussion and a shattered elbow.

He had a vague memory of that drive out of town, how

he'd decided to head south toward Utah. He had known he was leaving Cassie forever, and his heart had cracked into sharp little pieces that gouged him just as painfully as his broken ribs.

"Where did you go?"

He blinked back to the present, to the soft, beautiful woman beside him who had suffered the consequences of that decision. "What?"

"Just now. You looked like you were miles away."

"I was remembering. Regretting. I should never have left. I should have stayed and fought Briggs."

Her eyes softened and she reached across the vehicle and touched his arm. "You would have lost. He might have killed you."

"Maybe. But at least I would have known I tried."

"Small consolation that would have been to you in your grave. No. I can't believe I'm actually saying this, but I'm glad you made the choice you did."

He stared at her, taking his eyes off the road for several beats too long. When he realized he had just narrowly missed hitting a reflector pole, he yanked the Range Rover into the nearest pullout and shoved it into Park.

"How can you say that? Running out on you was unforgivable."

"No it wasn't. You broke my heart when you left, I won't lie about that. But broken hearts eventually heal, even if they never quite fit together perfectly again." She was quiet for a moment, then she grabbed his hand. "If you had been killed, Zack, I never would have recovered."

After her low admission, he didn't say anything for several moments, just gazed at her with a bemused kind of wonder in his eyes, then with a muffled groan he reached for her.

The kiss was soft and sweet and so full of tenderness she melted against him, her bones dissolving inside her skin.

They had shared dozens of kisses in this last week. Hundreds of them. But she sensed something deeper in this embrace, as if they had both crossed some invisible line.

A heavy tractor trailer passed them, and its wake rattled the windows of the Range Rover. Zack groaned and pressed his forehead against hers. "I don't deserve you."

"You deserve whatever you want out of life." She touched his cheek. "You always have."

"You're what I want. Whether I deserve you or not." He drew away suddenly and shoved the Range Rover into gear. "Come on. Let's go buy a pickup truck."

A little disoriented by the shift in the conversation, she blinked at him. "You're serious? I thought you were only teasing!"

His lopsided grin left her as breathless as his kiss. "Sweetheart, I wouldn't joke about something as important as this."

Driving with one hand, he grabbed her fingers suddenly with the other and pressed a kiss on her palm. "Seriously, Cass. I know nothing I do will bring back the last ten years. But I'd like to re-create at least one thing from that time."

"You're crazy! You can't just walk into a dealership at two in the afternoon on the Fourth of July and walk out with a new pickup truck!"

"Watch me."

She did just that. Not that she had much choice. The

sales manager at the small dealership didn't quite know how to deal with an immovable force like Zack Slater with his mind set on something.

The two of them —Cassie and LeRoy Thomas, his nametag read—just stood back and watched, while Zack quickly perused the inventory on the lot.

"What's your favorite color?" he asked her at one point while he peered under the hood of one big beast.

"I don't know," she answered helplessly, unable to believe he was actually doing this. "Um, I like the sage color of this one."

She didn't think he would appreciate the observation that when he stood next to it, the color perfectly matched the green flecks in his eyes.

"Sage it is, then," he said, poking his head up. "LeRoy, my friend, let's talk."

A half hour later, after some hard-core negotiations that made her head spin, Zack was the proud owner of a hulking three-quarter-ton pickup with all the extras and a price tag that left her feeling slightly ill.

He took her to a late lunch at a pizza place in Idaho Falls. On the way out of the restaurant he offered her the choice of driving home the new truck or the sleek Range Rover.

Home. She really liked the sound of that. Pretending to consider, she cocked her head, looking at both vehicles in the parking lot. "You take the truck," she finally said. "It's your new toy."

He grinned with such boyish excitement that she fell in love with him all over again.

She loved Zack Slater. The sweetness of admitting it to herself flowed through her like pure honey.

She loved his strength and his laughter and his decency.

As certain as she was that this was right between them—that she wanted to take this next step with him—by the time they drove under the wooden Lost Creek Ranch sign, her nerves were stretched thin, her body taut with restless anticipation.

When she parked the Range Rover next to the shiny new truck that gleamed in the late afternoon sun, she was chagrined to realize her hands were shaking, just a little. She climbed out, then shoved them in the pockets of her jeans to hide her nerves.

"Let me just grab a couple of...of quilts." She felt herself blush furiously. "I'm afraid I, um, don't have any strawberries."

"That's okay." He smiled. "Strawberries aren't what I'm hungry for, anyway."

Her mouth went dry and she had to grab the railing of the porch steps to steady herself. He followed her up the steps, and she was almost painfully aware of him as she unlocked the door.

Inside her little cabin he seemed to take up all the available air, leaving her breathless and a little dizzy.

She cleared her throat. "I'll just grab those quilts."

She turned away and nearly jumped out of her skin when he reached out and rested a strong hand on her shoulder. The heat of his fingers scorched through the soft cotton of her shirt as he turned her to face him.

His eyes were intent, searching, and she knew all her sudden anxieties must be glaringly obvious on her far-too-transparent features.

"Do you want me to leave?"

She shook her head fiercely.

"We don't have to do anything you're not ready for. Slow and easy, remember? That's what I promised. I meant every word. We don't even have to go anywhere. We can sit right out on your porch swing and watch the fireworks from here, okay? You can always make me go jump in the cold stream out back if I start misbehaving."

While he spoke, her nerves slid away. She had nothing to be afraid about. Not with Zack. A soft smile captured her mouth at the sincerity in his eyes. He probably would march right to the stream out back if she commanded him.

"You are a very sweet man, Zack Slater," she murmured.

He snorted. "You know me better than that. I just want to do everything right this time."

"So far you're doing a pretty darn good job." She smiled again, sultry this time, and stepped forward to press a kiss to his strong jaw where a hint of late-afternoon shadow rasped against her mouth. She liked it so much she kissed him again. And once more.

He stood motionless while she tasted his skin and meandered her way to his mouth. He wanted slow and easy. She could give him slow and easy. She brushed her lips across his, then back again with leisurely attention to every centimeter of his mouth.

His eyes fluttered closed and he leaned into her. Under her hands, his heart pounded hard and fast in erotic contrast to the unhurried pace of their kiss.

He seemed content to let her take the lead in the kiss, and she reveled in the heady power of his response. As she explored his mouth, she could feel the hard jut of his arousal at her hip, feel his breathing accelerate, grow labored.

When she gripped a handful of shirt and licked at the corner of his mouth, he groaned and parted his lips slightly, just enough for her to slip her tongue inside. But still he didn't move.

She knew the exact moment when his thin hold on control snapped apart. One moment he was motionless under her sensual onslaught. The next, he shuddered and his arms whipped up, twisting in her hair as he gripped her head and ravaged her mouth.

With a sigh of surrender she wrapped her arms around his neck and pressed her body to him.

She couldn't wait another hour, another moment, another second. She wanted him now, right here.

The dying sun sent long, stretched-out shafts of light through a break in the curtains to dapple the furniture and wood floor as she grabbed his hand and pulled him into her small bedroom.

He dug his boot heels into the floor just inside the doorway, his eyes intent and searching on her face. "Are you sure, Cass? There's no going back after this."

She smiled. "I couldn't be more sure than I am right this moment. Kiss me, Slater."

His mouth quirked a little at the order but he promptly obeyed, his hands busy untucking her shirt and exploring the sensitive skin above her hips. She shivered as those hard, rough hands moved closer to her breasts, to her nipples that ached and burned for his touch.

The next few moments were a flurry of buttons and snaps and zippers yanking free.

Finally no barriers remained between them. All her nerves came fluttering back like a flock of magpies to chatter noisily at her.

No man had ever seen her naked except him, and that

had been a decade ago. She was suddenly painfully aware of all her imperfections, every single extra calorie she had ever indulged in over the years.

He didn't appear to notice. At least not judging by the stunned expression on his face.

"I thought I remembered everything about you in exquisite detail," he murmured. "Every curve, every hollow. I can't believe I forgot the sheer impact of the whole package."

"Oh, stop." Hot color saturated all those curves and hollows as he gazed at her with stark longing in his eyes.

He grinned. "Get used to it, sweetheart. I'm just getting warmed up."

She decided the only way out of this was distraction. "That's too bad," she murmured. "Because I'm already very, very warm. And getting warmer by the second."

"Let's see." He stepped forward and kissed her, skimming one sneaky hand from her shoulders down her back to the curve of one rear cheek, pulling her against him. She gasped as fluttery little nerve impulses rocketed through her everywhere her skin brushed his.

"Mmm. You're right. Very warm," he murmured against her mouth.

They stood that way for a long time, wrapped together and rediscovering each other while the room darkened around them.

At last he lowered her to the bed. His hands were strong and hard and clever. He knew exactly how and where to touch her—where to linger, where to tease with fleeting caresses.

She closed her eyes, lost to the swirl of sensation and the steadily building heat he stoked so adroitly. When she opened them, she found him watching her, his eyes heavy with passion. Their gazes locked and stayed that way while his hands caressed her intimately. A restless, aching need gripped her and she curved into his fingers, nearly crying out from the tangle of emotions that bound them so tightly.

Still watching her, he lowered his mouth to hers. The kiss was fierce and possessive and demanding—and she found it every bit as arousing as his hands on her flesh.

"Please," she begged, unable to stand the slow, ex-quisite yearning another instant. His thumb stroked a particularly sensitive spot just then, hidden in folds of flesh, and she sobbed his name as she climaxed in a wild tumble of color and light and sensation.

He entered her while her body still seethed and shiv-ered. She gasped as tight, unused muscles had to stretch to accommodate his size.

Muscles corded in his neck as he eased deeper. She wasn't sure if his growled words were an oath or a prayer. "You're so tight."

"I'm sorry. I just haven't done this in a…in a long time."

He froze, his hot gaze piercing the soft, satiated fog enveloping her. "How long?"

She flushed and focused on the hard blade of his col-larbone. "Oh, ten years. Give or take a month or so."

He blinked but not before she saw the stunned disbe-lief in his eyes. "You haven't been with anyone at all?"

Did they have to talk about this right now, when she could hardly find her breath? When he was invading every inch of her soul? Apparently so. She knew that stubborn look in his eyes and knew he wouldn't let it drop.

"I've been a little busy raising my niece," she retorted.

"When was I supposed to fit in any torrid sexual encounters? In between changing her diapers or before I picked her up from school? I'm sorry. It just wasn't a priority."

The stunned look in his eyes began to give way to something else. Something that looked like an awed kind of wonder. "It shouldn't matter to me. It *doesn't*. I would have understood, Cass, if you had been involved with someone else. You had every right."

"Yes, I did. I just don't view making love with someone lightly. It was...never the right situation with anyone else."

"And this is right, isn't it? Between us?"

She nodded, helpless to do anything else.

"I love you, Cassidy Jane."

The gruff words stole what little breath remained in her lungs. If she'd had any left, it wouldn't have lasted long as he surged deeply inside her, his body taut and hard.

She gasped and rose to meet him, clinging to him as the need spiraled inside her again with each deep, steady movement.

"I love you," he repeated, and the words sent her soaring over the edge once more. An instant later he followed her with a low, exultant moan.

While she floated, featherlight, back to earth, he switched their positions so she was sprawled over him, listening to his ragged breathing while his hands stroked her skin.

A few minutes later, just as she thought she might be able to think straight again, she heard a tremendous boom and saw a sparkle of red and gold through that slim spear of open curtain.

She gasped. "Oh no! We're missing the fireworks!"

His hand curved over her hipbone. "I wouldn't exactly say that."

"But your new truck. You wasted all that money for nothing!"

Hard muscles rippled against her as he shrugged. "We'll use it next year. Make it our own annual tradition."

Would they have a "next year" together? She wanted fiercely to believe it. But even here in the sanctuary of his arms, she couldn't shake the niggling voice warning her that nothing lasts forever.

She had learned that lesson all too well.

In the meantime she needed to do all she could to protect whatever tiny remnants of her heart he hadn't already snatched for his own.

It worked.

He couldn't believe she was here, in his arms. That his weeks of planning, of hoping, had paid off.

Zack watched her sleep, fascinated by the steady rise and fall of her chest under the sheet, the fluttering of her eyelids, the little half smile that played around her mouth.

She was here. And she was his.

He had to be the luckiest son of a gun who ever lived. When he arrived at Salt River three weeks ago, he figured nothing short of a miracle could have convinced her to give him another chance.

Heaven knew, he didn't deserve one.

Yet here she was, warm and soft and cuddly as she slept curled against him.

Somehow she had turned to that steely core of courage inside her and taken a huge leap of faith into his arms. He could only guess what it must have cost her. If she had left *him* a decade ago like a thief in the night—without any kind of explanation—he wasn't sure he would be so willing to let her back into his life. Especially if he believed all that time that she left with another man.

She was a far better person than he was. He had always known that. Loving and generous and sweet.

For a man who had lived most of his life in a hard, unforgiving world, was it any wonder Cassidy Harte had been irresistible?

She was still irresistible, even though the years had changed her. Now that optimistic, artless girl had become a woman. A little less optimistic, maybe. A little more wary, but still as loving and generous as she had been when he lost his heart to her.

He pressed a soft kiss to her forehead. Not to wake her, simply because he still couldn't believe she was here.

She stirred, then her eyes fluttered open. A dazed kind of smile tilted that luscious mouth a little as their gazes met, then color flared across her cheekbones.

"What time is it?" She tried to peer around him to her alarm clock.

"Early. About four-thirty."

She groaned and buried her head under the pillow. "I have to get up in an hour to make breakfast."

"Or, since you're already awake, we could find something more interesting to do for an hour."

She pulled the pillow away and squinted at him. "You're inhuman. I figured four—or was it five?—times would be enough for you."

He couldn't stop the pure, sinful smile stealing over his mouth. "No. I'm very, very human. And I don't think I will ever get enough of you."

The disgruntled look in her eyes began to fade as he reached for her. It didn't take him long to make it disappear entirely, replaced by soft, dreamy desire.

Afterward, he held her tight, her head tucked under his chin.

"Marry me, Cassie."

The words slipped out of him like horses over downed barbed wire. Why had he blurted it out like that? So much for waiting, taking the time and effort to repair the damage he had done by leaving her.

He could tell the words shocked her. She went deep-water still and slid away from him. "Wha-what?"

He couldn't go back now—it was too late for that—so he plodded gamely forward. "I love you. I never stopped loving you. I fell for you all those years ago. For ten years the memory of that time has stalked me. Haunted me. I love you. I want to marry you."

She jumped out of bed as if the sheets were ablaze and scrambled for a silky robe tossed over a chair.

Panic skittered around her, through her. "Don't do this to me, Zack. This is not fair. You can't just blow back into town and expect everything to be the same."

"I don't. I hope we can build something even better than what we had before." He sat up, the sheets bunched at his hips and that wide, hard chest bare, looking so gorgeous her mouth watered. She jerked her gaze away, to something safe like the pale-pink dawn breaking outside her bedroom window.

How could he throw this at her? It was far too much, far too soon. She was still a little light-headed about having taken this giant step and spent the night in his arms.

"Slow and easy. Wasn't that what you said?"

"Yeah. That's what I said."

"This is not slow and easy! This is jumping straight from *hello* to picking out china patterns together. I… I need more time, Zack. I'm sorry. I'm just not ready yet."

A cold, hard knot of terror lodged in her throat at the very idea of committing to a future with him. She was being a yellow-bellied coward and she hated herself for it.

But the cruel lessons of the past were just too ingrained in her psyche.

She had a sudden memory of a pretty little blue heeler her brother Matt bought at a livestock auction a few years ago. The dog's previous owner must have been one mean son of a gun because she quailed, her belly slunk low to the ground and her tail between her legs, whenever Matt tried to work with her.

It had taken months of hard work and patience before her brother could gain the dog's trust.

She knew exactly how that poor bitch felt right now. So afraid to let down her guard. To believe this was any more than just another vicious trick—an outstretched hand that concealed a harsh stick.

"I'm sorry," she repeated. "I'm not ready."

"You still love me, though. Admit it."

She shoved her hands in the pockets of her robe to conceal their trembling. "Sometimes love is not enough. Ten years ago I might have thought it was. But I know better now."

He was silent, his expression resigned, regretful. "You think I'm going to leave you again, don't you?"

She wanted to deny his words but she couldn't. Until this moment she hadn't realized just how afraid she was that he would do exactly that.

Her silence spoke far more loudly than words. He nodded. "Okay. I won't pressure you, Cassie. I'll wait. We have the rest of our lives."

She wanted so fiercely to believe him.

But still she cowered.

Chapter Ten

The nervous jitters fluttering through her before the Independence Day parade nearly a week earlier seemed like tiny rippling waves in a spring breeze compared to this tidal wave of terror.

Cassie shifted in the leather passenger seat of Zack's new truck, adjusted her seat belt, tried to find a comfortable spot for her trembling hands.

Everything's going to be fine, she assured herself, trying hard not to give in to the fierce urge to gnaw her lip to shreds.

"You okay?" Zack asked, with such calm serenity she wanted to punch him. Hard.

Just dandy. She blew out a breath. "No. No, I'm not okay."

He sent her a reassuring smile. "Relax. Everything will be fine. We'll all try to get along."

"Right. Relax. You spent maybe six months with my brothers and that was ten years ago. I've lived with them my entire life. I know exactly what they're like. Everything is *not* going to be fine."

They were on their way to Sunday dinner at the Diamond Harte, and she wouldn't have been more terrified if she were standing barefoot in a nest full of rattlers.

The whole thing had been her idea, she was chagrined to admit. She wasn't sure what kind of evil demon had planted this seed in her head, but she had blurted out the invitation a few days before when she had been lying in his arms, sated and relaxed.

They had both been spending a lot of time in that condition in the last week. Not that she had any regrets. It had been incredible, far better than her memories of before. They laughed together, they talked together, they did everything but broach the subject of the future.

Friday was supposed to have been her last day at the Lost Creek under the terms of their agreement, but neither of them had given it much thought, too wrapped up in rediscovering each other.

"Do you want to forget it?" Zack asked her now. "I could just drop you off and make myself scarce for a couple hours if you want me to."

She blew out a breath. Matt and Jesse both knew she was bringing Zack to dinner. She had called them the day before to warn them. It wouldn't have been fair to just spring it on them out of the blue.

They knew she was seeing him again, and neither was happy about it. She winced remembering their identical, very vocal reactions to the news when she had called them.

But she knew if she and Zack had any future at all—

that future she didn't want to think about—they had to confront the past first.

"No," she answered firmly. "We're going to have to do this eventually. We can't keep hiding out from them like we're holed up in Robber's Roost waiting for the posse to catch up to us. One of these days my brothers are going to see that I'm all grown up and can live my own life. Make my own decisions."

"How bad can it be?" He grinned. "I'll let them each punch me around a few times—I figure I deserve at least that much for breaking their baby sister's heart—then we'll all have a beer and move on."

She slugged his shoulder, more for the cocky grin than his words. "Don't even joke about it. That's exactly what I'm afraid of. I'm fairly fond of that pretty face of yours. I'd hate to see my obstinate brothers mess it up."

He grabbed her hand. "Don't worry about your brothers, I can hold my own. Physically or otherwise." He kissed the fingers he held. "Everything is going to be fine, Cass. Just watch."

If she closed her eyes, she could almost believe him.

The Diamond Harte was exactly as he remembered it—big and sprawling and as brightly polished as a prize rodeo buckle.

Of all the ranches he'd seen in the years his father had dragged him around like a worn-out saddle, the Harte ranch stood out in his memory as one of the cleanest, most efficient operations he'd ever had the pleasure of working.

They pulled up in front of the ranch house, a massive stone and log structure that had always intimidated him a little. Immediately two little dynamos—a redhead and a tiny brunette with long dark hair—hopped down from a swing on the front porch and rushed to their vehicle.

Before he could play the gentleman and open the passenger door for Cassie, they did it for him, all but climbing onto her lap.

"Aunt Cassie! It's been forever since we've seen you!" the darker one exclaimed. He looked closer at her and immediately saw Melanie Harte's silvery-gray eyes looking back at him. This one must be Lucy.

"I know, sweetheart. I'm sorry I didn't make it last week for dinner. I've been really busy at work and with... with things."

"Guess what? Maisy had kittens. They're all black-and-white except one that has ginger stripes. Do you want to see them?"

She laughed. "I will later, okay." She gestured toward him. "Zack, these beautiful creatures are my nieces, Lucy and Dylan. Lucy, Dylan, this is Zack Slater. A friend of mine."

He smiled. "Hi, ladies."

Instantly the girls' enthusiasm switched off like a burned-out bulb. The happy welcome in their eyes faded, and they nodded politely to him, their faces stiff.

Obviously, they had heard about the evil Zack Slater who had blown back into town to ruin their beloved aunt's life once again.

If he couldn't win over a couple of ten-year-olds, he was in serious trouble with the rest of her family. He was racking his brain trying to come up with something harmless and friendly to say when Cassie beat him to it.

"Where is everybody?"

"Mom and Sarah are in the kitchen," Lucy said. "Dad's checking on one of the horses down at the barn, and Jesse's not here yet. He had some stuff to do at the police station and said he'd be a little late."

Cassie lifted an eyebrow. "On Sunday?"

"Sarah said he was waiting for a fax or something. She said it was something real important."

Zack pulled their contribution from behind the seat— a heavy, cast-iron Dutch oven filled with the makings for Cassie's world-famous blueberry cobbler and a huge plastic container loaded with pasta salad—then he followed her up the porch steps and into the ranch house.

Inside, he heard the low, musical murmur of women's voices as they neared the kitchen but it stopped in midnote when they walked into the big, airy room.

One woman stood at the professional stove stirring something while the other sat at the table husking corncobs. Their eyes turned wary, the way the girls' had, when they saw him.

Beside Zack Cassie fidgeted and cleared her throat. "Sorry we're a little late."

"You're fine. Matt hasn't even started the charcoal for the steaks yet," the shorter of the two women said.

With a nervous smile Cassie introduced him to the women. Ellie Harte, Matt's new wife, was an older version of her daughter, small and slender with auburn hair and sparkling green eyes. Sarah, who was apparently brave enough to be willing to marry wild, reckless Jesse Harte, was tall and willowy with a long sweep of wheat-colored hair.

Their expressions were polite and curious but far from friendly. Unless he found a way to break the ice, he could see they were all in for a long, awkward afternoon.

"What can I do to help?" he asked as Cassie moved

containers around in the big refrigerator to make room for her salad. "I can fire up the charcoal if you'd like."

"Matt gets a little territorial when it comes to his barbecue," Ellie said.

Then he was probably real testy about breaking bread with the man he thought had taken his wife. Zack winced. Maybe Cassie was right to be so nervous. Maybe they should have put this off a little longer.

No. There was no sense in waiting. He owed Matt an explanation and an apology and he might as well get it over with. Not here at the house, though. If the man wanted to take a swing at him, he wouldn't do it in front of the nervous eyes of the women and Zack didn't want to deprive him of the chance. He figured he owed him that, as well.

"I think I'll just take a stroll around and see how much the ranch has changed in the past ten years."

"I'll come with you," Cassie offered.

He shook his head. "Why don't you stay and visit? I'd rather go alone."

She sent him a searching look, then nodded and squeezed his hand in gratitude or for luck, he wasn't certain.

He found Matt Harte with his elbows resting on the split rail of a corral fence watching a filly canter around inside.

Cassie's oldest brother, the man who had raised her from the age of twelve, narrowed his gaze as Zack approached but said nothing, waiting for him to make the first move.

He had always liked and respected Matt Harte. The man had nerves of steel and the best natural horse instincts of anybody Zack had ever met. It didn't surprise

him at all that in the past ten years the Diamond Harte
had become world-renowned for raising and training
champion cutters.

That didn't make what he had to do any easier.

He joined Matt at the fence. "She's a pretty little thing,
isn't she?" he murmured, nodding toward the filly.

"Yeah. She's shaping up to be a real goer. I thought
her gait was a little off this morning but she looks like
she's fine now. Ellie said as much but I had to check for
myself. I guess I should listen to my vet more often."

They lapsed into an awkward silence. Zack didn't have
the first clue where to begin.

"I know you don't want me here," he finally said.

Matt turned around and leaned against the fence, elbows propped on the rail and his expression shuttered.
"If I had my way, you'd just ride right on back out of
town the way you came."

"I'm not going to do that."

He received only a grunt in return and sighed. This
was much harder than he'd expected. "Look, you can
think whatever you want about me for walking out on
your sister. You couldn't think any worse of me than I
do of myself for that. But I didn't leave with Melanie. I
swear it."

Matt gave him a sidelong glance as if testing his sincerity. "So you say. But you still left."

He nodded. "I had my reasons. I thought they were
good ones at the time."

"And now?"

"I don't know," he answered honestly. "I don't think I
was ready to be the kind of man Cassie deserves."

"And I'm supposed to believe everything's different

now? That you're not going to get itchy feet in a few days or a few weeks and walk away from her again?"

"To be blunt, Harte, it really doesn't matter what you believe. Just what she believes."

Matt muttered a pungent oath. "I'm not going to let you break her heart again. She grieved over you for a long time. Too damn long. And I know she blamed herself that Melanie ran off and left me with Lucy so tiny."

His chest ached at the words. "I owe Cassie more apologies than I can ever give for hurting her. I'd like to spend the rest of my life trying to make it up to her. And I'm also sorry I betrayed your trust in me. You were a man I liked and respected. Even if I hadn't been engaged to Cassie, for that reason alone I never would have touched your wife."

He paused. "I drove out of town alone ten years ago, Harte. I know you don't believe me and there's not a damn thing I can do to prove it, but it's God's honest truth."

A muscle worked in the other man's cheek as he gazed at the ranch house. "You're right. I'll never really know if Melanie left with you or not. It doesn't really matter. If not you, she would have latched on to some other saddle bum to take her anywhere but here. All I know is she walked away and never looked back. Just like you did."

Although he felt about as uncomfortable as a short-tailed bull in fly season talking about this with another man—and Cassie's brother to boot—he plunged forward. "I love your sister. I never stopped loving her in all these years. I hope as a recently married man maybe you can understand a little about that."

He paused, feeling his ears redden while Matt appeared to become suddenly fascinated with something on his boots. "I want to marry her," he went on gamely.

"But I won't come between her and her family. You and Jesse mean too much to her."

If Matt was surprised by that, he didn't show his hand.

"I know the past is always going to be there between the two of us. Maybe you're always going to wonder if I'm one of the men who messed with your wife. I can swear up and down that I didn't, but if you don't think you can get beyond that, do you think you can just pretend, for Cassie's sake? Hate me all you want on your own time. But can we at least try to be polite to each other around her?"

The other man was silent for several moments then he shrugged. "Let's see how you treat her first. Now what's this I hear about you running a spread near Durango? Cattle or horses?"

Zack breathed out a sigh of relief. He couldn't exactly say Matt had welcomed him back with open arms. But he hadn't shoved his face in the dirt, either.

"Cattle," he answered. "Only a couple hundred head. It's beautiful country there but not as beautiful as Star Valley."

As the conversation shifted from women to the far more comfortable topic of ranching, he relaxed a little.

One brother down, one to go.

With her stomach still snarled into knots, Cassie stood on the wide flagstone patio watching Zack and Matt leaning against the corral fence, deep in conversation. If only they were a little closer, she might be able to read their lips.

"What do you think they're talking about?" she asked Ellie.

Her sister-in-law shaded her eyes with her hand to follow Cassie's gaze. "I don't know. But at least nobody's throwing punches yet."

"It's early in the game," Sarah put in. "Wait until Jesse shows up."

Cassie groaned. "You two are not helping."

The quiet, pretty schoolteacher who had captured Jesse's wild heart was immediately apologetic. "Sorry. I shouldn't have said that. I was only joking. For what it's worth, Matt has too much control to punch anyone, and I made Jesse promise to behave himself. Everything will be fine."

Why did everybody else seem to think that but her? She huffed out a breath. "So, um, what do you think?" she asked, anxious for her friends' opinion.

"About what?" Ellie asked, her eyes dark green with teasing laughter.

"About him." she said impatiently. "Zack."

"He seems very polite," Sarah offered.

"He must have plenty of sand in his gut to walk right out first thing and face Matt," Ellie added.

Sarah cocked her head, her expression thoughtful as she gazed at the pasture where the two men stood admiring the horses. "And I have to admit, I can see why a woman might find him moderately attractive," she said.

Ellie snorted. "Moderately attractive. Right. That's like saying Matt is moderately stubborn. The man's beautiful. Movie-star gorgeous, Cass."

"He is, isn't he?" She smiled as the tremors in her stomach changed from nerves to that familiar achy awareness.

After a moment Ellie touched her arm, her green eyes worried. "But *gorgeous* and *good for you* aren't the same thing at all. Are you sure you know what you're doing?"

Did she? No. She was still scared to death whenever she thought about the future, but she was beginning to feel the first fledgling stirs of hope.

"I still love him," she said simply. "I never stopped."

Ellie studied her, that anxious look still on her face, then it faded away as she smiled. "Then that's good enough for me."

"Me, too," Sarah piped in, with uncharacteristically poor grammar but with a sincerity that brought tears to Cassie's eyes.

"Thank you. Both of you." On impulse, she hugged them both, grateful once more to fate for handing her such wonderful sisters and friends—and that her brothers had been smart enough to snatch them up.

"Just be careful," Ellie murmured.

Oh, it was far too late for that, she thought. She was way beyond careful. When she stepped away from the embrace, she decided her curiosity couldn't wait any longer. "I think I'll just go see for myself what they're talking about."

"Tell your brother to get up here and start the coals, or it will be midnight before we eat."

She hummed a little as she walked down to the corral, her heart suddenly much lighter than it had been driving to the ranch. Maybe Zack was right. Maybe everything would be fine, after all.

When she reached the men, Zack's smile of greeting warmed her to her toes. She slipped her hand into his and was met with a look of surprise, then deep pleasure at her gesture that told him she wouldn't hide their relationship behind her fear.

"Your wife sent me to tell you to start the coals," she told Matt. "Those steaks aren't going to grill themselves."

Matt's relaxed grin took her by surprise. She might have expected thick tension between the two men with their history, but they seemed to be getting along like a couple of hogs rolling in mud.

"Yeah, she's a bossy little thing, isn't she?" he answered, looking toward the house and his wife with such an expression of joy and love on his face that tears burned behind her eyes.

Was it happiness she felt for her brother and his bride? Or envy?

Whatever, she blinked them back as he headed toward the house. "What were you two talking about?" Her voice came out a little ragged around the edges, but Zack didn't appear to notice.

"Oh, this and that. I told him I'm interested in buying this little filly for my ranch when she's trained. He told me he'd think about it."

"Did you…did you talk about Melanie?"

"Yeah."

She frowned impatiently at him. "And?"

He shrugged. "I told him I didn't leave with her, but he's a hard man to read. I think he's far more concerned about you than about Melanie at this point. I tried to assure him my intentions toward you are honorable."

"Oh. That's really too bad," she teased.

His laughter sounded rough. "If I had my way, I'd drag you back into that barn over there, find a nice soft pile of hay and then…" He whispered something in her ear that sent heat rushing through her like the blast from a welder's torch.

She shivered in reaction, but before she could answer, raised voices sounded on the patio, destroying the moment. With a groan of resignation, she eased away from the sultry promise of that low voice in her ear.

"That would be brother number two. The hotheaded one. Your hay pile idea sounds like a very smart one. Let's go."

She yanked his hand to lead him toward the barn and outbuildings, but he shook his head, gripping her fingers. "Come on, sweetheart. We've come this far. Don't chicken out on me now."

She blew out a breath. "I was afraid you were going to say that."

Squaring her shoulders, she walked beside Zack toward the house, her hand still wrapped in his. They were almost to the patio when Jesse marched out to meet them.

She had expected him to be angry, but the sheer cold fury in his eyes stunned her.

"Get away from him, Cass," Jesse growled. "Right now. Go on into the house."

An answering anger flared and she stepped forward, chin out. "I haven't taken orders from you since I was fourteen years old. I'm not about to start now."

"Do it, Cassie."

She was dismayed—and disgusted—to see dark violence in his eyes, etched into his features.

"Forget it," she snapped. "You're a little old for settling things with your fists, don't you think? Not to mention the fact that around here you're supposed to be upholding the law, not shattering it."

"That's exactly what I'm doing. Slater, I'm going to have to ask you to come with me down to the station."

Zack's laughter held little humor. "You're arresting me for dating your sister? Don't you think that's a little extreme?"

"I'm not arresting you for anything. I just have some questions to ask you."

Cassie stepped between them. "Stop it. This is ridiculous. We're here to share Sunday dinner with the family, and that's just what we're going to do. If you have a problem with that, Jess, maybe you need to go eat somewhere else."

Zack certainly didn't need Cassie to fight his battles for him but he was absurdly touched that she stood up to her brother, chin up and her hand still in his, clenching as if she was ready to take Jesse on if he made one wrong move.

He wanted to kiss her right there, but he had a pretty strong feeling that that wouldn't go over well given the current climate.

He glanced toward the wide flagstone patio where the rest of her family gathered and the first flickers of unease stirred to life in his gut.

Something was wrong.

Seriously wrong.

Matt and his wife both looked stunned, their faces ashen, and the other woman—Jesse's fiancée, Sarah—looked as if she was ready to cry.

He jerked back to the heated conversation next to him. Cassie was still upbraiding her brother for his lack of manners and his immaturity.

He held a hand out to stop her. "What's going on?" he asked slowly. "This isn't about some personal vendetta, is it?"

The police chief's voice was hard as a whetstone. "No. I'm investigating a homicide, Slater. And right now you're my prime suspect. I need you to come in for questioning."

Beside him, he felt Cassie jerk her shoulders back. "A homicide? Are you crazy? We haven't had a homicide in Salt River in years."

"Right. This one is about ten years old. Remember that skeleton Ron Atkins found a few months ago in the foothills of his ranch? The state crime lab was finally able to make an identification."

A feeling of dread settled over him. "And?"

"And Matt wasted his money getting a divorce in absentia. Apparently he's been a widower all these years. The bones belonged to Melanie."

The color leached from Cassie's face. "Oh, no."

"After her fingerprints were found on some of the items found with her body, the state crime lab ran dental records and they matched perfectly. No question it was Melanie."

She was going to be sick.

The smell of charcoal and starter fluid wafting from the grill suddenly seemed greasy—the heat of the afternoon too heavy and oppressive—and she pulled her hand away from Zack's to press it to the churning of her stomach.

Melanie was dead. Murdered. She could hardly believe it.

She had hated her manipulative, amoral sister-in-law passionately even before she thought Zack had run off with her, but she had never wished her dead.

All these years when she thought of Melanie it had been with malice and hateful anger for the future Cassie thought she had stolen from her. And all these years, the object of her hatred had been dead, buried in a shallow grave just a few miles away from the Diamond Harte.

Her stomach heaved again and she had to breathe hard to battle back the nausea.

She shifted her horrified gaze from her brother to Zack and found him watching her with an odd, stony expression on his features. It was only after she looked closer and saw the deep shadows of hurt in his eyes that she realized she had subconsciously stepped away from him as if she couldn't wait to put as much distance as possible between them.

She wanted to apologize but she was afraid it was too late.

"I didn't kill Melanie." He addressed his words to Jesse but his gold-flecked eyes locked with hers. "What motive would I possibly have?"

"That's something I'm sure we can discuss down at the station."

"I don't think so."

Jesse stepped forward, and she recognized the barely restrained violence simmering under the surface of his calm. "I don't believe that was a request, Slater."

"You really think that gives you enough evidence to arrest me, only because I was the last person seen with the woman a decade ago?"

A muscle flexed in Jesse's jaw but he didn't answer, which she supposed was answer enough.

"In that case, as I said, I'll have to pass," Zack murmured, his voice dripping with irony. "I'm always happy to cooperate with the law. I'll answer any questions, but unless the rules have changed since the last time I heard the drill, I believe I have the right to an attorney present for our little chat. I can send my plane to Denver for him and have him here in a few hours. Would that be convenient for you?"

She recognized his statement for what it was, a not-so-subtle reminder to Jesse and everyone else—including her—that he was no longer the dirt-poor ranch hand he'd been a decade ago, that he had money and influence now and wouldn't be railroaded into a murder charge.

Jesse looked as if he couldn't wait for an excuse to take a swing at him, but Matt stepped forward and rested a warning hand on his shoulder.

The motion jarred her out of the dream-like, surreal state she'd slipped into.

Matt. And Lucy. Dear heavens. How was this going to affect them? Her stomach shuddered again, and she tasted bile in her throat. Poor Lucy. Though she and Matt had tried to shield her as much as possible, children at school whispered to each other. She knew they did.

It had been hard enough on Lucy to believe her mother had abandoned her. Now, when she finally had a real family, all the talk about Melanie would resurface and Lucy would be hurt all over again.

She blinked when she realized Zack was speaking to her in a cold, distant voice she hated.

"I'm sure you can find a ride back to the Lost Creek, Cassie. If you'll all excuse me, I need to make some phone calls."

He turned on his heels, leaving stunned silence behind him. For a moment—only a moment—she was torn by conflicting loyalties. Her family would need her. Matt and Lucy would need her.

But she couldn't let him leave. Not like this. She turned to follow him, but Jesse grabbed her arm.

"Let him go," he ordered.

"Back off, Jess."

She and Sarah both said the words at exactly the same moment, only Cassie snarled like an angry bobcat while Sarah just murmured them in her soft, compelling voice.

She was pretty sure Jesse responded more to Sarah's request than her order, but she didn't wait around to thank her after he let her go. With her heart pounding, she raced around the house and caught up with Zack just as he was climbing into the shiny sage-green pickup she had picked out for him.

She skidded to a stop and stood there for a moment, scrambling for words.

"I'm sorry," she finally whispered, the only thing she could come up with as shock and misery choked her throat.

His expression was grim, closed. "For what? Believing I could be capable of murdering Melanie?"

She wanted to say she didn't believe it. That she could never believe it. But she had to admit that a tiny dark corner of her heart—the raw bruise that had never completely healed, had never been able to completely forgive him for leaving her—raised ugly doubts.

He *had* been the last one seen with Melanie. Jesse and others had seen them kissing outside the Renegade and then they had driven off together. Who knew what might have happened after that?

She'd been tempted to wring Melanie's neck more than a few times herself for what she'd put Matt through in their short, stormy marriage.

No. She swallowed hard. The tender man who painted her toenails and held her so gently and blew raspberries on her stomach would never use violence against a woman.

Never.

She couldn't believe it.

"I know you couldn't have killed her," she said firmly.

"But a part of you wonders, right? Unless your brother comes up with another suspect in a hurry, part of you will always wonder."

She opened her mouth as if to deny it, then closed it, shattering his heart into a thousand tiny pieces.

How could he blame her? Ten years ago he had broken her heart, had left her without a word. He couldn't blame anyone but himself if she had a hard time believing him after he betrayed her so completely.

He couldn't blame her but he also knew he couldn't live with a woman unable to trust him. They couldn't build a future on something so flimsy, or it would crumble to dust in the first hard wind.

A bitter laugh threatened to choke him. Hard wind, hell. This accusation of murder was a tornado coming out of the blue.

"I told you what happened that night," he said gruffly. "She came on to me, I turned her down. I couldn't let her drive home in her condition and I didn't want to leave her drunk at the Renegade at the mercy of any unscrupulous cowboy who came along. I tried to give her a ride home. When she wouldn't let up, I finally kicked her out of my truck. Whatever happened to her after that is anybody's guess. I didn't kill her."

Even as he said the words, deep down in the pit of his gut, he knew differently. He was as responsible for her death as if he'd been the one who pulled the trigger.

She must have run into trouble after he'd driven away. He should never have left her unprotected and alone on the road, no matter how much she might have provoked him.

A good man, a decent man, never would have abandoned a woman alone in the dark.

A no-account drifter, on the other hand, would do just that.

"Go on back to your family, Cass," he said gently. "This will be tough on them. They're going to need you."

She glared at him, but there were tears gathering in her eyes. His Cassie, who hardly ever cried. His heart wept along with her.

"Damn you, Zack. Don't you do this to me again."

"Do what?"

"Push me away. Make my decisions for me. You didn't give me the choice to stand beside you once. Don't do it again."

He couldn't drag her through this kind of ugliness. He had to push her away, no matter how badly he wanted to yank her against him and bury her head against his chest.

If he listened hard, he could almost hear the sound of his dreams shattering around his feet. The future stretched out ahead of him, bleak and empty. A vast gray expanse without her laughter and her sparkling blue eyes and the miracle of her love.

He had never deserved any of it. All this time he thought the money and power he'd spent a decade accumulating had made a difference, that he would finally be worthy of her.

But she was right all this time. Everything he had accomplished didn't matter at all.

He would always be the worthless son of a drunk saddle bum. And now he was under suspicion for murder.

No. It was better this way.

"Goodbye, Cassie. I didn't say that before and I'm sorry for that. I should have."

He slid into the truck but her outstretched hand kept him from closing the door behind him.

"You're...you're leaving?"

"Not right away. But I'm going to be busy for a while trying to fight this, then I'll be heading back to Denver. I'm sure you won't want to stay at the Lost Creek anymore now that the sale has gone through. Claire is capable of taking over for you—you've more than fulfilled your part of our deal. I'll send your check here."

"I don't want your money."

Tears seeped from her eyes, trickling down her cheeks into the corner of her mouth. Everything in him cried out to reach for her, but he knew he couldn't.

If he did—if he touched her—he wouldn't be able to let her go.

"Take it. Open your café. Be happy."

At his words, her outstretched hand curled into a fist and she pressed it against her stomach.

He closed the door of the truck and started it up, then drove away from the Diamond Harte without looking back.

This was the sort of day she usually loved.

Cassie stood at the sink in the modern kitchen of the Rendezvous Ranch, gazing out the window at the rain drizzling down outside. The sky was dark for late afternoon, the trees dripping heavily.

When she was a girl, her mother used to call these stormy summer afternoons "do nothing" days and that's exactly what they would do. Curl up on the porch swing with a book or play go-fish at the kitchen table or scavenge through each item in the cedar chest that always graced the foot of her parents' bed, brimming with history.

Those days had been rare and precious, when she could have her busy mother to herself. She closed her eyes, remembering soft hands, a tender smile, a lap just perfect for cuddling in.

Her parents had died when she was twelve, on the cusp of becoming a woman. She used to wonder if being without her mother during those critical teen years had somehow left her broken, a puzzle with a few pieces missing.

Growing up in a household of big, macho men, she had never had anyone to give her advice about being a girl. About how to talk to boys and what to wear and how to fix her hair. As a result, she had treated most of the boys she went to school with just like she treated her brothers. She hadn't known any better. And they had responded in kind, considering her just one of the gang.

Maybe that's why Zack had so completely swept her off her feet. He'd treated her like a woman, even from the beginning.

No. No matter what had happened in her past, she somehow knew that she would have fallen just as hard for the tawny, dangerous cowboy with the sweet smile.

If her mother hadn't died in that crash, what advice would she give now to her heartbroken daughter?

Forget him and move on? Or go after him, even though he wanted nothing to do with her?

Ten years ago if she had the first inkling where he might have gone, she would have gone after him, no question about it. But she had changed over the years.

This time she knew exactly where he was—still hunkered down at the Lost Creek since Jesse had ordered him not to leave town until he was either arrested or cleared in Melanie's murder.

She might know where he was, but she couldn't go to him. Not this time.

He didn't want her beside him.

No matter how she tried to convince him she knew he had nothing to do with Melanie's death, he still pushed her away. She thought she knew why—once more his damned nobility gave him some stupid, misguided notion that she deserved better than a man under suspicion for murder.

There was no one better. Why couldn't he see that? Zack Slater was the best thing that had ever happened to her.

She sighed and watched the sky weep while her heart wanted to cry right along with it. The rain she usually loved only reinforced how miserable and off-kilter she felt here.

It was kind of Wade to offer her a job at the Rendezvous, but she missed the Lost Creek. She missed her little cabin. She missed Jean and Kip and Claire and Greta.

Most of all she missed Zack.

"Something smells good in here."

The deep voice interrupted her reverie, and she looked up to see her new employer in the doorway wearing a long rain slicker and Stetson. He looked ruggedly handsome, like something out of a cologne commercial, and she wondered a little desperately why she couldn't have fallen in love with someone like him.

Despite Zack's claim that Wade might have been involved in whatever he'd stumbled onto the night he left Salt River, she still couldn't believe it.

Wade was nice and safe, and he wouldn't have made a habit of crushing her heart like it was made of toothpicks.

She managed to summon a smile. "Beef and barley soup and homemade bread. I know it wasn't on the week's menu we worked out, but it seemed just the thing for such a drizzly day."

She thought she saw just a hint of irritation flicker across his dark eyes, then he smiled. "That sounds perfect. I'm sure the guests will understand about the change in plans."

She cleared her throat, suddenly uncomfortable. "I'm sorry. I guess I should have cleared it with you first."

"No, it's fine."

At the Lost Creek she had enjoyed full autonomy in the kitchen. If she had wanted to serve cold cereal for dinner, Jean would have just laughed and gone along with it. But she was learning that Wade liked to have a hand in every aspect of his guest ranch.

She couldn't really blame him. While only a few miles away on horseback from the Lost Creek, the Rendezvous was in a completely different stratosphere when it came to its guests.

Wade's ranch catered to a far more exclusive clientele than the Lost Creek.

While Jean tried to bring in young families and older people—average folks yearning to experience the romance of the Old West for a while—the Rendezvous attracted movie stars and Wall Street tycoons and media moguls. Movers and shakers who wanted to be close to Jackson without the annoying crowds.

Her humble beef and barley soup had probably been a lousy idea. Big surprise there. She hadn't done a single thing right since she came here.

"I'm sorry," she said again.

Wade waved one hand dismissively while he removed his Stetson with the other one. "Don't worry about it. How are you settling in?"

Somehow she managed to find another smile. "Fine. Your kitchen is wonderful."

Wade studied her for a long moment until she began to squirm, then he smiled. "I hope this doesn't sound too forward of me but I designed it with you in mind. I always knew you would end up here, one way or another."

Okay. This was getting a little creepy. What was she supposed to say to that? She didn't have the heart to tell him the Rendezvous was just a brief resting place on her journey to her ultimate goal. As soon as the dust settled from this ridiculous murder charge against Zack and he left again, she would make an offer on Murphy's.

She would, she assured that hateful little voice raising doubts in her mind. She just needed a little more time.

"You made the right decision coming here." Wade moved behind her to grab a bottle of imported water from the refrigerator. "Distancing yourself from that... that son of a bitch Slater was the right thing to do. I tried to tell you he was no-good. Sooner or later, he'll be arrested for murder. That kind of ugliness should never have to touch you."

He reached out and rested his hand on her shoulder, and she fought the instinct to flinch away.

What on earth was the matter with her? Wade had been her friend for a long time. She shouldn't have this edginess around him.

"I'm not so sure about that arrest," she finally said, compelled to defend Slater even though he clearly didn't want her involved. "If Jesse had enough evidence against him, Zack would already be in jail."

"He will be. Just wait. If there was one thing I learned when I was on the force, it's that the wheels of justice roll slowly sometimes. But Slater will get what's coming to him. I guarantee it. He's going to find out we don't let men like him get away with killing innocent women around here."

Melanie? Innocent? A raw laugh almost escaped her throat, but she swallowed it back just in time, somehow sensing Wade wouldn't appreciate the irony. More than likely he would be horrified at her callous attitude toward her late sister-in-law.

Before she could answer, Wade changed the subject. "What are you planning for dessert?"

The shift in conversation so disoriented her that it took her several moments to gather her thoughts. "I, ah, I'm not sure."

A little frown wrinkled his tanned forehead. "Oh. Well, I'm sure it will be something delicious. I'll check back later. Remember, dinner is at seven sharp."

After he shoved his hat on and left, she gazed out once more at the gloomy late-afternoon sky. Dear heavens, she hated it here. She wanted to go home. Not to the Diamond Harte, to the Lost Creek. And to Zack.

Her fierce longing to see him again—to talk to him, to assure herself he was okay—was a physical ache inside her, grinding away at her spirit.

She forced her attention back to dinner. She needed to come up with something spectacular for dessert to make up for the soup disaster, and she didn't have any time to waste wishing for the moon.

At the Lost Creek she would have served jam and

butter with the homemade bread, but she suspected that wouldn't win her very many points here.

What about crêpes Suzette? They were relatively easy to make and always generated excitement, what with all that flaming brandy. It might be a little extravagant as a counterpoint to the soup but maybe a little flash wouldn't be such a bad thing.

So, brandy. Where could she find some? She did a quick mental inventory of the kitchen supplies she had seen throughout her week of working at the Rendezvous. Wade kept the spirits tucked away in one of the higher cupboards, didn't he?

She had to pore through several before she found it. There. Tucked away in a corner of the kitchen, on the top shelf with several other bottles. She pulled a stool over and climbed up, immediately spying the orange liqueur she would also need.

She was just reaching for the decanter of brandy when she spied something else in the rear of the cupboard.

A box, no more than six inches long and maybe four inches deep. Small and wooden, it seemed out of place amid the richly colored bottles.

The wood was smooth, cool in her hands as she picked it up and she heard a clink and rattle from inside. What might be inside? Someone's forgotten bank stash? Heirloom jewelry? A secret diary?

Her dark mood momentarily gave way to curiosity as she remembered those rainy days spent with her mother pawing through the old cedar chest.

This box was also cedar, the kind a woman might keep treasured letters inside. As she worked the catch and lifted the lid, the evocative smell wafted to her.

She closed her eyes, once more in her parents' bedroom looking at old photographs and bronzed baby shoes and bits of lace pillowcase her grandmother had tatted as a new bride.

This box was lined in red velvet, she saw when she opened her eyes again, the contents obviously precious to someone.

Why? she wondered. It was jewelry all right, but instead of old cameos and pearls that might have belonged to someone's ancestors, at first glance it seemed to be nothing but cheap costume jewelry. A gaudy necklace, spangled bracelets, a pair of dangly earrings.

She had seen these things before. She blinked, racking her mind to remember where. A long time ago. Someone she knew had owned similar pieces.

She couldn't think who or where or when until she moved them aside and saw something else at the bottom of the pile of trinkets. A photograph, facedown, with no writing on the back.

She pulled it out, and nervousness skittered down her spine like a closet full of spiders.

With trembling hands she turned over the picture, then gasped.

It was a Polaroid of a woman she knew all too well, with dark curly hair and troubled gray eyes.

Melanie.

She wore a tight, flashy dress along with every one of the items in the box.

And judging by the pool of blood puddling under her head and the empty look in those gray eyes, she was very, very dead.

Chapter Eleven

She stared at the box in her hands, vaguely aware of the drumming of her pulse, her rapid, shallow breathing.

Her mind raced, trying to figure out what it meant. Why would this be here, tucked away in the kitchen of the Rendezvous Ranch? Had Wade somehow been involved in Melanie's death? Was this box some kind of grisly souvenir?

Her vision dimmed at the thought, and she had to step down from the stool before she toppled to the ground.

What other explanation could there be?

Zack had tried to warn her about Wade, but she hadn't listened. Now she saw his claims in an entirely different light. Had Wade really been involved in the drug ring Zack said he'd stumbled on the night he left? Had he been one of the men who had brutally kicked and beaten Zack before ordering him out of town?

Get up to 4
FREE FABULOUS BOOKS
You Love!

To thank you for being a loyal reader we'd like to send you up to 4 FREE BOOKS, absolutely free.

Just write "YES" on the Loyal Reader Voucher and we'll send you up to 4 Free Books and Free Mystery Gifts, altogether worth over $20, as a way of saying thank you for being a loyal reader.

Try **Essential Suspense** featuring spine-tingling suspense and psychological thrillers with many written by today's best-selling authors.

Try **Essential Romance** featuring compelling romance stories with many written by today's best-selling authors.

Or **TRY BOTH!**

We are so glad you love the books as much as we do and can't wait to send you great new books.

So don't miss out, return your Loyal Reader Voucher Today!

Pam Powers

LOYAL READER
FREE BOOKS VOUCHER

YES! I Love Reading, please send me up to 4 FREE BOOKS and Free Mystery Gifts from the series I select.

Just write in "YES" on the dotted line below then return this card today and we'll send your free books & gifts asap!

➡ _ _YES_ _ ⬅

Which do you prefer?

☐ **Essential Suspense**
191/391 MDL GNR4

☐ **Essential Romance**
194/394 MDL GNR4

☐ **BOTH**
191/391 & 194/394
MDL GNSG

FIRST NAME	LAST NAME

ADDRESS

APT.#	CITY

STATE/PROV.	ZIP/POSTAL CODE

She had struggled to believe Zack's claims. The idea of a mild-mannered, kind man like Wade—a pillar of the community, active in church and civic responsibilities—wrapped up in something so ugly seemed ludicrous.

It didn't seem so outrageous now.

She stared at the picture in her hand, at that beautiful face with the wide, empty eyes, and her stomach churned.

Had Melanie been linked to the drug activity Zack claimed to have seen? She wouldn't have been surprised to know her sister-in-law had been abusing drugs. It fit the pattern of an unhappy, self-destructive woman.

Melanie hadn't died of an overdose, though, but of a bullet to the brain. Had Wade put it there?

She began to shiver. Why, in heaven's name, would he have left this here tucked away in a back cupboard of his kitchen? He must have known she would eventually find it.

Maybe that's exactly what he wanted.

A chill gusted over her, colder than any January wind. Why? Why would he possibly want her to see this?

No. This must be some kind of hideous mistake. The logical, rational corner of her mind still couldn't imagine Wade could be capable of this. A box full of costume jewelry wasn't proof of anything.

The picture, though. That was a fairly damning piece of the puzzle.

Jesse. She should call Jesse. He would know what to do. Hands shaking, her breathing ragged, she rushed to the phone hanging on the kitchen wall and dialed her brother's cellular number.

She was just punching in the last number when the door opened. She froze, her finger poised above the five, and the box in her other hand just as Wade walked back into the kitchen.

In one quick movement, she shoved the box behind her back and hung up the phone.

"Did you forget something?" she asked, hoping he couldn't hear the panic she tried to hide behind a thin, crackly sheen of false cheerfulness.

He narrowed his gaze at her, looking from the phone and then back to her. "Is everything okay? You're looking a little pale."

"Fine. Everything's just fine." *Breathe,* she ordered herself as her knees started to wobble.

"Are you sure? Maybe you need to sit down."

"No. I promise, I'm fine."

If anyone in her right mind could consider ready to jump out of her skin any minute now at all close to *fine*.

"Am I interrupting something?"

"No. I was…was just trying to figure out what to fix for dessert."

"That's why I came back. I had a couple of suggestions for something to serve after your, uh, delicious soup."

If she hadn't been so terrified, she would have been offended by that not-so-subtle dig.

"I was thinking a cheesecake might be nice. Or some kind of torte. I believe we have fresh raspberries."

She made a noncommittal sound, willing him to leave the kitchen. When she didn't answer beyond that, his gaze narrowed. "Are you sure you're all right, Cassidy? You look as if you've seen a ghost."

Maybe because she had. "No. I… I'm fine. Just a little tired."

"What do you have there?"

"Where?"

"Behind your back. What are you hiding?"

She shuddered out a quick breath, her mind scrambling. "It's, um, a surprise. For dessert."

He fingered his hat. "Please don't take this the wrong way, but I'm not really all that fond of surprises. Why don't you just tell me what you're planning?"

"Crêpes Suzette," she blurted out. "It's one of my specialties."

"Oh." He smiled. "That sounds very elegant. Very French. I don't believe we've ever served that at the Rendezvous. Okay. Good. I'll see you at dinner, then."

To her vast relief he started to walk back out of the kitchen. She forced her breathing into a slow, measured cadence. But just before he reached the door, he stopped, his head turned toward the liquor cabinet.

To her horror she suddenly realized the door to the cupboard was still wide open, the stepstool in front of it. There was nothing she could do to hide either at this point.

If he was indeed the one who'd stashed the gruesome little box there, he would know she had discovered it.

He turned back to her, his mouth suddenly grim, then walked closer. "What are you hiding?" he repeated.

"Nothing. Just…nothing." She was too frightened to come up with anything more coherent than that.

"Oh, dear. This is a problem. You found it, didn't you?"

"Found what? I don't know what you're talking about."

"You were never a very good liar, Cassidy. You shouldn't have gone snooping around. It wasn't very polite."

She tried one more time to bluff her way through. "I'm not lying. I was…was just looking for some brandy for the dessert. For crêpes Suzette you pour brandy over the crêpes and set them ablaze. It's really quite dramatic."

His sigh was resigned. "I'm afraid I can't let you leave, now that you know."

"I don't know anything. I swear."

"You're a smart woman, Cassidy. That's one of the things I've always admired about you. That and your lush beauty. You're like a rare rose blooming in a weed patch." He reached a hand out and traced one finger down her cheek, and it took every ounce of strength to keep from flinching. "We could have made a wonderful team together."

Even though her stomach heaved and she was very much afraid she was going to be sick all over him, she mustered a smile. "We still can."

"It's too late for that. Far too late. You shouldn't have gone snooping."

He was crazy. He had to be. He left the box there in plain sight, where anyone could have stumbled on it, then he accused her of going searching for it. Real fear began uncoiling inside her. He wouldn't let her leave. Not after this.

"You're very much like her."

"Like who?" She barely paid attention to him as her mind chased in circles trying to come up with an escape route. There were two doors in the kitchen, one to the back porch of the lodge, the other to the dining room. She mentally scanned her options and decided her chances were better outside.

He would be on her in a second, though, unless she came up with something to delay him.

"Like Melanie," Wade went on, his voice conversational, as if he were talking about something benign, mundane.

"I loved her. I never wanted to hurt her." His sigh sounded wistful, melancholy. "We were going to leave Star Valley. Make a new start, just the two of us. I was working on getting the money."

"By dealing drugs with Carl Briggs?"

She hadn't meant to say that, it just slipped out. Wade's dark eyes widened with surprise for just a moment, then his expression hardened. "How did you know about that?"

She didn't answer, just tried to focus on escaping.

"That bastard Slater told you, didn't he? He doesn't know how to keep his mouth shut. I knew we should have finished him off that night."

She swallowed hard as his words confirmed everything Zack had said and more.

"Carl and me and a few of the other boys had a good thing going," Wade went on, apparently not expecting any involvement in the conversation from her. "We were the middlemen. It was a perfect setup. Who would have suspected a podunk small-town Wyoming police department was a distribution hub for the intermountain West? We could have gotten away with it forever. Then that night everything went wrong."

He glared at her as if it had all been her fault.

"First that no-account drifter of yours turned up where he had no business, then I came home to find Melanie at my place in town, drunk and acting crazy. She wanted to leave that night. I told her I needed a few more weeks to come up with enough money. She said she couldn't wait, that she had to get out of town and didn't have any more patience for what she called my stupid little schemes. She shouldn't have said that."

His expression darkened until she hardly recognized him as the same kind, decent man she had always believed him to be.

She cleared her throat, compelled despite her own instincts of self-preservation to hear of Melanie's fate. "What happened?"

"I had to prove to her I was onto something big, to convince her to wait just a few more weeks, so I showed her the blow still in the truck. We were delivering it the next morning to our contacts.

"If she had only stayed quiet, everything would have been fine. But she started going on about how she wanted in. If I refused, she said she would go public with the whole thing and expose us all."

A vague plan began to form in her mind, and Cassie began edging toward the stove, hoping he wouldn't notice.

To her relief, he seemed to be too wrapped up in the past. "I tried to shut her up, but she kept going on and on about how she deserved my share since she took pity on me and slept with me."

He closed his eyes as if to block out the memories, and Cassie took advantage of his distraction to step closer to the stove.

"I didn't know what else to do. She wouldn't shut up. She even picked up the phone and said she was calling the sheriff right then. I knew if she told anybody, Carl would kill *me* for showing her the merchandise. I pulled out my gun, just to scare her. She laughed at me and kept dialing."

"So you shot her."

He opened his eyes as if he were surprised to see her still there.

"I shot her. I didn't want to. I cried the whole time I dug that grave out at the Atkins place. I loved her. I never wanted to hurt her." His lips narrowed. "I don't want to hurt you, either, Cassidy. You shouldn't have gone snooping around."

"You shouldn't have left this in the back of the liquor cabinet, then, where anybody could have stumbled on it."

She held out the photograph, and for a moment he froze, then he reached out and snatched it from her, examining the grisly scene as if it was a Monet water-color.

"Wasn't she beautiful?" he murmured. "Like an angel."

She chose that moment to move, while he was distracted by the picture. In one motion, she picked up the heavy stockpot of soup—the soup he had been so disdainful of—and hurled it into his face.

As the boiling liquid hit him, Wade screamed a terrible, high-pitched scream and went down on his knees, his hands over his face. She knew this was likely her only chance for survival so she didn't wait around.

In seconds she had rushed out the back door. Although she knew it was costing her precious time, she quickly hefted one of the sturdy Adirondack lawn chairs on the back porch and wedged it under the door-knob as a further delaying tactic, then took off running.

The sky had darkened even more, and after just a few yards she was soaked and shivering in her jeans and sweatshirt.

A short distance from the house she caught a lucky break. Wade had left his horse tied up to a hitching post near the driveway, obviously intending to ride out again after he finished nagging her about dessert.

The horse was skittish as this strange, dripping-wet woman ran up to him out of nowhere. He whinnied and danced around on his lead, but Cassie hadn't spent her whole life around horses for nothing. She grabbed the reins firmly and wasted a few more valuable seconds trying to calm the animal with soft words.

When the fractious horse was finally under control, she quickly mounted. Although the stirrups were set for Wade's much longer legs, she dug the heels of her sneakers into his side. The horse apparently got the message and the two of them hurtled off through the rain.

She wasn't conscious of any kind of plan beyond escaping whatever grim fate Wade had in store for her. But as the horse galloped away from the Rendezvous, she realized exactly where she was heading.

To the Lost Creek.

To safety.

To Zack.

It was over.

Despite the steady drizzle, Zack nudged his mount a little higher up the trail above the Lost Creek, loath to leave the mountain just yet. He wanted one last look at this place he had come to love so much—at the bright, shining future he had cupped in his hands for only a few precious moments before it had trickled through his fingers.

He was leaving in the morning at first light, Jesse Harte's edicts about not leaving town be damned. His lawyers could wrangle over the particulars. Until the county prosecutor determined there was enough evidence to charge him, they had no legal basis to keep him here.

And he couldn't stay any longer.

It was too painful being so close to Cassie, to know she was just through the trees at her new job working for that son of a bitch Lowry. Just a few miles away but forever out of his reach.

For a few magical weeks she had been his again. The world had gleamed with promise. Possibilities. He closed his eyes, his mind filled with images of her: laughing at something he said, her smile wide and her eyes bright; bustling about the heat of the ranch kitchen with flushed cheeks and that look of concentration on her features; her body taut beneath him, around him, as he made love to her.

He should have known this time with her wouldn't last. It had been a chimera, a fleeting glimpse at something he could never hope to own.

The identification of Melanie Harte's remains—and the subsequent wide net of suspicion cast on him—had effectively shattered that future.

The irony of the past didn't escape him. He had left her a decade ago in an effort to protect her from a no-good son of a bitch like him. He was doing the same now.

Once more he faced charges for a crime he didn't commit—this time for a heinous crime against a member of her own family—and the injustice of it made him want to climb to the highest spot he could find and shake his fists at the sky.

So close. He'd been so close to grabbing the prize, the only thing he had ever wanted. A home, a place to belong, with the woman who had owned his heart since she was just eighteen.

And now he had nothing. Less than nothing. A few memories that cut his heart like a fresh blade.

He drew in a ragged breath and dismounted at a spot where the trees thinned. Below him the Star Valley spread out, little clusters of population surrounded by acres and acres of farms and ranches.

The dark clouds overhead saturated the valley with color. The countryside looked fresh and clean and verdant.

A place where he would always be an outsider.

He couldn't stay anymore. If Jesse Harte wanted him here to face charges, he could damn well charge him with something or cut him free. This had been just a brief, wonderful interlude that ended in disaster, and now he needed to get back to his real life.

His solitary, empty, colorless life.

He sighed, fighting the primitive urge to keep on riding until he reached the Rendezvous, then toss Cassie over his saddle and ride off into the mountains with her.

No. He couldn't. He had to head back to the Lost Creek, to spend one more night at the guest ranch he now owned and didn't know what to do with.

He didn't feel right about turning around and selling it to someone else. Not when he had promised Jean Martineau he would care for her ranch with the same care she had always given it.

He would just have to hire someone to run it. Would Cassie consider the job? he wondered, then discarded the idea just as quickly. She would excel at managing the place, he had no doubt about that whatsoever. But he could never ask her to work for him on a permanent basis, even if he thought for a minute she might even consider it.

What a mess. He'd been so damn sure his plans to

woo her again would eventually succeed that he hadn't planned for failure at all.

With another deep sigh of regret, he shoved his boot in the stirrup and swung into the saddle. He spared one last look at the pristine valley below before nudging the horse back down the trail.

He had only ridden a hundred yards when he heard something crash through the undergrowth on the trail ahead of him, hidden from view by the thick brush. Moose and elk often frequented the thickly wooded area. They were about the only thing big enough to make that kind of noise, he thought, then he heard a high whinny and the unmistakable sound of a horse at full gallop.

Damn. What kind of idiot takes a muddy, steep trail like this at such a pace? Either the animal was out of control or its rider had some kind of a death wish.

He spurred his own mount as fast as safety dictated to catch up with the rider. As he burst around the bend, he saw a muscular buckskin being urged hell-for-leather down the trail. At first he thought the rider was a foolish boy who had been caught out in the weather unprepared, judging by the lack of rain gear and the short dark hair plastered to his head.

Then, as the rider turned around to see who followed, Zack had a quick impression of delicate, pale features, and realized the rider was no boy.

It was Cassie. And she looked scared to death.

He thought for a moment she was going to keep hurtling down the mountainside, but she finally reined in the buckskin. The horse skidded to a stop then stood, sides heaving, while Zack caught up with her.

He dismounted and rushed to her, his arms out. She slid almost bonelessly into them, stumbling when she reached the ground. She would have fallen if he hadn't held her so tightly to his chest. He realized she was trembling, from cold or shock, he wasn't sure, and his gut clutched with dread.

"What is it? What's happened?" Urgency sharpened his voice.

Her voice sounded dazed, thready. "He killed her. We have to get out of here. I think I heard him following me."

She tried to pull away from him, her face tight with fear, but he held her fast. "Who? Slow down!"

"Wade. He...he killed Melanie. I stumbled onto proof at the Rendezvous. I tried to hide it from him, but I couldn't and he... I think he was going to hurt me, too. I threw a pot of soup at him and ran. All I could think about was coming here, to the Lost Creek. To you."

His arms tightened around her, and she rested her cheek against his chest only for a moment, then drew back frantically.

"We can't stay here. I think he's crazy. Who knows what he'll do if he finds us. Come on. We have to get to the ranch and call Jesse."

And she needed to get out of this rain and her wet clothes before she caught pneumonia. Already he could see signs of hypothermia in her bloodless lips and dazed expression. He pulled off his oiled slicker and wrapped her in it. She was trembling so much he didn't think she would be able to stay in the saddle much longer. "I think you and your horse are both done for. You can ride with me."

She opened her mouth as if she to argue, then closed it again, obviously deciding there wasn't time.

Grateful for the strength of the big, rawboned bay he'd been riding since his arrival at the ranch, he mounted first, then reached down and helped her up behind him. She clung tightly as he urged the horse down the trail, the buckskin plodding tiredly behind.

She wrapped her arms around him, soaking in the heat that emanated from his powerful back. Although deep tremors still shook her body, for the first time since that gruesome discovery—no, for the first time since the week before, when Jesse had growled out the news about Melanie's death and Zack had pushed her away— she began to feel safe and warm again.

As they rode, she explained her discovery to him, about stumbling onto that terrible box and the story Wade had told her of Melanie's death.

"How did you get away?" he asked, shifting in the saddle so he could see her through the gathering darkness.

She winced. "I, um, threw a pot of hot beef and barley soup on him and ran out the door."

"Soup? You threw *soup* at a man threatening to kill you? A man who has already murdered at least one person who stood in his way?"

Feeling warmer by the second, she clenched her teeth at the stunned disbelief in his voice. "Yeah, I know. It was a waste of good soup. How about the next time a murderer comes after me, I'll ask you first before I make any kind of move to protect myself?"

Before he could answer, they heard a loud rustling in the thick brush twenty yards or thirty yards ahead of them. Both horses alerted, tails raised. With a soft command to the bay, Zack reined in the horse, his head up like a tawny mountain lion scenting danger.

Although there was a good hour of daylight left, the steady rain created a thick, misty curtain that limited visibility. All she could hear was the heavy pounding of her pulse and the musical drip of raindrops plinking off the leaves.

"Is it Wade?" she whispered through the fear in her throat.

He squeezed one of her hands wrapped around his middle. "I'm not sure. Probably not. A man doesn't quickly recover from having a pot of beef and barley soup hurled at him."

He gave her that lopsided grin she loved so much, then it slid away. "Damn. I wish I'd brought a revolver with me."

A revolver? Did he really think he might need a weapon? She had never wanted to put Zack in danger. All she had been thinking about was escape. Now her mind reeled with a dozen scenarios, each more grim than the last.

After a moment they heard nothing else down the trail so Zack cautiously urged his horse on. Before they could make it even ten yards, Wade stepped out of the brush, holding a shiny black handgun aimed right at them.

Cassie swallowed a shriek, and her grip tightened convulsively around Zack.

All signs of the benign, friendly man she had known had disappeared, replaced by an angry stranger. Wade's face was a dusky red, as if he had spent way too much time in the sun. Odd, since it was so cloudy. It took her several seconds to realize he must have been burned by the soup broth.

"Oh, this is perfect," he drawled. "It couldn't be more perfect. I can take care of two problems at once."

Horrified, Cassie stared at him. What had she done? She had led Wade right to them, now here they were unarmed and completely at his mercy. Dear heavens. She should have escaped to the Diamond Harte. It was several miles farther, but Wade wouldn't have been able to storm into the ranch house.

And even if he had managed to catch up with her, at least Zack would have been safe.

"How did you find me?" she asked, and cursed her voice for trembling.

"It wasn't hard. When you stole my horse, I knew you would come here. To him. Slater." He said the name like the vilest curse. "Besides, you left a trail a mile wide for me to follow. I just can't figure out why you're still so hot for him after what he did. I would have been so good to you."

"Like you were for Melanie?"

The words tumbled out before she could swallow them down, and she winced. When would she ever learn to shut her big mouth?

If possible, more color suffused his face. "You don't know anything about that. I loved her." He gestured emphatically with the hand holding the gun, and she held her breath, waiting for the bullet to dig into her flesh. Or worse, for Zack to be hit.

He appeared to be struggling to regain control. A moment later he pointed the gun at them again. "Get down. Both of you."

Inside the circle of her arms, Zack's already taut frame tensed even more. "Why?"

"I'm the one with the gun. Because I said so, damn it. Now get off the damn horse."

Her legs were shaking just like the rest of her, and she had to grip Zack's hand tightly to keep from falling as she dismounted. Once she reached the ground, he climbed down from the horse to join her, then moved in front of her, shielding her body with his.

Wade noted the gesture with a cold smile. "You really think you're going to take me on? It looks to me like I'm the one holding all the aces here. My Colt .45 trumps your bare hands any day."

The bare hands in question clenched convulsively. This must be horrible for Zack. Forced to stand helplessly and do nothing while they both literally stared death in the face.

Wade pointed the gun at Zack suddenly. "Cassidy, you tie up the horses. Mine, too. We wouldn't want them to wander back to the ranch and raise any suspicions. Oh, and make sure those knots are tight, too, unless you want to watch your loverboy die right here."

With cold, shaking hands, she obeyed then stood aside while Wade double-checked her knots.

"All right. Now walk," Wade ordered, his voice hard.

"Where are you taking us?" Zack asked.

She suspected even before Wade answered.

"There's an old, abandoned cabin between the Rendezvous and the Lost Creek," he said. "Jean and I keep it maintained for the tourists to see what an authentic Western homestead was like. It's the perfect place for a lovers' tryst."

His laugh raised her hackles. "And for a lovers' spat."

They walked single file through the heavy timber on what looked like little more than a deer trail, Cassie in the lead, Zack a few steps behind her and Wade coming up the rear, his gun trained on them both. Even with the warmth of Zack's oiled slicker, she was still wet and cold.

What did it matter if she was shivering? She was going to die in a few moments, anyway.

"So you're going to kill us both and make it look like a murder-suicide?" Zack broke the silence, his voice almost casual. She marveled at his grit—how was he so calm when she could barely make one foot move in front of the other?

"That's the general idea."

"You used to be a cop. I'm sure you're aware those kind of crime scenes aren't easy to fake."

"I'll make it look good. Trust me. It won't be too hard. Everyone knows you and Cassie are on the outs now, that she and everybody else think you murdered Melanie. I've got the proof right here."

Eyes focused on the trail ahead of her for some kind of weapon, she barely heard a thump as he patted the pocket of his slicker. He must have brought the box with Melanie's picture and her jewelry.

"Your poor grief-stricken brother will be smart enough to put it together, Cass. The minute the police chief sees this in your cold, dead hands, he'll know you found evidence that your lover killed Melanie. Even he'll be able to figure out you must have confronted Slater with it, forcing him to kill you. Then, unable to live with his crimes, he turned his gun on himself. It's very romantic, really. The perfect setup."

It *was* perfect. Given his overwhelming animosity toward Zack, Jesse would be quick to jump to such a conclusion.

She couldn't let Wade get away with it, she thought fiercely. Not only because she didn't want to die here on this cold, rainy mountainside, but for Zack's sake.

It wasn't fair. He had been unfairly blamed for too many things, only because he was an outsider.

Through a break in the trees she saw the outline of a structure ahead and knew they were almost at the old cabin. They didn't have much time. She had to figure something out.

She was just wondering if she could create a diversion long enough for Zack to get away when he coughed behind her. She surreptitiously turned her head to look at him and their gazes met. The sun had almost slipped behind the mountains to the west but she had enough light left to see him mouth a single word to her.

Run.

She stumbled on the trail, then righted herself with a small, emphatic shake of her head that sent drops of rain flying from her wet hair. No. She wouldn't leave him here at Wade's mercy, even if she had more than the slightest chance in hell of escaping.

Turning her gaze back to the trail for some kind of a weapon, she felt rather than heard his resigned sigh.

An instant later the world erupted into a flurry of motion. She felt something shove her off the trail—Zack, she assumed, trying to get her out of harm's way. She rolled through the slippery grass and looked up just in time to see Zack smash his elbow into Wade's face. The other man sagged to his knees from the impact, blood spurting wildly from his nose, but he didn't drop the gun.

While Wade still reeled from the unexpected attack, Zack dived in low, hoping to catch him off guard. For long terrible moments the men grappled for the weapon. They were evenly matched, both hardened by years of ranch work. Wade was an inch or two taller and maybe thirty pounds heavier, but Zack didn't have an ounce of spare flesh on him.

Besides, he was fighting for his life. For *their* lives.

She crouched in the wet grass for long moments while the two men fought for possession of the revolver. Without even really focusing on it, she managed to pry a rock the size of a frying pan out of the mud and waited for a chance to use it as a weapon if she had to. It was slick and heavy in her hands and she only prayed she could hang on to it.

She wanted to help—do anything—but she was afraid whatever she did might distract Zack enough to give Wade the advantage.

Zack seemed to be gaining the upper hand. They were locked so closely together she couldn't tell exactly what was happening, but she could tell Wade was hampered by the blood still gushing from his nose. With one powerful lunge, Zack tumbled him to the ground, his hand on the wrist holding the gun. They rolled again until both of them were covered in mud and she could no longer see the gun.

Wade was tiring, she realized. Zack almost had him overpowered.

And then the gun went off.

Her breath tangling in her lungs, Cassie could only stare at the two men still snarled together as the echo of the gunshot boomed across the mountainside.

Which one had been hit?

She felt a scream build up inside her an instant later, when Zack slumped over on his back, a crimson stain blossoming across his chest. The breath she had been holding escaped with a hollow gurgle and she swayed, her vision dimming around the edges.

Wade stood over him, wiping the blood that still seeped from his broken nose with the back of his hand. "Stupid bastard," he growled, his breathing ragged.

The words and the angry disdain behind them spurred her to action. Praying for strength, she hefted the stone high above her head and rushed toward him, bringing the heavy weight crashing down against his head with her last ounce of energy.

It struck with the same hollow, thumping sound of a car driving over a pumpkin.

He crumpled to the ground, out cold, and she snatched the gun out of his motionless hand, then rushed to Zack.

The wound was bleeding profusely, seeping out in all directions, and she did her best to stanch the flow with his sweater.

Dear God. Please let him be all right.

"Why did you have to be such a damn hero?" she growled.

His breathing was irregular, and beneath his tan, his face wore an unnatural pallor. He grabbed her hand and his grip was weak. "Cass, I'm sorry."

"For what?" she asked.

"For making you cry. I hate making you cry." He coughed and more blood bubbled out of his wound, then his eyes fluttered shut again and stayed that way.

"You are not going to die," she vowed, only vaguely aware of the tears seeping down her cheeks to mix with the rain. "I'm not letting you leave me again."

She had to get him dry and go for help but she knew she didn't have much time. Wade could wake up any moment. He wouldn't have the gun since the cold weight of it was tucked into the waistband of her jeans, but he could still finish Zack off if he regained consciousness before she returned with help.

Although she knew it would take precious moments, she knew she had to secure him somehow. How? she wondered, near frantic. The horses! Zack's horse and the buckskin both had coiled ropes hanging from their saddles.

With fear for Zack coursing through her veins, she ran down the deer trail, slipping and sliding through the mud in her haste. When she reached the horses, she grabbed as much rope as she could find, then untied the reins of Zack's big blood bay and vaulted into the saddle.

He was much more surefooted than she had been as they rode up the narrow trail toward the cabin.

She wanted to rush to Zack first but she could see that Wade was already beginning to stir. He hadn't regained full consciousness and she contemplated hitting him again with the rock. But it was one thing to bean a man who had just shot the man you loved. It was quite another to strike an inert figure who was still only half-conscious.

Before he could come back all the way, she quickly shoved him over with a knee in his back and trussed his hands together behind him, deeply grateful for all the time Matt had spent with her teaching her how to hitch a good knot.

She left him with his face in the mud while she tied his legs together then used the other rope to bind him to the nearest tree, a sturdy pine.

Only after he was secured could she turn her attention to Zack. She skidded toward him, sick to see how much the angry red stain on his sweater had spread in the five minutes she'd been gone. "Zack. Come on. Wake up. We've got to get you to the cabin so you can stay dry while I go for help. Please! Wake up."

Her breath came out in heaving sobs when he didn't even flutter his eyelids and she whispered a plea for help. What could she do? Even on a good day, she didn't have the strength to drag two hundred pounds of hard-muscled man that far—especially not one bleeding heavily from a gunshot wound to the chest.

And this had *not* been a good day.

She had to get help fast, but she couldn't leave him here like this in the rain. Her mind whirled through her options for a few seconds, then she somehow managed to haul him a few feet until he lay under the spreading branches of a nearby spruce tree.

He didn't move at all while she situated him but she blocked her mind from the very real possibility that his gunshot wound might prove fatal.

She wasn't going to let him die.

Quickly rifling through the bay's saddlebags, she found the emergency survival kit Jean always insisted the Lost Creek guests rode with. Inside among the other supplies was a thin plastic rain jacket and an emergency space blanket.

She worked as fast as she could, wrapping his own slicker—the one he had lent her—around him along with the rain jacket, then she constructed a primitive rain shelter over his upper body by draping the silvery material of the blanket over the branches just above his head.

That would keep the worst of the rain away from him, at least.

It was only after she finished that she realized her vision was obstructed not from the elements but from the steady tears that still coursed down her cheeks.

The next fifteen minutes passed in a blur as she bowed low over the horse's head and raced through the darkness toward the Lost Creek. Fortunately, Zack's horse was as eager to be home as she and he knew the trail far better.

By the time she reached the ranch, the adrenaline rush that had carried her through the last hour, since that horrible discovery in Wade's kitchen, began to ebb. Every muscle in her body strained and ached and she could barely manage to breathe past the cold ball of helpless dread lodged in her throat.

At the ranch she was baffled to see several police

vehicles parked out front, Jesse's Bronco among them. How had he known? she wondered as she burst up the stairs and into the lodge with her last ounce of energy.

Her brother was standing just inside the door, surrounded by what looked like the entire Salt River police force. His face went slack with shock when he saw her.

"Please. I need help." It was the only thing she could manage to say through her racing lungs.

Jesse rushed to her, taking in her bedraggled state and the blood and muck she knew was smeared all over her soaked sweatshirt. "Cassie. What the hell happened? Are you hurt?" His eyes sharpened with anger. "Where is he? Where is that son of a bitch? If he hurt you, I swear I'm going to rip him apart with my bare hands."

She blinked, finally realizing how odd it was to find him at the ranch. He had no way of knowing what Wade had done.

"What are you doing here?" she managed to ask, her voice weak and raspy.

"I've come for Slater. No way in hell was I going to let the bastard skip town. I finally managed to convince the county attorney to file charges against him for killing Melanie."

She gazed at her brother's hard, angry features. Of course, she thought hysterically, what else would he be doing? He was here to arrest Zack, who even now lay bleeding to death because he had stepped in front of a bullet.

For her.

The trauma and terror and terrible fear that had been nipping at her heels finally caught up with her.

She began to laugh, a bitter, grating, horrible sound. "You can't arrest him, Jesse. Not if he's already dead."

Chapter Twelve

He awoke to grinding, white-hot pain just below his left collarbone and the disorienting sensation of knowing he was in a completely unfamiliar place.

It had to be some kind of hospital. The walls were white, clinical, and he could hear the whoosh and beep of medical equipment. He looked down and saw a bandage wrapped around his chest.

What happened? Where the hell was he?

He closed his eyes, trying to remember what might have brought him here. For a moment he had only brief fragments of memory. Images, really.

Cassie.

A rainy mountainside.

Lowry…

He hitched in a breath as memories tumbled back like hard stones being thrown at him. Lowry. Cassie. A bitter struggle.

Where was she? Had she been hurt?

He had to find her! He struggled to rise, but a steady hand suddenly held him down. "Whoa there, cowboy. You don't want to move too much, I promise, or you're going to find yourself in a world of hurt."

A man with a steely gray buzz cut and a white coat stood over him writing on a clipboard. He knew this man. He squinted, trying to place him, then it came to him. Old Doc Wallace at the Salt River Clinic.

He swallowed, aware suddenly that his throat felt as if he'd gulped down a plateful of desert sand.

"Cassie," he managed to rasp out.

The doctor gestured with his thumb toward the door, where Zack thought he heard raised voices.

Hers, he realized. Sweet relief coursed through him. She couldn't have been hurt too badly if she was outside his door yelling at someone. He thought he heard the words *owe* and *apology* and *pigheaded*.

"Who else?" he asked.

Doc Wallace rolled his eyes. "Whole damn town, seems like. Her whole family got here right after they brought you in. I believe Chief Harte is the one being, uh, reprimanded out there. Jean Martineau and most of her Lost Creek staff showed up a few minutes ago. I think the police officers who rode up that mountain after you and Lowry are still hanging around. You're quite the hero. Lowry, in case you're wondering, has a concussion but he's being treated at the sick bay over at the jail."

Zack closed his eyes again, remembering those terrible moments on the trail when he was sure the son of a bitch was going to kill them both. When he had known he wouldn't be able to save her.

"Cassie's okay? You're sure?"

"More scared than anything. She had a mild case of hypothermia but she's fine."

The doc finished scribbling in the chart, then closed it with a wry smile. "Since you haven't bothered to ask about yourself, I'll tell you anyway. You are one lucky cowboy. I don't know how but that bullet missed just about everything important. You lost a lot of blood but you're stable enough now that I can send you on to Idaho Falls for surgery."

Surgery. Great. He grimaced. He hated hospitals, always had. But they sure beat the alternative—bleeding to death in the muddy mountainside above the Lost Creek.

As if he'd read his thoughts, the doc gestured toward the door to the trauma room. The shouting had died down, Zack noted. "That's one hell of a woman you got there," Wallace said. "You never would have made it if she'd had one ounce less grit."

Zack wanted to correct him but he didn't. Yeah, Cassie was one hell of a woman. He would never argue there.

But she wasn't his.

He remembered her kneeling next to him, tears coursing down her cheeks, and his chest felt tight and achy from more than just a lousy bullet hole.

"She's itching to come in," the doc said. "You up to a visitor?"

He nodded and kept his gaze trained on the door for the next few moments, trying not to focus on the pain, until she opened it cautiously, peeking around the door.

He was startled to see a whole crowd milling around outside behind her. What were they all doing there? An instant later she slipped inside the door, then closed it behind her, shutting out the noisy waiting area.

Her eyes looked red and puffy, and smears of shadow underscored them. She looked tired, he thought with concern. If he hadn't felt so weak himself, he would have ripped out this damn IV line and climbed right out of the bed so she could lie down for a few minutes.

Unfortunately, he had a sneaking suspicion he would end up on the floor if he tried it.

For all her fatigue, she moved quickly to his side. "How do you feel?"

"Like I've tangled with a couple of bull moose." His voice sounded rough, raspy, and he cleared it before continuing. "The doc says I should be fine once they patch me up."

"Oh, Zack. I'm so glad." To his dismay, two tears slipped out from her spiky dark lashes and were quickly followed by several more.

He grabbed her hand and wrapped his fingers tightly around it. "Hey. Don't cry. Everything's okay."

"I was so afraid you wouldn't make it."

He squeezed her fingers. "The doc says I wouldn't have if you hadn't been there."

"You wouldn't have been shot in the first place if not for me! I'm so sorry I dragged you into it."

He breathed deeply of her wildflower scent. "Don't say that. I don't want to think about what might have happened if he had found you alone."

"I would have figured something out," she mumbled.

"Yeah. More beef and barley soup."

Although he knew it wasn't wise, he couldn't restrain himself an instant longer. With his good arm he reached out and snagged his fingers in her hair, then brought her face to his. Her mouth tasted sweet and pure and he wanted to stay there forever just drinking her in. "Thanks for saving my life," he murmured.

She sniffled, and more tears slid down her cheeks. "Right back at you."

She edged away, grabbing a tissue off the small table next to his bed. "Jean tells me you were planning on leaving tomorrow."

The hurt in her eyes stabbed at him like a sharp scalpel. "I had to go, Cassie. I'm sorry. It was too hard staying here with the way things were between us."

"The only reason for that was because of your stubbornness! You're the one who pushed me away."

Only because he was trying to protect her, just as he had pushed her off the trail to safety so he could take on Lowry. He didn't know how to answer, so decided to keep his mouth shut.

After a moment she spoke again. "So Doc says you'll probably have to spend a few days at the medical center in Idaho Falls. Will you be heading to Denver when you get out?"

Did she want him to go? Was this her way of telling him to get lost?

"I don't know. I guess that's something I'll have to figure out."

"Well, let me know when you make up your mind."

The scalpel twisted a little harder. "I will."

"Good." She paused. "I just want to know what forwarding address to give my family."

He stared at her, his vision a little gray around the edges. The damn medications must be making his head fuzzy. "What did you just say?"

She gazed back with an innocent expression. "You don't really think I'm going to let you just ride off into the sunset again, do you?"

He cleared his throat. "Cassie…"

"No. I'm sorry, Zack, but this time I'm sticking to you like flypaper. Wherever you go, I'm going right along with you. Denver. Durango. Timbuktu. It doesn't matter."

Dazed by her conviction, he could only stare at her for several long moments. "You would be willing to leave your family?" he asked when he could find his voice again. "Star Valley? Everything you love here? All for some no-account drifter?"

She shook her head emphatically. "No. But I would leave in a heartbeat for you."

Gripping his hand tightly, she brought it to her chest, where he felt her heartbeat strong and true beneath her shirt. "I love you, Zack Slater. I have never stopped loving you. When I saw you lying so still on that mountainside, I realized nothing else matters but that. Whatever happened in the past can stay there for all I care. We have the rest of our lives ahead of us and we can build whatever kind of future we want."

"What do you see in that future?" He found he was suddenly desperate to know exactly where she was heading with this.

"Simple. We're going to get married and have babies together and live happily ever after."

Oh, hell. He felt the sting of tears behind his own eyes as wave after wave of love for her washed over him, purifying him, healing him. He could see that future vividly, and he wanted to reach for it so fiercely he trembled with it.

"Is that a proposal?" he managed to ask through the joy exploding inside him.

She smiled that slow, sweet Cassie smile that had haunted him for so long, for all the years and miles between them.

"No, Slater," she murmured softly against his mouth. "It's a promise."

* * * * *

Also by Maisey Yates

Harlequin Desire

Take Me, Cowboy
Hold Me, Cowboy
Seduce Me, Cowboy
Claim Me, Cowboy
Want Me, Cowboy

HQN Books

Shoulda Been a Cowboy (prequel novella)
Part Time Cowboy
Brokedown Cowboy
Bad News Cowboy
A Copper Ridge Christmas (ebook novella)
The Cowboy Way
Hometown Heartbreaker (ebook novella)
One Night Charmer
Tough Luck Hero
Last Chance Rebel
Slow Burn Cowboy
Down Home Cowboy
Wild Ride Cowboy
Christmastime Cowboy

For more books by Maisey Yates,
visit www.maiseyyates.com.

WANT ME, COWBOY

Maisey Yates

Chapter One

November 1, 2018
Location: Copper Ridge, Oregon

WIFE WANTED—

Rich rancher, not given to socializing. Wants a wife who will not try to change me. Must be tolerant of moods, reported lack of sensitivity and the tendency to take off for a few days' time in the mountains. Will expect meals cooked. Also, probably a kid or two. Exact number to be negotiated. Beard is non-negotiable.

November 5, 2018
Revised draft for approval by 11/6

WIFE WANTED—

~~Rich rancher, not given to socializing.~~ Successful rancher searching for a wife who enjoys rural living. ~~Wants a wife who will not try to change me. Must be tolerant of moods, reported lack of sensitivity, and the tendency to take off for a few days' time in the mountains.~~ Though happy with my life, it has begun to feel lonely, and I would like someone to enhance my satisfaction with what I have already. I enjoy extended camping trips and prefer the mountains to a night on the town. ~~Will expect meals cooked. Also, probably a kid or two. Exact number to be negotiated. Beard is nonnegotiable. I~~ I'm looking for a traditional family life, and a wife and children to share it with.

"This is awful."

Poppy Sinclair looked up from her desk, her eyes colliding with her boss's angry gray stare. He was holding a printout of the personal ad she'd revised for him and shaking it at her like she was a dog and it was a newspaper.

"The *original* was awful," she responded curtly, turning her focus back to her computer.

"But it was all true."

"Lead with being less of an asshole."

"I *am* an asshole," Isaiah said, clearly unconcerned with that fact.

He was at peace with himself. Which she admired on some level. Isaiah was Isaiah, and he made no apologies for that fact. But his attitude would be a problem if the man wanted to find a wife. Because very few other people were at peace with him just as he was.

"I would never say I want to—" he frowned ""—enhance my enjoyment.' What the hell, Poppy?"

Poppy had known Isaiah since she was eighteen years old. She was used to his moods. His complete lack of subtlety. His gruffness.

But somehow, she'd never managed to get used to *him*. As a man.

This grumpy, rough, bearded man who was like a brick wall. Or like one of those mountains he'd disappear into for days at a time.

Every time she saw him, it felt as if he'd stolen the air right from her lungs. It was more than just being handsome—though he was. A lot of men were handsome. His brother Joshua was handsome, and a whole lot easier to get along with.

Isaiah was... Well, he was her very particular brand of catnip. He made everything in her sit up, purr...and want to be stroked.

Even when he was in full hermit mode.

People—and interacting with them—were decidedly not his thing. It was one reason Poppy had always been an asset to him in his work life. It was her job to sit and take notes during meetings...and report her read on the room to him after. He was a brilliant businessman, and fantastic with numbers. But people...not so much.

As evidenced by the ad. Of course, the very fact that he was placing an ad to find a wife was both contradicting to that point—suddenly, he wanted a wife!—and also, somehow, firmly in affirmation of it. He was placing an ad to find her.

The whole situation was Joshua's fault. Well, probably Devlin and Joshua combined, in fairness.

Isaiah's brothers had been happy bachelors until a couple of years ago when Devlin had married their sister Faith's best friend, Mia.

Then, Joshua had been the next to succumb to matrimony, a victim of their father's harebrained scheme. The patriarch of the Grayson family had put an ad in a national newspaper looking for a wife for his son. In retaliation, Joshua had placed an ad of his own, looking for an unsuitable wife that would teach his father not to meddle.

It all backfired. Or...front fired. Either way, Joshua had ended up married to Danielle, and was now happily settled with her and her infant half brother who both of them were raising as their son.

It was after their wedding that Isaiah had formed his plan.

The wedding had—he had explained to Poppy at work one morning—clarified a few things for him. He believed in marriage as a valuable institution, one that he wanted to be part of. He wanted stability. He wanted children. But he didn't have any inclination toward love.

He didn't have to tell her why.

She *knew* why.

Rosalind.

But she wouldn't speak her foster sister's name out loud, and neither would he. But she remembered. The awful, awful fallout of Rosalind's betrayal.

His pain. Poppy's own conflicted feelings.

It was easy to remember her conflicted feelings, since she still had them.

He was staring at her now, those slate eyes hard and glinting with an energy she couldn't quite pin down.

And with coldness, a coldness that hadn't been there before Rosalind. A coldness that told her and any other woman—loud and clear—that his heart was unavailable.

That didn't mean her own heart didn't twist every time he walked into the room. Every time he leaned closer to her—like he was doing now—and she got a hint of the scent of him. Rugged and pine-laden and basically lumberjack porn for her senses.

He was a contradiction, from his cowboy hat down to his boots. A numbers guy who loved the outdoors and was built like he belonged outside doing hard labor.

Dear God, he was problematic.

He made her dizzy. Those broad shoulders, shoulders she wanted to grab on to. Lean waist and hips—hips she wanted to wrap her legs around. And his forearms…all hard muscle. She wanted to lick them.

He turned her into a being made of sensual frustration, and no one else did that. Ever. Sadly, she seemed to have no effect on him at all.

"I'm not trying to mislead anyone," he said.

"Right. But you *are* trying to entice someone." The very thought made her stomach twist into a knot. But jealousy was pointless. If Isaiah wanted her…well, he would have wanted her by now.

He straightened, moving away from her and walking across the office. She nearly sagged with relief. "My money should do that." As if that solved every potential issue.

She bit back a weary sigh. "Would you like someone who was maybe…interested in who you are as a person?"

She knew that was a stupid question to ask of Isaiah Grayson. But she was his friend, as well as his employee.

So it was kind of…her duty to work through this with him. Even if she didn't want him to do this at all.

And she didn't want him to find anyone.

Wow. Some friend she was.

But then, having…complex feelings for one's friend made emotional altruism tricky.

"As you pointed out," he said, his tone dry, "I'm an asshole."

"You were actually the one who said that. I said you *sounded* like one."

He waved his hand. "Either way, I'm not going to win Miss Congeniality in the pageant, and we both know that. Fine with me if somebody wants to get hitched and spend my money."

She sighed heavily, ignoring the fact that her heart felt an awful lot like paper that had been crumpled up into a tight, mutilated ball. "Why do you even *want* a wife, Isaiah?"

"I explained that to you already. Joshua is settled. Devlin is settled."

"Yes, they are. So why now?"

"I always imagined I would get married," he said simply. "I never intended to spend my whole life single."

"Is your biological clock ticking?" she asked drily.

"In a way," he said. "Again, it all comes back to logic. I'm close to my family, to my brothers. They'll have children sooner rather than later. Joshua and Danielle already have a son. Cousins should be close in age. It just makes sense."

She bit the inside of her cheek. "So you…just think you can decide it's time and then make it happen?"

"Yes. And I think Joshua's experience proves you can

make anything work as long as you have a common goal. It *can* be like math."

She graduated from biting her cheek to her tongue. Isaiah was a numbers guy unto his soul. "Uh-huh."

She refused to offer even a pat agreement because she just thought he was wrong. Not that she knew much of anything about relationships of…any kind really.

She'd been shuffled around so many foster homes as a child, and it wasn't until she was in high school that she'd had a couple years of stability with one family. Which was where she'd met Rosalind, the one foster sibling Poppy was still in touch with. They'd shared a room and talked about a future where they were more than wards of the state.

In the years since, Poppy felt like she'd carved out a decent life for herself. But still, it wasn't like she'd ever had any romantic relationships to speak of.

Pining after your boss didn't count.

"The only aspect of going out and hooking up I like is the hooking up," he said.

She wanted to punch him for that unnecessary addition to the conversation. She sucked her cheek in and bit the inside of it too. "Great."

"When you think about it, making a relationship a transaction is smart. Marriage is a legal agreement. But you don't just get sex. You get the benefit of having your household kept, children…"

"Right. Children." She'd ignored his first mention of them, but… She pressed her hands to her stomach unconsciously. Then, she dropped them quickly.

She should not be thinking about Isaiah and children or the fact that he intended to have them with another woman.

Confused feelings was a cop-out. And it was hard to deny the truth when she was steeped in this kind of reaction to him, to his presence, to his plan, to his talk about children.

The fact of the matter was, she was tragically in love with him. And he'd never once seen her the way she saw him.

She'd met him through Rosalind. When Poppy had turned eighteen, she'd found herself released from her foster home with nowhere to go. Everything she owned was in an old canvas tote that a foster mom had given her years ago.

Rosalind had been the only person Poppy could think to call. The foster sister she'd bonded with in her last few years in care. She'd always kept in touch with Rosalind, even when Rosalind had moved to Seattle and got work.

Even when she'd started dating a wonderful man she couldn't say enough good things about.

She was the only lifeline Poppy had, and she'd reached for her. And Rosalind had come through. She'd had Poppy come to Rosalind's apartment, and then she'd arranged for a job interview with her boyfriend, who needed an assistant for a construction firm he was with.

In one afternoon, Poppy had found a place to live, gotten a job and lost her heart.

Of course, she had lost it, immediately and—in the fullness of time it had become clear—irrevocably, to the one man who was off-limits.

Her boss. Her foster sister's boyfriend. Isaiah Grayson.

Though his status as her boss had lasted longer than his status as Rosalind's boyfriend. He'd become her fiancé. And then after, her ex.

Poppy had lived with a divided heart for so long. Even after Isaiah and Rosalind's split, Poppy was able to care for them both. Though she never, ever spoke to Rosalind in Isaiah's presence, or even mentioned her.

Rosalind didn't have the same embargo on mentions of Isaiah. But in fairness, Rosalind was the one who had cheated on him, cost him a major business deal and nearly ruined his start-up company and—by extension—nearly ruined his relationship with his business partner, who was also his brother.

So.

Poppy had loved him while he'd dated another woman. Loved him while he nursed a broken heart because of said other woman. Loved him when he disavowed love completely. And now she would have to love him while she interviewed potential candidates to be his wife.

She was wretched.

He had said the word *sex* in front of her like it wouldn't do anything to her body. Had talked about children like it wouldn't make her...yearn.

Men were idiots. But this one might well be their king.

"Put the unrevised ad in the paper."

She shook her head. "I'm not doing that."

"I could fire you." He leaned in closer and her breath caught. "For insubordination."

Her heart tumbled around erratically, and she wished she could blame it on anger. Annoyance. But she knew that wasn't it.

She forced herself to rally. "If you haven't fired me yet, you're never going to. And anyway," she said, narrowing her tone so that the words would hit him with a point, "I'm the one who has to interview your prospective brides. Which makes this my endeavor in many ways.

I'm the one who's going to have to weed through your choices. So I would like the ad to go out that I think has the best chance of giving me less crap to sort through."

He looked up at her, and much to her surprise seemed to be considering what she said. "That is true. You will be doing the interviews."

She felt like she'd been stabbed. She was going to be interviewing Isaiah's potential wife. The man she had been in love with since she was a teenage idiot, and was still in love with now that she was an idiot in her late twenties.

There were a whole host of reasons she'd never, ever let on about her feelings for him, Rosalind and his feelings on love aside.

She loved her job. She loved Isaiah's family, who she'd gotten to know well over the past decade, and who were the closest thing she had to a family of her own.

Plus, loving him was just…easy to dismiss. She wasn't the type of girl who could have something like that. Not Poppy Sinclair whose mother had disappeared when she was two years old and left her with a father who forgot to feed her.

Her life was changing though, slowly.

She was living well beyond what she had ever imagined would be possible for her. Gray Bear Construction was thriving; the merger between Jonathan Bear and the Graysons' company a couple of years ago was more successful than they'd imagined it could be.

And every employee on every level had reaped the benefits.

She was also living in the small town of Copper Ridge, Oregon, which was a bit strange for a girl from Seattle, but she did like it. It had a different pace. But that meant there was less opportunity for a social life. There were fewer people to interact with. By default she, and the other folks in town, ended up spending a lot of their free time with the people they worked with every day. There was nothing wrong with that. She loved Faith, and she had begun getting close to Joshua's wife recently. But it was just… Mostly there wasn't enough of a break from Isaiah on any given day.

But then, she also didn't enforce one. Didn't take one. She supposed she couldn't really blame the small-town location when the likely culprit of the entire situation was *her*.

"Place whatever ad you need to," he said, his tone abrupt. "When you meet the right woman, you'll know."

"I'll know," she echoed lamely.

"Yes. Nobody knows me better than you do, Poppy. I have faith that you'll pick the right wife for me."

With those awful words still ringing in the room, Isaiah left her there, sitting at her desk, feeling numb and ill used.

The fact of the matter was, she probably *could* pick him a perfect wife. Someone who would facilitate his life, and give him space when he needed it. Someone who was beautiful and fabulous in bed.

Yes, she knew exactly what Isaiah Grayson would think made a woman the perfect wife for him.

The sad thing was, Poppy didn't possess very many of those qualities herself.

And what she so desperately wanted was for Isaiah's perfect wife to be *her*.

But dreams were for other women. They always had been. Which meant some other woman was going to end up with Poppy's dream.

While she played matchmaker to the whole affair.

Chapter Two

"I put an ad in the paper."

"For?" Isaiah's brother Joshua looked up from his computer and stared at him like he was waiting to hear the answers to the mystery of the universe.

Joshua, Isaiah and their younger sister, Faith, were sitting in the waiting area of their office, enjoying their early-morning coffee. Or maybe enjoying was overstating it. The three of them were trying to find a state of consciousness.

"A wife."

Faith spat her coffee back into her cup. "What?"

"I placed an ad in the paper to help me find a wife," he repeated.

Honestly, he couldn't understand why she was having such a large reaction to the news. After all, that was how Joshua had found his wife, Danielle.

"You can't be serious," Joshua said.

"I expected you of all people to be supportive."

"Why *me*?"

"Because that's how you met Danielle. Or you have you forgotten?"

"I have not forgotten how I met my wife. However, I didn't put an ad out there seriously thinking I was going to find someone to marry. I was trying to prove to dad that *his* ad was a stupid idea."

"But it turned out it wasn't a stupid idea," Isaiah said. "I want to get married. I figured this was a hassle-free way of finding a wife."

Faith stared at him, dumbfounded. "You can't be serious."

"I'm serious."

The door to the office opened, and Poppy walked in wearing a cheerful, polka-dotted dress, her dark hair swept back into a bun, a few curls around her face.

"Please tell me my brother is joking," Faith said. "And that he didn't actually put an ad in the paper to find a wife."

Poppy looked from him back to Faith. "He doesn't joke, you know that."

"And you know that he put an ad in the paper for a wife?" Joshua asked.

"Of course I know," Poppy responded. "Who do you think is doing the interviews?"

That earned him two slack-jawed looks.

"Who else is going to do it?" Isaiah asked.

"You're not even doing the interview for your own wife?" Faith asked.

"I trust Poppy implicitly. If I didn't, she wouldn't be my assistant."

"Of all the… You are insane." Faith stormed out of the room. Joshua continued to sit and sip his coffee.

"No comment?" Isaiah asked.

"Oh, I have plenty. But I know you well enough to know that making them won't change a damn thing. So I'm keeping my thoughts to myself. However," he said, collecting his computer and his coffee, "I do have to go to work now."

That left both Isaiah and Poppy standing in the room by themselves. She wasn't looking at him; she was staring off down the hall, her expression unreadable. She had a delicate profile, dark, sweeping eyelashes and a fascinating curve to her lips. Her neck was long and elegant, and the way her dress shaped around her full breasts was definitely a pleasing sight.

He clenched his teeth. He didn't make a habit of looking at Poppy that way. But she was pretty. He had always thought so.

Even back when he'd been with Rosalind he'd thought there was something…indefinable about Poppy. Special.

She made him feel… He didn't know. A little more grounded. Or maybe it was just because she treated him differently than most people did.

Either way, she was irreplaceable to him. In the running of his business, Poppy was his barometer. The way he got the best read on a situation. She did his detail work flawlessly. Handled everything he didn't like so he could focus on what he was good at.

She was absolutely, 100 percent, the most important asset to him at the company.

He would have to tell her that sometime. Maybe buy her another pearl necklace. Though, last time he'd done that she had gotten angry at him. But she wore it. She was wearing it today, in fact.

"They're right," she said finally.

"About?"

"The fact that you're insane."

"I think I'm sane enough."

"Of course you do. Actually—" she let out a long, slow breath "—I don't think you're insane. But, I don't think this is a good idea."

"Why?"

"This is really how you want to find a wife? In a way that's this…impersonal?"

"What are my other options? I have to meet someone new, go through the process of dating… She'll expect a courtship of some kind. We'll have to figure out what we have in common, what we don't have in common. This way, it's all out in the open. That's more straightforward."

"Maybe you deserve better than that," she said, her tone uncharacteristically gentle.

"Maybe this is better for *me*."

She shook her head. "I don't know about that."

"When it comes to matters of business, there's no one I trust more than you. But you're going to have to trust that I know what will work best in my own life."

"It's not what I want for you."

A strange current arced between them when she spoke those words, a spark in her brown eyes catching on something inside him.

"I appreciate your concern."

"Yes," she echoed. "My concern."

"We have work to do. And you have wife applications to sort through."

"Right," she said.

"Preference will be given to blondes," he said.

Poppy blinked and then reached up slowly, touching her own dark hair. "Of course."

And then she turned and walked out of the room.

Isaiah hadn't expected to receive quite so many responses to his ad. Perhaps, in the end, Poppy had been right about her particular tactic with the wording. It had certainly netted what felt to him to be a record number of responses.

Though he didn't actually know how many women had responded to his brother's personal ad.

He felt only slightly competitive about it, seeing as it would be almost impossible to do a direct comparison between his and Joshua's efforts. Their father had placed an ad first, making Joshua sound undoubtedly even nicer than Poppy had made Isaiah sound.

Thereafter, Joshua had placed his own ad, which had offered a fake marriage and hefty compensation.

Isaiah imagined that a great many more women would respond to that.

But he didn't need quantity. He just needed quality.

And he believed that existed.

It had occurred to him at Joshua and Danielle's wedding that there was no reason a match couldn't be like math. He believed in marriage; it was romance he had gone off of.

Or rather, the kind of romance he had experience with.

Obviously, he couldn't dispute the existence of love. His parents were in love, after all. Forty years of marriage hadn't seemed to do anything to dampen that. But then, he was not like his mother. And he wasn't like his father. Both of them were warm people. *Compassionate*. And those things seemed to come easily to them.

Isaiah was a black-and-white man living in a world filled with shades of gray. He didn't care for those shades, and he didn't like to acknowledge them.

But he wasn't an irrational man. Not at all.

Yet he'd been irrational once. Five years with Rosalind and they had been the best of his life. At least, he had thought so at the time.

Then she had betrayed him, and nearly destroyed everything.

Or rather, he had.

Which was all he had needed to learn about what happened to him and his instincts under the influence of love.

He'd been in his twenties then, and it had been easy to ignore the idea that his particular set of practices when it came to relationships meant he would be spending his life without a partner. But now he was in his thirties, and that reality was much more difficult to ignore. When he'd had to think about the future, he hadn't liked the idea of what he was signing himself up for.

So, he had decided to change it. That was the logical thing to do when you found yourself unhappy with where you were, after all. A change of circumstances was not beyond his reach. And so, he was reaching out to grab it.

Which was why Poppy was currently on interview number three with one of the respondents to his ad. Isaiah had insisted that anyone responding to the ad come directly to Copper Ridge to be interviewed. Anyone who didn't take the ad seriously enough to put in a personal appearance was not worthy of consideration, in his opinion.

He leaned back in his chair, looking at the neat expanse of desk in front of him. Everything was in its place in his office, as it always was. As it should be. And soon, everything in his personal life would be in place too.

Across the hall, the door to Poppy's office opened and a tall, willowy blonde walked out. She was definitely his type in the physical sense, and the physical mattered quite a bit. Emotionally, he might be a bit detached, but physically, everything was functioning. Quite well, thank you.

In his marriage-math equation, sex was an important factor.

He intended to be faithful to his wife. There was really no point in making a lifelong commitment without fidelity.

Because of that, it stood to reason that he should make sure he chose in accordance with his typical physical type.

By the time he finished that thought process the woman was gone, and Poppy appeared a moment later. She was glaring down the hall, looking both disheveled and generally irritated. He had learned to recognize her moods with unerring accuracy. Mostly because it was often a matter of survival. Poppy was one of the few people on earth who wasn't intimidated by him. He should be annoyed by that. She was his employee, and ought to be a bit more deferential than she was.

He didn't want her to be, though. He liked Poppy. And that was a rarity in his world. He didn't like very many people. Because most people were idiots.

But not her.

Though, she looked a little bit like she wanted to kill him at the moment. When her stormy, dark eyes connected with his across the space, he had the fleeting thought that a lesser man would jump up and run away, leaving his boots behind.

Isaiah was not that man.

He was happy to meet her. Steel-capped toe to pointy-toed stiletto.

"She was stupid," Poppy pronounced.

He lifted a brow. "Did you give her an IQ test?"

"I'm not talking about her intelligence," Poppy said, looking fierce. "Though, the argument could be made that any woman responding to this ad…"

"Are you about to cast aspersions on my desirability?"

"No," she said. "I cast those last week, if you recall. It would just be tiresome to cast them again."

"Why is she stupid?" he pressed.

"Because she has no real concept of what you need. You're a busy man, and you live in a rural…area. You're not going to be taking her out to galas every night. And I know she thought that because you're a rich man galas were going to be part of the deal. But I explained to her that you only go to a certain number of business-oriented events a year, and that you do so grudgingly. That anyone hanging on your arm at such a thing would need to be polished, smiling, and, in general, making up for you."

He spent a moment deciding if he should be offended by that or not. He decided not to be. Because she was right. He knew his strengths and his limitations.

"She didn't seem very happy about those details. And that is why I'm saying she's stupid. She wants to take this…job, essentially. A job that is a life sentence. And she wants it to be about her."

He frowned. "Obviously, this marriage is not going to be completely about me. I am talking about a *marriage* and not a position at the company." Though, he supposed he could see why she would be thinking in those terms. He had placed an ad with strict requirements. And he supposed, as a starting point, it *was* about him.

"Is that true, Isaiah? Because I kind of doubt it. You don't want a woman who's going to inconvenience you."

"I'm not buying a car," he said.

"Aren't you?" She narrowed her eyes, her expression mean.

"No. I realize that."

"You're basically making an arranged marriage for yourself."

"Consider it advanced online dating," he said. "With a more direct goal."

"You're having your assistant choose a wife for you." She enunciated each word as if he didn't understand what he'd asked of her.

Her delicate brows locked together, and her mouth pulled into a pout. Though, she would undoubtedly punch him if he called it a pout.

In a physical sense, Poppy was not his type at all. She was not tall, or particularly leggy, though she did often wear high heels with her 1950s housewife dresses. She was petite, but still curvy, her hair dark and curly, and usually pulled back in a loose, artfully pinned bun that allowed tendrils to slowly make their escape over the course of the day.

She was pretty, in spite of the fact that she wasn't the type of woman he would normally gravitate toward.

He wasn't sure why he was just now noticing that. Perhaps it was the way the light was filtering through the window now. Falling across her delicately curved face. Her mahogany skin with a bit of rose color bleeding across her cheeks. In this instance, he had a feeling the color was because she was angry. But, it was lovely nonetheless.

Her lips were full—pouty or not—and the same rose color as her cheeks.

"I don't understand your point," he said, stopping his visual perusal of her.

"I'm just saying you're taking about as much of a personal interest in finding a wife as someone who was buying a car."

He did not point out that if he were buying a car, he would take it for a test drive, and that he had not suggested doing anything half so crass with any of the women who'd come to be interviewed.

"How many more women are you seeing today?" he asked, deciding to bypass her little show of indignation.

"Three more," she said.

There was something in the set of her jaw, in the rather stubborn, mulish look on her face that almost made him want to ask a question about what was bothering her.

But only almost.

"Has my sister sent through cost estimates for her latest design?" he asked.

Poppy blinked. "What?"

"Faith. Has she sent through her cost estimates? I'm going to end up correcting them anyway, but I like to see what she starts with."

"I'm well aware of the process, Isaiah," Poppy said. "I'm just surprised that you moved on from wife interviews to your sister's next design."

"Why would you be surprised by that? The designs are important. They are, in fact, why I am a billionaire."

"Yes. I know," Poppy said. "Faith's talent is a big reason why we're all doing well. Believe me, I respect the work. However, the subject change seems a bit abrupt."

"It *is* a workday."

Deep brown eyes narrowed in his direction. "You're really something else, do you know that?"

He did. He always had. The fact that she felt the need to question him on it didn't make much sense to him.

"Yes," he responded.

Poppy stamped.

She stamped her high-heel-clad foot like they were in a black-and-white movie.

"No, she hasn't sent it through," Poppy said.

"You just stomped your foot at me."

She flung her arms wide. "Because you were just being an idiot at me."

"I don't understand you," he said.

"I don't need you to understand me." Her brow furrowed.

"But you *do* need me to sign your paychecks," he pointed out. "I'm your boss."

Then, all the color drained from her cheeks. "Right. Of course. I do need that. Because you're my boss."

"I am."

"Just my boss."

"I've been your boss for the past decade," he pointed out, not quite sure why she was being so spiky.

"Yes," she said. "You have been my boss for the past decade."

Then, she turned on her heel and walked back into her office, shutting the door firmly behind her.

And Isaiah went back to his desk.

He had work to do. Which was why he had given Poppy the task of picking him a wife. But before he chased Faith down for those estimates, he was going to need some caffeine. He sent a quick text to that effect to Poppy.

There was a quick flash of three dots at the bottom of the message box, then they disappeared.

It popped up again, and disappeared again. Then finally there was a simple: of course.

He could only hope that when he got his coffee it wasn't poisoned.

Three hours and three women later, Poppy was wishing she had gone with her original instinct and sent the middle finger emoji to Isaiah in response to his request for coffee.

This was too much. It would be crazy for anyone to have their assistant pick their wife—a harebrained scheme that no self-respecting personal assistant should have to cope with. But for her especially, it was a strange kind of emotional torture. She had to ask each woman questions about their compatibility with Isaiah. And then, she had to talk to them about Isaiah. Who she knew better than she knew any other man on the face of the earth. Who she knew possibly better than she knew anyone else. And all the while his words rang in her ears.

I'm your boss.

She was his *employee*.

And that was how he saw her. It shouldn't surprise her that no-nonsense, rigid Isaiah thought of her primarily as his employee. She thought of him as her friend.

Her best friend. Practically family.

Except for the part of her that was in love with him and had sex dreams about him sometimes.

Though, were she to take an afternoon nap today, her

only dreams about Isaiah would involve her sticking a pen through his chest.

Well, maybe not his chest. That would be fatal. Maybe his arm. But then, that would get ink and blood on his shirt. She would have to unbutton it and take it off him…

Okay. Maybe she was capable of having both dreams at the same time.

"Kittens are my hard line," the sixth blonde of the day was saying to her. All the blondes were starting to run together like boxes of dye in the hair care aisle.

"I…" Poppy blinked, trying to get a handle on what that meant. "Like… Sexually… Or?"

The woman wrinkled her nose. "I mean, I need to be able to have a kitten. That's nonnegotiable."

Poppy was trying to imagine Isaiah Grayson with a kitten living in his house. He had barn cats. And he had myriad horses and animals at his ranch, but he did not have a kitten. Though, because he already had so many animals, it was likely that he would be okay with one more.

"I will… Make a note of that."

"Oh," the woman continued. "I can also tie a cherry stem into a knot with my tongue."

Poppy closed her eyes and prayed for the strength to not run out of the room and hit Isaiah over the head with a wastebasket. "I assume I should mark that down under special skills."

"Men like that," the woman said.

Well, maybe that was why Poppy had such bad luck with men. She couldn't do party tricks with her tongue. In fairness, she'd never tried.

"Good to know," Poppy continued.

Poppy curled her hands into fists and tried to keep

herself from... She didn't even know what. Screaming. Running from the room.

One of these women who she interviewed today might very well be the woman Isaiah Grayson slept with for the rest of his life. The last woman he ever slept with. The one who made him completely and totally unavailable to Poppy forever.

The one who finally killed her fantasy stone-cold.

She had known that going in. She had. But suddenly it hit her with more vivid force.

I am your boss.

Her boss. Her boss. He was her boss. Not her friend. Not her lover. Never her lover.

Maybe he didn't see his future wife as a new car he was buying. But he basically saw Poppy as a stapler. Efficient and useful only when needed.

"Well, I will be in touch," Poppy stated crisply.

"Why are *you* interviewing all the women? Is this like a sister wives thing?"

Poppy almost choked. "No. I am Mr. Grayson's assistant. Not his wife."

"I wouldn't mind that," Lola continued. "It's always seemed efficient to me. Somebody to share the workload of kids and housework. Well, and sex."

"Not. His. Wife." Poppy said that through clenched teeth.

"He should consider that."

She tightened her hold on her pen, and was surprised she didn't end up snapping it in half. "Me as his wife?"

"Sister wives."

"I'll make a note," Poppy said drily.

Her breath exited her body in a rush when Lola finally left, and Poppy's head was swimming with rage.

She had thought she could do this. She had been wrong. She had been an idiot.

I am your boss.

He was her boss. Because she worked for him. Because she had worked for him for ten years. Ten years.

Why had she kept this job for so long? She had job experience. She also had a nest egg. The money was good, she couldn't argue that, but she could also go get comparable pay at a large company in a city, and she now had the experience to do that. She didn't have to stay isolated here in Copper Ridge. She didn't have to stay with a man who didn't appreciate her.

She didn't have to stay trapped in this endless hell of wanting something she was never going to have.

No one was keeping her here. Nothing was keeping her here.

Nothing except the ridiculous idea that Isaiah had feelings for her that went beyond that of his assistant.

Friends could be friends in different cities. They didn't have to live in each other's pockets. Even if he had misspoken and he did see them as friends—and really, now that she was taking some breaths, she imagined that was closer to the truth—it was no excuse to continue to expose herself to him for twelve hours a day.

He was her business life. He was her social life. He was her fantasy life. That was too much for one man. Too much.

She walked into his office, breathing hard, and he looked up from his computer screen, his gray eyes assessing. He made her blood run hotter. Made her hands shake and her stomach turn over. She wanted him. Even now. She wanted to launch herself across the empty space and fling herself into his arms.

No. It had to stop.

"I quit," she said, the words tumbling out of her mouth in a glorious triumph.

But then they hit.

Hit him, hit her. And she knew she could take them back. Maybe she should.

No. She shouldn't.

"You *quit*?"

"It should not be in my job description to find you a wife. This is ludicrous. I just spent the last twenty minutes talking to a woman who was trying to get me to add the fact that she could tie a cherry stem into a knot with her tongue onto that ridiculous, awful form of yours underneath her '*skills*.'"

He frowned. "Well, that is a skill that might have interesting applications..."

"I know that," she said. "But why am I sitting around having a discussion with a woman that is obviously about your penis?"

Her cheeks heated, and her hands shook. She could not believe she had just... Talked about his penis. In front of him.

"I didn't realize that would be a problem."

"Of course you didn't. Because you don't realize *anything*. You don't care about anything except the bottom line. That's all you ever see. You want a wife to help run your home. To help organize your life. By those standards *I* have been your damned wife for the past ten years, Isaiah Grayson. Isn't that what you're after? A personal assistant for your house. A *me* clone who can cook your dinner and...and...do wife things."

He frowned, leaning back in his chair.

He didn't speak, so she just kept going. "I quit," she

repeated. "And you have to find your own wife. I'm not working with you anymore. I'm not dealing with you anymore. You said you were my boss. Well, you're not now. Not anymore."

"Poppy," he said, his large, masculine hands pressing flat on his desk as he pushed himself into a standing position. She looked away from his hands. They were as problematic as the rest of him. "Be reasonable."

"No! I'm not going to be reasonable. This situation is so unreasonable it isn't remotely fair of you to ask me to be reasonable within it."

They just stayed there for a moment, regarding each other, and then she slowly turned away, her breath coming in slow, harsh bursts.

"Wait," he said.

She stopped, but she didn't turn. She could feel his stare, resting right between her shoulder blades, digging in between them. "You're right. What I am looking for is a personal version of you. I hadn't thought about it that way until just now. But I am looking for a PA. In all areas of my life."

An odd sensation crept up the back of her neck, goose bumps breaking out over her arms. Still, she fought the urge to turn.

"Poppy," he said slowly. "I think you should marry me."

Chapter Three

When Poppy turned around to face him, her expression was still. Placid. He wasn't good at reading most people, but he knew Poppy. She was expressive. She had a bright smile and a stormy frown, and the absence of either was…concerning.

"Excuse me?"

"You said yourself that what I need is someone like you. I agree. I've never been a man who aims for second best. So why would I aim for second best in this instance? You're the best personal assistant I've ever had."

"I doubt you had a personal assistant before you had me," she said.

"That's irrelevant," he said, waving a hand. "I like the way we work together. I don't see why we couldn't make it something more. We're good partners, Poppy."

Finally, her face moved. But only just the slightest bit. "We're good partners," she echoed, the words hollow.

"Yes," he confirmed. "We are. We always have been. You've managed to make seamless transitions at every turn. From when we worked at a larger construction firm, to when we were starting our own. When we expanded, to when we merged with Jonathan Bear. You've followed me every step of the way, and I've been successful in part because of the confidence I have that you're handling all the details that I need you to."

"And you think I could just... Do that at your house too?"

"Yes," he said simply.

"There's one little problem," Poppy said, her cheeks suddenly turning a dark pink. She stood there just staring for a moment, and the color in her face deepened. It took her a long while to speak. "The problem being that a wife doesn't just manage your kitchen. *That* is a housekeeper."

"I'm aware of that."

"A wife is supposed to..." She looked down, a pink blush continuing to bleed over her dark skin. "You don't feel that way about me."

"Feel what way? You know my desire to get married has nothing to do with love and romance."

"Sex." The word was like a mini explosion in the room. "Being a wife does have something to do with sex."

She was right about that, and when he had made his impromptu proposal a moment earlier, he hadn't been thinking of that. But now that he was...

He took a leisurely visual tour of her, similar to the one he had taken earlier. But this time, he didn't just appreciate her beauty in an abstract sense. This time, he allowed it to be a slightly more heated exploration.

Her skin looked smooth. He had noticed how lovely it was earlier. But there was more than that. Her breasts looked about the right size to fit neatly into his hands, and she had an extremely enticing curve to her hips. Her skirts were never short enough to show very much of her leg, but she had nice ankles.

He could easily imagine getting down on his knees and taking those high heels off her feet. And biting one of her ankles.

That worked for him.

"I don't think that's going to be a problem," he said.

Poppy's mouth dropped open and then snapped shut. "We've never even… We've never even kissed, Isaiah. We've never even almost kissed."

"Yes. Because you're my assistant."

"Your assistant. And you're my foster sister's ex-fiancé."

Isaiah gritted his teeth, an involuntary spike of anger elevating his blood pressure. Poppy knew better than to talk about Rosalind. And hell, she had nothing to do with Poppy. Not in his mind, not anymore.

Yes, she was the reason Poppy had come to work for him in the first place, but Poppy had been with him for so long her presence wasn't connected with the other woman in any way.

He wasn't heartbroken. He never had been, not really. He was angry. She'd made a fool of him. She'd caused him to take his focus off his business. She'd nearly destroyed not only his work, but his brother's. And what would eventually be their sister's too.

All of it, all the success they had now had nearly been taken out by his own idiocy. By the single time he'd allowed his heart to control him.

He would never do that again.

"Rosalind doesn't have anything to do with this," he said.

"She's in my life," Poppy pointed out.

"That's a detail we can discuss later." Or not at all. He didn't see why they were coming close to discussing it now.

"You don't want to marry me," Poppy said.

"Are you questioning my decision-making, Poppy? How long have you known me? If there's one thing I'm not, it's an indecisive man. And I think you know that."

"You're a dick," Poppy said in exasperation. "How dare you… Have me interviewing these women all day… And then… Is this some kind of sick test?"

"You threatened to quit. I don't *want* you to quit. I would rather have you in all of my life than in none of my life."

"I didn't threaten to quit our friendship."

"I mostly see you at work," he said.

"And you value what I do at work more than what you get out of our friendship, is that it?"

That was another question he didn't know how to answer. Because he had a feeling the honest answer would earn him a spiked heel to the forehead. "I'm not sure how the two are separate," he said, thinking he was being quite diplomatic. "Considering we spend most of our time together at work, and my enjoyment of your company often dovetails with the fact that you're so efficient."

Poppy let out a howl that would not have been out of place coming from an enraged chipmunk. "You are… You are…"

Well, if her objection to the marriage was that they had never kissed, and never almost kissed, and he didn't want to hear her talk anymore—and all those things were true—he could only see one solution to the entire situation.

He made his way over to where Poppy was standing like a brittle rose and wrapped his arms around her waist. He dragged her to him, holding her in place as he stared down at her.

"Consider this your almost-kiss," he said.

Her brown eyes went wide, and she stared up at him, her soft lips falling open.

And then his heart was suddenly beating faster, the unsettled feeling in his gut transforming into something else. Heat. Desire. He had never looked at Poppy this way, ever.

And now he wondered if that had been deliberate. Now he wondered if he had been purposefully ignoring how beautiful she was because of all the reasons she had just mentioned for why they shouldn't get married.

The fact she was his assistant. The fact that she was Rosalind's foster sister.

"Isaiah…"

He moved one hand up to cup her cheek and brought his face down closer to hers. She smelled delicate, like flowers and uncertainty. And he found himself drawn to her even more.

"And this will be your kiss."

He brought his lips down onto hers, expecting… He didn't know what.

Usually, sexual attraction was a straightforward thing for him. That was one of the many things he liked about sex. There was no guesswork. It was honest. There was never anything shocking about it. If he saw a woman he thought was beautiful, he approached her. He never wondered if he would enjoy kissing her. Because he always wanted to kiss her before he did. But Poppy...

In the split second before their mouths touched, he wondered. Wondered what it would be like to kiss this woman he had known for so long. Who he had seen as essential to his life, but never as a sexual person.

And then, all his thoughts burned away. Because she tasted better than anything he could remember and her lips just felt right.

It felt equally right to slide his fingertips along the edge of her soft jawline and tilt her face up farther so he could angle his head in deep and gain access. It felt equally right to wrap both arms around her waist and press her body as tightly to his as he possibly could. To feel the soft swell of her breasts against his chest.

And he waited, for a moment, to see if she was going to stick her claws into him. To see if she was going to pull away or resist.

She did neither. Instead, she sighed, slowly, softly. Sweetly. She opened her mouth to his.

He took advantage of that, sliding his tongue between her lips and taking a taste.

He felt it, straight down to his cock, a lightning bolt of pleasure he'd had no idea was coming.

Suddenly, he was in the middle of a violent storm when only a moment ago the sky had been clear.

He had never experienced anything like it. The idea that Poppy—this woman who had been a constant in his world—was a hidden temptress rocked him down to his soul. He had no idea such a thing was possible.

In his world, chemistry had always been both straight-forward and instant. That it could simply exist beneath the surface like this seemed impossible.

And yet, it appeared there was chemistry between himself and Poppy that had been dormant all this time.

Her soft hands were suddenly pressed against his face, holding on to him as she returned his kiss with surprising enthusiasm.

Her enthusiasm might be surprising, but he was damn well going to take advantage of it.

Because if chemistry was her concern, then he was more than happy to demolish her worry here and now.

He reversed their positions, turning so her back was to his desk, and then he walked her backward before sliding one arm beneath her ass and picking her up, depositing her on top of the desk. He bent down to continue kissing her, taking advantage of her shock to step between her legs.

Or maybe he wasn't taking advantage of anything. Maybe none of this was calculated as he would like to pretend that it was. Maybe it was just necessary. Maybe now that their lips had touched there was just no going back.

And hell, why should they? If she couldn't deny the chemistry between them... If it went to its natural conclusion...she had no reason to refuse his proposal.

He slid one hand down her thigh, toward her knee, and then lifted that leg, hooking it over his hip as he drew her forward and pressed himself against her.

Thank God for the fullness of her skirt, because it was easy to make a space for himself right there between her legs. He was so hard it hurt.

He was a thirty-six-year-old man who had a hell of a lot more self-control now than he'd ever had, and yet, he felt more out of control than he could ever remember being before.

That did not add up. It was bad math.

And right now, he didn't care.

Slowly, he slid his other hand up and cupped her breast. He had been right. It was exactly the right size to fill his palm. He squeezed her gently, and Poppy let out a hoarse groan, then wrenched her mouth away from his.

Her eyes were full of hurt. Full of tears.

"Don't," she said, wiggling away from him.

"What?" he asked, drawing a deep breath and trying to gain control over himself.

Stopping was the last thing he wanted to do. He wanted to strip that dress off her, marvel at every inch of uncovered skin. Kiss every inch of it. He wanted her twisting and begging underneath him. He wanted to sink into her and lose himself. Wanted to make her lose herself too.

Poppy.

His friend. His assistant.

"How dare you?" she asked. "How dare you try to manipulate me with…with *sex*. You're my friend, Isaiah. I trusted you. You're just…trying to control me the way you control everything in your life."

"That isn't true," he said. It wasn't. It might have started out as…not a manipulation, but an attempt to prove something to both of them.

But eventually, he had just been swept up in all this. In her. In the heat between them.

"I think it is. You… I quit."

And then she turned and walked out of the room, leaving him standing there, rejected for the first time in a good long while.

And it bothered him more than he would have ever imagined.

Poppy was steeped in misery by the time she crawled onto the couch in her pajamas that evening.

Her little house down by the ocean was usually a great comfort to her. A representation of security that she had never imagined someone like her could possess.

Now, nothing felt like a refuge. Nothing at all. This whole town felt like a prison.

Her bars were Isaiah Grayson.

That had to stop.

She really was going to quit.

She swallowed, feeling sick to her stomach. She was going to quit and sell this house and move away. She would talk to him sometimes, but mostly she had to let the connection go.

She didn't mean to him what he did to her. Not just in a romantic way. Isaiah didn't... He didn't understand. He didn't feel for people the way that other people felt.

And he had used the attraction she felt for him against her. Her deepest, darkest secret.

There was no way a woman without a strong, preexisting attraction would have ever responded to him the way she had.

It had been revealing. Though, now she wondered if it had actually been revealing at all, or if he had just always known.

Had he known—all this time—how much she wanted him? And had he been...laughing at her?

No. Not laughing. He wouldn't do that. He wasn't cruel, not at all. But had he been waiting until it was of some use to him? Maybe.

She wailed and dragged a blanket down from the back of the couch, pulling it over herself and curling into a ball.

She had kissed Isaiah Grayson today.

More than kissed. He had... He had touched her.

He had *proposed* to her.

And, whether it was a manipulation or not, she had felt…

He had been hard. Right there between her legs, he had been turned on.

But then, he was a man, and there were a great many men who could get hard for blowup dolls. So. It wasn't like it was that amazing.

Except, something about it felt kind of amazing.

She closed her eyes. Isaiah. He was… He was absolutely everything to her.

She could marry him. She could keep another woman from marrying him.

Great. And then you can be married to somebody who doesn't love you at all. Who sees you as a convenience.

She laughed aloud at that thought. Yes. Some of that sounded terrible. But… She had spent most of her life in foster care. She had lived with a whole lot of people who didn't love her. And some of them had found her to be inconvenient. So that would put marrying Isaiah several steps above some of the living situations she'd had as a kid.

Then there was Rosalind. Tall, blond Rosalind who was very clearly Isaiah's type. While Poppy was…not.

How would she ever…cope with that? With the inevitable comparisons?

He hates her. He doesn't hate you.

Well. That was true. Rosalind had always gone after what she wanted. She had devastated Isaiah in the process. So much so that it had even hurt Poppy at the time. Because as much as she wanted to be with Isaiah, she didn't want him to be hurt.

And then, Rosalind had gone on to her billionaire. The

man she was still with. She traveled around the world and hosted dinner parties and did all these things that had been beyond their wildest fantasies when they were growing up.

Rosalind wasn't afraid of taking something just for herself. And she didn't worry at all about someone else's feelings.

Sometimes, that was a negative. But right about now... Poppy was tempted—more than a little bit tempted—to be like Rosalind.

To go after her fantasy and damn the feelings and the consequences. She could have him. As her husband. She could have him...kissing her. She could have him naked.

She could be *his*.

She had been his friend and his assistant for ten years. But she'd never been his in the way she wanted to be.

He'd been her friend and her boss.

He'd never been hers.

Had anyone ever been hers?

Rosalind certainly cared about Poppy, in her own way. If she didn't, she wouldn't have bailed Poppy out when she was in need. But Rosalind's life was very much about her. She and Poppy kept in touch, but that communication was largely driven by Poppy.

That was...it for her as far as family went. Except for the Graysons.

And if she married Isaiah...they really would be her family.

There was a firm, steady knock on her door. Three times. She knew exactly who it was.

It was like thinking about him had conjured him up.

She wasn't sure she was ready to face him.

She looked down. She was wearing a T-shirt and no bra. She was definitely not ready to face him. Still, she got up off the couch and padded over to the door. Because she couldn't *not*...

She couldn't not see him. Not right now. Not when all her thoughts and feelings were jumbled up like this. Maybe she would look at him and get a clear answer. Maybe she would look at him and think, *No, I still need to quit.*

Or maybe...

She knew she was tempting herself. Tempting him.

She hoped she was tempting him.

She scowled and grabbed hold of her blanket, wrapping it tightly around her shoulders before she made her way to the door. She wrenched it open. "What are you doing here?"

"I came to talk sense into you."

"You can't," she said, knowing she sounded like a bratty kid and not caring at all.

"Why not?"

"Because I am an insensible female." She whirled around and walked back into her small kitchen, and Isaiah followed her, closing the front door behind him.

She turned to face him again, and her heart caught in her throat. He was gorgeous. Those cold, clear gray eyes, his sculpted cheekbones, the beard that made him more approachable. Because without it, she had a feeling he would be too pretty. And his lips...

She had kissed those lips.

He was just staring at her.

"I'm emotional."

He said nothing to that.

"I might actually throw myself onto the ground at any moment in a serious display of said emotion, and you won't like it at all. So you should probably leave."

Those gray eyes were level with hers, sparking heat within her, stoking a deep ache of desire inside her stomach.

"Reconsider." His voice was low and enticing, and made her want to agree to whatever commandment he issued.

"Quitting or marrying you?" She took a step back from him. She couldn't be trusted to be too close to him. Couldn't be trusted to keep her hands to herself. To keep from flinging herself at him—either to beat him or kiss him she didn't know.

"Both. Either."

Just when she thought he couldn't make it worse.

"That's not exactly the world's most compelling proposal."

"I already know that my proposal wasn't all that compelling. You made it clear."

"I mean, I've heard of bosses offering to give a raise to keep an employee from leaving. But offering marriage…"

"That's not the only reason I asked you to marry me," he said.

She made a scoffing sound. "You could've fooled me."

"I'm not trying to fool you," he said.

Her heart twisted. This was one of the things she liked about Isaiah. It was tempting to focus on his rather grumpy exterior, and when she did that, the question of why she loved him became a lot more muddled. Because he was hot? A lot of men were hot. That wasn't it. There was something incredibly endearing about the fact that he said what he meant. He didn't play games. It simply wasn't in him. He was a man who didn't manipulate. And that made her accusation from earlier feel…wrong.

Manipulation wasn't really the right way to look at it. But he was used to being in charge. Unquestioned.

And he would do whatever he needed to do to get his way, that much she knew.

"Did you take the kiss as far as you did because you wanted to prove something to me?"

"No," he said. "I kissed you to try and prove something to *me*. Because you're right. If we were going to get married, then an attraction would have to be there."

"Yes," she said, her throat dry.

"I can honestly say that I never thought about you that way."

She felt like she'd just been stabbed through the chest with a kitchen knife. "Right," she said, instead of letting out the groan of pain that she was tempted to issue.

"We definitely have chemistry," he said. "I was genuinely caught off guard by it. I assume it was the same for you."

She blinked. He really had no idea? Did he really not know that her response to him wasn't sudden or random?

No. She could see that he didn't.

Isaiah often seemed insensitive because he simply didn't bother to blunt his statements to make them palatable for other people. Because he either didn't understand or care what people found offensive. Which meant, if backed into a corner about whether or not he had been using the kiss against her, he would have told her.

"I'm sorry," she said.

Now he looked genuinely confused. "You're apologizing to me. Why?"

"I'm apologizing to you because I assumed the worst about you. And that wasn't fair. You're not underhanded. You're not always sweet or cuddly or sensitive. But you're not underhanded."

"You like me," he pointed out.

He looked smug about that.

"Obviously. I wouldn't have put up with you for the past ten years. Good paying job or not. But then, I assume you like me too. At least to a degree."

"We're a smart match," he said. "I don't think you can deny that."

"Just a few hours ago you were thinking that one of those bottle blondes was your smart match. You can see why I'm not exactly thrilled by your sudden proposal to me."

"Are you in love with someone else?"

The idea was laughable. She hadn't even been on a date in...

She wasn't counting. It was too depressing.

"No," she said, her throat tightening. "But is it so wrong to want the possibility of love?"

"I think love is good for the right kind of people. Though my observation is that people mostly settle into a partnership anyway. The healthiest marriage is a partnership."

"Love is also kind of a thing."

He waved a hand. "Passion fades. But the way you support one another... That's what matters. That's what I've seen with my parents."

She stared at him for a long moment. He was right in front of her, asking for marriage, and she still felt like he was standing on the other side of a wall. Like she couldn't quite reach him. "And you're just...never going to love anyone."

"I *have* loved someone," he said simply.

There was something so incredibly painful about that truth. That he had loved someone. And she had used the one shot he was willing to give. It wasn't fair. That Rosalind had gotten his love. If Poppy would have had it, she would have preserved it. Held it close. Done anything to keep it for always.

But she would never get that chance. Because her vivacious older foster sister had gotten it first. And Rosalind hadn't appreciated what she'd had in him.

It was difficult to be angry at Rosalind over what had happened. Particularly when her and Isaiah being together had been painful for Poppy anyway. But right now... Right now, she was angry.

Because whole parts of Isaiah were closed off to Poppy because of the heartbreak he'd endured.

Or maybe that was silly. Maybe it was just going to take a very special woman to make him fall in love. And she wasn't that woman.

Well, on the plus side, if you don't marry him, you'll give him a chance to find that woman.

She clenched her teeth, closing her eyes against the pain. She didn't think she could handle that. It was one terrible thing to think about watching him marry another woman. But it was another, even worse thing to think about him falling in love with someone else. If she were good and selfless, pure and true, she supposed that's what she would want for him.

But she wasn't, and she didn't. Because if he fell in love, that would mean she wasn't going to get what she wanted. She would lose her chance at love. At least, the love she wanted.

How did it benefit her to be that selfless? It just didn't.

"I'll think about it," she said.

Chapter Four

"I'm not leaving here until I close this deal," he said.

"I'm not a business deal waiting to happen, Isaiah."

He took a step toward her, and she felt her resolve begin to weaken. And then, she questioned why she was even fighting this at all.

He was the one driving this train. He always was.

Because she loved him.

Because he was her boss.

Because he possessed the ability to remain somewhat detached, and she absolutely did not.

She could watch him trying to calculate his next move. She could see that it was difficult for him to think of this as something other than a business deal.

No, she supposed that what Isaiah was proposing *was* a business deal. With sex.

"You can't actually be serious," she said.

294 WANT ME, COWBOY

"I'm always serious."

"I get that you think you can get married and make it not about...*feelings*. But it's... I can't get over the sex thing, Isaiah. I can't."

There were many reasons for that, not the least of which being her own inexperience. But she was not going to have that discussion with him.

"The kiss was good." He said it like that solved everything. Like it should somehow deal with all of her concerns.

"A kiss isn't sex," she said lamely. As if pointing out one of the most obvious things in the world would fix this situation.

"Do you think it's going to be a problem?"

"I think it's going to be weird."

Weird was maybe the wrong word. Terrifying.

Able to rip her entire heart straight out of her chest.

"You're fixating," he said simply. "Let's put a pin in the sex."

"You can't put a pin in the sex," she protested.

"Why can't I put a pin in the sex?"

"Because," she said, waving her hand in a broad gesture. "The sex is like the eight-hundred-pound gorilla in the room. In lingerie. It will not be ignored. It will not be...pinned."

"Put a pin in it," he reiterated. "Let's talk about everything else that a marriage between the two of us could offer you."

She sputtered. "Could offer *me*?"

"Yes. Of course, I don't expect you to enter into an arrangement that benefits only me. So far, I haven't presented you with one compelling reason why marriage between the two of us would be beneficial to you."

"And you think that's my issue?"

"I think it's one issue. My family loves you. I appreciate that. Because I'm very close to my family. Anyone I marry will have to get along with my family. You already do. I feel like you love my family…"

She closed her eyes. Yes. She did love the Grayson family. She loved them so much. They were the only real, functional family she had ever seen in existence. They were the reason she believed that kind of thing existed outside the land of sitcoms. If it weren't for them, she would have no frame of reference for that kind of normalcy. A couple who had been together all those years. Adult children that loved their parents enough to try to please them. To come back home and visit. Siblings who worked together to build a business. Who cared for each other.

Loud, boisterous holiday celebrations that were warm and inviting. That included her.

Yes, the Grayson family was a big, fat carrot in all of this.

But what Isaiah didn't seem to understand was that he was the biggest carrot of all.

An inescapably sexual thought, and she had been asked to put a pin in the sex. But with Isaiah she could never just set the sex aside.

"You love my ranch," he said. "You love to come out and ride the horses. Imagine. You would already be sleeping there on weekends. It would be easy to get up and go for a ride."

"I love my house," she protested.

"My ranch is better," he said.

She wanted to punch him for that. Except, it was true. His gorgeous modern ranch house with both rustic and modern details, flawlessly designed by his sister, was a feat of architectural engineering and design. There was not a single negative thing she could say about the place.

Set up in the mountains, with a gorgeous barn and horses and all kinds of things that young, daydreamer Poppy would have given her right arm to visit, much less inhabit.

He had horses. And he'd taught her to ride a year earlier.

"And I assume you want children."

She felt like the wind had been knocked out of her. "I thought we weren't going to talk about sex."

"We're not talking about sex. We're talking about children."

"Didn't your parents tell you where babies come from?"

His mouth flattened into a grim line. "I will admit there was something I missed when I was thinking of finding a wife through an ad."

She rolled her eyes. "Really?"

"Yes. I thought about myself. I thought about the fact that I wanted children in the abstract. But I did not think about what kind of mother I wanted my children to have. You would be a wonderful mother."

She blinked rapidly, fighting against the sting of sudden tears. "Why would you think that?"

"I know you. I've watched the way you took care of me and my business for the last ten years. The way you handle everything. The details in my professional life, Joshua and Faith's, as well. I've seen you with Joshua's son."

"I was basically raised by wolves," she pointed out. "I don't know anything about families."

"I think that will make you an even better mother. You know exactly what not to do."

She huffed out a laugh. "Disappearing into a heroin haze is a good thing to avoid. That much I know."

"You know more than that," he said. "You're good with people. You're good at anticipating what they want, what they need. You're organized. You're efficient."

"You make me sound like an app, Isaiah."

"You're warm and…and sometimes sweet. Though, not to me."

"You wouldn't like me if I were sweet," she pointed out.

"No. I wouldn't. But that's the other thing. You know how to stand up to me." The sincerity on his face nearly killed her. "We would be good together."

He sounded so certain. And she felt on the opposite side of the world from certain.

This was too much. It really was. Too close to everything she had ever dreamed about—without one essential ingredient. Except… When had she really ever been allowed to dream?

She had watched so many other people achieve their dreams. While she'd barely allowed herself to imagine…

A life with Isaiah.

Children.

A family of her own.

Isaiah had simply been off-limits in her head all this time. It had made working with him easier. It had made being his friend less risky.

But he was offering her fantasy.

How could she refuse?

"Your parents can't know it's fake," she said.

"Are you agreeing?"

She blinked rapidly, trying to keep her tears back. "They can't know," she repeated.

"It's not fake," he said simply. "We'll have a real marriage."

"They can't know about the ad. They can't know that you just… Are hiring me for a new position. Okay?"

"Poppy…"

"They can't know you're not in love with me."

She would die. She would die of shame. If his wonderful, amazing parents who only ever wanted the best for their children, who most certainly wanted deep abiding love for Isaiah, were to know this marriage was an arrangement.

"It's not going to come up," he said.

"Good. It can't." Desperation clawed at her, and she wasn't really sure what she was desperate for. For him to agree. For him to say he had feelings for her. For him to kiss her. "Or it's off."

"Agreed."

"Agreed."

For a moment she thought he *was* going to kiss her again. She wasn't sure she could handle that. So instead, she stuck her hand out and stood there, staring at him. He frowned but took her offered hand, shaking it slowly.

Getting engaged in her pajamas and ending it with a handshake was not the romantic story she would need to tell his family.

He released his hold on her hand, and she thought he was going to walk away. But instead, he reached out and pulled her forward, capturing her mouth with his after all, a flood of sensation washing over her.

And then, as quickly as it began, the kiss ended.

"No. It's not going to be a problem," he said.

She expected him to leave then. He was supposed to leave. But instead, he dipped his head and kissed her again.

She felt dizzy. And she wanted to keep on kissing him. This couldn't be happening. It shouldn't be happening.

But they were engaged. So maybe this had to happen.

She didn't know this man, she realized as he let out a feral growl and backed her up against her wall. This was not the cool, logical friend she had spent all these years getting to know. This was...

Well, this was Isaiah as a man.

She had always known he was a man. Of course she had. If she hadn't, she wouldn't have been in love with him. Wouldn't have had so many fantasies about him. But she hadn't *really* known. Not like this. She hadn't known what it would be like to be the woman he wanted. Hadn't had any idea just how hot-blooded a man as detached and cool as he was on a day-to-day basis could be when sex was involved.

Sex.

She supposed now was the time to bring up her little secret.

But maybe this was just a kiss, maybe they weren't going to have sex.

He angled his head then, taking the kiss deeper. Making it more intense. And then he reached down and gripped the hem of her T-shirt, pulling it up over her head.

She didn't have a bra on underneath, and she was left completely exposed. Her nipples went tight as he looked at her, as those familiar gray eyes, so cold and rational most of the time, went hot.

He stared at her, his eyes glittering. "How did I not know?"

"How did you not know what?" Her teeth chattered when she asked the question.

Only then did she realize she was afraid this would expose her. Because while she could handle keeping her love for Isaiah in a little corner of her heart while she had access to his body—while she claimed ownership of him, rather than allowing some other woman to have him—she could not handle him knowing how she felt.

She'd had her love rejected too many times in her life. She would never subject herself to that again. Ever.

"How did I not know how beautiful you were?" He was absolutely serious, his sculpted face looking as if it was carved from rock.

She reached out, dragged her fingertips over his face. Over the coarse hair of his beard.

She could touch him now. Like this.

The kiss in his office had been so abrupt, so shocking, that while she had enjoyed it, she hadn't fully been able to process all that it meant. All the changes that came with it.

She didn't touch Isaiah like this. She didn't touch him ever.

And now… She finally could.

She frowned and leaned forward, pressing her lips slowly against his. They were warm, and firm, and she couldn't remember anything in the world feeling this wonderful.

Slowly, ever so slowly, she traced the outline of his bottom lip with her tongue.

She was tasting him.

Ten years of fantasies, vague and half-realized, and they had led here. To this. To him.

She slid her hands back, pushing them through his hair as she moved forward, pressing her bare breasts to his chest, still covered by the T-shirt he was wearing.

She didn't want anything between them. Nothing at all.

Suddenly, pride didn't matter.

She pulled away from him for a moment, and his eyes went straight down to her breasts again.

That would be her salvation. The fact that he was a man. That he was more invested in breasts than in feelings.

He was never going to see how she felt. Never going to see the love shining from her eyes, as long as he was looking at her body. And in this, in sex, she had the freedom to express everything she felt.

She was going to.

Oh, she was going to.

She wrapped her arms around his neck and pushed forward again, claiming his mouth, pouring everything, every fantasy, into that moment.

He growled, his arm wrapping around her waist like a steel band, the other one going down to her thighs as he lifted her up off the ground, pulling her against him. She wrapped her legs around his waist and didn't protest at all when he carried them both from the kitchen back toward her bedroom.

She knew exactly where this was going.

But it was time.

If she were totally, completely honest with herself, she knew why she hadn't done this before.

She was waiting for him.

She always had been.

A foolish, humiliating truth that she had never allowed herself to face until now. But it made pausing for consideration pointless.

She was going to marry him.

She was going to be with him.

There was nothing to think about.

There was a small, fragile bubble of joy in her chest, something she had never allowed herself to feel before. And it was growing inside her now.

She could have this. She could have him.

She squeaked when he dropped her down onto the bed and wrenched his shirt up over his head. She lay back, looking at him, taking in the fine, sculpted angles of his body. His chest was covered with just the right amount of dark hair, extending in a line down the center of his abs, disappearing beneath the waistband of his jeans.

She was exceptionally interested in that. And, for the first time, she hoped she was going to have those questions answered. That her curiosity would be satisfied.

He moved his hands to his belt buckle and reality began to whisper in her ear as he worked through the loops.

She didn't know why reality had showed up. It was her knee-jerk reaction to good things, she supposed.

In her life, nothing stayed good for long. Not for her. Only other girls got what they wanted.

The fact of the matter was, she wasn't his second choice after her much more beautiful foster sister.

She wasn't even his tenth choice.

She had come somewhere down the line of she-didn't-even-want-to-know-how-many bar hookups and the women who had been in her office earlier today.

On the list of women he might marry, Poppy was below placing an ad as a solution.

That was how much of a last resort she was.

At least this time you're a resort at all. Does it really matter if you're the last one?

In many ways, it didn't. Not at all.

Because she wanted to be chosen, even if she was chosen last.

He slowly lowered the zipper on his jeans and all of her thoughts evaporated.

Saved by the slow tug of his underwear, revealing a line of muscle that was almost obscene and a shadow of dark hair before he drew the fabric down farther and exposed himself completely, pushing his pants and underwear all the way to the floor.

She tried not to stare openmouthed. She had never seen a naked man in person before. And she had never counted on seeing Isaiah naked. Had dreamed about it, yes. Had fantasized about it, sure. But, she had never really imagined that it might happen.

"Now it's your turn," he said, his voice husky. Affected.

"I…"

She was too nervous. She couldn't make her hands move. Couldn't find the dexterity to pull her pajama pants down. And, as skills went, taking off pajama pants was a pretty easy one.

He took pity on her. He leaned forward, cupping her chin and kissing her, bringing himself down onto the bed beside her and pressing his large, warm palm between her shoulder blades, sliding his hand down the line of her back, just beneath the waistband of those pajamas. His hand was hot and enticing on her ass, and she arched her hips forward, his erection brushing against the apex of her thighs.

She gasped, and he kissed her, delving deep as he did, bringing his other hand around to cup her breast, his thumb sliding over her nipple, drawing it into an impossibly tight bud.

She pressed her hands against his chest, and just stared at them for a moment. Then she looked up at his face and back down at her hands.

She was touching his bare chest.

Isaiah.

It was undeniable.

He was looking down at her, his dark brows locked together, his expression as serious as it ever was, and it was just...*him*.

She slid her hands downward, watching as they traveled. Her mouth went dry when she touched those ab muscles, when her hands went down farther. She paused, holding out her index finger and tracing the indention that ran diagonally across his body, straight toward that place where he was most male.

She avoided touching him there.

She didn't know *how*.

But then, he took hold of her hand, curved his fingers around it and guided her right toward his erection.

She held back a gasp as he encouraged her to curl her fingers around his thick length.

He was so hot. Hot and soft and hard all at once. Then she looked back up, meeting his eyes, and suddenly, it wasn't so scary. Because Isaiah—a man who was not terribly affected by anything at all in the world, who seemed so confident in his ability to control everything around him—looked absolutely at a loss.

His forehead had relaxed, his eyes fluttering closed, his lips going slack. His head fell back. She squeezed him, and a groan rumbled in his chest.

Right now, she had the control, the power.

Probably for the first and only time in their entire relationship.

She had never felt anything like this before. Not ever.

A pulse began to beat between her legs, need swamping her. She felt hollow there, the slickness a telltale sign of just how much she wanted him too. But she didn't feel embarrassed about it. It didn't make her feel vulnerable. They were equals in this. It felt...exhilarating. Exciting. Right here in her little bed, it felt safe. To want him as much as she did.

How could it not, when he wanted her too?

Experimentally, she pumped her hand along his length, and he growled.

He was beautiful.

Everything she'd ever wanted. She knew he'd been made for her. This man who had captured her heart, her fantasies, from the moment she'd first met him.

But she didn't have time to think about all of that, because she found herself flipped onto her back, with Isaiah looming over her. In an easy movement, he reached between them and yanked off her pants and underwear.

He made space for himself between her legs, gripping his arousal and pressing it through her slick folds, the intimacy of the action taking her breath away, and then the intense, white-hot pleasure that assaulted her when he hit that perfect spot cleared her mind of anything and everything.

He did it again, and then released his hold on himself,

flexing his hips against her. She gasped, grabbing his shoulders and digging her fingers into his skin.

His face was a study in concentration, and he cupped her breast, teasing her nipple as he continued to flex his hips back and forth across that sensitive bundle of nerves.

Something gathered low in her stomach, that hollow sensation between her legs growing keener...

And he didn't stop. He kept at it, teasing her nipple, and moving his hips in a maddening rhythm.

The tension within her increased, further and further until it suddenly snapped. She gasped as her climax overtook her, and he captured that sound of pleasure with his mouth, before drawing back and pressing the himself into the entrance of her body. And then, before she had a chance to tense up, he pressed forward.

The shocking, tearing sensation made her cry out in pain.

Isaiah's eyes clashed with hers.

"What the hell?"

Chapter Five

Isaiah was trying to form words, but he was completely overtaken by the feel of her around his body. She was so tight. So wet. And he couldn't do anything but press his hips forward and sink even deeper into her in spite of the fact that she had cried out with obvious pain only a second before.

He should stop. But she was kissing him again. She was holding him against her as she moved her hips in invitation. As her movements physically begged him to stay with her.

Poppy was a virgin.

He should stop.

He *couldn't* stop.

He couldn't remember when that had ever happened to him before. He didn't know if it ever had. He was all about control. It was necessary for a man like him. He had to override his emotions, his needs.

Right now.

But she was holding him so tight. She felt…so good. He had only intended to give her a kiss before he left. And he *had* intended to go. But he'd been caught up…in her. Not in triumph over the fact that he had convinced her to marry him.

No, he had been caught up in *her*.

In the wonder of kissing her. Uncovering her. Exploring her in a way he had never imagined he might.

But he'd had no idea—none at all—that she was this inexperienced.

Poppy was brash. She gave as good as she got. She didn't shy away from anything. And she hadn't shied away from this either.

She still wasn't.

Her hands traveled down to cup his ass, and she tugged at him, as if urging him on.

"Isaiah," she whispered. "Isaiah, please."

And he had no choice but to oblige.

He moved inside her, slowly at first, torturing them both, and trying to make things more comfortable for her.

He had no idea how he was supposed to have sex with a damned virgin. He never had before.

He had a type. And Poppy was against that type in every single way.

But it seemed to be working just fine for him now.

She pressed her fingertips to his cheek, then pulled him down toward her mouth. She kissed him. Slow and sweet, and he forgot to have control.

He would apologize later. For going too fast. Too hard. But she kept making these sounds. Like she wanted it. Like she liked it. She wrapped her legs around his hips and urged him on, like she needed it. And he couldn't slow down. Couldn't stop. Couldn't make it better, even if he should.

He should make her come at least three more times before he took his own pleasure, but he didn't have the willpower. Not at all.

His pleasure overtook him, squeezing down on his windpipe, feeling like jaws to his throat, and he couldn't pull back. Not now. When his orgasm overtook him, all he could hear was the roar of his own blood in his ears, the pounding of his heartbeat. And then Poppy arched beneath him, her nails in his shoulders probably near to drawing blood as she let out a deep, intense cry, her internal muscles flexing around him.

He jerked forward, spilling inside her before he withdrew and rolled over onto his back. He was breathing hard, unable to speak. Unable to think.

"Poppy..."

"I don't want to talk about it," she said, crawling beneath a blanket beside him, covering herself up. She suddenly looked very small, and he was forced to sit there and do the math on their age difference. It wasn't that big. Well, eight years. But he had never thought about what that might mean.

Of course, he had never known her to have a serious relationship. But then, he had only had the one, and he had certainly been having sex.

"We should talk about it."

"Why?" Her eyes were large and full of an emotion he couldn't grab hold of. But it echoed in him, and it felt a lot like pain. "There's really nothing to talk about. You know that my... My childhood was terrible. And I don't see why we have to go over all the different issues *that* might've given me."

"So you've been avoiding this."

It suddenly made sense why she had been so fixated on the sex aspect of his proposal. He'd been with a lot of women. So he had taken for granted that sex would be sex.

Of course, he had been wrong. He looked down at her, all vulnerable and curled into a ball. He kissed her forehead.

It hadn't just been sex. And of course poor Poppy had no reference at all for what sex would be like anyway.

"I'm sorry," he said.

"Don't be sorry. But I... I need to be alone."

That didn't sit well with him. The idea of leaving her like this.

"Please," she said.

He had no idea how to handle a woman in this state. Didn't know how to...

He usually wasn't frustrated by his difficulty connecting with people. He had a life that suited him. Family and friends who understood him. Who he knew well enough to understand.

Usually, he understood Poppy. But this was uncharted territory for the two of them, and he was at a loss for the right thing to do.

"If you really need that."

She nodded. "I do."

He got up, slowly gathering his clothes and walking out of the bedroom. He paused in her living room, holding those clothes in his hands. Then he dropped them. He lay down on her couch, which he was far too tall for, and pulled a blanket over himself.

There. She could be alone. In her room. And tomorrow they would talk. And put together details for their upcoming wedding.

He closed his eyes, and he tried not to think about what it had felt like to slide inside her.

But that was all he thought about.

Over and over again, until he finally fell asleep.

Poppy's eyes opened wide at three in the morning. She padded out into the hall, feeling disoriented. She was naked. Because she'd had sex with Isaiah last night.

And then she had sent him away.

Because… She didn't know why. She hated herself? She hated him? And everything good that could possibly happen to her?

She'd panicked. That was the only real explanation for her reaction.

She had felt stripped and vulnerable. She had wanted—needed— time to get a hold of herself.

Though, considering how she felt this morning, there probably wasn't enough time in the entire world for her to collect herself.

She had asked him to leave. And he'd left.

Of course he had.

She cared for that man with a passion, but he was not sensitive. Not in the least. Not even a little bit.

You asked him to go. What do you want from him?

It was silly to want anything but exactly what she had asked for. She knew it.

She padded out toward the living room. She needed something. A mindless TV show. A stiff drink. But she wasn't going to be able to go back to sleep.

When she walked into the living room, her heart jumped into her throat. Because there was a man-shaped something lying on her couch.

Well, it wasn't just man-shaped. It *was* a man.

Isaiah. Who had never left.

Who was defying her expectations again.

He'd been covered by a blanket, she was pretty sure, considering the fact that there was a blanket on the floor bunched up next to him. But he was still naked, sprawled out on her couch and now uncovered. He was...

Even in the dim light she could see just how incredible he was. Long limbs, strong muscles. So hard. Like he was carved from granite.

He was in many ways a mystery to her, even though she knew him as well as she knew anyone. If not better.

He was brilliant with numbers. His investments, his money management, was a huge part of what made Gray Bear Construction a success. He wasn't charismatic Joshua with an easy grin, good with PR and an expert way with people. He wasn't the fresh-faced wunderkind like Faith, taking the architecture world by storm with designs that outstripped her age and experience. Faith was a rare and unique talent. And Jonathan Bear was the hardest worker she had ever met.

And yet, Isaiah's work was what kept the company moving. He was the reason they stayed solvent. The reason that everything he had ever been involved with had been a success in one way or another.

But he was no pale, soft, indoor man. No. He was rugged. He loved spending time outdoors. Seemed to thrive on it. The moment work was through, Isaiah was out on his ranch. It amazed her that he had ever managed to live in Seattle. Though, even then, he had been hiking on the weekends, mountain biking and staying in cabins outside the city whenever he got the chance.

She supposed in many ways that was consistent enough. The one thing he didn't seem to have a perfect handle on was people. Otherwise, he was a genius.

But he had stayed with her.

In spite of the fact that she had asked him not to. She wasn't sure if that was an incredible amount of intuition on his part or if it was simply him being a stubborn ass.

"Are you just going to stand there staring at me?"

She jumped. "I didn't know you were awake."

"I wasn't."

"You knew I was looking at you," she said, shrinking in on herself slightly, wishing she had something to cover up her body.

Isaiah, for his part, looked completely unconcerned. He lifted his arms and clasped his hands, putting them behind his head. "Are you ready to talk?"

"I thought it was the woman who was supposed to be all needy and wanting to talk."

"Traditionally. Maybe. But this isn't normal for me. And I'm damn sure this isn't normal for you. You know, on account of the fact that you've never done this before."

"I said I didn't want to talk about my hymenal status."

"Okay."

He didn't say anything. The silence between them seemed to balloon, expand, becoming very, very uncomfortable.

"It wasn't a big deal," she said. "I mean, in that I wasn't waiting for anything in particular. I was always waiting for somebody to care about me. Always. But then, when I left home… When I got my job with you…" She artfully left out any mention of Rosalind. "That was when I finally felt like I fit. And there just wasn't room for anything else. I didn't want there to be. I didn't need there to be."

"But now, with me, you suddenly changed your mind?"

She shifted, covering herself with her hand as she clenched her thighs more tightly together. "It's not that I changed my mind. I didn't have a specific No Sex Rule. I just hadn't met a man I trust, and I trust you and…and I got carried away."

"And that's never happened to you before," he said, keeping his tone measured and even. The way he handled people when he was irritated but trying not to show it. She knew him well enough to be familiar with that reaction.

"No," she admitted. Because there was no point in not telling him.

"You wanted this," he said, pushing into a sitting position. "You wanted it, didn't you?"

"Yes," she said. "I don't know how you could doubt that."

"Because you've never wanted to do this before. And then suddenly… You did. Poppy, I knew I was coercing you into marriage, but I didn't want to coerce you into bed."

"You didn't. We're engaged now anyway and… It was always going to be you," she blurted out and then quickly tried to backtrack. "Maybe it was never going to happen for me if I didn't trust and know the person. But I've never had an easy time with trusting. With you, it just kind of…happened."

"Sex?"

"Trust."

"Come here."

"There?"

He reached out and took hold of her wrist, and then

he tugged her forward, bringing her down onto his lap in an elegant tumble. "Yes."

He was naked. She was naked. She was sitting on his lap. It should feel ridiculous. Or wrong somehow. This sudden change.

But it didn't feel strange. It felt good.

He felt good.

"I'm staying," he said.

"I asked you to leave," she pointed out.

"You didn't really want me to."

"You can't know that," she said, feeling stubborn.

It really wasn't fair. Because she *had* wanted him to stay.

"Normally, I would say that's true. But I know you. And I knew that you didn't really want me to leave you alone *alone*."

"You knew that?"

"Yes, even I knew that," he said.

She lifted her hand, let it hover over his chest. Then he took hold of it and pressed it down, over his heart. She could feel it thundering beneath her palm.

"I guess you can stay," she whispered.

"I'm too tall for this couch," he pointed out.

"Well, you can sleep on the floor."

That was when she found herself being lifted into the air as Isaiah stood. "I think I'll go back to your bed."

She swallowed, her heart in her throat, her body trembling. Were they really going to… Again?

"It's not a very comfortable bed," she said weakly.

"I think I can handle it."

Then he kissed her, and he kept on kissing her until they were back in her room.

Whatever desire she had to protect herself, to withdraw from him, was gone completely.

For the first time in her life, she was living her dream in Isaiah's arms. She wasn't going to keep herself from it.

Chapter Six

Poppy was not happy when he insisted they drive to work together the next day.

But it was foolish for them to go separately. He was already at her house. She was clearly resisting him taking over every aspect of the situation, and he could understand that. But it didn't mean he could allow for impracticality.

Still, she threw him out of the bedroom, closed herself in and didn't emerge until it was about five minutes to the time they were meant to be there.

She was back in her uniform. A bright red skirt that fell down to her knees and a crisp, white top that she had tucked in. Matching red earrings and shoes added to the very Poppy look.

"Faith and Joshua are going to have questions," she said, her tone brittle as she got into the passenger seat of his sports car.

"So what? We're engaged."

"We're going to have to figure out a story. And… We're going to have to tell your parents. Your parents are not going to be happy if they're the last to know."

"We don't have to tell my siblings we're engaged."

"Oh, you just figure we can tell them we knocked boots and leave it at that?" Her tone told him she didn't actually think that was a good idea.

"Or not tell them anything. It's not like either of them keep me apprised of their sexual exploits."

"Well, Joshua is married and Faith is your little sister."

"And?"

"You are an endless frustration."

So was she, but he had a feeling if he pointed that out at the moment it wouldn't end well for him.

This wasn't a real argument. He'd already won. She was here with him, regardless of her protestations. He'd risk her wrath when it was actually necessary.

"Jonathan will not be in today, if that helps. At least, he's not planning on it as far as I know."

She made a noise halfway between a snort and clearing her throat. "The idea of dealing with Jonathan bothers me a lot less than dealing with your siblings."

"Well. We have to deal with them eventually. There's no reason to wait. It's not going to get less uncomfortable. I could probably make an argument for the fact that the longer we wait the more uncomfortable we'll get."

"You know. If you could be just slightly less practical sometimes, it would make us mere mortals feel a whole lot better."

"What do you mean?"

"Everything is black-and-white to you. Everything is…easy." She looked like she actually meant that.

"That isn't true," he said. "Things are easy for me when I can line them out. When I can make categories and columns, so whenever I can do that, I do it. Life has variables. Too many. If you turn it into math, there's one answer. If the answer makes sense, go with that."

"But life *isn't* math," she said. "There's not one answer. We could hide this from everyone until we feel like not hiding it. We could have driven separate cars."

"Hiding it is illogical."

"Not when you're a woman who just lost her virginity and you're a little embarrassed and don't necessarily want everyone to know."

"You know," he said, his tone dry, "you don't have to walk in and announce that you just lost your virginity."

"I am aware of that," she snapped. She tapped her fingernails on the armrest of the passenger door. "You know. You're a pretty terrible cowboy. What with the sports car."

"I have a truck for the ranch. But I also have money. So driving multiple cars is my prerogative."

She made a scoffing sound. And she didn't speak to him for the rest of the drive over.

For his part, Isaiah wasn't bothered by her mood. After she had come to speak to him in the early hours of the morning, he had taken her back to bed where he had kept her up for the rest of the night. She had responded to every touch, every kiss.

She might be angry at him, but she wanted him. And that would sustain them when nothing else would.

The whole plan was genius, really.

Now that they'd discovered this attraction between them, she really was the perfect wife for him. He liked her. She would be a fantastic mother. She was an amazing partner, and he already knew it. And then there was this…this heat.

It was more than he'd imagined getting out of a relationship.

So he could handle moments of spikiness in the name of all they had going for them.

They drove through the main street of town in silence, and Isaiah took stock of how the place looked, altered for Christmas. All the little shops adorned with strings of white lights and evergreen boughs.

It made him wonder about Poppy's life growing up. About the Christmases she might have had.

"Did you celebrate Christmas when you were a child?" he asked.

"What?"

"The Christmas decorations made me wonder. We did. Just…very normal Christmases. Like movies. A tree, family. Gifts and a dry turkey."

She laughed. "I have a hard time believing your mother ever made a dry turkey."

"My grandma made dry turkey," he said. "She died when I was in high school. But before then…"

"It sounds lovely," Poppy said. "Down to the dry turkey. I had some very nice Christmases. But there was never a routine. I also had years where there was no celebration. I don't have…very strong feelings about Christmas, actually. I don't have years of tradition to make into something special."

When they pulled into the office just outside of town, he parked, and Poppy wasted no time in getting out of the car and striding toward the building. Like she was trying to outrun appearing with him.

He shook his head and got out of the car, following behind her. Not rushing.

If she wanted to play a game, she was welcome to it. But she was the one who was bothered. Not him.

He walked into the craftsman-style building behind her, and directly into the front seating area, where his sister, Faith, was curled on a chair with her feet underneath her and a cup of coffee beside her.

Joshua was sitting in a chair across from her, his legs propped up on the coffee table.

"Are you having car trouble?" Faith directed that question at Poppy.

Poppy looked from Isaiah to Joshua and then to Faith. And he could sense when she'd made a decision. Her shoulders squared, her whole body became as stiff as a board, as if she were bracing herself.

She took a deep breath.

"No," she said. "I drove over with your brother because I had sex with him last night."

Then she swept out of the room and stomped down the hall toward her office. He heard the door slam decisively behind her.

Two heads swiveled toward him, wide eyes on his face.

"What?" his sister asked.

"I don't think she could have made it any clearer," he said, walking over to the coffeepot and pouring himself a cup.

"You had sex with Poppy," Joshua confirmed.

"Yes," Isaiah responded, not bothering to look at his brother.

"You... *You.* And Poppy."

"Yes," he said again.

"Why do I know this?" Faith asked, covering her ears.

"I didn't know she was going to make a pronounce-ment," Isaiah said. He felt a smile tug at his lips. "Though, she was kind of mad at me. So. I feel like this is her way of getting back at me for saying the change in our rela-tionship was simple."

Faith's eyes bugged out. "You told her that it was sim-ple. The whole thing. The two of you...*friends*... *Poppy*, an employee of the past ten years... *Sleeping together*." Faith was sputtering.

"It was good sex, Faith," he commented.

Faith's look contorted into one of abject horror, and she withdrew into her chair.

"There's more," Isaiah said. "I'm getting married to her."

"You are...*marrying Poppy*?" Now Faith was just get-ting shrill.

"Yes."

"You don't have to marry someone just because you have sex with them," Joshua pointed out.

"I'm aware of that, but you know I want to get mar-ried. And considering she and I have chemistry, I figured we might as well get married."

"But... Poppy?" Joshua asked.

"Why *not* Poppy?"

"Are you in love with her?" Faith asked.

"I care about her more than I care about almost any-one."

"You didn't answer my question," Faith said.

"Did no one respond to your ad?" Joshua was clearly happy to skip over questions about feelings.

Isaiah nodded. "Several women did. Poppy inter-viewed six of them yesterday."

Joshua looked like he wanted to say something that he bit back. "And you didn't like any of them?"

"I didn't meet any of them."

"So," Faith said slowly, "yesterday you had her interviewing women to marry you. And then last night you… hooked up with her."

"You're skipping a step. Yesterday afternoon she accused me of looking for a wife who was basically an assistant. For my life. And that was when I realized… She's actually the one I'm looking for."

"That is… The least romantic thing I've ever heard," Faith said.

"Romance is not a requirement for me."

"What about Poppy?"

He lifted a shoulder. "She could have said no."

"Could she have?" Faith asked. "I mean, no offense, Isaiah, but it's difficult to say no to you when you get something in your head."

"You don't want to hear this," Isaiah said, "but particularly after last night, I can say confidently that Poppy and I suit each other just fine."

"You're right," Faith said, "I don't want to hear it." She stood up, grabbing her coffee and heading back toward her office.

"I hope you know what you're doing," Joshua said slowly.

Isaiah looked over at his brother. "What about any of this doesn't look like I know what I'm doing?"

"Getting engaged to Poppy?" Joshua asked.

"You like Poppy," Isaiah pointed out.

"I do," Joshua said. "That's my concern. She's not like you. Your feelings are on a pretty deep freeze, Isaiah. I shouldn't have to tell you that."

"I don't know that I agree with you," he said.

"What's your stance on falling in love?"

"I've done it, and I'm not interested in doing it again."

"Has Poppy ever been in love before?" Joshua pressed.

Isaiah absolutely knew the answer to this question, not that it was any of his brother's business how he knew it. "No."

"Maybe she wants to be. And I imagine she wants her husband to love her."

"Poppy wants to be able to trust someone. She knows she can trust me. I know I can trust her. You can't get much better than that."

"I know you're anti-love... But what Danielle and I have..."

"What you and Danielle have is statistically improbable. There's no way you should have been able to place an ad in the paper for someone who is the antithesis of everything you should need in your life and fall madly in love with her. Additionally, I don't want that. I want stability."

"And my life looks terribly unstable to you?" Joshua asked.

"No. It doesn't. You forget, I was in a relationship for five years with a woman who turned out to be nothing like what I thought she was."

"You're still hung up on Rosalind?"

Isaiah shook his head. "Not at all. But I learned from my mistakes, Joshua. And the lesson there is that you can't actually trust those kinds of feelings. They blind you to reality."

"So you think I'm blind to reality?"

"And I hope it never bites your ass."

"What about Mom and Dad?"

"It's different," he said.

"How?"

"It's different for you too," Isaiah said. "I don't read people like you do. You know how to charm people. You know how to sense what they're feeling. How to turn the emotional tide of a room. I don't know how to do that. I have to trust my head because my heart doesn't give me a whole lot. What works for you isn't going to work for me."

"Just don't hurt her."

"I won't."

But then, Isaiah suddenly wasn't so sure. She was already hurt. Or at least, annoyed with him. And he wasn't quite sure what he was supposed to do about it.

He walked back toward Poppy's office and opened the door without knocking. She was sitting in her chair at her desk, not looking at anything in particular, and most definitely fuming.

"That was an unexpected little stunt," he said.

"You're not in charge of this," she pointed out. "If we are going to get married, it's a partnership. You don't get to manipulate me. You're not my boss in our marriage."

His lips twitched. "I could be your boss in the bedroom."

The color in her cheeks darkened. "I will allow that. However, in real life…"

"I get it."

He walked toward her and lowered himself to his knees in front of her, taking her chin in his hand. "I promise, I'm not trying to be a dick."

"Really?" He felt her tremble slightly beneath his touch.

He frowned. "I never try to be. I just am sometimes."

"Right."

"Joshua and Faith know. I mean, they already knew about the ad, and there was no way I was getting it by them that this wasn't related to that in some way."

"What did they say?"

"Joshua wants to make sure I don't hurt you."

She huffed a laugh. "Well. I'm team Joshua on that one."

"When do you want to tell my parents?" he asked. "We have our monthly dinner in three weeks."

"Let's…wait until then," she said.

"You want to wait that long?"

"Yes," she said. "I'm not…ready."

He would give her that. He knew that sometimes Poppy found interactions with family difficult. He'd always attributed that to her upbringing. "I understand. In the meantime, I want you to move your things into my house."

"But what about *my* house?" she asked.

"Obviously, you're coming to live on my ranch."

"No sex until we get married." The words came out fast and desperate.

He frowned. "We've already had sex. Several times."

"And that was…good. To establish our connection. It's established. And I want to wait now."

"Okay," he said.

She blinked. "Good."

He didn't think she'd hold to that. But Poppy was obviously trying to gain a sense of power here, and he was happy to give it to her.

Of course, that didn't mean he wouldn't try to seduce her.

Chapter Seven

Poppy didn't have time to think much about her decision over the next few days. Isaiah had a moving company take all of her things to his house, and before she knew it, she was settling into a routine that was different from anything she had ever imagined she'd be part of.

They went to work together. They spent all day on the job, being very much the same Poppy and Isaiah they'd always been. But then they went home together.

And sexual tension seemed to light their every interaction on fire. She swore she could feel his body heat from across the room.

He had given her a room, her own space. But she could tell he was confused by her abstinence edict.

Even she was wondering why she was torturing herself.

Being with him physically was wonderful. But she felt completely overwhelmed by him.

She'd spent ten years secretly pining for him. Then in one moment, he'd decided he wanted something different, something more, and they'd been on their way to it. Isaiah had snapped his fingers and changed her world, and she didn't recognize even one part of it anymore.

Not even the ceiling she saw every morning when she opened her eyes.

She had to figure out a way to have power in this relationship. She was the one who was in love, and that meant she was at a disadvantage already. He was the one who got to keep his house. He was the one with the family she would become a part of.

She had to do something to hold on to her sanity.

It was hard to resist him though. So terribly hard.

When she felt lonely and scared at night, worrying for the future in a bedroom that was just down the hall from his, she wished—like that first night—that he would do a little less respecting of her commandments. That he would at least try to tempt her away from her resolve. Because if he did, she was sure it would fail.

But he didn't. So it was up to her to hang on to that edict.

No matter what.

Even when they had to behave like a normal couple for his parents' sakes.

And she was dreading the dinner at his parents' house tonight. With all of her soul.

Dreading having to tell a vague story about how they had suddenly realized their feelings for each other and were now making it official.

The fact that it was a farce hurt too badly.

But tonight they would actually discuss setting a wedding date.

A wedding date.

She squeezed her eyes shut for a moment, and then looked up at the gorgeous, custom-made cabinets in Isaiah's expansive kitchen. Maybe she should have a glass of wine before dinner. Or four. To calm her nerves.

She was already dressed and ready to go, but Isaiah had been out taking care of his horses, and she was still waiting for him to finish showering.

Part of her wished she could have simply joined him. But she'd made an edict and she should be able to stick to it.

She wondered if there was any point in preserving a sanity that was so frazzled as it was. Probably not.

Isaiah appeared a moment later, barefoot, in a pair of dark jeans with a button-up shirt. He was wearing his cowboy hat, looking sexy and disreputable, and exactly like the kind of guy who had been tailor-made for her from her deepest fantasies.

Or, maybe it was just that *he* was her fantasy.

Then he reached into his pocket and pulled out a black velvet box.

"No," she said.

He held it up. "No?"

"I didn't… I didn't know you were going to…"

"You have to have a ring before we see my parents."

"But then I'm going to walk in with a ring and they're going to know." As excuses went, it was a weak one. They were going to inform his parents of their engagement anyway.

They were engaged.

It was so strange. She didn't feel engaged to him.

Maybe because you won't sleep with him?

No. Because he doesn't love me.

She had a snotty response at the ready for her internal critic. Because really.

"They won't know you're engaged to me. And even so, were not trying to make it a surprise. We're just telling them in person."

The ring inside the box was stunning. Ornately designed, rather than a simple solitaire.

"It's vintage," he said. "It was part of a museum collection, on display in Washington, DC. I saw it online and I contacted the owner."

"You bought a vintage ring out of a museum." It wasn't a question so much as a recitation of what he'd just said.

"It was a privately owned collection." As if that explained it. "What?" he asked, frowning after she hadn't spoken for a few moments. "You don't look happy."

She didn't know how to describe what she was feeling. It was the strangest little dream come true. Something she would never have even given a thought to. Ever. She never thought about what kind of engagement ring she might want. And if she had, she would have asked for something small, and from the mall. Not from...*a museum collection.*

"I know how much you like vintage. And I know you don't like some of the issues surrounding the diamond trade."

She had gone on a small tirade in the office after seeing the movie *Blood Diamond* a few years ago. Just once. It wasn't like it was a cause she talked about regularly. "You...listened to that?"

"Yes," he responded.

Sometimes she wondered if everybody misunderstood him, including her. If no one knew just how deeply he held on to each moment. To people. Remembering a detail like that wasn't the mark of an unemotional man. It seemed...remarkably sentimental for him to remember such a small thing about her. Especially something that—at the time—wouldn't have been relevant to him.

She saw Isaiah as such a stark guy. A man who didn't engage in anything unnecessary. Or hold on to anything he didn't need to hold on to.

But that was obviously just what he showed the world. What he showed her.

It wasn't all of him.

It was so easy to think of him as cold, emotionless. He would be the first person to say a relationship could be a math equation for him, after all.

But remembering her feelings on diamonds wasn't math. It was personal.

There was no other man on earth—no other person on earth—who understood her the way Isaiah Grayson did.

She hadn't realized it until this moment. She'd made a lot of accusations about him being oblivious, but she was just as guilty.

And now...

She wanted to wear his ring. The ring he'd chosen for her with such thought and...well, extravagance. Because who had ever given her that kind of thought before? No one.

And certainly no one had ever been so extravagant for her.

Only him.

Only ever him.

He walked over to where she was sitting and took the ring out of the box, sliding it onto her finger. He didn't get down on one knee. But then, that didn't surprise her.

More to the point, it didn't matter.

The ring itself didn't even matter. It was the thought. It was the man.

Her man.

It was how much she wanted it that scared her. That was the real problem. She wanted to wear his ring more than she wanted anything in the world.

And she was going to take it.

"Are you ready to go to dinner?"

She swallowed hard, looking down at the perfect, sparkly rock on her finger.

"Yes," she said. "I'm ready."

Isaiah felt a sense of calm and completion when they pulled into his parents' house that night. The small, modest farmhouse looked the same as it ever did, the yellow porch light cheery in the dim evening. It was always funny to him that no matter how successful Devlin, Joshua, Faith or Isaiah became, his parents refused to allow their children to buy them a new house. Or even to upgrade the old one at all.

They were perfectly happy with what they had.

He envied that feeling of being content. Being so certain what home was.

He liked his house, but he didn't yet feel the need to stop changing his circumstances. He wasn't settled.

He imagined that this new step forward with Poppy would change that. Though, he would like it if she dropped the sex embargo.

He wasn't quite sure why she was so bound by it, though she had said something about white weddings and how she was a traditional girl at heart, even though he didn't believe any of it since she had happily jumped into bed with him a few weeks earlier.

It was strange. He'd spent ten years not having sex with Poppy. But now that they'd done it a few times, it was damn near impossible to wait ten days, much less however long it was going to be until their wedding. He was fairly confident she wouldn't stick to her proclamation that whole time, though. At least, he had been confident until nearly three weeks had passed without her knocking on his bedroom door.

But then, Poppy had been a twenty-eight-year-old virgin. Her commitment to celibacy was much greater than his own. He might have spent years abstaining from relationships, but he had not abstained from sex.

They got out of the car, and she started to charge ahead of him, as she had done on the way into the office that first morning after they'd made love. He was not going to allow that this time.

He caught up with her, wrapping his arm around her waist. "If you walk into my parents' living room and announce that we had sex I may have to punish you."

She turned her head sharply, her eyes wide. "Punish me? What sort of caveman proclamation is that?"

"Exactly the kind a bratty girl like you needs if you're plotting evil."

"I'm *not* plotting evil," she said, her cheeks turning pink.

He examined her expression closely. Knowing Poppy like he did, he could read her better than he could read just about anyone else. She was annoyed with him. They certainly weren't back on the same footing they had been.

But she wanted him. She couldn't hide that, even now, standing in front of his parents' home.

"But you're a little bit intrigued about what I might do," he whispered.

She wiggled against him, and he could tell she absolutely, grudgingly was intrigued. "Not at all."

"You're a liar."

"You have a bad habit of pointing that out." She sounded crabby about that.

"I don't see the point of lies. In the end, they don't make anything less uncomfortable."

"Most people find small lies a great comfort," she disagreed.

"I don't," he said, a hot rock lodging itself in his chest. "I don't allow lies on any level, Poppy. That, you do have to know about me."

He'd already been in a relationship with a woman who had lied to him. And he hadn't questioned it. Because he'd imagined that love was somehow the same as having two-way trust.

"I won't lie to you," she said softly, brushing her fingertips over his lips.

Instantly, he felt himself getting hard. She hadn't touched him in the weeks since he'd spent the night in her bed. But now was not the time.

He nodded once, and then tightened his hold on her as they continued to walk up the porch. Then he knocked.

"Why do you knock at your parents' house?"

"I don't live here."

The door opened, and his mother appeared, looking between the two of them, her eyes searching.

"Isaiah? Poppy."

"Hi," Poppy said, not moving away from his hold.

"Hi, Mom," Isaiah said.

"I imagine you have something to tell us," his mom said, stepping away from the door.

Isaiah led Poppy into the cozy room. His father was

sitting in his favorite chair, a picture of the life he'd had growing up still intact. The feeling it gave him… It was the kind of life he wanted.

"We have something to tell you," Isaiah said.

Then the front door opened again and his brother Devlin and his wife, Mia, who was heavily pregnant, walked into the room.

"We brought chips," Mia said, stopping cold when she saw Isaiah and Poppy standing together.

"Yay for chips," Poppy said.

Then Joshua, Danielle and baby Riley came in, and with the exception of Faith, the entire audience was present.

"Do you want to wait for Faith?" his mom asked.

"No," Isaiah said. "Poppy and I are engaged."

His mother and father stared at them, and then his mother smiled. "That's wonderful!" She closed the distance between them and pulled him in for a hug.

She did the same to Poppy, who was shrinking slightly next to him, like she was her wilting namesake.

His father made his way over to them and extended his hand; Isaiah shook it. "A good decision," his dad said, looking at Poppy. And then, he hugged her, kissing her on the cheek. "Welcome to the family, Poppy."

Poppy made a sound that was somewhere between a gasp and a sob, but she stayed rooted next to his side.

This was what he wanted. This feeling. There was warmth here. And it was easy. There was closeness.

And now that he had Poppy, it was perfect.

Poppy didn't know how she made it through dinner. The food tasted like glue, which was ridiculous, since Nancy Grayson made the best food, and it always tasted like heaven. But Poppy had a feeling that her taste buds were defective, along with her very soul. She felt…wonderful and awful. All at once.

The Graysons were such an amazing family, and she loved Isaiah's parents. But they thought Isaiah and Poppy were in love. They thought Isaiah had finally shared his heart with someone.

And he didn't understand their assumptions. He thought they wanted marriage for him. A traditional family. But that wasn't really what they wanted.

They wanted his happiness.

And Isaiah was still… He was still in the same place he had always been, emotionally. Unwilling to open up. Unwilling to take a risk because it was so difficult. They thought she'd changed him, and she hadn't.

She was…enabling him.

She was enabling him and it was terrible.

After dinner, Poppy helped Nancy clear the dishes away.

"Poppy," she said. "Can I talk to you?"

Poppy shifted. "Of course."

"I've always known you would be perfect for him," Nancy said. "But I'm hesitant to push Isaiah into anything because he just digs in. They're all like that to a degree… But he's the biggest puzzle. He always has been. Since he was a boy. Either angry and very emotional, or seemingly emotionless. I've always known that wasn't true. People often find him detached, but I think it's because he cares so much."

Poppy agreed, and it went right along with what she'd been thinking when he'd given her the ring. That there were hidden spaces in him he didn't show anyone. And that had to be out of protection. Which showed that he did feel. He felt an awful lot.

"He's a good man," Nancy continued. "And I think he'll be a good husband to you. I'm just so glad you're going to be the one to be his wife, because you are exactly what he needs. You always have been."

"I don't... He's not difficult." Poppy looked down at her hands, her throat getting tight. "He's one of the most special people I know."

Nancy reached out and squeezed Poppy's hands. "That's all any mother wants the wife of her son to think."

Poppy felt even more terrible. Like a fraud. Yes, she would love Isaiah with everything she had, but she wasn't sure she was helping him at all.

"I have something for you," Nancy said. "Come with me."

She led Poppy back to the master bedroom, the only room in the house Poppy had never gone into. Nancy walked across the old wooden floor and the threadbare braided rug on top, moving to a highboy dresser and opening up a jewelry box.

"I have my mother's wedding band here. I know that you like...old-fashioned things. It didn't seem right for Danielle. And I know Faith won't want it. You're the one it was waiting for." Nancy turned, holding it out to Poppy.

Poppy swallowed hard. "Thank you," she said. "I'll save it until the... Until the wedding."

"It can stay here, for safekeeping, if you want."

"If you could," Poppy said. "But I want to wear it. Once Isaiah and I are married." Married. She was going to marry Isaiah. "Thank you."

Nancy gave Poppy another hug, and Poppy felt like her heart was splintering. "I know that your own mother won't be at the wedding," Mrs. Grayson said. "But we won't make a bride's side and a groom's side. It's just going to be our family. You're our family now, Poppy. You're not alone."

"Thank you," Poppy said, barely able to speak.

She walked back out into the living room on numb feet to find Isaiah standing by the front door with his hat on. "Are you ready to go?" he asked.

"Yes," she said.

She got another round of hugs from the entire family, each one adding weight to her already burdened conscience.

When they got out, they made their way back to the car, and as soon as he closed the door behind them, Poppy's insides broke apart.

They pulled out of the driveway, and a tear slid down her cheeks, and she turned her face away from him to keep him from seeing.

"I can't do this."

Chapter Eight

"What?"

"I can't do this," she said, feeling panic rising inside her now. "I'm sorry. But your parents think that I've... transformed you in some way. That I'm healing you. And instead, I'm enabling you to keep on doing that thing you love to do, where you run away from emotion and make everything about…"

"Maybe I just don't feel it," he said. "Maybe I'm not running from anything because there isn't anything there for me to run from. Why would you think differently?"

"Because you loved Rosalind…"

"Maybe. Or maybe I didn't. You're trying to make it seem like I feel things the exact same way other people do, and that isn't fair. I don't."

"I'm not trying to. It's just that your parents think—"

"I don't give a damn what my parents think. You were

the one who wanted them to believe this was a normal kind of courtship. I don't care either way."

"Of course you don't."

"This is ridiculous, Poppy. You can't pull out of our agreement now that everybody knows."

"I could," she said. "I could, and I could quit. Like I was going to do."

"Because you would find it so easy to leave me?"

"No!"

"You're doing this because you feel guilty? I don't believe it. I think you're running away. You accuse me of not dealing with my feelings. But you were a twenty-eight-year-old virgin. You've refused to let me touch you in the time since we first made love, and now that you've had to endure hugs from my entire family suddenly you're trying to escape like a feral cat."

"I am not a feral cat." The comparison was unflattering.

And a little bit too close to the truth.

"I think you are. I think you're fine as long as somebody leaves a can of tuna for you out by the Dumpster, but the minute they try to bring you in the house you're all claws and teeth."

"No one has ever left me a can of tuna by a Dumpster." If he wanted claws, she was on the verge of giving them to him. This entire conversation was getting ridiculous.

"This isn't over." He started to drive them back toward his house.

"It is," she protested.

"No."

"Take me back to *my* house," she insisted.

"My house *is* your house. You agreed to marry me."

"And now I'm *un*agreeing," she insisted.

"And I think you're full of shit," he said, his tone so sharp it could have easily sliced right through her. "I think you're a hypocrite. Going on about what I need to do. Worrying about my emotional health when your own is in a much worse place."

She huffed, clenching her hands into fists and looking away from him. She said nothing for the rest of the drive, and then when they pulled up to the house, Isaiah was out of the car much quicker than she was, moving over to her side and pulling open the door. Then he reached into the car, unbuckled her and literally lifted her out as though she were a child. Holding her in his arms, he carried her up the steps toward the house.

"What the hell are you doing?" she shouted.

"What I should have done weeks ago."

"Making the transformation from man to caveman complete?"

He slid his hand down toward her ass and heat rioted through her. Even now, when she should be made of nothing but rage, she responded to him. Dammit.

"Making you remember why we're doing this."

"For your convenience," she hissed.

"Because I can't want another woman," he said, his voice rough, his eyes blazing. "Not now. And we both know you don't want another man."

She made a poor show of kicking her feet slightly as he carried her inside. She could unman him if she wanted to, but she wouldn't. And they both knew it.

"You can't do this," she protested weakly. "It violates all manner of HR rules."

"Too bad for you that I own the company. I *am* HR."

"I'm going to organize an ethics committee," she groused.

"This is personal business. The company has nothing to do with it."

"Is it? I think it's business for you, period, like everything else."

"It's personal," he ground out, "because I've been inside you. Don't you dare pretend that isn't true. Though it all makes sense to me now. Why you wanted me to stay away from you for the past few weeks."

"Because I'm just not that into you?" she asked as he carried her up the stairs.

"No. Because you're *too* into it."

She froze, ice gathering at the center of her chest. She didn't want him to know. He had been so clueless up until this point.

"You're afraid that I'll be able to convince you to stay because the sex is so good."

Okay. Well, he was a little bit onto it. But not really.

Just a little bit off base, was her Isaiah.

"You're in charge of everything," she said. "I didn't think it would hurt you to have to wait."

"I don't play games."

"Sadly for you, the rest of the world does. We play games when we need to. We play games to protect ourselves. We play games because it's a lot more palatable than wandering around making proclamations like you do."

"I don't understand games," he said. He flung open the door to his bedroom and walked them both inside. "But I understand this." He claimed her mouth. And she should have... She should have told him no. Because of course he would have stopped. But she didn't.

Instead, she let him consume her.

Then she began to consume him back. She wanted

him. That was the problem. As much as everything that had happened back at the Grayson house terrified her, she wanted him.

Terrified. That wasn't the word she had used before. Isaiah was the one who had said she was afraid. And maybe she was. But she didn't know what to do about it.

It was like the time she had gone to live with a couple who hadn't been expecting a little girl as young as she was. They had been surprised, and clearly, their house hadn't been ready for a boisterous six-year-old. There had been a list of things she wasn't allowed to touch. And so she had lived in that house for all of three weeks, afraid to leave feet print on the carpet, afraid of touching breakable objects. Afraid that somehow she was going to destroy the beautiful place she found herself in simply because of who she was.

Because she was the wrong fit.

That was what it had felt like at the Graysons' tonight. Like she was surrounded by all this lovely, wonderful love, and somehow, it just wasn't for her. Wasn't to be.

There was more to it than that, of course, but that was the *real* reason she was freaking out, and she knew it.

But it didn't make her *wrong*.

It also didn't make her want to stop what was happening with Isaiah right now.

She was lonely. She had been a neglected child, and then she had lived in boisterous houses full of lots of children, which could sometimes feel equally lonely. She had never had a close romantic relationship as an adult. She was making friends in Copper Ridge, but moving around as often as she had made it difficult for her to have close lifelong friends. Isaiah was that friend, essentially.

And being close to him like this was a balm for a wound that ran very, very deep.

"You think this is fake?" he asked, his voice like gravel.

He bent down in front of her, grabbing hold of her skirt and drawing it down her legs without bothering to take off her shoes. Her shirt went next.

"Sit down," he commanded, and her legs were far too weak to disobey him. He looked up at her, those gray eyes intent on hers. "Take your bra off for me."

With shaking hands, she found herself obeying him.

"I imagine you're going to report me to HR for this too." The smile that curved his lips told her he didn't much care.

"I might," she responded, sliding her bra down her arms and throwing it onto the floor.

"Well, then I might have to keep you trapped here so you can't tell anyone."

"This is a major infraction."

"Maybe. But then again. I am the boss. I suppose I could choose to reprimand you for such behavior."

"I… I suppose you could."

"You're being a very bad girl," he said, hooking his fingers in the waistband of her panties and pulling them down to her knees. "Very bad."

Panic skittered in her stomach, and she had no idea how to respond. To Isaiah being like this, so playful. To him being like this and also staring at her right where he was staring at her.

"You need to remember who the boss is," he said, moving his hands around her lower back and sliding them down to cup her ass. Then he jerked her forward, and she gasped as he pressed a kiss to the inside of her thigh.

Then he went higher, and higher still, while she trembled.

She couldn't believe he was about to do this. She wanted him to. But she was also scared. Self-conscious. Excited. It was a whole lot of things.

But then, everything with Isaiah was a lot.

He squeezed her with both hands and then moved his focus to her center, his tongue sliding through her slick folds. She clapped her hand over her mouth to keep from making an extremely embarrassing noise, but she had a feeling he could still hear it, muffled or not.

Because he chuckled.

Isaiah, who was often humorless, chuckled with his mouth where it was, and his filthy intentions were obvious even to her.

And then he started to show her what he meant by punishment. He teased her with his tongue, with his fingers, with his mouth. He scraped her inner thigh with the edge of his teeth before returning his attention to where she was most needy for him. But every time she got close he would back off. He would move somewhere else. Kiss her stomach, her wrist, her hand. He would take his attention off of exactly where she needed him.

"Please," she begged.

"Bad girls don't get to come," he said, the edge in his voice sharp like a knife.

Those words just about pushed her over the edge all on their own.

"I thought you said you didn't play games," she choked out.

"Let me rephrase that," he said, looking up at her, a wicked smile curving his mouth. "I only play games in the bedroom."

He pressed two fingers into her before laughing at her again with his tongue, taking her all the way to the edge again before backing off. He knew her body better than she did, knew exactly where to touch her, and where not to. Knew the exact pressure and speed. How to rev her up and bring her back.

He was evil, and in that moment, she felt like she hated him as much as she had ever loved him.

"Tell me what you want," he said.

"You *know.*"

"I do," he responded. "But you have to tell me."

"You're mean," she panted.

"I'm a very, very mean man," he agreed, sounding unrepentant as he slid one finger back through her folds. Tormenting. Teasing. "And you like it."

"I don't," she insisted.

"You do. Which is your real problem with all of this. You want me. And you want this. Even though you know you probably shouldn't."

"Well, what about you?" she asked, breathing hard. "You want it too. Or you wouldn't be trying so hard to convince me to go through with this marriage. Maybe *you* should beg."

"I'm on my knees," he said. "Isn't that like begging?"

"That's not—"

But she was cut off because his lips connected with that most sensitive part of her again. She could do nothing but feel.

She was so wet, so ready for him, so very hollow and achy that she couldn't stand for him to continue. It was going to kill her.

Or she was going to kill him. One of the two.

"Tell me," he whispered in her ear. "Tell me what you want."

"You," she said.

"Me?"

"You. Inside me. Please."

She didn't have to ask him twice.

Instead, she found herself being lifted up, brought down onto the bed, sitting astride him. He maneuvered her so her slick entrance was poised just above his hardness. And then he thrust up, inside her.

She gasped.

"You want to be in charge? Go ahead."

It was a challenge. And it gave her anything but control, when she was so desperate for him, when each move over him betrayed just how desperate she was.

He knew it too. The bastard.

But she couldn't stop, because she was so close, and now that she was on top she could…

Stars exploded behind her eyes, her internal muscles pulsing, her entire body shaking as her orgasm rocked her. All it had taken was a couple of times rocking back and forth, just a couple of times applying pressure where it was needed.

He growled, flipping her over and pinning her hands above her head. "You were just a bit too easy on me."

He kissed her then, and it was like a beast had been unleashed inside him. He was rough and untamed, and his response called up desire inside her again much sooner than she would have thought possible.

But it was Isaiah.

And with him, she had a feeling it would always be like this.

Always?

She pushed that mocking question aside.

She wasn't going to think about anything beyond this, right now.

She wasn't going to think about what she had told him before he carried her upstairs. About what she believed she deserved or didn't, about what she believed was possible and wasn't.

She was just going to feel.

This time, when the wave broke over her, he was swept up in it too, letting out a hoarse growl as he found his own release.

And when it was over, she didn't have the strength to get up. Didn't have the strength to walk away from him.

Tomorrow. Tomorrow would sort itself out.

Maybe for now she could hang on to the fantasy.

Poppy woke up in the middle of the night, curled around Isaiah's body. Something strange had woken her, and it wasn't the fact that she was sharing a bed with Isaiah.

It wasn't the fact that her resolve had weakened quite so badly last night.

There was something else.

She couldn't think what, or why it had woken her out of a dead sleep. She rolled away from him and padded into the bathroom that was just off his bedroom. She stood there for a moment staring at the mirror, at the woman looking back at her. Who was disheveled and had raccoon eyes because she hadn't taken her makeup off before allowing Isaiah to rock her world last night.

And then it suddenly hit her.

Because she was standing in a bathroom and staring at the mirror, and it felt like a strange kind of déjà vu.

It was the middle of the month. And she absolutely should've started her period by now.

She was two days late.

And she and Isaiah hadn't used a condom.

"No," she whispered.

It was too coincidental.

She went back into the bedroom and dressed as quickly and quietly as possible. And then she grabbed her purse and went downstairs.

She had to know.

She wouldn't sleep until she did. There were a few twenty-four-hour places in Tolowa, and she was going over there right now.

And that was how, at five in the morning in a public restroom, Poppy Sinclair's life changed forever.

Chapter Nine

When Isaiah woke up the next morning, Poppy wasn't in bed with him. He was irritated, but he imagined she was still trying to hold on to some semblance of control with her little game.

She was going to end up agreeing to marry him. He was fairly confident in that. But what he'd said about her being like a stray cat, he'd meant. She might not like the comparison, but it was true enough. Now that he wanted to domesticate her, she was preparing to run.

But her common sense would prevail. It didn't benefit her *not* to marry him.

And she couldn't deny the chemistry between them. He wasn't being egotistical about that. What they had between them was explosive. It *couldn't* be denied.

When he got downstairs, he saw Poppy sitting at the kitchen table. She was dressed in the same outfit she'd been wearing last night, and she was staring straight ahead, her eyes fixed on her clenched fists.

"Good morning," he said.

"No, it isn't," she responded. She looked up at him, and then she frowned. "Could you put a shirt on?"

He looked down at his bare chest. He was only wearing a pair of jeans. "No."

"I feel like this is a conversation we should have with your shirt on." She kept her gaze focused on the wall behind him.

He crossed his arms over his chest. "I've decided I like the conversations I have with you without my shirt better."

"I'm not joking around, Isaiah."

"Then you don't have time for me to go get a shirt. What's going on?"

"I'm pregnant." She looked like she was delivering the news of a death to him.

"That's…" He let the words wash over him, took a moment to turn them over and analyze what they made him feel. He felt…calm. "That's good," he said.

"Is it?" Poppy looked borderline hysterical.

"Yes," he said, feeling completely confident and certain now. "We both want children."

It was sooner than he'd anticipated, of course, but he wanted children. And…there was something relieving about it. It made this marriage agreement feel much more final. Made it feel like more of a done deal.

Poppy was his.

He'd spent last night in bed with her working to affirm that.

A pregnancy just made it that much more final.

"I broke up with you last night," she pointed out.

"Yes, you did a very good impression of a woman who was broken up with me. Particularly when you cried out my name during your… Was it your third or fourth orgasm?"

"That has nothing to do with whether or not we should be together. Whether or not we should get married."

"Well, now there's no question about whether or not we're getting married. You're having my baby."

"This is not 1953. That is not a good enough reason to get married."

He frowned. "I disagree."

"I'm not going to just jump into marriage with you."

"You're being unreasonable. You were more than willing to jump into marriage with me when you agreed to my proposal. Now suddenly when we're having a child you can't *jump into* anything? You continually *jump into* my bed, Poppy, so you can't claim we don't have the necessary ingredients to make a marriage work."

"Do you love me?" There was a challenge in her eyes, a stubborn set to her chin.

"I care very much about you," he responded.

It was the truth. The honest truth. She was one of the most important people in his life.

"But you're not in love with me."

"I already told you—"

"Yes. You're not going to do love. Well, you know what? I've decided that it feels fake if we're not in love."

"The fact that you're pregnant with my child indicates it's real enough."

"You don't understand. You don't understand anything."

"You sound like a sixteen-year-old girl having an argument with her parents. You would rather have some idealistic concept that may never actually happen than make a family with me?"

"I would rather… I would rather none of this was happening."

It felt like a slap, and he didn't know why.

That she didn't want him. Didn't seem to want the baby. He couldn't sort out the feeling it gave him. The sharp, stabbing sensation right around the area of his heart.

But he could reason through it. He was right, and her hysterics didn't change that.

There was an order to things. An order of operations, like math. That didn't change based on how people felt.

He understood…nothing right now. Nothing happening inside him, or outside him.

But he knew what was right. And he knew he could count on his brain.

It was the surest thing. The most certain.

So he went with that.

"But it is happening," he said, his voice tight. "You are far too practical to discard something real for some silly fantasy."

Her face drained of color. "So it's a *fantasy* that someone could love me."

"That isn't what I meant. It's a fantasy that you're going to find someone else who can take care of you like I can. Who is also the father of your child. Who can make you come the way that I do."

"Maybe it's just easy for me. You don't know. Neither do I. I've only had the one lover."

That kicked up the fire and heat in his stomach, and he shoved it back down because this was not about what he felt. Not about what his body wanted.

"Trust me," he bit out. "It's never this good."

"I can't do this." She pressed a balled-up fist to her eyes.

"That's too bad," he said. "Because you will."

Resolve strengthened in him like iron. She was upset. But there was only one logical way forward. It was the only thing that made sense. And he was not going to let her take a different route. He just wasn't.

"I don't have to, Isaiah."

"You want your child growing up like you did? Being shuffled between homes?"

She looked like he'd hit her. "Foster care is not the same as sharing custody, and you know that. Don't you dare compare the two. I would have been thrilled to have two involved parents, even if I did have to change houses on the weekends. I didn't have that, and I never have had that. Don't talk about things you don't understand."

"I understand well enough. You're being selfish."

"I'm being *reasonable*!"

Reasonable.

Reasonable to her was them not being together. Reasonable to her was shoving him out of her life now that he'd realized just how essential she was.

"How is it reasonable to deny your child a chance at a family?" he asked. "All of us. Together. At my parents' house for dinners. Aunts and uncles and cousins. How is it unreasonable for me to want to share that with you instead of keeping my life and yours separate?"

"Isaiah…"

He was right, though. And what he wanted wasn't really about what he wanted. It was about logic.

And he wasn't above being heavy-handed to prove that point.

"If you don't marry me, I'm going to pursue full custody of our child," he said, the words landing heavily in the room.

Her head popped up. "You what?"

"And believe me, I'll get it. I have money. I have a family to back me up. I can make this very difficult for you. I don't want to, Poppy. That's not my goal. But I will have my way."

The look on her face, the abject betrayal, almost made him feel something like regret. Almost.

"I thought you were my friend," she said. "I thought you cared about me."

"I do. Which is why I'm prepared to do this. The best thing. The right thing. I'm not going to allow you to hurt our child in the name of friendship. How is that friendship?"

"Caring about someone doesn't just mean running them over until they do what you want. Friendship and caring goes both ways." She pressed her hand to her chest. "What I feel—*what I want*—has to matter."

"I know what you *should* want," he insisted.

If she would only listen. If she could, she'd understand what he was doing. In the end, it would be better if they were together. There was no scenario where their being apart would work, and if he had to play hardball to get her there, he damn well would.

"That isn't how wanting works. It's not how feelings work." She stood up, and she lifted her fist and slammed it down onto his chest. "It's not how any of this works, you robot."

He drew back, shock assaulting him. Poppy was one of the only people who had never looked at him that way before. Poppy had always taken pains to try to understand him.

"I'm a robot because I want to make sure my child has a family?" he asked, keeping his voice low.

"Because you don't care about what I want."

"I *want* you to want what *I* want," he said, holding her fist against his chest where she had hit him. "I want for this to work. How is that not feeling?"

"Because it isn't the *right feeling*."

Those words were like a whip cracking over his insides.

He had *never* had the right feelings. He already knew that. But with Poppy his feelings hadn't ever felt wrong before. *He* hadn't felt wrong before.

She'd been safe. Always.

But not now. Not now he'd started to care.

"I'm sorry," he said, his voice low. "I'm sorry I can't open up my chest and rearrange everything for you. I'm sorry that you agreed to be engaged to me, and then I didn't transform into a different man."

"I never said that's what I wanted."

"It *is* what you wanted. You wanted being with me to look like being with someone else. And you know what? If you weren't pregnant, I might've been able to let you walk away. But it's too late now. This is happening. The wedding is not off."

"The wedding *is* off," she insisted.

"Look at me," he said, his voice low, fierce. "Look at me and tell me if you think I was joking about taking custody."

Her eyes widened, her lips going slack. "I've always cared about you," she said, her voice shaking. "I've always tried to understand you. But I think maybe I was just pretending there was a heart in your chest when there never was."

"You can fling all the insults you want at me. If I'm really heartless, I don't see how you think that's going to make a difference."

Then she let out a frustrated cry and turned and fled the room, leaving him standing there feeling hollowed out.

Wishing that he was exactly what she had accused him of being.

But if he were heartless, then her words—her rejection—wouldn't feel like a knife through his chest.

If he were a robot, he wouldn't care that he couldn't find a way to order his feelings exactly to her liking.

But he did care.

He just had no idea what to do about it.

Chapter Ten

Ultimately, it wasn't Isaiah's threats that had her agreeing to his proposal.

It was what he'd said about family.

She was angry that it had gotten inside her head. That it had wormed its way into her heart.

No. Angry was an understatement.

She was *livid*.

She was also doing exactly what he had asked her to do.

The date for their wedding was now Christmas Eve. Of all the ridiculous things. Though, she supposed that would give her a much stronger association with the holiday than she'd had before.

His family was thrilled.

Poppy was not.

And she was still sleeping in her own room.

After that lapse when she had tried to break things off with him a week earlier, she had decided that she really, *really* needed Isaiah not to touch her for a while.

For his part, he was seething around the house with an intensity that she could feel.

But he hadn't tried to change her mind.

Which was good. Because the fact of the matter was he *would* be able to change her mind. With very little effort.

And besides the tension at home, she was involved in things that made her break out in hives.

Literally.

She had been itchy for three days. The stress of trying to plan a wedding that felt like a death march was starting to get to her.

The fact that she was going wedding-dress shopping with Isaiah's mother and sister was only making matters worse.

And yet, here she was, at Something New, the little bridal boutique in Gold Valley, awaiting the arrival of Nancy and Faith.

The little town was even more heavily decorated for the holidays than Copper Ridge. The red brick buildings were lined with lights, wreaths with crimson bows on every door.

She had opted to drive her own car because she had a feeling she was going to need the distance.

She sighed heavily as she walked into the store, the bell above the door signaling her arrival. A bright, pretty young woman behind the counter perked up.

"Hi," she said. "I'm Celia."

"Hi," Poppy said uncomfortably. "I have an appointment to try on dresses."

"You must be Poppy," she said.

"I am," Poppy said, looking down at her hands. At the ring that shone brightly against her dark skin. "I'm getting married."

"Congratulations," Celia said, as though the inane announcement wasn't that inane at all.

"I'm just waiting for..." The words died on her lips. Her future mother-in-law and sister-in-law. That was who she was waiting for.

Isaiah's family really would be her family. She knew that. It was why she'd said yes to this wedding. And somehow it hadn't fully sunk in yet. She wondered if it ever would.

The door opened a few moments later and Faith and Nancy came in, both grinning widely.

"I'm so excited," Faith said.

Poppy shot her an incredulous look that she hoped Nancy would miss. Faith of all people should not be that excited. She knew Isaiah was only marrying Poppy because of the ad.

Of course, no one knew that Isaiah was also marrying her because she was pregnant.

"So exciting," Poppy echoed, aware that it sounded hollow and lacking in excitement. She was a great assistant, but she was a lousy actress.

Celia ushered them through endless aisles of dresses and gave them instructions on how to choose preferred styles.

"When you're ready," Celia said, "just turn the dresses out and leave them on the rack. I'll bring them to you in the dressing room."

Poppy wandered through her size, idly touching a few of the dresses, but not committing to anything. Meanwhile, Faith and Nancy were selecting styles left and right.

She saw one that caught her eye. It looked as though it was off the shoulder with long sleeves that came to a point over the top of her hand and loops that would go over her middle finger. It was understated, sedate. Very Grace Kelly, which was right in Poppy's wheelhouse. The heavy, white satin was unadorned, with a deep sheen to it that looked expensive.

She glanced at the price tag. *Incredibly* expensive.

It was somewhat surprising that there was such an up-scale shop in the small community of Gold Valley, but then the place had become something of a destination for brides who wanted to make a day of dress shopping, and the cute atmosphere of the little gold rush town, with its good food and unique shops, made for an ideal girls' day out.

"Don't worry about that," Nancy said.

"I can't not worry about it," Poppy said, looking back at the price.

"Isaiah is going to pay for all of it," Nancy said. "And he made sure I was here to reinforce that."

"I know it's silly to be worked up about it," Poppy said. "Considering he signs my paychecks. But the thing is… I don't necessarily want to just take everything from him. I don't want him to think that…"

"That you're marrying him for his money?" Faith asked.

"Kind of," Poppy said.

"He isn't going to think that," Nancy said with authority. "He knows you."

"Yes," Poppy said slowly. "I just…" She looked at them both helplessly. "He's not in love with me," she said.

Faith knew, and there was no reason that Poppy's future mother-in-law shouldn't know too. She'd thought she wanted to keep it a secret, but she couldn't bear it anymore, not with the woman she was accepting as family.

"I love him," Poppy said. "I want to make that clear. I love him, and I told him not to let on that this was…a convenient marriage. For my pride. But I can't lie to you." She directed that part to his mother. "I can't lie to you and have you think that I reached him or changed him in a way that I haven't. He still thinks this marriage is the height of practicality. And he's happy to throw money at it like he's happy to throw money at any of his problems. He's not paying for this wedding because he cares what I look like in the wedding dress."

She swallowed hard. "He's paying for it because he thinks that making me his wife is going to somehow magically simplify his life."

Nancy frowned. "You love him."

"I do."

"You've loved him for a long time, haven't you?"

Poppy looked down. She could see Faith shift uncomfortably out of the corner of her eye.

"Yes," Poppy confirmed. "I've loved him ever since I met him. He's a wonderful person. I can see underneath all of the… Isaiah. Or maybe that's not the right way of putting it. I don't even have to see under it. I love who he is. And that…not everybody can see just how wonderful he is. It makes it like a secret. My secret."

"I'm not upset with you," Nancy said, taking hold of the wedding dress Poppy was looking at and turning it outward. "I'm not upset with you at all. You love him, and he came barreling at you with all of the intensity that he has, I imagine, and demanded that you marry him because he decided it was logical, am I right?"

"Very."

"I don't see what woman in your position could have resisted."

If only his mother knew just how little Poppy had resisted. Just how much she wasn't resisting him…

"I should have told him no."

"Does he know that you love him?" Faith asked.

"No," Poppy said.

And she knew she didn't have to tell either of them to keep it a secret. Because they just would.

"Maybe you should tell him," Faith pointed out.

Poppy bit back a smart remark about the fact that Faith was single, and had been for as long as Poppy had known her, and Faith maybe didn't have any clue about dealing with unrequited love.

"Love isn't important to him," Poppy said. "He *likes* me. He thinks that's enough."

Nancy shook her head. "I hope he more than likes you. Otherwise that's going to be a cold marriage bed."

Faith made a squeaking sound. "Mom. Please."

"What? Marriage is long, sweetheart. And sometimes you get distant. Sometimes you get irritated with each other. In those times all you've got is the spark."

Faith slightly receded into one of the dress racks. "Please don't tell me any more about your spark."

"You should be grateful we have it," Nancy said pointedly at her daughter. "It's what I want for you in your marriage, whenever you get married. And it's certainly what I want for Poppy and Isaiah."

Poppy felt her skin flushing. "We're covered there."

"Well, that is a relief."

She wasn't going to tell them about the baby. Not now. She was just going to try on wedding dresses.

Which was what they did.

For the next two hours, Poppy tried on wedding dresses. And it all came down to The One. The long-sleeved beauty with the scary price tag and the perfect train that fanned out behind her like a dream.

Celia found a veil and pinned it into Poppy's dark hair. It was long, extending past the train with a little row of rhinestones along the edge, adding a hint of mist and glitter.

She looked at herself in the mirror, and she found herself completely overwhelmed with emotion.

She was glowing.

There, underneath the lights in the boutique, the white dress contrasted perfectly with her skin tone. She looked like a princess. She felt like one.

And she had...

She looked behind her and saw Nancy and Faith, their eyes full of tears, their hands clasped in front of them.

She had a family who cared about this. Who was here watching her try on dresses.

Who cared for her. For her happiness.

Maybe Isaiah didn't love her, but she loved him. And... His mother and sister loved her. And that offered Poppy more than she had ever imagined she might have.

It was enough. It would be.

Nancy came up behind Poppy and put a hand on Poppy's shoulder. "This is the one. Let him buy it for you. Believe me, he'll cause enough trouble over the course of a lifetime with him that you won't feel bad about spending his money this way."

Poppy laughed, then wiped at a tear that fell down her cheek. "I suppose that's true."

"I'm going to try to keep from hammering advice at you," Nancy said. "But I do have to say this. Love is an amazing thing. It's an inexhaustible resource. I've been married a long time. And over the course of that many decades with someone, there are a lot of stages. Ebbs and flows. But if you keep on giving love, as much as you have, you won't run out. Give it even when it's not flowing to you. Give it when you don't feel like it. If you can do that… That's the best use of love that I can think of. It doesn't mean it's always easy. But it's something you won't regret. Love is a gift. When you have it, choosing to give it is the most powerful thing you can do."

Poppy looked back at her reflection. She was going to be a bride. And more than that, she was going to be Isaiah's wife. He had very clear ideas about what he wanted and didn't want from that relationship. He had very definite thoughts on what he felt and didn't feel.

She had to make a decision about that. About what she was going to let it mean to her.

The problem was, she had spent a lot of years wanting love. Needing love. From parents who were unable to give it for whatever reason. Because they were either too captivated by drugs, or too lost in the struggle of life. She had decided, after that kind of childhood, after the long years of being shuffled between foster homes, that she didn't want to expose herself to that kind of pain again.

Which was exactly what Isaiah was doing.

He was holding himself back. Holding his love back because he'd been hurt before. And somehow…somehow she'd judged that. As if she was different. As if she was well-adjusted and he was wrong.

But that wasn't true.

It was a perfect circle of self-protection. One that was the reason why she had nearly broken the engagement off a week ago. Why she was holding herself back from him now.

And they would never stop.

Not until one of them took a step outside that self-created box.

She could blame her parents. She could blame the handful of foster families who hadn't been able to care for her the way she had needed them to. She could blame the ones who had. The ones she had loved deeply, but whom she had ultimately had to leave, which had caused its own kind of pain.

She could blame the fact that Isaiah had been unavailable to her for all those years. That he had belonged to Rosalind, and somehow that had put him off-limits.

But blame didn't matter. The reasons didn't really matter.

The only thing that mattered was whether or not she was going to change her life.

No one could do it for her.

And if she waited for Isaiah to be the first to take that step, then she would wait forever.

His mother was right. Love was a gift, and you could either hoard it, keep it close to your chest where it wouldn't do a thing for anyone, or you could give it.

Giving her love was the only thing that could possibly open up that door between them. If she wanted him to love her, wanted him to find the faith to love her, she'd have to be the first one to stop protecting herself.

Poppy would have to open up her arms. Stop holding them in front of her, defensive and closed off.

Which was the real problem. Really, it had been all along.

That deeply rooted feeling of unrequited love that she'd had for Isaiah had been incredibly important to her. It had kept her safe. It had kept her from going after anyone else. It had kept her insulated.

But she couldn't continue that now.

Not if she wanted a hope at happiness. Not if she wanted even the smallest chance of a relationship with him.

Someone was going to have to budge first. And she could be bitter about the fact that it had to be her, but there was no point to that.

It was simple.

This wasn't about right or wrong or who should have to give more or less. Who should have to be brave.

She could see that she should.

And if she loved him… Well. She had to care more for him and less for her own comfort.

"I think I might need to give a little bit more love," Poppy said softly.

"If my son doesn't give back to you everything that you deserve, Poppy, you had better believe that I will scar him myself."

"I do believe it," Poppy said.

And if nothing else, what she had learned in that moment was invaluable.

Somebody was in her corner.

And not only had she heard Nancy say it, Poppy believed it. She couldn't remember the last time that had been true.

This was family.

It was so much better than she had ever imagined it could be.

Chapter Eleven

It was late, and Isaiah was working in his home office. His eyes were starting to get gritty, but he wasn't going to his room until he was ready to pass out. It was the only way he could get any sleep at all these days.

Lying in bed knowing she was just down the hall and he couldn't have her was torture. Distance and exhaustion were the only things he could do to combat the restlessness.

He looked up, catching his reflection in the window, along with the reflection of the lamp on his desk.

It was dark out. So dark he couldn't see anything. But he knew the view well. The mountains and hills that were outside that window. A view he had carefully curated after growing tired of the gray landscape of Seattle.

Poppy had been out shopping all day, and he hadn't seen her since she'd left that morning. But he had been thinking about her.

It was strange. The way his feelings for her were affected. A borderline obsession with a woman who should feel commonplace to him in many ways. She had been a part of his office furniture for the past decade.

Except, she'd always been more than that.

Yes. That was true. She always had been.

She was remarkable, smart and funny. Funny in a way he could never really manage to be. More than once, he had wished he could capture that sweetness and hold it to himself just for a little while.

Not that she was saccharine. No. She had no issues taking strips off his hide when it was necessary.

She was also so damn sexy he couldn't think of anything else, and she was starting to drive him insane.

He didn't have any practice with restraint. Over the years, he had been involved mostly in casual hookups, and the great thing about those was they could absolutely happen on his schedule. If the woman didn't matter, then all that was needed was time spent in an appropriate location, and a woman—any woman—would eventually indicate she was available.

But now, he was at the point where not just any woman would do. He needed Poppy.

She was still withholding herself from him, and he supposed he could understand. What with the fact that he had made threats to take her child away if she didn't fall in line. It was entirely possible he wasn't her favorite person at the moment.

That bothered him.

He wasn't very many people's favorite person. But Poppy liked him. At least, she had always seemed to. And now, he had found a very unique way of messing that up.

He'd had a lot of friendships not go the distance. Admittedly, this was quite the most creative way he'd had one dissolve. Proposing, getting that same friend pregnant, and then forcing her to marry him.

Not that he was *forcing* her. Not *really*. He was simply giving her a set of incredibly unpleasant options. And forcing her to choose the one she found the least unpleasant.

He supposed he could take some small measure of comfort in the fact that he wasn't the *least* pleasant option.

But then, that had more to do with the baby than with him.

He sighed heavily.

He'd never felt this way about a woman before. The strange sense of constant urgency. To be with her. To fix things with her. The fact that she was angry with him actively bothered him even when she wasn't in the room displaying that anger.

He could feel it.

He could actually feel someone else's emotion. Stronger than his own.

If he wasn't so fed up, he might marvel at that.

He didn't know what was happening to him.

He was obsessing about the desire. Fixated on it. Because that he understood. Sex, he understood.

This need to tear down all the walls inside him so that he could…

He didn't know.

Be closer to her? Have her feel him, his emotions, so difficult and hard to explain, as keenly as he felt hers?

They'd been friends for ten years. Now they were lovers.

His feelings were like nothing he'd ever felt for a friend or a lover.

The door opened behind him, and he didn't have to turn to see that it was Poppy standing in the doorway. She was wearing her favorite red coat that had a high collar and a tightly belted waist, flaring out at her hips. Her hands were stuffed in her pockets, her eyes cast downward.

"How was your day?"

Her voice was so soft it startled him. He turned. "Good. I wish it were over."

"Still working?"

"Yes. Faith is interested in taking on a couple more projects. I'm just trying to make sure everything balances out."

"I chose a wedding dress."

He had half expected her to say that she had chosen a burlap sack. Or nothing at all. As a form of protest.

"I'm glad to hear it," he said, not quite sure what she wanted him to say. Not quite sure where this was leading at all.

"I've missed you."

The words landed softly, then seemed to sing down deep into his heart. "I've seen you every day for the past week."

"That isn't what I meant." A small crease appeared between her brows as she stared at him. "I'm not going to say I miss the way we used to be. Because I don't. I like so much of what we have now better. Except…we don't have it right now. Because I haven't let you get close to me. I haven't let you touch me."

She pushed away from the door jamb and walked slowly toward him. His eyes were drawn downward, to the wicked, black stilettos on her feet. And to her bare legs. Which was odd, because she was wearing a coat as if she had been outside in the cold, and he would have thought she would have something to cover her skin.

"I've missed you touching me." she said, her voice growing husky. "I've missed touching you."

She lifted her hands, working the button at the top of her coat, and then the next, followed by the next. It exposed a V of brown skin, the soft, plump curve of her breasts. And a hint of bright yellow lace.

She made it to the belt, working the fabric through the loop and letting the coat fall open before she undid the button behind it, and the next button, and the next. Until she revealed that she had nothing on beneath the coat but transparent yellow lace. Some sort of top that scooped low around her full breasts and ended above her belly button, showing hints of dark skin through the pattern, the darker shadows of her nipples.

The panties were tiny. They covered almost nothing, and he was pleased with that. She left the heels on, making her legs look impossibly long, shapely and exactly what he wanted wrapped around him.

"What did I do to deserve this?" he asked.

It wasn't a game. Not a leading question. He genuinely wanted to know.

"Nothing," she said. She took a step toward him, lifted the delicate high heel up off the ground and pressed her knee into the empty space on the chair, just beside his thigh.

She gripped the back of the chair, leaning forward. "You haven't done anything at all to deserve this. But I want it. I'm not sure why I shouldn't have it. I think… I think this is a mess." Her tongue darted out, slid over her lips, and he felt the action like a slow lick. "*We* are a mess. We have been. For a long time. Together. Apart. But I'd rather be a mess with you than just a mess who lives in your house and wears your ring. I'd rather be a mess with you inside of me. We're going to get married. I'm having your baby. We're going to have to be a family. And I don't know how to…fix us. I don't know how to repair the broken spaces inside of us. I don't know if it's possible. But nothing is going to be fixed, nothing at all if we're just strangers existing in the same space. If I'm still just your personal assistant when I'm at work."

"What are you going to be when you're at work?"

"Your personal assistant. And your fiancée. And later, your wife. We can't separate these things. Not anymore. We can't separate ourselves."

She pressed her fingertips against his cheek and dragged her hand back, sliding her thumb over his lower lip. "I'm so tired of being lonely. Feeling like…nobody belongs to me. That I don't belong to anyone."

Those words echoed inside him, and they touched something raw. Something painful. He felt… He felt as if they could be words that were coming out of his own mouth. As if she was putting voice to his own pain, a pain he had never before realized was there.

"I want you," she said.

He reached out, bracing his hands on her hips, marveling at the erotic sight of that contrast. His paler hand over the deep rich color of her skin.

A contrast. And still a match.

Deep and sexual and perfect.

He leaned forward and pressed a kiss to her breast, to the bare skin just above the edge of lace. And she gasped, letting her head fall back. It was the most erotic sight. Perfect and indulgent, and something he wanted to hold on to and turn away from with matching intensity.

He wanted her to make him whole. He wanted to find the thing that she was talking about. That depth. That sense of belonging.

Of not being alone.

Of being understood.

He had never even made that a goal. Not even when he'd been with Rosalind. He'd never imagined that a woman might…understand him. He didn't quite understand himself. No one ever had.

He was different. That was all he knew.

He didn't know how to show things the way other people did. Didn't know how to read what was happening right in front of him sometimes.

Was more interested in the black-and-white numbers on a page than the full-color scene in front of him.

He couldn't change it. Didn't know if he would even if he could. His differences were what had made him successful. Made him who he was. But there were very few people willing to put up with that, with him.

But Poppy always had.

She had always been there. She had never—except for the day when she'd hit him in the chest and called him a robot—she had never acted like him being different was even a problem.

Maybe she was the one who could finally reach him. Maybe she was the one he could hold on to.

"I want you," he said, repeating her words back to her.

"I'm here," she said, tilting his face up, her dark eyes luminous and beautiful as she stared down at him. "I'm giving myself to you." She leaned forward, her lips a whisper from his. "Can I be yours, Isaiah?"

"You already are."

He closed the distance between them and claimed her mouth with his.

It was like a storm had exploded. He pulled her onto his lap, wrapping his arms around her tightly as he kissed her. As he lost himself in her. He wanted there to be nothing between them. Not the T-shirt and jeans he was wearing, not even the beautiful lace that barely covered her curves.

Nothing.

Nothing but her.

A smile curved his lips. She could maybe keep the shoes. Yes, he would love for her to have those shoes on when he draped her legs over his shoulders and thrust deep inside her.

"I want you so much," he said. The words were torn from him. Coming from somewhere deep and real that he wasn't normally in touch with. "I think I might die if I don't have you."

"I've been in front of you for ten years," she whispered, kissing the spot right next to his mouth, kissing his cheek. "Why now?"

Because he had seen her. Because she had finally kissed him. Because...

"I don't see the world the way everyone else does," he whispered. "I know that. Sometimes it takes an act of God for me to really notice what's happening in front of me. To pull me out of that space in my head. I like it there. Because everything makes sense. And I put people in their place, so I can navigate the day with everything just where I expect it. I can never totally do that with you, Poppy. You always occupied more spaces than you were supposed to.

"I hired you, but you were never only my assistant. You became my friend. And then, you wouldn't stay there either. I put control above everything else. I always have. It's the only way to... For me to make the world work. If I go in knowing exactly what to expect, knowing what everything is. What everyone is. And that's how I didn't see. But then...the minute our lips touched, I knew. I knew, and I can't go back to knowing anything different."

"You like blondes," she pointed out.

"I don't," he responded.

"Rosalind was blonde," Poppy said, brazenly speaking the name she usually avoided at all costs. "And there have been a string of them ever since."

"I told you. I like certainty. Blondes are women I'm attracted to. At least, that was an easy way to think of it. I like to bring order to the world in any way I can."

"And that kept you from looking at me?"

He searched her face, trying to get an idea of what she was thinking. He searched himself, because he didn't know the answer. She was beautiful, and the fact that he hadn't been obsessed with her like this for the past decade was destined to remain a mystery to him.

"Maybe."

She touched his face, sliding her palms back, holding him. "You are not difficult," she said. "Not to me. I like you. All of you."

"No," he responded, shaking his head. "You... You put up with me, I'm sure. And I compensate for the ways that I'm difficult by..."

"No, Isaiah. I like all of you. I always have. There's no putting up with anything."

He hadn't realized how much words like that might mean. Until they poured through him like sunshine dipping down into a low, dark valley. Flooding him with light and warmth.

When he'd been younger, he'd had a kind of boundless certainty in his worldview. But as he'd gotten older— as he'd realized that the way he saw things, the way he perceived interactions and emotions, was often different from the other people involved—he'd started questioning himself.

The older he'd gotten the more he'd realized. How difficult people found it to be his friend. How hard he found it sometimes to carry on a conversation another person wanted to have when he just wanted to charge straight to the point.

How much his brother Joshua carried for him, with his lightning-quick response times and his way with words.

Which had made him wonder how much his parents had modified for him back before he'd realized he needed modification at all.

And with that realization came the worry. About how much of a burden he might be.

But not to Poppy.

He reached up and wrapped his fingers around her slender wrists, holding her hands against his face. He looked at her. Just looked. He didn't have words to respond to what she had said.

He didn't have words.

He had nothing but his desire for her, twisting in his gut, taking him over. Control was the linchpin in his life. It was essential to him. But not now. Now, only Poppy was essential. He wanted her to keep touching him.

Control could wait. It could be set aside for now.

Because letting go so he could hold on to this—to her—was much more important.

It was necessary.

He slid her hands back, draping her arms over his shoulders so she was closer to him, so she was holding on to him. Then he cradled her face, dragging her mouth to his, claiming her, deep and hard and long. Pouring everything that he felt, everything he couldn't say, into this kiss. Into this moment.

He pulled away, sliding his thumb across her lower lip, watching as heat and desire clouded her dark eyes. He could see her surrender to the same need that was roaring through him.

"I always have control," he mumbled, pressing a kiss to her neck, another, and then traveling down to her collarbone. "Always."

He pressed his hand firmly to the small of her back, holding her against him as he stood from the chair, then lowered them both down onto the floor.

He reached behind her and tugged at the top she was wearing. He didn't manage to get hold of the snaps, and he tore the straps, the elastic popping free, the cups falling away from her breasts.

He didn't have to tell her he was out of control. She knew. He could see it. In the heat and fire burning in her dark eyes, and in the subtle curve of her full lips.

She knew that he was out of control, for her. And she liked it.

His efficient, organized Poppy had a wild side. At least, she did with him.

Only for him.

Suddenly, the fact that she had never been with another man before meant everything. This was his.

She was his.

And it mattered.

More than he would have ever thought it could. He had never given thought to something like that before. He didn't know why he did now. Except... Poppy.

Poppy, who had always been there.

She was a phenomenon. Someone he couldn't understand, someone he wasn't sure he wanted to understand. He didn't mind her staying mysterious. An enigma he got to hold in his arms. As long as this burning bright glory remained.

If he stopped to think, she might disappear. This moment might vanish completely, and he couldn't bear that.

She tore at his clothes too, wrenching them away from his body, making quick work of his shirt before turning her attention to his pants.

As she undressed him, he finished with her clothes, capturing her nipple in his mouth, sucking it in deep. Tasting her. Relishing the feel of her, that velvet skin under his tongue. The taste of her.

It wasn't enough. It never would be. Nothing ever would be.

He felt like his skin was hypersensitized, and that feeling ran all the way beneath his skin, deeper. Making him feel...

Making him *feel*.

He pressed his face into the curve of her neck, kissing her there, licking her. She whimpered and shifted beneath him, wrapping her fingers around his thick length, squeezing him. He let his head fall back, a hoarse groan on his lips.

"Not like that," he rasped. "I need to... No, Poppy. I need you."

"But you have me." She looked innocent. Far too innocent for the moment.

She stroked him, sliding her fingers up and down his length. Then she reached forward, planting her free hand in the center of his chest and pushing him backward slightly. He didn't have to give. He chose to. Because he wanted to see what she would do. He was far too captivated by what might be brewing beneath the surface.

Her breasts were completely bare for him. And then she leaned forward, wrapping her lips around the head of his erection, sliding down slowly as she took all of him into her mouth.

He gritted his teeth, her name a curse on his lips as he grabbed hold of her dark curls and held on tightly while she pleasured him with her mouth. He was transfixed by the sight of her. By the way she moved, unpracticed but earnest. By the way she made him feel.

"Have you ever done this before?" He forced the words out through his constricted throat.

The answer to that question shouldn't matter. It was a question he never should have asked. He'd never cared before, if one of his partners had other lovers. He would have said he preferred a woman with experience.

Not with Poppy. The idea of another man touching her made him insane.

She licked him from base to tip like a lollipop, and then looked up at him. "No."

He swore, letting his head fall back as she took him in deep again.

"Does that matter to you?" she asked, angling her head and licking him.

"Don't stop," he growled.

"Does it matter, Isaiah?" she repeated. "Do you want to be the only man I've ever touched like this? Do you want to know you that you're the only man I've ever seen naked?"

His stomach tightened, impossibly. And he was sure he was going to go right over the edge as her husky, erotic words rolled over him.

"Yes," he bit out.

"Why?"

"Because I want you to be mine," he said, his tone hard. "Only mine."

"I said I was yours," she responded, stoking the length of him with her hand as she spoke. "You're the only man I've ever wanted like this."

His breath hissed out through his teeth. "Me?"

"The only one. From the time you hired me when I was eighteen. I could never… I wanted to date other men. But I just couldn't. I didn't want them. Isaiah, I only wanted you."

Her dark eyes were so earnest as she made the confession, so sincere. That look touched him, all the way down. Even to those places he normally felt were closed off.

She kissed his stomach, up higher to his chest, and then captured his lips again.

"I want you," she said. "Please."

She didn't have to ask twice. He lowered her onto her back and slipped his fingers beneath the waistband of those electric yellow panties, sliding his fingers through her slick folds slowly, slowly, drawing out all that slick wetness, drawing out her pleasure. Until she was whimpering and bucking beneath him. Until she was begging him.

Then he slipped one finger deep inside her, watched as

her release found her. As it washed over her like a wave. It was the most beautiful thing he'd ever seen.

But it wasn't enough.

He pulled her panties off and threw them onto the floor, positioning himself between her thighs, pressing himself to the entrance of her body and thrusting in, rough and decisive. Claiming her. Showing her exactly who she belonged to.

Just as he belonged to her.

He lost himself completely, wrapped in her, consumed by her. That familiar scent, vanilla and spice, some perfume Poppy had always worn, mingling with something new. Sweat. Desire. Skin.

What they had been collided with what they were now.

He gripped her hips, thrust into her, deep and hard, relishing her cry of pleasure as he claimed her. Over and over again.

She arched underneath him, crying out his name, her fingernails digging into his skin as her internal muscles pulsed around him.

And he let go. He came on a growl, feral and unrestrained, pleasure like fire over his skin, in his gut.

And when it was over, he could only hold her. He couldn't speak. Couldn't move. Didn't want to.

He looked down at her, and she smiled. Then she pressed her fingers to his lips.

He grabbed her wrist, kissed her palm. "Come to bed with me," he said.

"Okay."

Chapter Twelve

At three in the morning, Isaiah decided that they needed something to eat. Poppy sat on the counter wearing nothing but his T-shirt, watching as he fried eggs and bacon.

She wondered if this was…her life now. She could hardly believe it. And yet, she didn't want to believe anything different.

She ached just looking at this man.

He was so…him. Undeniably. So intense and serious, and yet now, there was something almost boyish about him with his dark hair falling into his eyes, his expression one of concentration as he flipped the eggs in the pan flawlessly without breaking a yolk.

But then, he was shirtless, wearing a pair of low-slung gray sweatpants that seemed perilously close to falling off. His back was broad and muscular, and she enjoyed the play of those muscles while he cooked.

Just that one moment, that one expression on his face, could come close to being called boyish. The rest of him was all man.

He served up the eggs and bacon onto a plate, and he handed Poppy hers, then set his on the counter beside her. He braced himself on the counter, watching her expectantly.

"Do you often have midnight snacks?" she asked.

"No," he said. "But then, tonight isn't exactly routine. Eat."

"Are you trying to fortify me so we can have sex again?"

His lips curved upward. "Undoubtedly."

"This bacon is tainted with ulterior motives," she said, happily taking a bite.

"You seem very sad about that."

"I am." She looked down, then back up, a bubble of happiness blooming in her chest.

"I wanted to make sure you were taken care of," he said, his voice suddenly serious. "Do you feel okay?"

"Yes," she said, confused for a moment.

"No…nausea, or anything like that?"

Right. Because of the baby. So he wasn't only concerned about her. She fought off a small bit of disappointment.

"I feel fine," she said.

"Good," he said.

"Because if I had morning sickness I'd have to miss work?" she asked, not quite certain why she was goading him.

"No. Because if you were sick it would upset me to see you like that."

Suddenly, she felt achingly vulnerable sitting here like this with him.

Isaiah.

She was having his baby. She'd just spent the past couple of hours having wild sex with him. And now she just felt…so acutely aware of who she was. With her hair loose and curly, falling into her face that was free of makeup. Without her structured dresses and killer high heels.

She was just Poppy Sinclair, the same Poppy Sinclair who'd bounced from home to home all through her childhood. Who had never found a family who wanted her forever.

Her throat ached, raw and dry.

His large hand cupped her chin, tilted her face upward. "What's wrong?"

Her heart twisted. That show of caring from him made the vulnerability seem like it might not be so bad. Except…even when he was being nice, it hurt.

She definitely liked a little bit of opposition in her life, and Isaiah was always around to provide that. Either because of her unrequited feelings, or because he was such an obstinate, hardheaded man.

Somehow, all of that was easier than…feeling. It was all part of remaining closed off.

This…opening up was hard, but she had expected that. She hadn't expected it to be painful even when nothing bad was happening.

"I was just thinking," she said.

"About?"

"Nothing specifically," she said.

Just about who she was, and why it was almost ludicrous that she was here now. With him. With so many beautiful things right within her reach.

A family. A husband. A baby.

Passion.

Love.

"You can tell me," he said, his gray eyes searching.

"Why do you *want* me to tell you?" she pressed.

"Because you're mine. Anything that is bothering you… Give it to me. I want to…help. Listen."

"Isaiah…" Her eyes burned.

"Did I make you cry?" He looked genuinely concerned by that. He lifted his hand, brushed his thumb beneath the corner of her eye, wiping away a tear she hadn't realized was there.

"You didn't," she said. She swallowed hard. "I was just… It's stupid."

"Nothing is stupid if it makes you cry."

"I was thinking, while I was sitting here watching you take care of me, that I don't remember what it's like to have someone care for me like this. Because… I'm not sure anyone ever really has. People definitely showed me kindness throughout my life—I'm not saying they didn't. There were so many families and houses. They blur together. I used to remember everyone's names, but now the earlier homes are fading into a blur. Even the people who were kind.

"I remember there was a family… They were going to take me to the fair. And I'd never been before. I was so excited, Isaiah. So excited I could hardly contain myself. We were going to ride a Ferris wheel, and I was going to have cotton candy. I'd never had it before." She took another bite of her bacon and found swallowing difficult.

"The next day, that family found out that the birth

mother of a sibling group they were fostering had given birth to another baby. Child services wanted to arrange to have the baby brought in right away. And…that required they move me. The baby had to be with her half siblings. It was right. It made sense."

"You didn't get to go to the fair."

She blinked and shook her head. A tear rolled down her cheek, and she laughed. "It's stupid to still be upset about it. I've been to the fair. I've had cotton candy. But I just… I can remember. How it hurt. How it felt like the world was ending. Worse, I think, is that feeling that nothing in the world is ever stable. That at any moment the rug is going to be pulled out from underneath me. That everything good is just going to vanish. Well, like cotton candy once it hits your tongue."

"I want to take care of you," he said, looking at her, his gray eyes fierce. "Always."

"Don't make promises you can't keep," she said, her stomach churning.

"Don't you trust me?"

She wanted to. But he didn't love her. And if they didn't share love, she wasn't sure what the bond was supposed to be. They had one. She didn't doubt that. And she loved him more than ever.

They would have the baby.

Once they were married it would feel better. It would feel more secure.

"I don't know if you can…understand. But… You've been one of the most constant people I've ever had in my life. Rosalind and I don't see each other very often, but she made sure I was taken care of. She didn't forget me. She's my family. And you… You're my family too."

"If you want to invite Rosalind to the wedding you can," he said.

She blinked. Stunned, because usually any mention of Rosalind's name earned her nothing but stony silence or barely suppressed rage. "She can come to our...wedding?"

"She matters to you," Isaiah said. "And what happened between the two of us isn't important anymore."

"It isn't?" Hope bloomed in her heart, fragile and new, like a tiny bud trying to find its way in early spring. "But she...broke your heart," Poppy finished.

"But now I have you. The rest doesn't matter."

It wasn't the declaration she wanted, but it was something. Better than the promise of a fair or cotton candy or anything like it.

And she wanted to hope.

So she did.

And she leaned forward and kissed him. With each pass of his lips over hers, she let go of a little more of the weight she carried and held on to him a little bit tighter.

Chapter Thirteen

Isaiah had actually taken a lunch break, which wasn't like him, and then it had turned into a rather long lunch. In fact, he had been out of the office for almost two hours, and Poppy couldn't remember the last time he had done that in the middle of the day. She was almost sure he never had, unless he'd taken her with him because it was a working lunch and he had needed somebody to handle the details.

It made her edgy to have him acting out of character.

At least, that's what she told herself. In reality, she just felt a little edgy having him out of her sight. Like he might disappear completely if she couldn't keep tabs on him. Like everything that had happened between them might be imaginary after all.

She tried to relax her face, to keep her concern from showing. Even though there was no one there to see it.

It was just… The situation made her feel tense all over. And she shouldn't. Last night had been…

She had never experienced anything like it. Never before, and the only way she would again was if…

If they actually got married.

If everything actually worked out.

She placed her hand lightly on her stomach and sent up a small prayer. She just didn't want to lose any of this.

She'd never had so much.

She sighed and stood up from her desk. She needed some coffee. Something to clear her head. Something to make her feel less like a crazy lady who needed to keep a visual on her fiancé at all times.

Of course, she *was* a crazy lady who wanted a visual on her fiancé at all times, but, it would be nice if she could pretend otherwise.

Then the door to her office opened and she turned and saw Isaiah standing there in the same black T-shirt and jeans he'd been wearing when he left. But his arm was behind his back, and his expression was…

She didn't think she had ever seen an expression like that on his face before.

"What are you doing?" she asked.

"I went out looking for something for you," he said, his expression serious. "It was harder to find than I thought it would be."

"Because you didn't know what to get me?"

"No. Because it turns out I had no idea where to find what I was looking for."

She frowned. "What's behind your back?"

"Roses would have been easy," he said, and then he moved his hand and she saw a flash of pink. He held out something that was shaped like a bouquet but was absolutely not.

She stood there and just…stared for a moment. Another diamond ring wouldn't have affected her as deeply as this gesture.

Seemingly simple and inexpensive.

To her…it was priceless.

"Cotton candy," she breathed.

"I just wanted to find you some to have with lunch." He frowned. "But now of course it isn't lunchtime anymore."

Isaiah in his most intense state, with his dark brows and heavy beard, holding the pinkest, fluffiest candy in the world, was her new favorite, absurd sight.

She held back a giggle. "Where did you go to get this?"

"There's a family fun center in Tolowa that has it, funnily enough."

"You drove all the way to… Isaiah." She took hold of the cotton candy, then wrenched it from his hand and set it on her desk before wrapping her arms around his neck and kissing him.

"It's going to melt," he said against her lips.

"Cotton candy doesn't melt."

"It shrinks," he pointed out.

"I love cotton candy, don't get me wrong. But I'd rather eat you," she returned.

"I worked hard for that."

She laughed and reached behind her, grabbing hold of the cotton candy and taking a bite, the sugar coating her lips and her tongue. Then she kissed Isaiah again, a sugary, sweet kiss that she hoped expressed some of what she felt.

But not all of it.

Because she hadn't told him.

She was afraid to.

Last night had been a big step of faith, approaching him and giving herself to him like that. It had been her *showing* him what was in her heart. But she knew that wasn't enough. Not really. She needed to say it too.

It had to be said.

She cupped his face and kissed him one more time, examining the lines by his gray eyes, the weathered, rugged look his beard gave him, that sharp, perfect nose and his lips... Lips she was convinced had been made just for her.

Other women had kissed them. She'd seen them do it. But it didn't matter. Because those lips weren't for those women. They were for her. They softened for her. Smiled for her. Only she reached those parts of Isaiah, and she had been the only one for a long time.

And yes, Rosalind had reached something in him Poppy hadn't managed to reach, but if she could do all these other things to him, if she could make him lose control, make him hunt all over creation for cotton candy, then maybe in the future...

It didn't matter. What might happen and what might not. There was only one thing that was certain. And that was how she felt.

She'd loved him for so long. Through so many things. Growing his business, enduring a heartbreak. Long hours, late nights. Fighting. Laughing. Making love.

She'd loved him through all of that.

And she'd love him forever.

Not telling him...worrying about what might happen was just more self-protection, and she was done with that.

"I love you," she said.

He went stiff beneath her touch, but she truly hadn't expected a different reaction. It was going to take him time. She didn't expect a response from him right away; she didn't even want one.

"I've always loved you," she said. "In the beginning, even when you were with Rosalind. And it felt like a horrible betrayal. But I wanted you. And I burned with jealousy. I wanted to have your intensity directed at me. And then when she… The fact that she got to be the only one to ever have it… It's not fair.

"I want it. I love you, Isaiah. I've loved you for ten years, I'll love you for ten more. For all my years. You're everything I could ever want. A fantasy I didn't even know I could create. And I just… I love you. I loved you before we kissed. Before we made love. Before you proposed to me and before I was pregnant. I just…love you."

His expression hadn't changed. It was a wall. Impenetrable and flat. His mouth was set into a grim line, his entire body stiff.

"Poppy…"

"Don't. Don't look at me like you pity me. Like I'm a puppy that you have to kick. I've spent too much of my life being pitied, Isaiah, and I don't want to be pitied by you."

"You have me," he said. "I promise that."

"You don't love me," she said.

"I can't," he said.

She shook her head, pain lancing her heart. "You won't."

"In the end, does it make a difference?"

"In the end, I suppose it doesn't make a difference, but on the journey there, it makes all the difference. *Can't* means there's nothing… Nothing on heaven or earth that could make you change. Won't means you're choosing this. You're choosing to hold on to past hurts, to pain. You're choosing to hold on to another woman instead of holding on to me. You accused me of clinging to a fantasy—of wanting a man who might love me, instead of taking the man who was right in front of me. But what you're doing is worse. You're hanging on to the ghosts of the past rather than hanging on to something real. I think you could love me. I think you might. But you have it buried so far down, underneath all this protection…"

"You don't understand," he said, turning away from her and pushing his fingers through his hair. "You don't understand," he repeated, this time more measured. "It's easy for you. You don't have that disconnect. That time it takes to translate someone's facial expression, what the words beneath their words are, and what it all means. Rosalind was the clumsiest liar, the clumsiest cheat in the entire world, and I didn't know. Because she said she loved me, and so I believed it."

Poppy let out a harsh, wounded breath. "And you don't believe me?"

"I didn't say that."

"But that's what it is. You don't trust me. If you trusted me, then this wouldn't be an issue."

"No," he said. "That isn't true. I felt like a tool when everything happened with Rosalind. She broke places in me I hadn't realized were there to be broken. I don't think you can possibly understand what it's like to be blindsided like that."

Her vision went fuzzy around the edges, her heart pounding so hard she thought she might faint.

"You don't… I just told you one small piece of what

it was like to grow up like I did. How anticipating what might happen tomorrow was dangerous because you might be in a whole new house with a bunch of strangers the next day. My life was never in my control. Ever. It was dangerous to be comfortable, dangerous to care. There was a system, there were reasons, but when I was a child all I knew was that I was being uprooted. Again and again."

"I'm sorry. I didn't mean…"

"We've all been hurt. No one gives us a choice about that. But what are you going to do about it? What is the problem? Say it out loud. Tell me. So that you have to hear for yourself how ridiculous this all is."

"It changed something in me," he said. "And I can't… I can't change it back."

"You *won't*. You're a coward, Isaiah Grayson. You're running. From what you feel. From what you *could* feel. You talk about these things you can't do, these things you can't feel. These things you can't understand. But you understand things other people never will. The way you see numbers, the way you fit it all together—that's a miracle. And if your brain worked like everyone else's, then you wouldn't be that person. You wouldn't be the man I love. I don't want you to change who you are. Don't you understand that? That's not what I'm asking for. I'm asking for you to hold on to me instead of her."

He took a step back, shaking his head slowly. "Poppy…"

"Where's my big, scary, decisive boss? My stubborn friend who doesn't back down? Or is this request terrifying because I'm asking for something that's not in your head? Something that's in your heart?"

Her own heart was breaking, splintering into a thousand pieces and falling apart inside her chest. She thought she might die from this.

She hadn't expected him to be able to give her a response today, but she hadn't known he was going to launch into an outright denial of his ability to ever, ever love her.

"Maybe I don't have a heart," he said, his voice hard. "Maybe I'm a robot, like you said."

"I don't think that's true. And I shouldn't have said that in the first place."

"But maybe you were closer to the truth than you want to believe. Maybe you don't love me like I am, Poppy. Maybe you just see things in me that aren't there, and you love those. But they aren't real."

She shook her head, fighting back tears. "I don't think that's true. I've been with you for a decade, Isaiah." She looked at his face, that wonderful, familiar face. That man who was destroying everything they'd found.

She wanted to hit him, rage at him. "I *know you*. I know you care. I've watched you with your family. I've watched you work hard to build this business with Joshua and Faith, to take it to the next level with the merger. You work so hard, and that's not…empty. Everything you've done to support Faith in her dream of being an architect…"

"It's her talent. I can't take the credit."

"Without you, the money wouldn't flow and that would be the end of it. You're the main artery, and you give it everything. You might not express how you care the way other people do, but you express it in a real, tangible way." He didn't move. Didn't change his expression. "You can love, Isaiah. And other people love you."

He said nothing. Not for a long moment.

"I would never take our child from you," he said finally.

"What?"

"I won't take our child from you. Forcing you to marry me was a mistake. This is a mistake, Poppy."

She felt like that little girl who had been promised a carnival, only to wake up in the morning and have her bags packed again.

The disappointment even came complete with cotton candy.

"You don't want to marry me?"

"I was forcing it," he said. "Because in my mind I had decided that was best, and so because I decided it, it had to be true. But… It's not right. I won't do that to you."

"How dare you? How dare you dump me and try to act like it's for my own good? After I tell you that I love you? Forcing me to marry you was bad enough, but at least then you were acting out of complete emotional ignorance."

"I'm always acting out of emotional ignorance," he said. "Don't say you accept all of me and then act surprised by that."

"Yeah, but sometimes you're just full of shit, Isaiah. And you hide behind those walls. You hide behind that brain. You try to outwit and outreason everything, but life is not a chess game. It's not math. None of this is. Your actions least of all. Because if you added up everything you've said and done over the past few weeks, you would know that the answer equaled love. You would know that the answer is that we should be together. You would know that you finally have what you want and *you're giving it away.*

"So don't try to tell me you're being logical. Don't try to talk to me like I'm a hysterical female asking something ridiculous of you. You're the one who's scared. You're the one who's hysterical. You can stand there with a blank look on your face and pretend that somehow makes you rational, but you aren't. You can try to lie to me. You can try to lie to yourself. But I don't believe it. I refuse."

She took a deep breath. "And I quit. I really do quit this time. I'm not going to be here for your convenience. I'm not going to be here to keep your life running smoothly, to give you what you want when you want it while I don't get my needs met in return. If you want to let me go, then you have to let me go."

She picked up the cotton candy. "But I'm taking this." She picked up her coat also, and started to walk past him and out of the room. Then she stopped. "I'll be in touch with you about the baby. And I will pay you back for the wedding dress if I can't return it. Please tell… Please tell your mom that I'm sorry. No. Tell them you're sorry. Tell them you're sorry that you let a woman who could never really love you ruin your chance with one who already does."

And then she walked out of the office, down the hall, past Joshua's open door and his questioning expression, through the lobby area, where Faith was sitting curled up in a chair staring down at a computer.

"Goodbye," Poppy said, her voice small and pained.

"What's going on?" Faith asked.

"I quit," Poppy said. "And the wedding is off. And… I think my heart is breaking. But I don't know what else to do."

Poppy found herself standing outside the door, waiting for a whole new life to start.

And, like so many times before, she wasn't confident that there would be anything good in that new life.

She took a breath. No. There would be something good. This time, there was the certainty of that.

She was going to be a mother.

Strangely, out of all this heartbreak, all this broken-ness, came a chance at a kind of redemption she had never really let herself believe in.

She was going to be a mother.

It would be her only real chance at having a good mother-daughter relationship. And yes, she would be on the other side of it. But she would give her child the best of herself.

A sad smile touched her lips. Even without meaning to, Isaiah had given her a chance at love. It just hadn't been the kind of love she'd been hoping for.

But…it was still a gift.

And she was going to cling to it with everything she had.

Chapter Fourteen

Isaiah wasn't a man given to excessive drinking, but tonight he was considering it.

By the time he had gotten home from work, Poppy had cleared out her things. He supposed he should have gone after her. Should have left early. But he had been…

He had been frozen.

He had gone through the motions all day, trying to process what had happened.

One thing kept echoing in his head, and it wasn't that she loved him, though that had wrapped itself around his heart and was currently battering at him, making him feel as though his insides had been kicked with a steel-toed boot.

Or maybe just a stiletto.

No, the thing that kept going through his mind was what she'd said about his excuses.

MAISEY YATES   401

He had known even as he said it out loud that he didn't really believe all the things he'd said. It wasn't true that he couldn't love her.

She had asked if he didn't trust her. And that wasn't the problem either.

He didn't trust himself.

Emotion was like a foreign language to him. One he had to put in effort to learn so he could understand the people around him. His childhood had been a minefield of navigating friendships he could never quite make gel, and high school and college had been a lot of him trying to date and inadvertently breaking hearts when he missed connections that others saw.

It was never that he didn't feel. It was just that his feelings were in another language.

And he often didn't know how to bridge the gap.

And the intensity of what he felt now was so sharp, so intense that his natural inclination was to deny it completely. To shut it down. To shut it off. It was what he often did. When he thought of those parts of himself he couldn't reach...

He chose to make them unreachable.

It was easier to navigate those difficult situations with others if he wasn't also dealing with his own feelings. And so he'd learned. Push it down. Rationalize the situation.

Emotion was something he could feel, hear, taste and smell. Something that overtook him completely. Something that became so raw and intense he wanted to cut it off completely.

But with her... He couldn't.

When he was making love with her, at least there was a place for all those feelings to go. A way for them to be expressed. There was something he could do with them. With that roaring in his blood, that sharp slice to his senses.

How could he give that to someone else? How could he... How could he trust himself to treat those emotions the way that they needed to be treated?

He really wanted a drink. But honestly, the explosion of alcohol with his tenuous control was likely a bad idea. Still, he was considering it.

There was a heavy knock on his front door and Isaiah frowned, going down the stairs toward the entry.

Maybe it was Poppy.

He jerked the door open and was met by his brother Joshua.

"What are you doing here?" Isaiah asked.

"I talked to Faith." Joshua shoved his hands in his pockets. "She said Poppy quit."

"Yes," Isaiah said. He turned away from his brother and walked toward the kitchen. He was going to need that drink.

"What did you do?"

"You assume I did something?" he asked.

Isaiah's anger rang a little bit hollow, considering he knew that it was his fault. Joshua just stared at him.

Bastard.

Was he so predictably destructive in his interpersonal relationships?

Yes.

He knew the answer to that without thinking.

"I released her from her obligation," Isaiah said. "She was the one who chose to leave."

"You released her from her obligation? What the hell does that mean?"

"It means I was forcing her to marry me, and then I decided not to." He sounded ridiculous. Which in and of itself was ridiculous, since *he* never was.

His brother pinched the bridge of his nose. "Start at the beginning."

"She's pregnant," Isaiah said.

Joshua froze. "She's..."

"She's pregnant," Isaiah repeated.

"How..."

"You know exactly how."

"I thought the two of you had an arrangement. Meaning I figured you weren't going to go...losing control," Joshua said.

"We had something like an arrangement. But it turned out we were very compatible. Physically."

"Yes," Joshua said, "I understood what you meant by compatible."

"Well, how was I supposed to know? You were just standing there staring at me." He rubbed his hand over his face. "We were engaged, she tried to break it off. Then she found out she was pregnant. I told her she had to marry me or I would pursue full custody—"

"Every woman's fantasy proposal. I hope you filmed it so you'll always have a memory of that special moment."

Isaiah ignored his brother. "It was practical. But then...then she wanted things I couldn't give, and I realized that maybe forcing a woman to marry me wasn't the best idea."

"And she's in love with you."

Isaiah sighed heavily. "Yes."

"And you said you couldn't love her back so she left?"

"No," he said. "I said I couldn't love her and I told her I wouldn't force her to marry me. And then she left."

"You're the one who rejected her," Joshua said.

"I don't know how to do this," Isaiah said, his voice rough. "I don't know how to give her what she wants while...while making sure I don't..."

He didn't want to say it because it sounded weak, and he'd never considered himself weak. But he was afraid of being hurt, and if that wasn't weakness, he didn't know what was.

"You can't," Joshua said simply, reading his mind. "Loving someone means loving them at the expense of your own emotional safety. Sorry. There's not another alternative."

"I can't do that."

"Because one woman hurt you?"

"You don't understand," Isaiah said. "It has nothing to do with being hurt once. Rosalind didn't just hurt me, she made a fool out of me. She highlighted every single thing that I've struggled with all my life and showed me how inadequate I am. Not with words. She doesn't even know what she did."

He took a deep breath and continued, "Connecting with people has always been hard for me. Not you, not the family. You all...know how to talk to me. Know how to deal with me. But other people? It's not easy, Joshua. But with her I thought I finally had something. I let my guard down, and I quit worrying. I quit worrying about whether or not I understood everything and just...was with someone for a while. But what I thought was happening wasn't the truth. Everything that should've been obvious was right in front of me."

"But that's not your relationship with Poppy. And it isn't going to be. She's not going to change into something else just because you admit that you're in love with her."

"Poppy is different," Isaiah said. "Whatever I thought I felt then, this is different."

"You love her. And if you don't admit that, Isaiah? Maybe you won't feel it quite so keenly, but you won't have her. You're going to…live in a separate place from the woman you love?"

"I won't be a good father anyway," Isaiah said.

"Why do you think that?"

"How am I going to be a good father when I can't… What am I going to teach a kid about relationships and people? I'm not wired like everyone else."

"And maybe your child won't be either. Or maybe my child will be different, and he'll need his uncle's help. Any of our children could need someone there with him who understands. You're not alone. You're not the only person who feels the way that you do."

Isaiah had never thought about that. About the fact that his own experiences might be valuable to someone else.

"But Poppy…"

"Knows you and loves you. She doesn't want you to be someone else."

Isaiah cleared his throat. "I accused her of that."

"Because she demanded you pull your head out of your ass and admit that you love her?"

"Yes," he admitted.

"Being alone is the refuge of cowards, Isaiah, and you're a lot of things, but I never thought you were a coward. I understand trying to avoid being hurt again. After everything I went through with my ex, I didn't want anything to do with a wife or another baby. But now I have

Danielle. I have both a wife and a son. And I'm glad I
didn't let grief be the deciding factor in my life. Because,
let me tell you something, that's easy. It's easy to let the
hard things ruin you. It's a hell of a lot braver to decide
they don't get to control you."

"It hurts to breathe," Isaiah said, his voice rough.
"When I look at her."

"If you aren't with her, it'll still hurt to breathe. She
just won't be beside you."

"I didn't want a wife so I could be in love," Isaiah said.
"I wanted one to make my life easier."

"You don't add another person to your life to make it
easier. Other people only make things harder, and you
should have a better understanding of that than most. You
accept another person into your life because you can't
live without them. Because easy isn't the most important
thing anymore. She is. That's love. And it's bigger than
fear. It has to be, because love itself is so damned scary."

"Why does anyone do it?" Isaiah asked.

"You do it when you don't have a choice anymore. I
almost let Danielle walk away from me. I almost ruined
the best thing I'd ever been given because of fear. And
you tell me why a smart man would do that? Why does
fear get to be the biggest emotion? Why can't love win?"

Isaiah stood there, feeling like something had shifted
under his feet.

He couldn't outrun emotion. Even when he suppressed
it, there was an emotion that was winning: fear.

He'd never realized that, never understood it, until
now.

"Think about it," Joshua said.

Then he turned and walked out of the house, leaving
Isaiah alone with his obviously flawed thinking.

He loved Poppy.

To his bones. To his soul.

He couldn't breathe for the pain of it, and he had no idea what the hell he was supposed to do with the damned fear that gnawed at his gut.

This had all started with an ad for a wife. With the most dispassionate idea any man had ever hatched.

Him, divorcing himself from feeling and figuring out a way to make his life look like he wanted it to look. To make it look like his parents' lives. His idea of home.

Only now he realized he'd left out the most important thing.

Love.

It was strange how his idea of what he wanted his life to be had changed. He had wanted to get married. He had wanted a wife. And he'd found a way to secure that.

But now he just wanted *Poppy*.

Whether they were married or not, whether or not they had perfect, domestic bliss and Sunday dinners just like his parents, whether they were in a little farmhouse or his monstrosity of a place... It didn't matter. If she was there.

Wherever Poppy was...that was his home.

And if he didn't have her, he would never have a home.

He could get that drink now. Stop the pain in his chest from spreading further, dull the impending realization of what he'd done. To himself. To his life. But he had to feel it. He had to.

He braced himself against the wall and lowered his head, pain starting in his stomach, twisting and turning its way up into his chest. Like a shard of glass had been wedged into the center of his ribs and was pushed in deeper with each breath.

He'd never lost love before.

He'd had wounded pride. Damaged trust.

But he'd never had a broken heart.

Until now.

And he'd done it to himself.

Poppy had offered him all he needed in the world, and he'd been too afraid to take it.

Poppy had lived a whole life filled with heartbreak. With being let down. He'd promised to take care of her, and then he hadn't. He was just another person who'd let her down. Another person who hadn't loved her like she should have been loved.

He should have loved her more than he loved himself.

He clenched his hand into a fist. He was done with this. With this self-protection. He didn't want it anymore.

He wanted Poppy.

Now. Always.

More than safety. More than breathing.

But he'd broken her trust. She'd already loved and lost so many people in her life, had been let down by parades of people who should have done better, and there was no logical reason for her to forgive him.

He just had to hope that love would be stronger than fear.

Chapter Fifteen

Poppy was a study in misery.

She had taken all her easily moved things and gone back to her house.

She wasn't going to flee the town. She loved her house, and she didn't really have anywhere else to go at the moment. No, she was going to have to sort that out, but later.

She wasn't entirely sure what she wanted. Where she would go.

She would have to find another job.

She could, she knew that. She had amply marketable skills. It was just that... It would mean well and truly closing the door on the Isaiah chapter of her life. Possibly the longest chapter she even had.

So many people had cycled in and out of her life. There had been a few constants, and the Graysons had been some of her most cherished friends. It hurt. Losing him like this. Losing them. But this was just how life went for her. And there was nothing she could do about it. She was always, forever at the mercy of people who simply couldn't...

She swallowed hard.

There was no real furniture left in her house after she'd moved to Isaiah's ranch. She had gathered a duffel bag full of clothes and a sleeping bag. She curled up in the sleeping bag on the floor in the corner of her bedroom and grabbed her cell phone.

There was one person she really owed a phone call.

She dialed her foster sister's number and waited.

"Hello?"

"I hope it's not too late," Poppy said, rolling to her side and looking out the window at the inky black sky.

It had the audacity to look normal out there. Clear and crisp like it was just a typical December night and not a night where her world had crashed down around her.

"Of course not. Jason and I were just getting ready to go out. But that can wait. What's going on?"

"Oh. Nothing... Everything."

"What's going on?" Rosalind repeated, her voice getting serious. "You haven't called in a couple of months."

"Neither have you," Poppy pointed out.

"I know. I'm sorry. I've never been very good at keeping in touch. But that doesn't mean I don't like hearing from you."

"I'm pregnant," Poppy blurted out.

The pause on the other end was telling. But when Rosalind finally did speak, her voice was shot through with excitement. "Poppy, congratulations. I'm so happy for you."

"I'm single," she said as a follow-up.

"Well, I figured you would have altered your announcement slightly if you weren't."

"I don't know what I'm going to do." She pulled her knees up and tucked her head down, holding her misery to her chest.

"If you need money or a place to stay... You know you can always come and stay with me and Jason."

Poppy did know that. Maybe that was even why she had called Rosalind. Because knowing that she had a place with her foster sister made her feel slightly less rootless.

She wouldn't need to use it. At least, she *shouldn't* need to use it. But knowing that Rosalind was there for her helped.

Right now, with the only other anchor in her life removed and casting her mostly adrift, Rosalind was more important than ever.

"Isaiah isn't being a terror about it, is he?" Rosalind asked.

"Not... Not the way you mean," Poppy said slowly. "It's Isaiah's baby."

The silence stretched even longer this time. *"Isaiah?"*

"Yes," Poppy said. "And I know... I know that's... I'm sorry."

"Why are you apologizing to me?" Rosalind sounded genuinely mystified.

"Because he's your...your ex. And I know I don't have a lot of experience with family, but you're the closest thing I have to a sister, and I know you don't...go dating your sister's ex-boyfriends."

"Well. Yes. I suppose so. But he's my *ex*. From a long time ago. And I'm with someone else now. I've moved on. Obviously, so has he. Why would you keep yourself from something you want just because…just because it's something other people might not think was okay? If you love him…"

Poppy realized that the guilt she felt was related to the fact that her feelings for Isaiah had most definitely originated when Isaiah had not been Rosalind's ex.

"I've had feelings for him for a long time," Poppy said quietly. "A really long time."

"Don't tell me you feel bad about that, Poppy," Rosalind said.

"I do," Poppy said. "He was your boyfriend. And you got me a job with him. In that whole time…"

"You didn't *do* anything. It's not like you went after him when we were together."

"No."

"I'm the cheater in that relationship." Rosalind sighed heavily. "I didn't handle things right with Isaiah back then. I cheated on him, and I shouldn't have. I should have been strong enough to break things off with him without being unfaithful. But I wasn't."

They'd never talked about this before. The subject of Isaiah had always been too difficult for Poppy. She'd been so angry that Rosalind had hurt him, and then so resentful that her betrayal had claimed such a huge part of his heart.

But Poppy had never really considered…how Rosalind's past might have informed what she'd done.

And considering happiness had made Poppy act a lot like a feral cat, she should have.

"He was the first person who treated me really well, and I felt guilty about it," Rosalind continued. "But gratitude isn't love. And what I felt for him was gratitude. When I met Jason, my whole world kind of turned over, and what I felt for him was something else. Something I had never experienced before.

"I caused a lot of trouble for Isaiah, and I feel bad about it. But you certainly shouldn't feel guilty over having feelings for him. You should... You should be with him. He's a great guy, Poppy. I mean, not for me. He's too serious and just...not *right* for me. But you've known him in a serious way even longer than I have, and if you think he's the guy for you..."

"We were engaged," Poppy said. "But he broke it off."

"What?"

"It's a long story." Poppy laughed. "A very Isaiah story, really. We got engaged. Then we slept together. Then I broke up with him. Then I got pregnant. Then we slept together again. Then we kind of...got back engaged... But then he...broke up with me because I told him I was in love with him."

"We really need to not have so much time between phone calls," Rosalind said. "Okay. So... You being in love with him...scared him?"

"Yes," Poppy said slowly.

She wasn't going to bring up Rosalind's part in the issues between Poppy and Isaiah. Mostly because Poppy didn't actually believe they were a significant part. Not specifically. The issues that Isaiah had with love and feelings were definitely on him.

"And you're just going to...let him walk away from what you have?"

"There's nothing I can do to stop him. He said he doesn't love me. He said he doesn't... He doesn't want a relationship like that. There's nothing I can do to change how he feels."

"What did you do when he said that?"

"I yelled at him. And then… I left."

"If I was in love with a guy, I would camp out on his doorstep. I would make him miserable."

"I have some pride, Rosalind."

"I don't," Rosalind said. "I'm a crazy bitch when it comes to love. I mean, I blew up a really good thing to chase after Jason."

"This is… It's different."

"But you love him."

"How many times can I be expected to care for someone and lose them? You know. Better than anyone, you understand what growing up was like for me. For us. People were always just…shuffling us around on a whim. And I just… I can't handle it. Not anymore."

"There's a really big difference between now and then," Rosalind pointed out. "We are not kids. This is what I realized, though a little bit late with Isaiah. I wasn't a child. I didn't have to go along. I had a choice. Child services and foster families and toxic parents don't get to run our lives anymore, Poppy. We are in charge now. You're your own caseworker. You are the one who gets to decide what kind of life you want to have. Who you want to live with. What you'll settle for and what you won't. You don't have to wait for someone to rescue you or accept it when someone says they can't be with you."

"I kind of do. He said…"

"What's the worst that could happen if you fight for him one more time? Just one more?"

Poppy huffed out a laugh. "I'll die of humiliation."

"You won't," Rosalind said. "I guarantee you, humiliation isn't fatal. If humiliation were fatal, I would have died twice before Jason and I actually got married. At *least*. I was insecure and clingy, and a lot of it was because of how our relationship started, which was my own fault. My fear of getting him dirty and losing him dirty, that kind of thing. But…now we've been married for five years, and…none of that matters. Now all that matters is that we love each other. That we have each other. Everything else is just a story we tell and laugh about."

"You know Isaiah. He was very certain."

"I don't actually know Isaiah as well as you do. But you're going to have a baby with him. And… Whether or not you get him in the end, don't you think what you want is worth fighting for? Not for the sake of the baby, or anything like that. But for you. Have you ever fought for *you* before, Poppy?"

She had started to. When Isaiah had broken things off. But…

She didn't know if she really had.

Maybe Rosalind was right. Maybe she needed to face this head-on. Again.

Because nobody controlled the show but her. Nobody told her when to be done except for her.

And pride shouldn't have the last word.

"I love you," Poppy said. "I hope you *know* that. I know we're different. But you've been family to me. And… You're responsible for some of the best things I have in life."

"Well, I'm going to feel guilty if Isaiah breaks your heart."

"Even if he does… I'll be glad he was in my life for as long as he was. I love him. And…being able to love someone like this is a gift. One I don't think I fully appreciated. With our background, just being able to admit my love without fear, without holding back… That's something. It's special. It's kind of a miracle."

"It really is," Rosalind said. "I had a rocky road to Jason. I had a rocky road to love, but Poppy, it's so worth it in the end. I promise you."

"I just hope Isaiah realizes how special it is. How amazing it is. His parents always loved him. He grew up in one house. He...doesn't know that not everyone has someone to love them."

"He might have had all of that, Poppy, but he's never had you. Don't sell yourself short."

Poppy tried to breathe around the emotion swelling in her chest. "If it all works out, you're invited to the wedding," Poppy said decisively.

"Are you sure?"

"Of course. You're my family. And the family I've created is the most important thing I have."

"Good," Rosalind said. "Then go fight for the rest of it."

Poppy would do that. She absolutely would.

Isaiah didn't know for sure that he would find Poppy at her house. He could only hope that he would.

If not, he would have to launch a search of the entire town, which everyone was going to find unpleasant. Because he would be getting in faces and asking for access to confidential records. And while he was confident that ultimately he would get his way, he would rather not cut a swath of rage and destruction through the community that he tried to do business in.

But, desperate times.

He felt like he was made entirely of feelings. His skin hurt from it. His heart felt bruised. And he needed to... He needed to find Poppy and tell her.

He needed to find her and he needed to fix this.

It was 6:00 a.m., and he had two cups of coffee in his hand when he pounded on the door of her house with the toe of his boot.

It took a couple of minutes, but the door finally opened and revealed Poppy, who was standing there in baggy pajama pants with polar bears on them, and a plain shirt. Her hair was exceptionally large and sticking out at all angles, one curl hanging in her face. And she looked...

Not altogether very happy to see him.

"What are you doing here?"

"I brought you coffee."

"Yesterday you brought me cotton candy, and you were still a dick. So explain to me why I should be compelled by the coffee." She crossed her arms and treated him to a hard glare.

"I need to talk to you."

"Well, that works, because I need to talk to you too. Though, I was not going to talk to you at six in the morning."

"Were you asleep?"

"Obviously. It's six in the morning." Then her shoulders slumped and she sighed, backing away from the door. "No. I wasn't sleeping."

He found himself relieved by that.

"I couldn't sleep at all," she continued. "Because I kept thinking about you. You asshole."

He found that extraordinarily cheering.

"I couldn't sleep either," he said.

"Well, of course not. You lost your assistant. And you had to get your own coffee as a result. Life is truly caving in around you, Isaiah."

"That isn't why I couldn't sleep," he said. "I talked to my brother last night."

"Which one?"

"Joshua. Who was not terribly impressed with me, I have to say."

"Well, I'm not sure who could be terribly impressed with you right at the moment."

She wasn't letting him off easy. And that was all right. He didn't need it to be easy. He just needed to fix it.

"I do feel," he said, his voice coming out so rough it was like a stranger's. "I feel a lot. All the time. It's just easier when I don't. So I'm very good at pushing down my emotions. And I'm very good at separating feelings from a moment. That way I have time to analyze what I feel later, instead of being reactionary."

"Because being reactionary is bad?"

"Yes. Especially when... When I might have read a situation wrong. And I do that a lot, Poppy. I'm a perfectionist. I don't like being wrong."

"This is not news to me," she said.

"I know. You've also known me long enough that you seem to know how to read me. And I... I'm pretty good at reading you too. But sometimes I don't get it right. Feelings are different for me. But it doesn't mean I don't have them. It does mean that sometimes I'm wrong about what's happening. And... I hate that. I hate it more than anything. I hate feeling like everything is okay and finding out it isn't. I hate feeling like something is wrong only to find out that it's not."

"You know everyone makes those mistakes," she said gently. "Nobody gets it completely right all the time."

"I do know that," he said. "But I get it wrong more often than most. I've always struggled with that. I've found ways to make it easier. I use organization. My interest in numbers. Having an assistant who helps me with the things I'm not so great at. All of those things have made it easier for me to have a life that functions simply. They've made it so I don't have to risk myself. So I don't have to be hurt.

"But I'm finding that they have not enabled me to have a full life. Poppy, I don't just want easy. That was a mistake I made when I asked you to find me a wife. I thought I wanted a wife so I could feel the sense of completeness in my personal life that I did my professional life. But what I didn't realize was that things felt complete in my professional life because I was with you every day."

He took a step toward her, wanting to touch her. With everything he had.

"I had you in that perfect space I created for you. And I got to be with you all the time," he continued. "Yours was one of the first faces I saw every morning. And you were always one of the last people I saw before I went home. There was a rightness to that. And I attributed it to…the fact that you were efficient. The fact that you were organized. The fact that I liked you. But it was more than that. And it always has been. It isn't that I didn't think of you when I decided to put an ad in the paper for a wife. You were actually the reason I did it. It's just that… I'm an idiot."

He paused and watched her expression.

"Are you waiting for me to argue with you?" She blinked. "I'm not going to."

"I'm not waiting for you to argue. I just want you to… I want you to see that I mean this. I want you to understand that I didn't do it on purpose. There's just so many layers of protection inside me, and it takes me days sometimes to sort out what's happening in my own chest.

"You are right. I hated it because it wasn't in my head.

I hated it because it all comes from that part of me that I find difficult. The part that I feel holds me back. It is amazing to have a brother like Joshua. Someone who's a PR expert. Who seems to navigate rooms and facial expressions and changes in mood seamlessly. I've had you by my side for that. To say the right thing in a meeting when I didn't. To give me your rundown on how something actually went so that I didn't have to."

"I already told you it's not hard for me to do that for you. The way you are doesn't bother me. It's just you. It's not like there's this separate piece of you that has these challenges and then there's you. It's all you. And I could never separate it out. I wouldn't even want to. Isaiah, you're perfect the way you are. Whether there is a label for this or not. Whether it's a disorder or it isn't. It doesn't matter to me. It's all you."

"I bet you resented it a little bit yesterday."

"You hurt me. You hurt me really badly. But I still think you're the best man I know. I still… Isaiah, I love you. You saying terrible things to me one day is not going to undo ten years of loving you."

The relief washing through him felt unlike anything he'd ever experienced before. He wanted to drop to his knees. He wanted to kiss her. Hold her. He wanted to unlock himself and let everything he felt pour out.

Why wasn't he doing that? Why was he standing there stiff as a board when that wasn't at all what he felt?

So he did.

He dropped down to his knees and he wrapped his arms around her, pressing his face against her stomach. Against Poppy and the life that was growing inside her.

"I love you," he whispered. "Poppy, I love you."

He looked up at her, and she was staring down at him,

bewildered, as he continued, "I just… I was so afraid to let myself feel it. To let myself want this. To let myself have it. I can't help but see myself as an emotional burden. When I think of everything you do for me… I think of you having to do that in our lives, and it doesn't feel fair. It feels like you deserve someone easier. Someone better. Someone you don't have to act as a translator for."

"I've had a long time to fall in love with other men, Isaiah. But you are the one I love. You. And I already told you that I don't see you and then the way you process emotion. It's all you. The man I love. All your traits, they can't be separated. I don't want them to be. You're not my project. You… You have no idea what you give to me. Because I've never told you. I talked with Rosalind last night."

"You did?"

"Yes." Poppy crouched down, so that they were eye to eye. "She told me I needed to fight for you. That we are not foster children anymore, and I can't live like someone else is in control of my destiny. And she's right. Whether or not you showed up at my house this morning, we were going to talk. Because I was going to come find you. And I was going to tell you again that I love you."

"I'm a lot of work," he said, his voice getting rough.

"I don't care. It's my privilege to have the freedom to work at it. No one is going to come and take me away and move me to a different place. No one is controlling what I do but me. If I choose to work at this, if I choose to love you, then that's my choice.

"And it's worth it. You mean everything to me. You hired me when I was an eighteen-year-old girl who had no job experience, who had barely been in one place for a year at a time. You introduced me to your family, and watching them showed me how love can function in those kinds of relationships. Your family showed me the way people can treat each other. The way you can fight and still care. The way you can make mistakes and still love."

"That's my family. It isn't me."

"I haven't gotten to you yet." She grabbed hold of his chin, her brown eyes steady on his. "You've told me how difficult it is for you to navigate people. But you still do it. You are so loyal to the people in your life. Including me.

"I watched the way you cared for Rosalind. Part of that was hiring me, simply because it meant something to her. Part of that was caring for her, and yes, in the end you felt like you made a mistake, like she made a fool out of you, but you showed that you had the capacity to care deeply.

"You have been the most constant steady presence in my life for the past decade. You've shown me what it means to be loyal. You took me with you to every job, every position. Every start-up. You committed to me in a way that no one else in my life ever has. And I don't know if you can possibly understand what that means for a foster kid who's had more houses than she can count."

Poppy stroked his face, her heart thundering hard, her whole body trembling. She continued, "You can't minimize the fact that you taught me that people can care that deeply. That they might show it in different ways, but that doesn't mean they don't care.

"I *do* know you have feelings, Isaiah. Because your actions show them. You are consistent month to month, year to year. It doesn't matter whether I misinterpret your reaction in the moment. You're always in it for the long haul. And that seems like a miracle to me." Her voice got thick, her eyes shiny. "You are not a trial, Isaiah Grayson. You are the greatest gift I've ever been given. And loving you is part of that gift."

The words washed over him, a balm for his soul. For his heart.

"I was afraid," he said. "Not just of being too much for you—" the words cut his throat "—but of losing you. I wish I were that altruistic. But I'm not. I was afraid because what I feel for you is so deep… I don't know what I would do if I lost you. If I… If I ruined it because of… Because of how I am."

"I *love* how you are." Poppy's voice was fierce. "It's up to me to tell you when something is wrong, to tell you when it's right. It doesn't matter how the rest of the world sees things, Isaiah. It matters how *we* see things. Here. Between us.

"Normal doesn't matter. Neither of us is normal. You're going to have to deal with my baggage. With the fact that I'm afraid I don't know how to be a mother because I never had one of my own. With the fact that sometimes my first instinct is to protect myself instead of fighting for what I feel. And I'm going to have to learn your way of communicating. That's love for everyone. Sometimes I'll be a bigger burden. And sometimes you will be. But we'll have each other. And that's so much better than being apart."

"I think I've loved you for a very long time. But it felt necessary to block it out. But once I touched you… Once I touched you, Poppy, I couldn't deny it. I can't keep you or my feelings for you in a box, and that terrifies me. You terrify me. But in a good way."

She lifted her hand, tracing a line down the side of

his face. "The only thing that terrifies me is a life without you."

"Will you marry me? This time I'm asking. Not because you're pregnant. Not because I want a wife. Because I want you."

"I will marry you," she said. "Not for your family. Not in spite of you, but because of you. Because I love you."

"I might be bad when it comes to dealing with emotion, but I know right now I'm the happiest man in the world."

His heart felt like it might burst, and he didn't hide from it. Didn't push it aside. He opened himself up and embraced all of it.

"There will have to be some ground rules," Poppy said, smiling impishly.

"Ground rules?"

"Yes. Lines between our personal and professional lives. For example, at home, I'm not making the coffee."

"That's a sacrifice I'm willing to make."

"Good. But that won't be the only one."

He wrapped his arms around her and pulled them both into a standing position, Poppy cradled against his chest. "Why don't I take you into your bedroom and show you exactly what sorts of sacrifices I'm prepared to make."

"I don't have a bed in there," she protested as he carried her back toward her room. "There's just a sleeping bag."

"I think I can work with that."

And he did.

Epilogue

December 24, 2018

WIFE FOUND—

Antisocial mountain man/businessman Isaiah Grayson married his assistant, his best friend and his other half, Poppy Sinclair, on Christmas Eve.

She'll give him a child or two, exact number to be negotiated. And has vowed to be as tolerant of his mood as he is of hers. Because that's how love works.

She is willing to stay with him in sickness and in health, in a mountain cabin or at a fancy gala. As long as she is with him. For as long as they both shall live.

She's happy for him to keep the beard.

They opted to have a small, family wedding on a mountain.

The fact that Poppy was able to have a family wedding made her heart feel like it was so full it might burst. The Grayson clan was all in attendance, standing in the snow, along with Rosalind and her husband.

Poppy peeked out from around the tree she was hiding behind and looked at Isaiah, who was standing next to Pastor John Thompson. The backdrop of evergreens capped with snow was breathtaking, but not as breathtaking as the man himself.

He wasn't wearing a suit. He was wearing a black coat, white button-up shirt and black jeans. He also had on his black cowboy hat. He hadn't shaved.

But that was what she wanted.

Him.

Not some polished version, but the man she loved.

This would be her new Christmas tradition. She would think of her wedding. Of their love. Of how her whole life had changed because of Isaiah Grayson.

For her part, Poppy had on her very perfect dress and was holding a bouquet of dark red roses.

She smiled. It was the fantasy wedding she hadn't even known she wanted.

But then, she supposed that was because she hadn't known who the groom might be.

But this was perfectly them. Remote, and yet surrounded by the people they loved most.

There was no music, just the deep silence of the forest, the sound of branches moving whenever there was a slight breeze. And Poppy came out from behind the tree when it felt like it was time.

She walked through the snow, her eyes never leaving

Isaiah's. She felt like she might have been walking down a very long aisle toward him for the past ten years. And that each and every one of those years had been necessary to bring them to this moment.

Isaiah didn't feel things the way other people did. He felt them deeper. It took longer to get there, but she knew that now she had his heart, she would have it forever.

She trusted it. Wholly and completely.

Just like she trusted him.

He reached out and took her hand, and the two of them stood across from each other, love flooding Poppy's heart.

"I told you an ad was a good idea," he whispered after they'd taken their vows and the pastor had told him to kiss the bride.

"What are you talking about?"

"It's the reason I finally realized what was in front of me the whole time."

"I think we would have found our way without the ad."

"No. We needed the ad."

"So you can be right?" she asked, holding back a smile.

He grinned. "I'm always right."

"Oh, really? Well then, what do you think is going to happen next?"

He kissed her again, deep and hard and long. "I think we're going to live happily-ever-after."

He was right. As always.

* * * * *

*When Jed Dalloway started over, ranching a
mountain plot for his recluse boss is what saved him.
So when hometown girl April Reed offers a deal
to develop the land, Jed tells her no sale.
But his heart doesn't get the message…*

*Read on for a sneak preview of
the next book in* New York Times *bestselling author
Allison Leigh's Return to the Double C miniseries,*
A Promise to Keep.

"Don't look at me like that, April."

She raised her gaze to his. "Like what?"

His fingers tightened in her hair and her mouth ran dry.
She swallowed. Moistened her lips.

She wasn't sure if she moved first. Or if it was him.

But then his mouth was on hers and like everything
else about him, she felt engulfed by an inferno. Or maybe
the burning was coming from inside her.

There was no way to know.

No reason to care.

Her hands slid up the granite chest, behind his neck,
where his skin felt even hotter beneath her fingertips, and
slipped through his thick hair, which was not hot, but
instead felt cool and unexpectedly silky.

His arm around her tightened, his hand pressing her
closer while his kiss deepened. Consuming. Exhilarating.

Her head was whirling, sounds roaring.

It was only a kiss.

But she was melting.

She was flying.

And then she realized the sounds weren't just inside her head.

Someone was laying on a horn.

She jerked back, her gaze skittering over Jed's as they both turned to peer through the curtain of white light shining over them.

"Mind getting at least one of these vehicles out of the way?" The shout was male and obviously amused.

"Oh for cryin'—" She exhaled. "That's my uncle Matthew," she told Jed, pushing him away. "And I'm sorry to say, but we are probably never going to live this down."

Don't miss
A Promise to Keep *by Allison Leigh,*
available March 2020 wherever
Harlequin Special Edition books and ebooks are sold.

Harlequin.com

Love Harlequin romance?

DISCOVER.

Be the first to find out about promotions,
news and exclusive content!

 Facebook.com/HarlequinBooks

 Twitter.com/HarlequinBooks

 Instagram.com/HarlequinBooks

 Pinterest.com/HarlequinBooks

 ReaderService.com

EXPLORE.

Sign up for the Harlequin e-newsletter and
download a free book from any series at
TryHarlequin.com

CONNECT.

Join our Harlequin community to
share your thoughts and connect
with other romance readers!
Facebook.com/groups/HarlequinConnection

HSOCIAL2020